Molly Hacker

IS TOO PICKY!

A novel by

LISETTE BRODEY

SABERLEE BOOKS

Published by
Saberlee Books
Los Angeles, CA

lisettebrodey.com
facebook.com/BrodeyAuthor
mollyhacker.com
twitter.com/lisettebrodey
saberleebooks@yahoo.com

@2011, Lisette Brodey
1st Edition: January 2012
2nd Edition: September 2013
3rd Edition: March 2016

Copy Editor: Laura Daly
Cover Design: Charles Roth
Original Character Conception: Megan Hansen
Author Photo: Robert Antal

ISBN: 978-0-9815836-3-1 (paperback)
ISBN: 978-0-9815836-4-8 (e-book)

Man-woman relationships – Fiction
Dating (social customs) – Fiction
Social life and customs – Fiction

Printed in the United States of America

To my mother, Jean Brodey, with love

I love her and that's the beginning of everything.
— F. Scott Fitzgerald

ACKNOWLEDGMENTS

To Laura Daly, my longtime friend and editor supreme. Thank you for not only editing this book, but also for editing Molly's blogs and for being a constant support.

To Lisa "Twitchy" McCallum, for the myriad ways you have supported me, but most of all for your extraordinary devotion and friendship.

To Charles Roth, for designing this beautiful new cover.

To Megan Hansen, for working with me to visualize and illustrate Molly's character for the original cover and for my blog. Thank you for your patience, your enthusiasm, your talent, and your friendship.

To Christy Leigh Stewart, for putting Molly's website together and being such a caring friend.

To Dara Brodey, for helping me with all things Italian.

To the amazing people who stood by me on the long road to getting this book out, waving and cheering me on, especially on the days when nothing was easy: Talatha Allen, Mark Cote, Tamara DeForest, Wright Gres, Janet Lee, Stuart Ross McCallum, Sheri A. Wilkinson, and Leigh Ann Wilson.

A special thank-you to Jaidis Shaw for your wise counsel, friendship, and support.

Molly Hacker

IS TOO PICKY!

Chapter 1: ANOTHER WEDDING

AUGUST 27th ... THIS YEAR

Three weddings ago, when my best girlfriend, Claudia Porter-Bellman, got married, I swore it would be the last one I would ever attend until I was the bride. Claudia Porter-Bellman—and people tell me I've got baggage.

I didn't, however, count on my mother's long-divorced best friend, Susan Decker, getting married again. Having tried every trick in and out of vogue to find a husband, Susan was ripe for success. But despite the odds being on her side, I figured Murphy's law would sabotage her efforts.

Cynical? Nah. It wasn't just Murphy or the fact that his law had wreaked so much havoc in my own life. It was simply that Susan just seemed too desperate, as opposed to my own state of being: nonchalantly desperate.

Back to Susan. One night, an insistent neighbor dragged her to a local community center for a fun night of number calling, and, bingo, six months later, she was engaged to a widower of two years.

He was a nice enough man, quite handsome, and seemed to truly care about her happiness. Luckily for me, Susan's good fortune veered far enough away from my own romantic hallucinations that I was able to attend the wedding without insane pangs of envy stabbing my chest like daggers.

I'll admit it: watching Susan and her new husband take their vows did fill me with a bit of "why the hell isn't that me up there?" but having to deal with the busybodies at the country club reception proved to be the real pebble in my Jimmy Choos. Although I had been wise enough to bring Tony Lostanza, my dear friend from high school who was estranged from his wife, my mom had already told a few friends (translation: it was broadcast to the world) that Tony was just an escort of sorts. As if that weren't bad enough, the ones who didn't know, but who knew Tony, were horrified that I was attending a wedding, of all occasions, with a married man.

That night, I was forced to fend off several not-so-subtle dirty looks, glances of pity accompanied by sad head shaking, and, once again, comments from those near and dear who felt compelled to remind me that if I weren't so darn picky, if I would just give a nice man a chance, I wouldn't have to bring another woman's husband to my mother's best friend's wedding.

If you think I just took all of this in stride, think again. I had no problem letting each and every person know that my business was just that, my business. With some people, I find the best way to deal with unwanted questions is to ask a few of my own. For example, when my aunt Pauline asked me why a pretty girl like me couldn't have brought a man who wasn't attached to someone else, I asked the thrice-divorced sister of my mother to explain to me how settling for three Mr. Wrongs had enhanced her life, and I inquired as to the price of divorce and whether her legal fees had been worth the paltry settlements she had received.

"Smart ass; stay single, Miss Picky," she snapped, and headed off to articulate her discontent to any random guest with ears willing to be mangled by a wart-nosed barfly.

I knew Pauline would shake off my admonishment the same way my cat shakes off my kisses. She had more important things to concern herself with: after all, a wedding was a perfect place to scour the crowd for Mr. Wrong number four. Pauline had a way of bypassing any man who didn't have one elbow on the bar and who was able to make it through an evening without slurring his words. Perhaps this had something to do with her less-than-stellar track record. I'm babbling. I need to refocus.

Twice that day, Tony had been asked to temporarily excuse himself so that the presiding snoop could have her way with me. Each time, he looked at me for the green light to do so, which, regrettably, I gave him. I don't understand why I should be polite to people who I know are about to say or do something rude. I know I said I had "no trouble" standing up to people, and for the most part I don't, but I should have told them that whatever they wanted to say could have been said in Tony's presence. In hindsight, I always have some pesky little regret; it's a bad habit, and I need to work on it.

"Molly, you're such a pretty woman," Naomi Hall-Benchley began. "And you're smart. But smart women often make foolish choices (blah, blah, cliché, blah) and being with a married man, even if he's 'just a friend,' is *not* a good choice. I've got great news for you. I've arranged a dinner for next week. Art (her long-suffering husband) has a new marketing VP who just moved here from Dallas. He's single, and he's looking. Great guy and quite the avid golfer."

I had never picked up a golf club in my life, but suddenly, looking at Naomi, it seemed like an excellent idea. She was the town's premier socialite and often looked more like a wax museum replica of herself than a real person. For years, I harbored fantasies of finding a wick on top of her head, lighting it, and watching her slowly burn to the ground. Just imagining the flames licking every inch of her skintight Herve Leger cocktail dress as her mascara kissed her melting pearls made me tingle with delight.

"And he makes oodles of money," she jabbered on, subtly glancing from side to side in hopes of being photographed. "What time is good for you? Shall we say seven p.m. next Friday?"

"You know, I'm busy that night. Sorry."

"No problem, we can reschedule!" She laughed. "Rescheduling is the least of our worries."

"How about the twelfth?" I asked, as I noticed Tony watching intently from the bar.

"But today is the twenty-seventh … the twelfth is two weeks away!"

"And the twelfth of never is even further away," I informed her, taking delight as her jaw dropped. I saw Tony laughing now; I knew he couldn't wait for a recap with his nightcap.

"You're ungrateful, Molly," she said, taking a swig of her vodka martini. "I have a perfectly fine man for you, and you refuse to give him a chance."

Now I was angry. "Have you ever met him?" I challenged her.

"Well, no," she said sheepishly. "Not yet."

"But he makes a good salary and loves golf. Those are your criteria for a hot prospect? Does he have a sense of humor? Is he sensitive? Does he do anything *but* play golf in his free time?"

"Well, I, I don't know …"

"No, you don't," I scolded. "You don't care about my happiness at all. You just want to be 'the one' who set up 'Picky Molly Hacker' and simultaneously score points with Art by playing matchmaker for his new vice president."

"Now, that's just silly—"

"Do you think if I were to meet someone new that I would want to do it with people watching, listening to our conversation, butting in to try and push us together? Do you realize this is the twenty-first century?"

"You're too picky, Molly Hacker. And if you don't wise up while you've still got something to offer a man, if indeed you do, you won't have all the things that life has to offer. Not to mention that children are best had while one is still fertile."

I started to roar fire but stopped myself. Tony was approaching, and I didn't know if his clothing was flame retardant.

3

I was thirty-two, and Naomi was only eight years older than I was. I wondered if she considered herself to be "old." But I chose a different question.

"Are you and Art in love?"

"How utterly inappropriate of you!" Naomi said, reeling in feigned horror. "Of course we are. Besides, I live very well. I have a beautiful home, beautiful children, and a full life."

"But are you in love with him? Is he in love with you?"

"Of course and of course! You're too picky, Molly Hacker, and deflecting the seriousness of your situation to me will not help you. I'm surprised you haven't found someone at the *Herald*. It's a fine newspaper with some very smart men working there."

By this time, Tony had arrived and put his arm around me, smiling at Naomi just to rattle her.

"If you don't mind, Naomi, I'll do things my own way. Call me funny, quirky, picky, or whatever you like, but I kind of had my heart set on love being part of the equation. Not that it's *any* of *your* business!"

Naomi finished her martini and put it on the tray of a passing waiter.

Tony smiled at her again, this time more broadly. Naomi and I took one last opportunity to scowl at one another, and I swore, no matter whose it was, I would *never* attend another wedding again until I attended my own. And I meant it. I sailed through the next year without attending one wedding, despite being invited to three.

So here I sit today, August twenty-seventh, just about a year after Susan's wedding, on a bright and beautiful summer day, glammed up in my dress, as I watch my younger sister, Hannah, get her hair pinned up with flowers for her big day. Hannah is bursting with joy. She's only twenty-six and is marrying her longtime guy, Matthew. Nobody ever told Hannah she was too picky.

Chapter 2: I WRITE ABOUT DEAD PEOPLE

Just about a month after Susan Decker's wedding, I was feeling down. Being the local features reporter for my town's newspaper, the *Swansea Herald*, I was informed by my editor that the society reporter had quit and that I would be doing her job, in addition to my regular duties, until the paper could budget for a suitable replacement.

Maybe in a parallel universe, this would have been a dream come true. Surely, covering high-society weddings and assorted galas for this New York bedroom community would pave the way for my own path to nuptial bliss. The possibilities were endless. Think of the men I could meet. Rich men. Maybe I could find one twice as rich as Art Benchley, and maybe I'd luck out and we'd find love, too. Not to mention the fun I'd have in watching Naomi's true color, GREEN, come out. But I was BLUE. And then I saw RED.

And the more I thought about it, the more disenchanted I became. I was in no mood to watch a bunch of rich people say, "I do," and write about the extravagant surroundings in which it all took place. The showers, the seventeen engagement parties, the rehearsal dinners, the wedding, the receptions ... oh, it was overwhelming. I didn't want any part of other people's weddings. Period.

Olivia Jackson, a bright young woman only a year out of college, had just started at the paper with an entry-level job writing obituaries. She was blown away by her good fortune (and my perceived insanity) when I asked my boss, Ray, if I could trade with Olivia and write OBITUARIES instead.

"You want to write about DEAD PEOPLE ... instead of glamorous society parties?" he asked. He scrunched up his face and stared at me, looking for some tell-tale sign that I was messing with him. "Hacks, you're not serious."

"I'm dead serious," I told him. "Besides, I'll still be doing my regular job. Dying isn't *that* morbid. We all do it at least once in our lives!"

"But you're so vibrant; you're so talented, so witty. Obits? Are you sure?"

"This is a job, Ray. My life is outside of this newspaper. I know why you chose me for the society gig, and though I appreciate the thought, I'll muddle through on my own."

"But, Hacks," he persisted, "I'm handing you a ticket to happiness on a silver platter. The opportunities! Think of them."

"Ray, maybe these aren't the opportunities *I* want. And maybe if I'm that wrapped up in the lives of others, I won't have time to find my soul mate—you know, the loving, sensitive, funny, complicated, intelligent, sweet guy that *I* want!"

"Molly Hacker, you're too picky," came the familiar mantra of the masses.

"Are you going to let me trade with Olivia or not?" I asked.

Ray shook his head. "Sure," he said. "It's your funeral."

I had determined way back in high school that life was like a treasure hunt. If you get to one destination and there's nothing there for you, take a clue from that, and it will lead you to the next stop, and so on. I had this amazing epiphany in my freshman year, when, like many of my classmates, I was turned down for the cheerleading squad. For about five minutes, I was heartbroken. It's not that I had ever wanted to be a cheerleader, but it was the cool thing to be, and rejection is never easy. If you've ever been pissed off because you weren't invited to a party you wouldn't have wanted to attend anyway, you'll likely get my drift.

My English teacher, Mr. Newman, had been walking by me in the hall as I stared blankly at the list of names that didn't include my own. "Molly, you've got one of the most inquiring minds in my class," he said. "Why don't you join the staff of the school paper? We could use someone with your innate curiosity and talent."

I was so thrilled at being wanted, especially at something I was truly good at, that I tossed my imaginary pom-poms into the air and began my semi-illustrious career as a reporter, never telling a soul that I wanted to be a psychologist and that my penchant for asking tough questions would be far more beneficial to the world with Dr. in front of my name.

It was while working at the paper that I became friends with Tony Lostanza. Tony was an enigma to many; he was a great football player with a 4.0 average. We became best friends and fell in love. Well, I fell in love with Tony; he fell in love with Victoria, the perky little cheerleader whom he eventually married and was legally separated from in time to take me to Susan Decker's wedding well over a decade and a half later.

When I got home to my apartment from work that evening, I felt the need to confess my bold career "move" to someone. I could call my mother. She would understand … sort of … but she'd be frustrated with me, and I couldn't take that. My dad would tell me that he was behind any choice I made, and he would mean it, but then he'd secretly worry that I was sabotaging my personal life and my career in one fell swoop. No doubt, he'd blame himself.

Once I told him that I'd always wanted to be a psychologist. "You'd be wonderful at that, Princess," he said, "but don't forget you'd be looking at several more years of school and clinical training." My translation: "You'll NEVER get married if you pursue psychology." No, the two are not mutually exclusive, and I have no idea what my dad was saying. He is so pro-education that I had to be imagining the worst. He was very likely just reminding me of what grad school entailed and asking me if I was up for that. But being so paranoid, I changed the subject because I figured no matter where the conversation went, it was bound to stress me out. Total coward; I know. I'm getting better, though.

I put my regrets on the back burner and went back to stirring the pot in which simmered my most recent career move. As much as I thought I wanted to share it with someone, was it necessary? After all, I could already imagine what they'd all have to say. Did I want to *hear* it?

My girlfriends would all lecture me about letting a golden opportunity slip through my fingers for a perfectly morbid one (and probably suggest *I* find a psychologist to snap me out of whatever crazy spell I was under). My kid sister, Hannah, would understand, but I didn't want to trouble her. She had a life. Only Tony would understand.

I called him on his cell phone and he sounded very agitated when he picked up.

"Hey, catch you at a bad time?" I asked.

"Uh … yup."

"I take it you're not alone."

"Metaphorically, yes," he said. "Physically, no."

I gathered he was with his wife.

"Listen, I just wanted to tell you something. It's not that important. You take care of business."

I heard a woman's voice screaming in the background. "Oh, don't bother hanging up, you hypocrite. I'm leaving anyway. Who's the pot calling the kettle black here, anyway?"

I heard a door slam and Tony sigh.

"She's gone."

"So I heard."

"You know, Molly, I never wanted to be a divorced man. Especially being a father. When I took those vows, I had every intention of keeping them, and despite the distance between us, I wanted to work it out." He paused. "I think."

"So what's the roadblock?" I asked.

"She's seeing someone, and she has been for two years."

"Damn! So why did she just call you a hypocrite?"

"She'd like to believe I have been having an affair, too. It would ease her conscience, though I'm not sure if she has one."

"Oh, Tony! It's my fault. This is SO my fault. I'll bet word got back to her because you came with me to Susan Decker's wedding."

"Don't worry about that, Molly."

"I'm a homewrecker and we're not even having an affair."

"Molly, did you hear me say she's been stepping out on me for two years? This isn't about you. Besides, there was distance between us long before that. I just wish I knew who this other man is. I've tried to find out, but he seems to live in the shadows somewhere."

"Ooooo, that's creepy."

"Yeah, it is. C'mon, kiddo, don't be a guilt sponge. This has nothing to do with you."

"I'll work on it," I said, pondering my most recent shortcoming, thereby making myself more of a guilt sponge if you can follow my somewhat skewed thinking.

Despite my psychologist/reporter instincts, I didn't want to ask him any more questions.

"I'm going to file for divorce in the morning. And for joint custody of Noah."

"I'm sorry."

"Don't be; this marriage has been dead for a long time. I just didn't know it. I've been grieving for a long time and didn't know it ... denial ... you know ... isn't just a river in Egypt—"

"But you just said there was distance for a long time."

"I married for better or for worse and put everything else aside. Molly, lots of people can have distance in their relationships and still be in denial about it. You know that. Whatever ... this marriage has bitten the dust. Bought the farm. Kicked the bucket. Okay?"

"Need an obit writer?" I asked.

"Say what?" he asked, distracted.

"You need some alone time," I told him. "And when you feel like talking, you know where to find me."

"You know, Molly, that's not a bad idea. I definitely need some alone time to figure out how I've been alone for so many years and never noticed. By the way, that's an excellent idea."

"What's an excellent idea?"

"An obituary. LOSTANZA MARRIAGE DEAD! Husband last to know. Doesn't give a flying fig anymore—"

"I'm sorry you're hurting, Tony. And you don't have to say 'fig' with me."

I heard what sounded like a chuckle. "I'm fine," he said. "Relieved. I don't know if we were ever right for each other. Getting married was just the thing to do back then. It was what people expected us to do because ... I should have ..."

"Because of what? You should have what?"

"I should have been pickier. Just like you, Molly Hacker."

I laughed. He always laughed with me, not at me.

"Catch you tomorrow," I said, as I hung up with every intention to plot (no pun intended) my quest to find Mr. Right.

My cell rang about a minute after we hung up. I was going through my mail, and I put the phone on speaker so I could multitask. I felt needed: Tony must be calling back to talk to me after all!

I didn't even bother with hello. "You know I'm right about using a stupid word like 'fig,' and you've called back to get those F bombs out of your system. Go ahead, sweetie, let 'em rip."

Instead of the stream of expletives I had expected to hear, a voice not belonging to Tony said to me: "Seymour Aaron Schlemecker. Noted ear, nose, and throat doctor."

The voice sounded familiar but I was out of sorts.

"Is this Dr. Schlemecker?" I asked.

"For God's sake, Hacks," Ray said. "Dr. Schlemecker is dead. He's your first obit. He was well loved in this town and heavily involved in the community. He was a good man. Find out everything you can about him and honor him well. Poor guy ... massive coronary. Went just like that."

"Oh, God," I said. "How sad."

"I've already given the society job to Olivia. I can't go back on my word."

"No, no," I said. "I wouldn't want you to do that. "I'll get on it,

Ray."

I hung up. "I'm Molly Hacker, " I said to myself. "I'm too picky, and I write about DEAD PEOPLE."

Chapter 3: THE LATE DOCTOR'S NEPHEW

LATER THAT SAME DAY ...

Moments after clicking Ray off, Captain Jack, my beautiful orange cat, came playfully bouncing onto my lap. If you're wondering about the name, there's no rhyme or reason to it. I love Johnny Depp but didn't name my cat for him. Captain Jack just had a dignified sound—for a male feline—and has since taken on many derivatives, the most common one being "C.J." or "Jackie." On days when I feed him and he immediately whines for more food, I call him "Oliver." (Please, Mom, I want some more!) He doesn't seem to mind any of them, but he seems to like the sound of "Wanna EAT?" the best of all. He doesn't understand it's not his name ... but that's okay.

He's not finicky at all (like Morris the Nine Lives cat in the old TV commercials), but once someone had the nerve to suggest to me that I subconsciously got a cat resembling famous finicky Morris so I'd have a partner in pickiness. When you start making comments like THAT to people, it's time to get a life! Sheesh! Okay, back to ME and my own shortcomings.

As I sat there thinking of the now-deceased doctor, I wondered if indeed I'd made a bad career choice after all, but as I had no real aspirations to be a star reporter anyway, it didn't matter. The important thing was to avoid being immersed in other people's weddings.

But I still needed comforting. I picked Captain Jack up and gave him a hug. If you have a cat, you likely know that cats *tolerate* hugs (if at all), and that few enjoy them. Jack's tolerance for affection ranged from one day to the next, but it never surpassed the duration of a three-minute egg timer, which I kept on the table next to my Laz-E Man Lounge chair. I would turn it over before picking Jack up. Usually, halfway through the low growl would sound, like thunder rumbling in the distance, and if I held him for too long, the growl would turn into a hiss and his back paws would push off my chest like an Olympic swimmer pushing off a wall. On rare occasions, Jack would hold still longer, but never longer than the egg timer.

Just as Jack was pushing away from "the wall," my cell rang again.

This time I wasn't assuming anything. I looked to see who was calling. I didn't recognize the number.

"Is this Molly Hacker?" the man asked.

"Who's calling, please?" I asked. Don't you just HATE it when people call you and want to know who YOU are without identifying themselves first? Arrrrrghhhh!

"This is Alan T. Cressman. My uncle died this morning, and the man at the newspaper told me that I should talk to you about his obituary. I know you were going to call me, but I'm anxious to get this done and make sure it's factual. I don't want to let my family down."

"I'm sorry for your loss," I told him, realizing that I might be saying that more and more and should work on variations so as not to stagnate or sound insincere.

"I'd prefer to meet with you in person. I could email or fax you this information, but if I see you in person, I can express my uncle's true essence as a human being. I would be forever grateful."

"Uh, well … " I said.

"The Starbucks on Holloway and East Main?" he asked. "In an hour?"

I remembered my "treasure hunt" philosophy and decided that in the interest of staying true to myself and keeping my job, I would meet him. I just couldn't shake the idea that I was being roped into a date.

You're paranoid, I told myself. "I'll see you in an hour," I told him.

I was still dressed from a day at work, and I looked fine. Why, then, did I take a quick shower, redo my makeup, and find the sweetest dress that hung in my closet? After all, I was meeting a guy I knew nothing about. I was meeting him to gather information about his deceased uncle. What in the world was I thinking?

On the drive to Starbuck's, it occurred to me that he had identified himself as "Alan T. Cressman." I wondered why that middle initial was important. I mean, if you're KNOWN by your middle initial, like "Michael J. Fox" or "Franklin D. Roosevelt," that's understandable. I'm Molly R. Hacker, but I don't introduce myself that way. I suppose it didn't matter, but things like that tend to fester in my brain.

"Alan T. Cressman," he said, putting his hand out to meet mine.

"Molly Hacker," I replied, resisting the temptation to insert my middle initial. Maybe under different circumstances I would have done so, but the man just lost a loved one. Sarcasm didn't live in that moment.

"Over here, in the corner," he said, leading the way with a nod of the head. "We'll have some privacy."

"Fine," I said, eyeing the fat briefcase he carried and wondering how much of it was meant for me. I also noticed him giving me the once over. He was a surprisingly nice-looking man, about thirty-five, I presumed, meticulously dressed and smelling of expensive cologne.

"What can I get you?" he asked as he held out my chair for me and then put his briefcase down in the empty chair.

"I'll just have a bottle of water," I said. "And maybe an almond biscotti if they have any."

"Super," he said.

I pondered the word "super." Had any man ever said that to me before? Did it matter if one had? Did the use of it have any serious implications? Was the use of the word "super" related to the use of his middle initial? Lots of people said "super," didn't they? Why was I even giving it a second thought?

"Here's your water," he said, taking a seat. "The almond biscotti has chocolate on top. Hope you don't mind."

"No, love it."

"Great," he said. "I wasn't sure. Some people are very picky about things. I can be that way myself."

If he only knew, I thought. Oh, Lord, I'll bet he's anal-retentive! How charming.

"I've got a mocha latte here," he informed me, "but to be quite honest, I could go for a good single malt whiskey."

Okay, don't ask me WHY, but in the spirit of being bright and cheerful, I reached into my bag and pulled out some Wrigley gum. "How 'bout some DOUBLE mint?"

He didn't get the joke. He just looked at me. "I don't chew gum," he said. "Especially with latte."

I should have given up, but I wanted him to know I was kidding. "Do you drink TRIPLE sec?" I asked.

He looked at me, then the corners of his mouth turned upwards.

"Ha!" he said. "Single malt, double mint, triple sec ... ha!"

I uttered a sound somewhere between amusement and utter mortification.

For forty-five minutes, Alan T. told me all about his uncle. I assured him I would write a fitting tribute and include as much of the information as I could, using a photo that the family had provided.

13

"I've never met an obituary writer before," he said. "I rather expected an old man or a college intern."

I was dying inside, mentally writing my own obituary as the pangs intensified.

"But I'm pleasantly surprised. Quite so," he said, resting his hand on mine.

I continued to internally deteriorate while maintaining a pleasant, fixed smile.

"I don't see a ring on your finger," he said.

"Nope," I said.

"You're not divorced, I hope," he said.

"No, never been married," I said. And if I *were* divorced? I thought.

"Neither have I," he said. "Perhaps I'm too choosy, but I'm looking for the right woman. What else do you do besides writing obituaries?"

He was checking me out. I wanted to retaliate by asking about his middle initial, but he had the upper hand and it was beginning to feel very sweaty on top of mine. I was ostensibly still working, he was grief stricken and not in his right mind, so I needed to remain professional. I slid my hand out from under his.

"I'm a reporter," I explained. "I'm just doing this temporarily in addition to my regular position until some new hires are made."

He brightened considerably. "I'm a vice president of a financial services company."

Nobody had ever said that to me before, especially with such gusto. I didn't know how to respond. He certainly looked the part; it was an excellent position, but he was sooooooooooo, well, you know.

"How nice," I said, not wanting any elaboration.

"Anything you want to know about mutual funds, annuities, CDs … just say the word." He winked at me and cocked his head.

"How very kind of you," I said, wondering if he was angling for a date or a new client.

"Who *is* Molly Hacker?" he said with great intensity.

Next he would be asking me if I were a tree, what kind of tree would I be? But I had that answer ready to go.

"A weeping willow!" I blurted out.

He seemed surprised. (A hangnail could throw this guy out of whack, I thought.)

"Molly Hacker is a weeping willow?"

"I didn't mean to say that," I stammered.

"That's an odd answer nonetheless. I find you intriguing. When can I see you again?" he pressed.

My cell could not have rung at a better time. It was Tony, taking me up on my offer to let him vent using real expletives! "%@#$! #(*$! You won't believe what that #@$&ing #@$* did after we last spoke! #$%$!"

Alan looked horrified. I suddenly realized my phone was still on speaker!

"Can you hold on, darling?" I said to Tony.

"Uh, sure ... " he said.

"I'd best be going," Alan T. said to me. "After all, my family is grieving. They need me and vice versa."

"It'll be in Wednesday's edition," I said cheerfully. "In the online edition, too."

He hastily picked up his fat briefcase and his middle initial and headed out the door.

"I owe you my life, Tony," I told him. I love you and I love your expletives."

★ ★ ★

"Excuse me," said a voice from behind after I hung up with Tony. "But you rock!"

I turned around to find an adorable rocker-type guy. He had a thick head of brown hair tied back into a ponytail, two earrings in one ear, raggedy designer jeans, and a faded, moderately tattered red T-shirt with "Malibu" on it. He had the most beautiful, exuberant smile.

Before I could speak (not that I knew what to say), he continued talking. "I've got to know. Did you pay someone to call you and curse like that? I don't do blind dates, but that's a clever way to get out of one."

"I was writing an obituary for him," I explained.

"Holy crap," he said. "You *really* didn't like that guy, did you?"

I burst out laughing and explained the situation to him. He laughed even louder.

"Well, I'm kind of relieved to hear that, " he said. "But my first impression makes a better story, you know?"

"Yeah, so it does," I said, still laughing.

"I'm Cody. Cody Cervantes."

"I'm Molly Hacker," I said, reaching out to shake his hand. He took my hand and held it, smiling as if he could feel the way I was tingling inside.

"Do you do any entertainment reporting?" he asked. "I'm a musician and an artist. I just had a gallery opening in town. Last week."

"Ah, Cervantes!" I said, "I remember that name … and no, I don't mean as the author of *Don Quixote*, I mean I remember hearing about your show. My colleague reviewed it. He said you did beautiful watercolors, very incongruous with your rocker look. Like you were painting your soul."

"That's about what I'm doing. In fact, I gave him that quote when he asked me to describe how I perceived my work."

That cheater, I thought. Should have attributed it to him.

"The passion and despair of my soul come out in my paintings. I almost go into a meditative state when I paint. My wild and crazy side comes out when I've got an acoustic guitar in my hands or a band behind me. I do alternative rock. Outgrew the heavy metal when I was twenty-nine … but hey, don't get me wrong; it's not Muzak."

"Looking at you," I said, "I am sure it's not."

He smiled, and his brown eyes twinkled.

Oh, Lord, I thought. Please tell me I didn't just come on to this guy.

"So, listen," he said. "At the risk of your phone ringing and that dude cursing again … " He looked out the plate glass window. "He's not, like, outside or anything, right? I mean, you don't have a hand signal or anything, do you?"

"I've got a hand signal," I said, "but I try to be a lady and save it only for desperate times."

He cracked up. No slight upward turn of the mouth followed by a "ha." He cracked up.

"I've been on the receiving end of that signal a few times, but I've used it on others even more. I'm a giver, not a receiver."

My double-entendre brain started working overtime. I had to slow my roll. Whew!

I laughed. "You're funny," I said. "And having someone ring my cell is a pretty good idea."

"Look, I heard that guy say he wanted to see you again, and I don't want to be Bozo Number Two, but I'd love it if you'd come to our gig at the Rolling Beetle next week. As my guest. I'd like that."

"I'd love to," I told him. "And you're *not* Bozo Number Two. You're Bozo Number Three. You should see the guy I met at lunch today."

He didn't even blink. He knew I was kidding, and he laughed loudly. It felt so good. He got my humor. I loved that about him. I reached into my bag and handed him my card. "Call me tomorrow with the info. I'll be there. I've got to get home now and open my laptop. It's been a long day and it's not over yet."

He looked at my card and then at me and grinned. "I can't wait to see you again."

"Me, too," I said.

As I walked to my car, I was feeling A-okay. I had followed my instincts and look where it had led. Two guys had asked me out within two hours and I had a "date" for next week.

Way to go! I told myself silently. I'll show them all yet.

Chapter 4: *T* STANDS FOR TROUBLE!

THE VERY NEXT DAY ...

"You're lucky I like you, Randy," I told my colleague. "Or you'd be in BIG TROUBLE, and your name would be mud!"

"Oh," he gasped. "What crime did I commit? Please, Molly Rose, don't change my name to Mud. Randy fits me to a T."

Ugh. There was that initial again. *T.* It could only stand for trouble.

"A capital *T* and that rhymes with *P*, and it stands for PERFECT," he continued.

I pretended not to hear him. "Didn't you ever hear of quoting someone?" I asked. "You don't take someone's words and make them your own because you wished you'd thought of it first. That is *so* lame."

Randy daintily patted his chest for relief and feigned fear. "Oh, no, Mommy, don't lock me up without dinner. That beautiful man's words were just *so* poetic, and I needed to impress someone special. Give me a break, puh-leeze."

He didn't know that I knew his real name was Harry. But he was about to find out.

"Why shouldn't I change your name?" I baited him. "YOU did. HARRY!"

"Oh, STOP!" he said, as a fake panic attack overwhelmed him. "Molly Rose Hacker, you must never, ever say that ghastly name again. You're not supposed to know that. But since you do, you must never say it again. Ever."

"Why not?" I said, enjoying myself immensely. "It's your name."

"My legal name is Randy. I have had it changed."

"Why didn't you change it to Horny instead of Randy? Would have been closer to the original."

He picked up his lime-flavored Perrier and took a sip to calm himself from his bogus shortness of breath.

"We *are* in a mood today!" he exclaimed. "And what do you know about Mr. Cody Cervantes, may I ask? Why so protective? Are you his new bodyguard? Oh, yes, sugar dumpling, I'll bet you'd LOVE that. What the heck, *I'd* LOVE that!"

Randy laughed raucously at his own joke.

"Oh, you are *so* not taking me seriously," I said, half-seriously. (I loved getting him going.)

He brushed some imaginary dust off his skintight black T-shirt as if the gesture of doing so somehow purified him.

"Come on, now Molly Rose. Dish to Randy."

He sat on the edge of his desk, crossed his legs, and put his chin in his right hand, staring at me with rapt attention. "I'm waiting."

"Okay, okay," I said. "I met Cody last night. In Starbucks."

"And we were in Starbucks because … ?"

"WE were in Starbucks because WE had to meet with Alan T. Cressman, nephew of my first obituary."

"Hmmm … *très intéressant.* I didn't know that WE met relatives of the dearly departed in coffeehouses."

"The guy wanted to meet me in person. It wasn't what you think. He wanted to give me firsthand information about his uncle because he wanted the obituary to reflect his true essence."

"Oh, puh-leeze! You fell for the 'true essence' line?"

"As a matter of fact," I said emphatically, "he told me that he had expected an old man or a college intern, not someone like me."

"Let Randy untangle the crossed wires in your head. Mr. Grieving Relative came into the office right after you left. Yes, he was indeed anxious to have the obituary taken care of in record time. However, it wasn't until he saw your photo on the wall that he asked Ray for your number."

I was flabbergasted. "No freakin' way! He KNEW what I looked like?"

Randy laughed with pure delight. "He *so* did, Molly Rose."

I grunted. I hated when people lied to me, and I hated being set up.

"Okay, so get over being duped and tell me about meeting that delicious Cody."

I told Randy the entire scenario. I was always amazed at how he could come up with a new physical motion to react to every word. He was ingenious at doing so.

"That's spectacular," he said. "But you're not the *only* one who met someone."

"And who is he?"

"Kyle Tillman," Randy said as his "bedroom eyes" expanded.

"I don't have to know *everything*!" I warned him.

"Well, he's new in town, fresh from the Big Apple, unscathed by the local cretins he could have encountered first. But luckily for him, he met me. We get along *fabulously*, and seriously, Gypsy Rose Lee, I think everything *is* coming up roses for us. We do have a lot in common. He's smart, sweet, sensitive, and he said I make him laugh."

"Cody found me funny, too," I interjected onto deaf ears.

"Yes, it's looking good," he continued. "I checked the weather report, and this time nothing is going to rain on my parade."

"I'm glad you met someone," I told him. "I hope it works out for you and Kyle. Just don't steal any of Cody's words if you interview him again, or life as you know it will cease to be a cabaret, old chum."

He gasped because it was what he liked to do, and then smiled.

"Race you to the altar," he said.

AND TWO DAYS AFTER THAT ONE ...

I was sitting at my desk, going through my notes for an op-ed piece I was going to write on government waste, but the only excess spending that I could think about was what I would wear to Cody's gig. I had spent the earlier part of that morning moping because Cody hadn't called, and I was certain that I had misread his cues. But at precisely 11:47 a.m., he called, apologizing for not having called sooner, and reaffirming his invitation to the Rolling Beetle.

So, not being able to previously focus because he *hadn't* called, I was now having trouble focusing because he *had* called. I was also vastly relieved that I would not have to tell Randy that I never heard from the guy again.

As was my usual routine, I ate lunch, a salad I'd made at home, at my desk. Randy and my other colleagues knew to ask a day in advance if they wanted me to join them at a local restaurant. (or "straunt," as I sometimes refer to them).

I was munching on a carrot, when a huge bouquet of flowers walked itself into my not-so-big office. It filled the room with a beautiful aroma, but I was too busy wondering whose legs were underneath it.

The bouquet sat down on the right side of my desk, revealing Alan T. Cressman to the left. I gulped.

"Hello, Molly. These are for you."

"Alan ... " I stammered.

He looked different. He was wearing khaki pants and a perfectly pressed sage green shirt, and he seemed far more relaxed than he had been a few nights ago. A lock of his wavy light brown hair fell playfully onto his forehead, and he was, dare I say it, rather cute.

"I want to thank you," he said. "That obituary you wrote for my uncle far exceeded my family's expectations. You put heart and soul into it. You captured his true essence."

I was just about to thank him when I noticed Randy practically standing behind where Alan was sitting, just over the threshold, gesturing wildly as he pointed to the flowers and heard Alan speak the words "true essence." Randy was somehow going to pay for this later, I decided, but I had to be professional, in spite of the fact that my beloved colleague and friend had other ideas.

I smiled more broadly than I normally would have, trying to cover up the suppressed laughter from Randy's antics. "That makes me feel *so* good, Alan. It does."

"I wasn't myself when I met you the other night," he said. "My uncle was special to me. Since I was a small boy, he made me feel special. He gave me that extra attention every kid needs, and the fact that he had three kids of his own didn't stop him. He was a wonderful man."

I suddenly wanted to cry.

"We were all devastated by his death, as I told you, but I was in shock, and I think I acted like some humorless stuffed shirt."

I wanted to protest, but I didn't know how. Alan seemed to pick up on that.

"I not only acted like a stuffed shirt," he continued, "but I was inappropriate, and I'm embarrassed about it."

"Don't be," I consoled him.

"No, I was. I was a jackass. That's why I didn't wear a suit and tie today. I wanted to erase your first impression of me and create a new one."

"Well, I did notice how nice you look," I told him.

He smiled warmly. "Molly, I have to confess something to you. I saw your photo out there in the hallway before I called you. You know, the 'Reporter of the Month' photo. I saw your name and thought you were beautiful. When your editor said you would be writing the obituary, although the timing was not optimal, I just couldn't pass up the opportunity to meet you."

"You wanted to meet me that much?"

"Yeah," he said. "I sort of, kind of, did."

"Oh, Alan, that's so sweet."

"The day I met you was hellish. I'm sure you didn't notice this, but I used my middle initial both times I identified myself—on the phone and in person. I had visions of you putting my photo up on the wall next to yours, you know, 'Dork of the Month.'"

I laughed. "No, I didn't go that far. As long as we're being honest with one another, I did notice the middle initial thing, but I didn't think twice about it."

"You noticed?" He laughed. "I love sharp women!"

I felt complimented.

"I can explain that, " he said.

"Please do." I was fascinated but tried to hide it.

"All day long I was making calls for my family. My father is also Alan, but my parents didn't want me to be a Junior, so I'm Alan Thomas Cressman, and my father is Alan Charles Cressman. Alan T. Alan C. Get it? So, as we're both known in the same business community, we differentiate with the initials. You must've thought I had starch in more places than my shirt."

I laughed. "Don't be silly. Honestly, Alan, it didn't faze me."

We chatted delightfully for another twenty minutes. Alan was terrific company and I discovered he loved to read, hike, play tennis, and do lots of things I enjoyed doing. When he asked me out, I almost instinctively said no, as I could not stop thinking about Cody. However, I quickly recovered and reminded myself that musicians invite a lot of people to their gigs, and Cody could have no more interest in me than trying to pad the audience. Opportunity had knocked, and I was letting it in.

I was proud of myself. I had turned down the social reporter job and within hours of being the temporary obit writer, I had met two men. Not bad. Not bad at all.

Alan had already told me that he'd never been married and was looking for the right woman. He was self-assured, financially stable, and quite handsome. I agreed to go out with him, and we made plans for a week from Saturday. I respected the fact that he wanted to spend more time with his family before going out on a date.

As he got up to go, he took my hand, kissed it, and smiled. "Do you mind if I call you before?" he said. "I feel so comfortable with you."

"I'll look forward to it."

He smiled and left my office. My thoughts of excess spending were exploding like fireworks. I might need an entire new wardrobe.

I don't need Naomi-Hall Benchley setting me up with Art's golf-playing, new-in-town colleague to get a date. I do just fine on my own, I bragged to myself.

"The Unsinkable Molly Rose!" Randy said, sticking his head in the door. "You agreed to go out with him. You're lining them up, girlfriend."

"Aren't I, though?" I said proudly.

"Just one thing, honey," Randy admonished. "The next time the guy brings you flowers, it would be nice if they weren't from a funeral home."

Now *I* was gasping. I started to protest, but I knew he was right. The huge bouquet on my desk had FUNERAL written all over them. He's a nice guy, I told myself. I can forgive this. I know I can.

Chapter 5: I GROW TIRED OF BUBBLES

THAT WEEKEND...

Claudia has been my best friend since junior high. Honestly, she was the most refreshingly honest and crazy girl in my class, and we shared *almost* everything. Hanging out with her was an adventure in itself, and if you asked Claudia, she'd have a lot of stories to tell about me.

After graduation, we attended different colleges, but we still remained close, chatting often about our lives and our romantic liaisons. But when Claudia met her future husband, she became more focused on him (and I don't blame her one bit). We grew somewhat apart but remained best friends in our hearts, still talking whenever time permitted.

When we both came back to Swansea after graduation, our friendship picked up more of its old steam. Claudia, then happily working in advertising and dating Colin, was all too eager to help me find my future husband. I loved the attention at first; she was never out of ideas. But I soon grew to realize that love is not a clever advertising concept (though many would disagree), and these crazy stunts and blind dates just didn't work for me anymore. Yet everyone in town wanted to set me up: my friends, my parents' friends, and even casual acquaintances. As much as I wanted to meet someone, I started to resent the intrusion.

It began to feel like everyone wanted to be "the one" to find me a husband. Even people like Naomi Hall-Benchley, who was an all-too-familiar acquaintance-slash-friend of some of my friends but never a friend of mine, developed an enormous interest in my marital status, as I previously mentioned.

That weekend, after meeting Alan and Cody, Claudia and I had plans for lunch and a trip to the mall. It was perfect timing; after all, I did need some new clothes for my upcoming dates. Dates, not date. The use of the plural can be invigorating at times.

Claudia, a tall, stunning African-American beauty, is often referred to by her friends as "Bubbling Brown Sugar" or "Champagne Claudia" because she is perpetually effervescent—positively indefatigable at times.

We were sitting in La Maison, each inspecting our respective salads, when Claudia asked me if I needed new clothes for anything special. I opened my mouth to tell her about Cody and Alan, but instead of words coming out, a forkful of salad went in.

"Do I need a reason to buy more clothes?" I asked. "Do you?"

She laughed. "Come to think of it, no, I guess you don't, but then again, Molly, you want to have something awesome in your closet in case you have a dating 911."

A sudden epiphany pounded furiously on my brain. In that moment, I decided it was best to keep everything to myself. All of my life I had involved my girlfriends in every aspect of my dating adventures, and nothing had ever worked out for me in the long run. Although I had wanted input, I decided I'd gotten way too much of it. Everyone had an opinion, and although I didn't realize it at the time, those opinions had begun to cloud my faith in my own judgment. Not only that, I felt as if I were dating under a microscope, and who can get intimate with anyone if you're being treated like a lab specimen between two pieces of glass?

"Geez, Claudia, it's not like I've got a closet full of rags!"

She took a sip of her Chardonnay. "You are *so* overly sensitive! You know what I mean; I'm hardly one to dis your wardrobe. After all, I'm the one who helped you pick most of it out!"

"Okay, then," I said. "There you have it. I'm good to go." I didn't want to tell her that lately Randy had become my shopping buddy and had the best eye for fashion of anyone I knew.

"How's Colin? How's work?" I asked.

"Colin is up for a promotion, totally deserved, and the buzz is that he's good to go. Work has been fun. This week, I had to create these characters for this client of ours—a gourmet supermarket—and it was riotous."

"Characters?" Anything to get her off the subject of my personal life.

"Yes," she explained. I had to take fruits and vegetables and give them names. For example, I took a cantaloupe and called her Mellonie. Get it? I named an ear of corn Cornelius, and a stalk of broccoli Brock Lee. Get it? "Brock Lee, Bruce Lee." I was going for the macho connection; eat your broccoli and kick ass like Bruce. This idiot in my department, Fred, who is *not* on the project, suggested naming cole slaw, Cole. I nixed his idea because cole slaw is a dish, anyway, it's not a vegetable unto itself, it wasn't clever, and it wasn't his job. So, after I said no, Fred goes over my head to my boss, and that *so* had me POed, but I won the battle. I knew I would, but he was just such a nuisance. It's just *so* annoying to have people butting into your business when you can do just fine on your own!"

"You know," I said, "I understand. You are *so* right."

"Oh, I always feel so much better when I talk to you," Claudia said, as she poked around in her Crab Louie.

"How about a media maven named Okra Winfrey?" I asked.

"Get real, Molly! That's so overdone and outdated. So, are you seeing anyone?" came the question that never died.

"Not at the moment," I told her.

"Molly, it's not just about sex. You need a man to talk to."

"Jeez, Claude. I'm not a freaking hermit. I talk to men. I KNOW men!"

"You talk to Captain Jack a lot, if I recall."

"He's a good listener," I said. "You'd be surprised."

"Wow. That reminds me. I have something hilarious to tell you. It's about this book I read, and it made me think of you."

Champagne Claudia was bubbling over. I was beginning to feel like flat soda.

"I can't wait to hear this," I said with an ever-so-slight twist of sarcasm in my voice.

"Okay, the book was about this woman who talked to her dog, Hugo, for years. Hugo was this adorable standard poodle, with brown curly hair, and this woman told him everything. She swore that Hugo understood, and he had this uncanny way of comforting her when she needed it the most. Anyway, Hugo died after fourteen years, and natch this woman is beyond heartbroken."

"That's so sad!" I said. "Gee, Claude, you're breaking my heart here."

"Just listen, will you? Okay, well, several months pass, and she's still grieving like crazy. Then, one day, in a rainstorm, she meets this stranger with dark, curly hair. They share a cab together, and he invites her out for a drink."

"Okay … "

"Well, during the course of the conversation, he admits to her that he has total amnesia and can't remember anything about his life except for the past three months. Nada. So she kind of likes this idea and thinks it's cool because he won't have any ex-wives or girlfriends to deal with, even though she worries that you-know-what might hit the fan someday."

"And this reminds you of me because—?"

"Patience. I'm getting there. So, anyway, as time goes on, she starts to notice that this guy just instinctively knows things about her. He doesn't know jack about himself, but he understands her in a way no human being ever has. Okay, so I'll cut to the chase. They have this amazing rapport and this awesome relationship. She suddenly starts to feel as if he is familiar to her. She starts recognizing some of his behavioral patterns and such."

"Oh, my God!" I said.

"That's right, after everything, she figures out that when Hugo died, he was reborn as a grown man, or perhaps he was born again into an amnesiac's body. Either way, she realizes that her lover is her dearly deceased dog. How cool is that? I mean, think about it. Who knows and loves us more than our pets? Our Grover is such a doll. I told Colin once that if Grover were a man, he'd be a super nice guy."

"So, what are you telling me, Claude? That if all else fails, on that dreaded day that I lose Jack, I can count on him coming back to me three months later as a guy with orange hair?"

"Hardly! But it *could* happen. Get real, Molly; I'm just telling you about a book I read, but I couldn't help thinking of you, and I wanted to say that you might want to pay more attention to what you spill to Jack." She laughed.

"That is great advice," I said, laughing. "And the book does sound rather amusing."

Claudia continued to bubble over for another forty-five minutes during lunch and for two more hours and as we traipsed through the mall.

In mid-traipse, Claudia tried about five more times to get the latest on my love life, and that was a good thing, because it made me feel all the more confident in my decision to go it alone without female intervention from start to finish. But I must admit, by the end of the day, I was very tired of bubbles.

LATER THAT SATURDAY NIGHT: EIGHTISH, MY APARTMENT

"These are for you," the male voice said, handing me the most vibrant bouquet of flowers I'd ever seen. "And they come directly to you from the best florist in town—no layovers at the local funeral home."

"Thank you, Randy," I said, noticing that he seemed a bit sad underneath his usual amusing self. "I'll get a vase."

"Oh, but you will let moi arrange these for you. One has to cut the stems precisely at the right angle for them to last longer."

"I wouldn't think of doing it myself," I said. I reached into a lower cabinet and pulled out a Waterford crystal vase that my former boyfriend,

27

Leo, had given me. At the time, the vase was filled with a dozen red roses. Later that same evening came a marriage proposal and a ring—but I'll get back to that traumatic upheaval a bit later on.

Anyway, this was the first time I was using the vase since Leo had given it to me, and it was far more emotional than I bargained for.

"Oh my," Randy said. "The Leonardo vase. And it's breaking your heart all over again. Don't try to hide it, Molly Rose, because I see that tear forming in the corner of your right eye. But that's okay; we must all face our fears in order to defeat them."

"I'll open a bottle of wine for us," I told him.

"Fantastic," he said, focusing on what he was doing. "As long as it's not fizzy."

"You know I don't do fizzy wine," I told him. "Besides, I had enough bubbles today already."

"Either you took a very long bubble bath or you spent the afternoon with Ms. Claudia. The latter, I presume?"

"You presume correctly," I said.

Randy and I, along with the wine and some cheese, relocated to the living room. "Now, tell me why you wanted to come by. And don't say that working full time with me five days a week isn't enough. Something is making you sad."

"English farmhouse cheddar," he said, cutting a piece of cheese and placing it on a cracker. "Exquisite."

"Randy, unless it's the cheese that's making you sad … "

"Okay, okay," he said. "You know I need a moment to collect myself."

He fiddled with the block of cheddar, cut a piece for me, and then sighed. He looked serious.

"I'm scared, Molly Rose," he said.

I had no idea what to think. "Of what? Of whom?"

"Of myself," came the reply.

"This new man you told me about, Kyle, is everything okay there?"

"I saw him last night. We went to an amazing production of *Rent* and then for a Thai dinner afterward. It was perfect. He wanted to get together tonight, but he said his new job has more 'social obligations' than he expected and that he was summoned to a cocktail party-slash-reception thingy tonight. Last moment. Events like that take planning; they're not thrown together at the last minute."

"Maybe his invitation was last minute. It doesn't mean the reception was. Don't you believe him?"

"You do have a point. God knows how many last-minute events we've been 'summoned' to attend."

"Precisely," I said. "Too many."

Randy took a sip of his wine and savored the flavor. "I do believe him, Molly Rose. It's just that I've been lied to so many times. My love life has been shakier than that tower of Pisa I made out of Jell-O for Leonardo's birthday. Oh, sorry. That name!"

"You can say his name," I told him. "I won't crumble. I won't lie down and die; I will survive!"

He laughed. "That song is my anthem!"

"Mine, too," I commiserated.

"Speaking of Jell-O, wouldn't it just be a lark if they hired J-Lo as their spokeswoman? Can't you just see Miss Lopez? 'Hi, I'm J-Lo for Jell-O!' Hell-O! I love it!"

"You're funny, Randy. But you're also stalling."

"I hate that you know me so well!"

"Well, if I didn't, you wouldn't be here, would you?"

"Heavens, no!" he said. "I love you because you understand my true essence." He burst out laughing.

"Oh, shut up!" I said, laughing along. "I should have never told you that. Now, start talking."

"Molly Rose, you of all people know how many times my heart has suffered because I dwelled in the Land of False Hope. But trust me when I say that this time I felt something different from anything I'd ever known before. When I met Kyle, I saw this nonpretentious, sincere, extraordinary someone who even upon meeting me could see through my ever-present facade and right into my soul. I just knew that he wasn't judging this book by its cover. My gut, my heart, my brain, and, well, we won't go *there*, all tell me he's the one."

"And you're afraid to go with it. You're afraid—"

"Of getting pulverized," he finished for me. "We all hide ourselves in different ways. Some people stuff everything way down and don't deal with anything. Of course, we both know that's impossible and that not dealing with something in a healthy way will only manifest itself in the most dysfunctional of ways. As you know, I usually deal by putting on The Randy Show. But if I find the right person, if Kyle is the right person, I won't have to hide in the center ring anymore. I won't have to be 'on' all the time because people expect it of me or because it's the best way I know to feel alive … or to at least look it. Do you know how many parties I've been invited to just because the host knew the soiree wouldn't be dull if I were around? Sometimes I hate the jokes I make; I'm just afraid if I stop, the real me will be painfully exposed. I have this recurring dream where I'm naked from the waist up, thank God, but my chest is made of glass, and people can see right inside me. They crowd around me and see my quivering, vulnerable heart. I get frightened, so I start making jokes, fast and furiously, until my chest turns back to opaque flesh, and nobody can see inside anymore."

I started to respond but realized the best thing I could do was to let him take a breath and keep on talking. Rarely did Randy open up like this, and I didn't want to give him any opportunity to veer off topic, as I would be unlikely to get him back. I liked listening to him. I couldn't help but think about how much I'd rather be a psychologist than a reporter.

"I'm all over the map here," he said, preparing another cracker for me, then for himself. "I'm so afraid I'll sabotage this because I'm afraid of getting hurt. I don't trust myself enough to trust *him*. Do I make any sense at all? Why can't I just roll with this and have faith that if it's meant to be, it will be. Why?"

I laughed. "Life is ironic, isn't it? You've come over here to ask me the same questions I pound myself with twenty-four/seven. I only wish I had the answers."

Randy and I talked until 3:00 a.m., stopping only to order some appetizers from a local gourmet shop. Not only did Randy's faith in me as a friend make the evening memorable, but through his doubts and insecurities, I was able to zoom in more clearly on my own before I lost focus again. We talked about everything, but mostly about our past relationships and how they affected our present ones (or in my case, lack of a present one). Thoughts of my ex, Leonardo, inhabited my dreams that night, utilizing some bizarre symbolism that I'm still working on deciphering. When I woke in a cold sweat, it occurred to me that I was trying to figure out the Leonardo da Vinci code and that Randy would appreciate my humor when I'd tell him the next day.

I realized that it had been a long time since I had a real conversation with a friend. It wasn't all about Randy; it wasn't all about me. It was about both of us; it was about life. When Randy spoke about living his life in the "center ring," I could relate to that. I felt as if I were living in the center ring, and everyone was focused on how to get me hooked up, myself included. Then there were the times I felt like a sideshow freak. Ladies and gentlemen, step right up and see the single, picky Molly Hacker screw up yet another relationship. Hurry, folks. The show is about to begin.

That evening was a turning point for me. I was closer to accepting what went wrong with Leo. And that was wonderful, but it left me with just one problem: now that I understood, what would I do with it? Move on, I told myself. Do you have any other freakin' choice?

Chapter 6: OKAY, I'LL TELL YOU SOMETHING ABOUT LEO

LATE SUNDAY MORNING ...

I managed just a few hours of restless sleep before I woke at 7:30 a.m. I was up for a mere two minutes to use the bathroom and feed a mewing Captain Jack before I threw myself at the mercy of my bed again. An internal dialogue took over the moment I shut my eyes. I couldn't nail down one thought and mull it over before five more demanded my attention. I felt as if I were drunk and dizzy and being spun around too fast on a dance floor. If my brain had an off switch, I didn't know where to find it, but suffocating myself with a pillow didn't do the trick.

I thought about every man I knew and every man I had just met: Randy, Leo, Tony, Alan T. Cressman, Cody, Art Benchley, Susan Decker's new husband, Claudia's husband, Ray, the mailman, and every guy I'd dated or had a relationship with in the last several years. My brain was torturing me. It was as if all of the men were draping their arms around one another's shoulders, kicking my brain like the Radio City Music Hall Rockettes, and singing, "If you don't know us by now, you will never, ever, ever know us ... " (With apologies to Harold Melvin and the Blue Notes for that ghastly visual.)

When I woke up close to noon on Sunday, my head felt as if it had been through a paper shredder. I thought about Randy and wondered how he was doing. I hoped that perhaps Kyle had called him and that they would be getting together. Then all of the men in my brain disappeared ... all except Leo.

I guess that leaves me no choice. If I want to tell my story, I will have to talk about Leo.

I met him in the fall. I was at this old-fashioned kiosk/café in the park, buying a bottle of water and some popcorn. After I paid, I turned to find this unusual free spirit behind me. I can't describe how I perceived him, because on paper, he won't sound that different from your typical attractive man. I think I'll just ramble a bit, and maybe you'll be able to decipher what I'm saying.

His clothing looked as if he had taken several different styles and combined them into one: his own. He had on faded, loose-fitting jeans, a long-sleeved tobacco-brown Henley shirt, a dark red Italian silk vest embroidered with an exquisite paisley pattern, and hiking boots. He had dark, slightly wild hair, and he wore black Ray-Ban sunglasses that made him look like a movie star, but at the same time made me want to rip them off his face so I could see his eyes.

"Where's the movie?" he asked, smiling.

Normally, I would have taken that as a pick-up line and maybe been a little bitchy in my response. (I said, maybe.) But he took my breath away, and I looked over at the empty bench where I'd been sitting.

"The movie is right here in the park; it's everything you can see from the park bench and some of what you can only infer or imagine," I told him. "I'm going back over to watch some more. It's *cinéma verité* at its finest."

"How about I get some popcorn and join you? If I'm not being too presumptuous—"

"No," I said, "not at all."

Everything felt honest and real. When Claudia told me about meeting Colin, when my sister, Hannah, told me about meeting Matthew, when Scarlett met Rhett—this had all of the elements of that "something special." Just as Randy had told me the other day about how he felt when he met Kyle, I understood. When I met Leo, I had this fluttery, flighty, frenetic feeling that life was going to get a whole lot more exciting.

Leo and I sat on the bench until the sun went down. Without excuses, he told me all the various things he did: he was an environmentalist and a political writer, a master carpenter, a runner, a vociferous reader, and a world traveler. He didn't tell me at the time that he came from an Italian family of some wealth, nor did he tell me exactly what he did for a living, which turned out to be a little bit of everything he liked and was good at doing.

He was brilliant and knew things I didn't know anyone knew. I'd met men before who would show off by quoting from the latest book they'd read or by repeating dialogue fresh from *Meet the Press*. I'd known men who wrote abhorrently mediocre poetry and wanted nothing more than to have women coddle them and tell them what sensitive, sexy, brilliant beings they were. Leo just told me things as they came up; he didn't force "interesting facts" into the conversation accidentally on purpose. He asked me all kinds of questions. He wanted to know what foods I enjoyed, what movies I liked, where I dreamed of traveling someday, if I thought animals understood more than humans thought they did, if I'd ever wished I could fly, if I had complex dreams, if I understood how soft, billowy clouds could turn to thunder. That was Leo.

The park closed at sundown, so we had to leave, but neither one of us wanted to separate. We knew that without discussing it. Leo took me to a new/used bookstore on a nearby side street where I'd never been. He showed me all kinds of books on topics I'd never thought about and asked me to show him what books I liked to read. When I dared choose a book of love sonnets, he bought it for me, quietly, and without the fanfare that would normally scare off the most interested woman.

Next door, in a sweet little French café, we had croissant sandwiches and coffee, and we talked as if we'd known each other forever.

And that was how I met Leo.

WELL, OF COURSE THERE'S MORE ...

And so, our relationship began as if we were already old friends. Leo believed in past lives, quite strongly, because he believed that the connections he had with some people throughout his lifetime (including me) were not accidental. He believed that we got along like old friends because indeed, we were. What we had meant to one another in another life or how it was resolved, he had no clue. But he believed there was a reason that we all come into contact with the people we meet, whether it was for the long or short run. Leo and I both expected it would be for the long run.

Leo worked doing many things because he loved many things, and he didn't want to be tied down to a nine-to-five job. He loved the flexibility of being his own boss. He had talents he was too humble to share with me. He was brilliant.

I can't even remember the day I knew I was in love with him. Maybe it happened that first day in the park, but Leo filled me up in places that I didn't even know had empty spaces. I was drawn to him emotionally, intellectually, sexually, spiritually, to just name a few ways. He had a wonderful sense of humor that didn't fit into any category; it was just eclectic, just like Leo.

A few months after we began dating, we spent our first Christmas together. He made me the most amazing nightstand for my bedroom because the one I had was too small, and the phone was always crashing to the floor. Leo learned carpentry from a very early age from his grandfather, who had learned his from his father. It is my most cherished possession. The craftsmanship is exquisite, but the love he put into making it, into designing it just for me, touched me more than I can appropriately address. Sorry, talking about him chokes me up.

Over the holidays, Leo and I spent some time with each other's families, and that was the first time my friends (except for Randy) had met him, and a few of his friends met me. We were just so much in love that we didn't feel like sharing one another much, at least not right away. Our life was one adventure after another. I never knew what he was going to suggest next.

"Baby, what do you say to bungee jumping?"

I didn't know what to think. I'd gone along with everything (joyously so), but this was not something I wanted to do.

"Uh … are you freakin' kidding me? I'd say the thought of it makes my stomach want to come out of my mouth!"

He laughed hard. "Me, too."

"Oh, thank God," I said.

"Quite frankly, it scares the hell out of me," he said. "But listen, Molly, even if it didn't, even if I wanted to do it, and you hated the idea, you don't have to be afraid to say no. I love you because you have a spirit that complements mine, because you have great passion and conviction, because you're funny and beautiful. But part of being passionate is saying, 'No way! I don't want to do that.' Do you hear what I'm saying?"

"Yeah, honey," I said, wondering if there was a bigger message behind his words. Was he trying to tell me that I didn't have to immerse my personality into his to be loved? Did he think that was what I was doing? I was so happy he let me off the bungee hook (metaphorically speaking), but I hated the way my insecurities grew like mental dandelions—brain weeds, if you like.

I loved and hated the notion that he knew me so well. Most of the time, it's wonderful to have your man understand you on such a deep level, but there are times it's convenient that he's clueless.

"Molly, I can see the wheels spinning, and they don't need to, you know?"

"Trying to tell me that I don't have all four tires on the pavement?" I said, in a meager attempt not to let things get too heavy.

Leo followed my lead and started singing "Just the Way You Are," a song we both detested. Leo, of course, had dibs on hating the song first.

About six months into our relationship, we'd gone to this wonderful Italian restaurant and unbeknown to us, the straunt had a piano player who began his first set at 9:30. He was a competent lounge lizard, but he didn't belong in *that* restaurant. Leo told me there are a lot of lizards in Italy, but this species belonged in a moderately priced hotel bar.

35

Anyway, this indigenous lizard opened his set by singing that song. Leo had his back to the piano, and as soon as heard the music begin, he began choking on his linguine, then trying to chase it down with *acqua frizzante*. The bubbles made him sneeze, and the lizard had sung just a few words past "Don't go changing, to try and please me … " when Leo started pulling a strand of linguine out of his nose.

We both became hysterical with laughter, then he took off on a comic side trip that made my stomach hurt more than bungee jumping could ever have done. "Would you love me if I sneezed linguine, and it was contagious?" he cooed. He started pulling the strand to the beat of the song. "What if I cried spinach and had marinara sauce dripping out of my ears? You wouldn't love me just the way I was, would you? That's such a bogus song. What if I did jumping jacks in the middle of the night in bed singing 'Jumpin' Jack Flash' and scared Captain Jack? What if I told Jack he couldn't eat until he was 'nimble and quick' and then jumped over a candlestick? You wouldn't love me then, would you? What if I had thick body hair that covered my entire back and shoulders? Would you be turned on?" (He knew I hated that!)

Leo grabbed a piece of bread and shoved it in his mouth, then proceeded to sing along with the lizard. "Would you wub me if I talked wib my mouf fulled like dis?"

I noticed the people at the tables on either side of us were in stitches, except for one couple two tables away who looked pretentiously aghast.

Leo sang along with the lizard, his mouth full of bread and the strand of linguine still in his nose. When the song was over, he disengaged all of the food from his face and delicately wrapped the "nose strand" in a paper napkin. We were still laughing, rejoicing in the fact that the song was over, when "That's Amore" filled the room. At least the lizard was right about something: it was amore.

Obviously, there's a lot more to tell about Leo, and if you're wondering how something so beautiful could end, I'm not sure I know. But I will tell you what happened. Eventually. There's only so much reminiscing I can do at once. My heart-to-heart with Randy evoked some powerful emotions in both of us.

I had two upcoming dates with two great guys. I had no business lamenting the past and coloring what could be a very bright future with another man. It was time for a good night's sleep.

Chapter 7: WILL CODY REMEMBER INVITING ME?

After I recovered from my "I Remember Leo" weekend, I came to work that Monday determined to move forward. Randy was in a better frame of mind. He had indeed gotten together with Kyle that Sunday, but he was still suffering from the fear of his wonderful new relationship coming undone. I reminded him of what he had told me many times, that anxiety can turn your worst fears into a self-fulfilling prophecy.

Randy and I were very good at boosting one another up, but we also fed off each other's insecurities. I begin mildly obsessing on the fact that Cody had not called again to confirm or to even say hello. More and more, I wondered if I should even show up at the Rolling Beetle and save myself the embarrassment of there being no ticket left at the door for me. Well, the gig was not until midweek. I had a couple more days to tramp through the mire.

"Molly Rose, if that man forgot that he invited you, then the shame is on him, not you."

"But couldn't he have called? I mean, wouldn't you have called?"

Randy sighed. "Honey, there are many things I would do, but I've also learned that everyone isn't just like me. As scintillating as I am, it would be boring if everyone were just like me. At the very least, you need to go. You have to climb every mountain, ford every stream ... you have to stop making excuses to not even try. You're going. If he forgets about you, I will so trash him in some subversive way that he'll never perform or paint in this town again. I'll have him blacklisted from every town that has a vowel in it."

I laughed. He had made me feel better. Then I went back to what I do best: worry.

Around three that afternoon, Alan called me, to let me know he was thinking about me and was looking forward to our date that weekend. We didn't talk long, but he said he had just wanted to hear the sound of my voice. The sound of my voice? That should have made me happy, but I wondered if he was one of those guys who falls deeply in love on the first date, freaks the woman out, and starts from scratch again.

I told myself I was being unfair and ridiculous. Here I was, having silly doubts about the man who didn't call me, and I was labeling the one who *did* call some kind of desperado. Were these men sitting around pinning undeserved labels on me? I reminded myself what a doll Cody was and what a truly nice man Alan was.

I was just nervous. Yes, I chalked all of my crazy thoughts up to nerves. Pickiness had nothing to do with any of it.

YEAH, THAT'S THE TICKET!

Two days passed, and I still hadn't heard from Cody. He had sounded so sincere about leaving a ticket for me, but I was irked he hadn't called to confirm. Then again, we didn't know one another, and he hadn't broken any promise to call, so I decided I would risk public humiliation at the box office and trust that he had remembered.

To say I felt relief to find a ticket waiting for me at the Rolling Beetle would be a vast understatement. I was saved from a potentially devastating, mortifying scene that I think would have set me back years. Not only was a ticket waiting, but the box office person said Cody had checked three times to make sure it was there. Someone was called over, and I was led to a small round table in the front of the room. I felt so special I didn't realize I was face to face with a gigantic speaker, and that its twin (and other family members) weren't all that far away.

A pleasant young woman with gads of tattoos and red and blue hair asked me what I wanted to drink and told me that she was given strict instructions to treat me like a queen. Suddenly, I was feeling like the rock star's girlfriend. I liked that, but then my lips started forming the word "groupie," and I didn't want to be considered one or to fend off their overzealous affection for my man. My man? I needed to regroup. Or did I need to regroupie? Why was I so ridiculously nervous? Why was I getting insanely ahead of myself? I might as well start worrying about the seating arrangements for our wedding while I was at it.

The room began filling up, and suddenly I saw Cody waving at me from backstage, holding up one finger (the index finger; don't get any silly thoughts, though I did squint to make sure I was seeing clearly) to let me know he'd be right out.

"Molly!" he said, grinning as he approached me with open arms. "Wow, I was hoping you'd show." He gave me a big bear hug.

"Of course I'm here," I told him. "I would never have accepted if I weren't planning to show."

"I wanted to call you, but I was just too crazed with rehearsals and studio work. I didn't want to hound you, either."

"You wouldn't have hounded me," I told him, trying to hide the fact that I was a bit miffed that he hadn't called. "You ain't nothin' but a hound dog."

He burst out laughing. "Yeah, I'm crying all the time."

Oh, Lord, please tell me I didn't initiate a duet of "Hound Dog." Please tell me I didn't.

Cody continued. "I ain't nothin' but a hound dog, but please be a friend of mine!"

I laughed nervously. I was stuck. I searched my brain for some witty repartee to dazzle him with, but I found nothing. I decided to get the ugly truth out of the way.

"I was afraid maybe you'd forgotten that you had invited me."

Cody's eyes opened wide. "Oh, effin' hell! Wow!" He smacked himself on the side of the head. "Nice going, Cervantes! Geez, I *should* be in the doghouse!"

"Oh, Cody, don't be—"

"I should have called," he said emphatically. "I should have. Damn, I'm sorry, Molly."

"It's okay."

"No, it's not. I don't want to come off like the flaky artist. Can I do one bonehead thing without tarnishing my image? I'm sorry. I'm not eighteen anymore, and I should have been more thoughtful."

I mentally slapped myself for having judged him so harshly.

Cody pulled up a chair, turned it around, and straddled his legs on either side of the back. "There's another band opening for us; they're going to do about four songs, and then we'll be on. After the show, I thought we could go somewhere and get to know each other."

I pondered his words. "Go somewhere and get to know each other." That was a perfectly normal thing to say. It had no overt carnal undertones. "Go somewhere and get to know each other." Sure, that was a fine thing to say. Just fine.

"Is that okay?" Cody asked. "Don't worry, we'll do better than Starbucks. I'll let you pick the place."

I sighed with relief and silently pummeled myself for being so ridiculous. "That sounds great, Cody. And I can't wait to hear your band. I did some research, you know. Your reviews are pretty awesome."

"Did you read the one my mother wrote or the one my father wrote? I think my brother wrote the best one ... kidding." He chuckled. "Thanks, Molly. That's sweet. I hope you agree with them."

He was showing humility. For an artist, that's a good thing. And I wasn't the only slightly insecure one; he had worried that *I* wouldn't show. Okay, so he could have called, but he apologized for that. I felt genuinely happy I had taken the chance and come.

MY POOR EARS!

I saw the speakers. I knew how close I was. Why didn't I ask for another table? I can answer that: I felt special being up close and near Cody.

The band that opened was loud. Not loud; LOUD. Screaming, crazy, hard-rock LOUD. This-headache-will-last-you-a-week LOUD to the gazillioneth power.

Cody's band, the Copper Spoons, was great, sort of Coldplayish with some Maroon 5 and some great alternative rock. Cody had a raspy, ultra-cool voice and was easily the hottest guy on stage, and I was his date. He was completely into his performance, but he did look at me and wink several times. I wondered if he noticed that my body was stiff and my head was bobbling. I loved the music, but the Copper Spoons were LOUD, too.

The sound in my head continued to reverberate way after Cody's band had finished playing two long sets, and I did not expect any decrease of pain in the foreseeable future. Seconds after the last song, a rush of people came forward, and I survived an interminable wait until every last one of them had cleared out. Cody kept looking over at me in frustration, as if he wanted to apologize for having to talk to everyone, but that's show business. I sat patiently in my chair, unintentionally giving occasional dirty looks to the closest speaker. Finally, Cody was free from the fans and friends.

"Oh, crap, Molly. I'm so used to this noise. It never occurred to me how loud it would be for you. I should have warned you, but I was thinking that if I asked you if you wanted to sit way back, you might get the idea I wanted to hide you or something."

At that moment, a very attractive blonde in a black leather skirt and a see-through fishnet red top with a black bra underneath sidled up next to Cody, turning ever so briefly to express her discontent with my presence.

"And this is who you've been blowing me off for?" she said, sneering at me.

Cody began to respond, but she cut him off.

"Save it, make word soup," she snapped. "All I wanted was to make things great happen for us and help you with your career. And just because I don't like creepy crawling little Barbie doll FREAKS and juvie biker chicks hanging all over you, you dump me for *this*?"

"Hey, helping me succeed isn't telling the dudes in the band what they should wear and what songs they should sing. And pushing fans away because you're jealous doesn't exactly do it for me, either. Nor does shadowing me twenty-four seven. But insulting my friend is the lowest—"

"Oh, please, Cody," she said, clearly unable to muster any kind of respectable defense. She looked at me. "You look so suburban. So clean-cut. What are you doing with Cody? You like that bad boy image? Taking a walk on the wild side? Isn't it past your curfew? Don't chicks like you break out in hives if they stay up this late?"

Cody started to seethe, but I stood up and faced her. "Put your claws back in. You might rip your little see-through top otherwise. And I can see by looking at *your* face that you must be up twenty-four seven. May I suggest a better foundation?"

"Oh, don't tell me!" she said. "You work in a department store behind a makeup counter. Or do you work at Cosmetic Town? That monstrous discount house that sells nothing but discontinued crapola!"

"It would be a perfectly respectable job if I did," I told her. "But I don't. You don't know anything about me. Maybe I should clue you in. Let's see. Where should I start? With my black belt in karate? Cody, got any spare boards around? Oh, never mind; her neck will do just fine."

"You don't think about touching me," she said, taking a few precautionary steps back. "Don't worry your little bleached head over it," I told her. "I'm germophobic."

"Bite me," she said.

I saw that Cody was nervously enjoying the catty repartee. I was ashamed to be partaking in such behavior but felt compelled to do so. Curiously, I found myself fighting back as Randy might do. (I'd learned a lot from him.)

"You won't last a week with him, you know," she continued. "He likes Mercedes; I guess tonight he just felt like driving an old Suburban."

"You're out of here, Barb," Cody said. "Make tracks and keep going."

She turned to me before she stormed out. "Like I said, sweetie, you won't last a week. Moldy cheese has a longer shelf life than you will. I got bitch fire, and it keeps me going strong!"

"Nice to meet you," I said, irritating her further by refusing to get further irritated.

Cody looked at me. "Oh, man, Molly. I'm so sorry. First I don't call; then I sit you right in front of the effin' speaker; then Barbarino attacks you … oh man."

"I've met her kind before," I assured him. "She wouldn't have acted that way if she wasn't jealous, so I'll just choose to take it all in stride."

"You rock," Cody said. "You know what she's doing, don't you, Molly? She wants you to think I'm a total player. She wants you to conjure up every stereotype of a musician out there until you find one or two that sends you running in the other direction. I'm thirty-five now; I've had my crazy fun, and I *still* want to have crazy fun, but not the kind that involves a different woman every night. I'd like to get to know you. I liked you the moment I heard your friend cursing into the phone. I think you're beautiful. And refreshing, and funny. Please, don't write any premature obituaries for you and me. Get to know me. Please."

A million questions raced through my head: good ones contradicting bad ones and vice versa. I fortified myself and tuned them all out. "I'd love to get to know you, Cody."

YES, I HAD A WONDERFUL TIME, THANK YOU

I had been so used to disastrous dates of late, that when I got home, I had to remind myself that I'd been on a great date with a hot guy. What I liked best about Cody was the ease with which we communicated, his willingness to talk about personal things, and how he didn't seem to take himself too seriously.

I also appreciated his sensitivity to my feelings. He was bothered by his ex attacking me as she did (but he loved the way I handled her), so when we got to the Moonlight Café & Bar, where we spent three hours together, he told me he wanted to talk about her just briefly enough to get her "off the canvas." He explained that when he began seeing her, she was much nicer, evolving over time into a jealous, controlling woman. He said that her name was Barbara Joan Reno and she had legally changed it to Barbarino. Like Cher or Madonna, just one name. He was so amused by it, I naturally thought to tell him about Alan T. Cressman with the glaring middle initial. However, had I done that, it would have slipped out that Alan was the guy from Starbucks (whom Cody thought I had gotten rid of) and that I had a date with Alan for that coming Saturday.

It all got very complicated in my head, so I nixed the idea, asking him instead how his group chose the name the Copper Spoons.

Cody explained that when he and some of his pals were in high school, there were a few "no-talent" bums who came from money and whose daddies bought them expensive music equipment that Cody and his talented friends coveted. So, years later, when Cody and two of his old friends formed a professional group (along with two new guys), they remembered their classmates who were born with "silver spoons" in their mouths and decided they would be the Copper Spoons.

Anyway, back to Barbarino for one last dis. Cody said that he had broken up with her months ago but that she refused to get the message. I couldn't help but be suspicious. I'd known guys (and women) who had dumped their significant others only to say hello again when their respective hormones were on fire. You know, ex-lovers with benefits. I decided I was being unfair to Cody by making such suppositions, but mostly, I was being unfair to me. I would never find my soul mate if I continued to doubt every word a man ever spoke to me. But then again, a girl can never be too careful. Or too picky.

Chapter 8: IS ALAN A FICUS OR A PALM?

RANDY IS AWOL WHEN I NEED HIM

I was exhausted going to work after a late-night weekday date, but I felt good. Being so picky, of course, I had all kinds of things nagging me that I wanted to share with Randy. To my great dismay, he wasn't feeling well and had opted to work from home that day.

I must note that Cody did call me to tell me he had "a blast." I appreciated that he was making a conscious effort to make up for not having called to confirm before our date. But then I began to wonder: did he call because it was the "right thing to do"? And then, and you'll think I'm awful, I couldn't help but ponder the use of the word "blast." It seemed to come out of the same dictionary as Alan's "super," but I convinced myself I was being unbelievably nitpicky, and the fact that Alan and Cody were so different just proved that certain words aren't reserved for a certain type.

I brooded over Randy's absence and emailed him several times to, well, *blast* him for not being at work when I needed him. Talking on the phone just wasn't the same.

Randy emailed me and told me not to pack a lunch the next day, a Friday, because he was taking me out to Le Chat Noir, one of the nicest restaurants in the area. I couldn't wait to tell him everything.

I then began to wonder why I always seemed to enjoy talking about dates more than actually being on dates.

OCTOBER 31 ... I HATE HALLOWEEN!

I've never been a big fan of Halloween, but Randy loves it. However, he believes Halloween should be separate from business, and he particularly chose Le Chat Noir because fine French restaurants do not encourage or even allow their employees to dress up.

"Molly Rose," Randy scolded me as we sat down. "Put on a happy face, girl, and don't concern yourself with something so silly as a man using 'blast' as slang. Although I will admit that a person's choice of verbiage can be a clue to his character. Perhaps you recall Ethan, with whom I had a short-lived relationship. The man refused to use contractions. I'd ask him to do something and he'd say, "Randy, I cannot do that now, but please do not be upset. I shall make up for it later."

"Oh, I'm *so* glad you brought that up, because you can be as quirky as me."

"Honey, Ethan was the quirky one! Who can go through life avoiding contractions, not to mention that he would not use slang at all. Most people say, 'Do the math,'; he says, 'Calculate the arithmetic!' "

"Sounds like a real control freak."

"Bingo," Randy said.

Ugh. Bingo! I hated that word, too, because, as I've already told you, it reminded me of how Susan Decker met her husband. Although I wouldn't be caught dead playing freakin' bingo, it irked me that she found a man before me.

A waiter came to our table, unobtrusively poured water in our glasses, then handed us menus. We ordered drinks and told him we needed time to peruse the specials.

"Order anything you like, darling," Randy said. "Now, what to have."

"OH MY GOD!" I said, startling Randy so much that his menu jumped out of his hands and back into them again.

"What is it?" he said, still panting from the scare I gave him.

I held the menu up to the right side of my face and then responded. "I cannot believe this, but I just figured it out. Alan is a plant!"

"Molly Rose, usually I can decipher almost anything that has fomented in that brain of yours, but I'm lost. Alan is a plant? A ficus or a palm? Do tell."

"I'm serious."

"That menu is beginning to look like a nasty growth on your face."

I continued to hold the menu up to block my face. "Look over there to your left," I stage whispered. "See the table under the framed poster of the black cat?"

"I see it," Randy said. "And a man and woman are sitting there. Oh my, it looks as if they've just finished lunch and are enjoying an espresso. Alert the media. Wait, we *are* the media."

"Don't you recognize him, Randy? That's Alan T. Cressman, and with him is the perpetual thorn in my side, Naomi Hall-Benchley!"

"Of course," Randy said. "I just didn't recognize him in profile. When he was at the office, I was checking out his—"

"Stop there," I warned him.

"His funeral home flowers," Randy said, laughing. "Molly Rose, get your head out of the gutter, child!"

45

I didn't believe him for a moment, so I gave him the evil eye.

"And of course I recognize Ms. Hall-Benchley. Now, do tell!" Randy said, suddenly forgiving me for my mini-outburst. "What do you surmise those two are doing together?"

"Her husband, Art, has a seat on the board of the newspaper. His grandfather was one of the founders. I think she knows Alan socially or through business, and maybe, when he had a death in his family, she told him to ask me out so she could get the lowdown on what I was like to go out with. He's a plant. I know it. Now that I think about it, a guy like that wouldn't normally seek out a date right after his beloved uncle dies. Who the heck does that? Uh huh … it's all starting to gel now."

"Send in the clowns," Randy said. "Molly Rose wants to join the circus. Oops, don't bother, they're here."

"I'm serious, Randy!" I realized I wasn't making much sense, even to myself, but my theories were coming fast and furious, and I couldn't control them.

"Honey, all that is gelling is mush. And when mush gels, well, you get gelled mush!" He laughed out loud at himself. I gave him a cold stare.

"Why don't you believe me? This is exactly something that she-devil would do. Once, at the house of a mutual friend who was having an engagement party, she sent this man over to talk to me, to feign interest in me, just to get the dirt on me. He repeated everything we talked about and then she broadcast our conversation to *everyone*. Naturally, her version was tainted by her twisted analysis of me. The guy wasn't interested in me, or vice versa, and he lived in London, as I later discovered, but she didn't want him to tell me that. So, don't tell me that Alan T. Cressman can't be a plant."

"But, Molly Rose, be reasonable. Why would she care enough to go to all of this trouble?"

"Because she is desperate to set me up with this new coworker of Art's. She wants to be the one to have found 'Picky Molly Hacker' a man, and at the same time, she'll score major points with Art for having done something so sublime for his coworker."

"Then why set you up with Alan? If you and Alan hit if off, then you won't be available for Art's coworker, and if that's her main mission here, she's sabotaging her own efforts!"

"Randy, listen, I'm trying to tell you that I don't think Alan is interested in me *at all*. Think about it: asking me out right after a death in the family, calling to hear 'the sound of my voice,' bringing me funeral home flowers ... he is Naomi's plant to get the dirt. All plants need dirt, don't they?"

"Hmmm ... that does sound plausible, and simultaneously ridiculous, but there could be many other explanations."

"Name one," I challenged him.

"Maybe Alan T. and Naomi H.B. are having an affair."

"Oh, God," I said. I pondered it for a moment. "No, no way. The sun rises and sets on her social status as Mrs. Arthur Benchley. No way she'd have an affair, especially in public at a place where anyone could see them. Like us."

"Damn, you're making sense now, and I *so* liked that scenario. Are you going to sit here through the entire meal with the menu attached to your right cheek? Ah, wait, you're in luck; they're leaving."

I peeked around my menu and saw them stand and shake hands. "Definitely not an affair; Alan is a plant. Maybe he's doing this for her because the Benchleys are major investment clients. Oh, how disgusting. Pimping himself out like that."

Randy was more relieved than I was when Alan and Naomi left.

"Okay, Molly Rose, what is rattling around in that head of yours?" he asked just as the waiter was approaching our table.

"I'll have the Niçoise salad," I said. "And a glass of your house wine. Whatever is white and dry."

"Coq au vin," Randy said. "*Et un Perrier avec lime, s'il vous plaît.*"

"*Merci,*" said the waiter, taking our menus.

"So, I assume you're going to cancel your date for Saturday, yes?" Randy asked.

"Hell, no!" I told him. "I'll keep the date, all right. But Alan will be in for the surprise of his life. If he's looking to dish the dirt with Naomi Hall-Benchley, I'll give him his money's worth."

Randy rolled his eyes. "Oh, delicious; I can't wait for the *après* party!"

FOOL ME ONCE, SHAME ON YOU: FOOL ME TWICE ...

When I returned to the office, there was a voicemail message from Alan. He told me that he had just been called out of town (sudden business trip to New York), and he begged my understanding and would I please give him a rain check for the following Saturday night.

Normally, I would have had to call an emergency conference with

47

Randy (or in the past, my girlfriends) to decide how to handle this, but since this was no longer a "real date," I decided waiting a week would only be to my advantage. Having just found out that Alan was a plant for Naomi, I needed time to strategize.

Alan was a stickler for details. He asked me to please leave him a message so he could be assured that I'd received his, and then told me that he would look forward to hearing "the sound of my voice." Leo always told me I had a distinct "sexy, sweet, and smoky" voice. (And no, I don't smoke.) Of course, Alan was just flattering me as part of a ruse, but I began thinking that taking pleasure in the sound of my voice was distinctly a "Leo pleasure" that no other man could ever have. Well, maybe Tony.

I debated whether to call Alan, but since his message said he was leaving for the airport, I banked on getting his voicemail, which was preferable to having him call me back.

Did he think I was so lamebrained that he could fool me twice? Shame on him. He was in for a date he wouldn't soon forget. HAAAAAAA.

Luckily, I did get his voicemail, and just to play along, I sexed up my voice to amuse myself. I was still in sexy voice mode when my cell rang back.

To my surprise and delight, it was Cody. He said he had a very late gig on Saturday, and wanted to know if I'd meet him for a late lunch or an early dinner on Sunday. We decided to play it by ear, and I was thrilled to be seeing him again.

Content to go home and spend a quiet evening with Captain Jack, I was not ready for yet another male to call for my attention, but it was Tony, my dear, sweet Tony.

"Hey, Molly. Glad I caught you."

"Something wrong?"

"No, honey. Something's right. I filed for divorce today, and I couldn't be happier to be moving on with my life. It took me a few days longer to file than I'd expected, but I feel so liberated just having processed the paperwork."

"And so now you're wondering why liberation can feel so sad," I told him.

"Exactly, Molly. This marriage has been long over. There's just something about the finality of it all. Like I've failed."

"Failing," I told him, "would be to live in limbo. You've already been separated, and you were 'apart' while you were still together. This *is* what you want, isn't it?" I suddenly wasn't so sure.

"Yes," he said adamantly. "I am very sure. As you know, this was a long time in coming and not something done hastily. I just don't know why I'm feeling so weird."

"Because change, whether good or bad, is scary to people. We are human beings, creatures of habit who tend to stick with the devil we know. Our brains are wired to fear change; it's true. You'll be just fine. What you're feeling is natural, Tony."

"I think you just nailed it," he said. "I should have married you."

"Well, then you wouldn't have Noah," I told him, pretending to take his comment in stride. "See, things work out for a reason."

"No, seriously, Molly, I never had the nerve to tell you this before, but … "

I had felt so on top of my game with my on-target analysis, and now Tony was throwing me for a loop.

"What?" I said, almost afraid to hear what he had to say.

"Molly, I shouldn't be telling you this on the phone."

"I'm not in a cliff-hanging mood, Tony, so you're going to have to finish what you started."

I heard him sigh heavily. I couldn't imagine what was coming.

"Molly, oh damn. Sorry, sweetie. I know I'm a jerk for starting this on the phone, but I just realized how disrespectful and wrong it would be to do it this way. It was just easier to get my courage up on my cell. But this is bull. I'm taking Noah out for Halloween tonight. You probably have a date tomorrow. Damn, I screwed this up."

The poor guy was beating himself up, and I didn't even know if he deserved it or not, but I loved him dearly, and it didn't make any difference.

"Forgive me," Tony said. "I promise I'll see you tomorrow. I know you hate waiting, but it would suck to have this conversation on the phone. Trust me."

"Okay," I said, "you win."

"Thanks, baby. And, hey, you are the wisest woman I know. Thank you for so easily and beautifully putting things into perspective for me. Okay, well, tomorrow then."

How can it be that when one is so filled with contradictions, questions, insanity, doubts, double doubts, and raw mental dizziness, one can so easily articulate what is contributing to the cerebral confusion of another and be left in the dark concerning oneself?

Chapter 9: IN HONOR OF HALLOWEEN, I SPILL MY GUTS

MORE ABOUT LEO AND ME ...

On the way home from work, I realized that I hadn't bought a thing for the trick-or-treaters. My mind had been on everything *but* treats.

Leo loved handing out goodies to the kids while in elaborate costume. He gave wings to children's imaginations by creating the phantasmagorical with a blend of everything creative he could conjure. During the almost-three years we were together, which included three Halloweens, Leo first dazzled me, quite unexpectedly, as Count Dracula.

Randy had stopped by my apartment with a friend that night and was so impressed with Leo's makeup that he presented him with a verbal award for having the "most amazing Max Factor moment," an unexpected honor that Leo reticently accepted, but did so with grace.

Doing it with Grace. Remember those four words. I'll get back to them. Promise.

Armed with goodies, I arrived home and quickly dumped everything into a large salad bowl. I exchanged my Kenneth Cole duds for my most respectable Vicky-Secret-But-Can-Pass-For Gap loungewear, picked up a folder filled with research notes I was doing for a feature, and waited for the doorbell to ring.

I found it hard to concentrate on where my local tax dollars were going while juggling thoughts of four men like bowling pins. First, there was my outrage at discovering that Alan was a plant for Naomi. I was imagining a plethora of plots in which Naomi and Alan would both be rewarded Molly-style for their pathetic plot against *me*.

Then, there was sweet and easy-to-be-with Cody. I was getting ahead of myself and trying to picture how and if our relationship would progress. Was he always so carefree? Was he *too* carefree? Was it over with that bimbo Barbarino? Did Cody have other women he was also seeing? Were we officially "seeing" one another? I didn't know how to classify our "relationship," and I seemed prone to always want to classify things. How did he classify me?

Also heavy on my mind was that quick but mysterious call from Tony. What in the world did he want to tell me? Why did he make that comment about how he should have married me? Where did that fit into anything after all of these years?

And, of course, it was Halloween, and there was Leo. Only there was no Leo. There were just mini-bags of Pepperidge Farm Goldfish and mini-bags of bite-sized chocolate chip cookies. Hearing my neighbor's door open, then close, I knew I was next. I opened the door to find Tigger, Eeyore, a small pirate, and a rather tall eleven-year-old with long blond hair who told me she was Donatella Versace. The accompanying adult, a cross between a Goth hooker and a traditional witch, never displayed any emotion or offered any explanation. Okay, I told myself, maybe it's not so unusual for an eleven-year-old to want to be Donatella Versace; I didn't care. I only cared that Donatella was Italian, and that made me think of Leo. Hell, everything made me think of Leo.

Enough about my Halloween visitors. Back to Leo.

Leo lived in a beautiful guesthouse on a property in New York's Hudson Valley, owned by his family. His parents, however, spent most of their time in Tuscany, Italy, where his father was born. The main house on the New York property was rented to wealthy families, usually foreigners who needed a temporary but fantastic place to reside. I loved the house and always thought that some day we'd live there together. Captain Jack and I spent weekends with Leo, and about three days a week, Leo would spend the night with us. My apartment was much closer to my job, and it was the practical thing to do. Sometimes I hate that word: practical.

This was the first time in my life that I was in a relationship with a man I truly loved. Everyone knew it. Claudia was genuinely happy for me, and she and others were always coming up with ways to help me "spice things up." They had lots of good ideas; that's why I went along with them, at first. But then they started getting a bit too *Cosmo* for me. I didn't need quizzes to determine if my sex life with Leo "Sizzled or Drizzled." It was fantastic; that's all *anybody* needed to know.

I did appreciate the fashion tips, the lingerie from Vicky's, and even the sometimes-wild ideas for creating unusual romantic outings. A "little help from my friends" was wonderful, but I didn't need it. *We* didn't need it.

My friends are wonderful. I don't mean to sound unappreciative. There were times when I needed a shoulder to cry on. Like all couples, there were times when Leo and I would have a fight. Sometimes he would just wander into a place where I couldn't reach him, and when I tried to do so, he either didn't let me in or couldn't understand why I wasn't in accord with his way of thinking. He was a bit of a wild card, but that's part of what made him exciting. He was stubborn and giving all at the same time.

Sometimes he talked too much; sometimes he seemed to be overly meditative. Those were the times that I got paranoid I might be losing him.

Leo hated that; he saw it as a lack of faith in him, and he'd let me know it. He would simultaneously tell me how exceptional I was while admonishing me not to idolize mundane obsessions and let frivolous worries consume me or, worse yet, terrorize me.

He was right. If something went wrong between us, I often forgot that such is life and that a disagreement doesn't mean that a relationship is over. I let his off times affect me more than mine affected him. I knew I had too much baggage, and even though it was Louis Vuitton, I wanted to be rid of it.

My natural tendencies to worry are innate. But it was when my dear friends grew extra helping hands, well, let's just say those helping hands became an octopus that strangled me. But I allowed it to happen; I take responsibility.

THE OCTUPUS THAT KILLED US

Two years and two months into our relationship, Leo presented me with the red roses, the Waterford vase, and a marriage proposal. He bought me a ring, and we decided to marry in a year's time. Leo said he had "loose ends" to tie up and "odd jobs" to finish, and I was involved in several long-term work projects. For many reasons, we found no reason to rush to the altar, but we did set a date.

Claudia is the kind of woman who was choosing bridesmaids dresses on her way out of the womb. The moment she and Colin got engaged, she and her mother were busy planning the event of a lifetime. Leo and I wanted something a bit more "us." We wanted a more informal wedding on the grounds of the estate: elegant but something that reflected our mutual love of the outdoors and our love of spontaneity without the frills and thrills that are a staple of so many weddings.

I told you earlier to remember the words "did it with Grace." In case you forgot, I'm reminding you.

I swear, I wasn't snooping, but I found "Grace" on Leo's cell phone. I knew he had an ex-girlfriend named Luciana, who lived out of town, but he had never mentioned anyone named Grace. To have asked him would have been akin to "Hey, baby, I was snooping and came across this name. Who is this chick, anyway, and should I be worried?" So, I wrote down the phone number, which was not local, and hoped I'd never need to think about it again.

It was shortly after that when Leo began taking more overnight trips than usual. He was vague about them but usually would say that he had family business to take care of, and that was often true, as he did manage the family estate and financial concerns.

Believe it or not, despite the name on the phone and my paranoid tendencies, nearly three years with Leo had taught me to have faith in myself, in my man, and in our love. Once in a while he seemed overwhelmed with sadness, but I instinctively felt it had nothing to do with me, and I knew to let him work it out. No matter how close two people are, we all have places within ourselves that we go to be alone. Respecting that in one's mate is something that I have always believed to be a tenet of true love.

Our life together was still filled with wonderful plans for the future. I started taking Italian at the local community college because Leo wanted me to experience life in Tuscany some day. I was truly fulfilled.

My friend Dina, who had only met Leo once, saw him on the street one day talking on his cell phone. She heard him say: "Okay, honey, I'll see you tomorrow." Assuming he was talking to me, she felt it necessary to pass on this uninteresting tidbit to Claudia, who informed her that she and Colin were having dinner that same night with Leo and me. That's when the helping hands grew into an octopus. Why did he say, "Okay, HONEY, see you TOMORROW?"

Assuming she was helping me, Claudia called immediately and wanted to chat. I found it odd that she wanted to make small talk when we would be seeing each other later, but she kept pressing me to stay on the phone, using the excuse that we couldn't have "girl talk" in front of the men. She kept asking me how we were doing, and I kept telling her we were fine. Were we? Was Leo having premarital jitters? I had known Claudia a very long time, and that was not small talk.

The next day, Leo left town again, and Claudia insisted on my giving her the number for "Grace" that I had tucked away. Reluctantly, I did so.

She called the number from a blocked phone and using an English accent, apologized for having the wrong number when Leo answered the phone.

I was mortified. They were right. He was having more than premarital jitters. He was having an affair. That was the consensus among my friends, and in no time at all, I was a believer. Four of them, Claudia, Dina, and our mutual friends Candy and Ellie, were brainstorming on what to do—with or without my participation.

I'm very close with my younger sister, Hannah, but I did not want to involve her. She is so sweet and exceptionally loyal, she would have put her own life on hold if she thought I was in pain. Hannah doesn't tend to complicate her life the way her big sister does, and she also would have been disappointed by the rush to judgment, as well I should have been.

This agony (and Leo's overnight trips) went on for several months. I began to notice a change in him. He seemed sad a lot of the time and would not talk about it.

Then, without my consent, Dina called "Grace," and a female voice answered. She asked if Leo was there. The woman seemed a bit confused but not upset and told her that Leo wasn't due until that Friday. She even asked if she could take a message for him, but, of course, Dina declined.

My loving and caring friends, coupled with my designer baggage, got the better of me. I finally confronted Leo.

It was a rainy Friday night, and Leo had just returned to his house, where I was waiting for him. He kissed me and looked sweetly at me, but he was sullen. It wasn't my imagination.

The rain pounded on the windows, and when the thunder began, Captain Jack darted under the couch for cover. Leo sat on the window seat and looked out the tall French windows at the storm. I had no doubts: he was trying to muster up the courage to break it off.

"I know what you're thinking," I told him.

He turned around. I could see he had been crying. He looked blankly at me. "What am I thinking, Molly?"

"You're thinking about her. The other woman."

He seemed unaffected by my revelation. "You're right. I am thinking of another woman."

I couldn't believe he could be so cold and just admit it like that, his voice flat and his watery brown eyes just staring at me.

"Why are you crying?" I asked. I didn't give him time to answer. After all, my friends and I *had* all the answers.

"You're sad because you don't know how to break it off with me. You've been seeing her for months, one, two overnight visits a week, and you think I haven't noticed? Do you think I'm an idiot? How long did you think I would suffer through this double life you've been leading?"

Leo shook his head. He still wasn't talking. That only fueled what was now becoming rage.

"Damn it, Leo! For someone so articulate who knows so much, where is all of that savvy now? Maybe for all of your talk, you're more effective in an alternate universe where you never have to deal with the reality of being faithful and true."

Leo didn't say a word. He just threw me some more rope, and I continued to hang myself.

"You've made a mockery of everything and mortified me in front of my friends. They all know. You haven't even tried to hide it."

"That's enough," he finally said, quietly but emphatically. "Quite enough."

"Fine," I said. "You talk. Tell me that you haven't been going to see another woman all of these months. Grace, isn't that her name? You've been cheating on me with Grace. How poetic. Maybe you've being doing it with Dignity, too."

He got up from the window seat and began pacing. I could see him constructing his thoughts. He looked as if he were going to explode.

"Shut up!" he screamed.

"Did you just tell *me* to shut up? Can't you even admit that her name is Grace?"

"Where do you get that ... oh, wait, my cell phone. How clever of you, Molly."

"Well, aren't I right?"

"Luciana," he said. "Luciana Luisa Grace. That was her name."

I was ready to throw the next punch when his use of the past tense jabbed me in the chest. "Was?"

"Was," he said. "She died this morning."

"Your ex-girlfriend, Luciana? She died? But ... how ... I'm so sorry ... but why didn't you just tell me what was going on? Why did you have to make all of these mysterious trips to see her?"

I had not let my inner voice guide me. I had allowed my friends, who read too much *Cosmo* and on occasion drank too many cosmopolitans, pull me out of a very secure place and into madness. I did not respect Leo's right to his space, yet at the same time, while I did not need be involved, he could have, NO, he *should* have at least told me what was going on.

"Listen, Molly, because I'm only going to tell you once. Yes, Luciana was my girlfriend before I met you. Our families always hoped we would marry some day. Luci had an amazing heart and a generous gift for helping others. I loved her. But I wasn't in love with her."

Leo stopped to swallow the lump in his throat and to pet Captain Jack, who had reluctantly come out of hiding to see what was going on. Frightened by the tension between us, Jack scurried back under the couch, and with difficulty, Leo resumed talking.

"Luci was far more traditional than me; she wanted different things from life, and although she never said it, I always felt as if I were disappointing her by being me. She would have taken me as I am, but she would not have been happy. Neither of us would have. But she couldn't see that when I left her; she only saw the destruction of what she perceived to be her future and the core of all her happiness."

I could see that Leo wanted to weep, but he was trying hard not to do so in front of me.

"It broke her heart when I left and moved to the estate. She got very depressed, morbidly so, and she did just the minimum to get through the day. I felt terrible knowing the state I'd left her in, but short of going back to her, nothing would have made her happy.

"She let things go, like her annual checkup with the gynecologist, and by the time her doctor had diagnosed the ovarian cancer, which is difficult to detect anyway, it was far too late. But, I blamed myself. I blamed myself for not having been able to love her, and I blamed myself for just walking away, leaving her to fall into such a state of depression that she neglected her health.

"Yes, I called her from time to time after our breakup, but I thought what she was going through was normal. I thought if I called too much I would be prolonging her agony and giving her false hope. It pained me terribly to leave her. It hurt for a long time. But then I met you. My life went on, and the wagons began circling hers."

"Oh, God, Leo."

"When her family told me that she was dying, and that she had never cared for another man after me, I felt I needed to be there. Not as her ex-boyfriend, but as the friend she had known for so many years. I owed her that. I owed myself that. I held her hand. I gave her medication. I read her poetry. I watched her sleep. I wiped her brow. I watched her die."

"You should have told me."

"Would you have been okay with it?" Leo asked, wiping a tear from his face.

I had never felt so defeated in all of my life. I honestly didn't know how to answer without lying to Leo or lying to myself. I didn't know how I would have felt.

"Leo … "

"Just answer the question. Would you have been okay with it?"

"It's not that simple."

"Yes or no," he said stoically.

"That's an impossible question to answer in hindsight. I know I certainly wouldn't have minded your spending time with a dying friend."

"But not as *much* time as I spent, right?"

"That's not fair," I protested.

"It's perfectly fair. Watching Luci die was harrowing enough without having to simultaneously contend with your disapproval. I couldn't let anyone or anything distract me."

"Am I just anyone?" I wanted to know.

"You know what I mean," he said, turning his head away and watching the flow of raindrops as they slid down the long window.

I was too angry to sit. I paced the room, quickly trying to gather my thoughts. I felt as if I had to say the right things at that moment or never have another chance to do so.

"Leo, you're the one who always says that nothing in life is black or white. Now here you are asking me to give you a black-or-white answer. That's so not you. It's downright unfair. And I hate having to be upset with you when you're mourning your friend. It makes me feel lower than low. How ironic that is because you're always telling me that no matter what happens in life, we shouldn't condemn ourselves."

"I don't want you to condemn yourself, Molly. I only asked you if you would have been okay with all of this had I told you. You can't answer me."

"Because I can't swear to what I would have felt. I could give a pat answer, but I couldn't be sure it would be the truth. How am I to know what I would have done? You never gave me the chance. You didn't trust me, and now you're judging me."

"I'm not judging you. I just did what I had to do. I couldn't risk your getting upset. I was already on emotional overload."

"You didn't trust me," I said. "You just didn't trust me."

"It's not that simple," Leo said.

"Right, nothing is black or white. Like I just said: gray answers are okay for you but not for me. Mine have to be black or white."

"I just watched a friend's life slip away. Can you respect that?"

"I am so deeply sorry. That's a tragic story and a painful loss for everyone who loved her. She was blessed to have you by her side. I hope you don't blame yourself for anything."

He looked at me as if he wanted to say something, but I suppose he decided it didn't matter, because he turned his head back to follow the path of the sliding raindrops.

He was in terrible pain, and so was I. There was nothing that could possibly have been resolved at that moment. I picked up my things and set out for the rainy drive home. I told myself it was a bad moment, but our love was strong enough to survive it. And it should have. I'll tell you more in a bit. Right after I dig the salt out of my wound.

Chapter 10: TONY SPILLS *HIS* GUTS!

I had invited Tony for lunch, but he said his stomach was in knots and didn't want me to go to any trouble preparing food he could only enjoy with his eyes.

Around two o'clock that Saturday, he arrived with a small but beautiful bouquet of flowers. I put them in a vase on an end table in my living room, where the floral palette perfectly picked up the colors of my window treatments. I didn't offer Tony a drink because he had brought his own bottle of spring water with him, so I just grabbed one of my own and sat down.

He started to fidget with the label on the bottle, eventually pulling it off entirely until there were only those little rubbery pieces of glue left. As he began to peel them off and roll them into little balls, he realized what he was doing and turned red.

"My God, what the hell am I doing?" He got up and walked across the room to the trash basket by the antique desk and threw the label and balled glue into it. He retained the look of mortification at his own behavior and then sat down again.

"Let me try to resurrect the person that you've come to associate with this face."

I laughed. Nervously, but I laughed.

"I feel so ridiculous for acting so ridiculous." He paused. "Well, that made a hell of a lot of sense, didn't it?"

Just as Tony was about to open his mouth, the doorbell rang again. I was as baffled as Tony, who seemed unnerved by it, rather than "saved" by it.

"Don't people know that Halloween is over?" he said irritably.

At the door was a delivery man hidden behind the most spectacular plant I'd ever seen. It was stunning.

"Who's it from?" I asked, realizing that was a dumb question to ask the delivery guy.

"Dunno," he said. "Should be a card with it. This was an out-of-town order that our shop handled. That's all I know. Never can get a good look at people over the phone." He grinned. I couldn't help but notice that he had a beautiful smile and that his ID tag read "Shawn."

Both my hands were occupied holding this enormous plant, and Tony jumped up and handed him a couple of bucks, took the leafy green wonder from me, and asked me where I wanted it.

"Gee, I don't know. Put it on the coffee table for now."

Tony obliged. I got the feeling he was not only feeling upset by this plant dwarfing his flowers, but the plant (a combination of several genera) seemed to exacerbate his anxiety. And no doubt, he caught Shawn smiling at me.

I sat down and stared at the card and the unopened envelope. I didn't want to upset Tony by reading it, but it was like an elephant sitting between us.

"Open the card, Molly. If you don't know who that thing is from, you'll never be able to give me your full attention."

I picked the card off the plastic clip that held it. Tony's use of the words "that thing" did not escape me. I read the card to myself, "I can't stop thinking about you. I miss you … " Then there was the beginning of either another sentence or the signature. I couldn't make it out at all, especially as someone from the floral shop had written it out, not the sender. I guessed that whoever wrote it got distracted and forgot to complete the card.

"Well?" Tony asked. "Anyone I know?"

"No," I told him. "And not anyone I want to know, either."

I knew immediately who had engineered this and couldn't help but be amused by the ridiculous irony. They were from Alan. He was out of town on a business trip (or so he said) and decided to get my attention by sending me a plant. Symbolism 101: a plant from a plant. The only interesting part about it was whether or not his unconscious mind was guilt-ridden and had chosen this plant to secretly expose himself for the fake that he was. Oh, what did it matter. But it was an exquisite combination of nature's botanical best.

"Okay, Tony, it's just me and you. Please don't explode on my couch; I just had it cleaned."

At that moment, Captain Jack came running from the bedroom, sniffed the plant and then the flowers, sniffed Tony, and satisfied that nothing too alien had encroached upon his territory, jumped into my lap, circled three times, and went to sleep.

"That was a quick inspection," Tony noted with as much humor as he could muster.

"And who says that cats don't take time to smell the flowers?"

We both laughed and then returned to the state of anxiety that Tony had created.

"Okay, so it's me, you, and the Jackster."

"I'm going to get this out, I promise."

"Now, would be good."

He shifted a few times in his seat, much like a cat or dog will do to get the most comfortable position, and began to speak. "Molly, oh, God, my best friend, Molly, who has endured heaven and hell with me for as long as I can remember."

"And vice versa," I said, which seemed to comfort him a bit.

"Molly, back in high school … "

As soon as I heard the words "high school," I felt as if I were about to study ancient history.

"I know it seemed to you that I never returned your feelings for me. I don't mean feelings of friendship, obviously. I mean, well, you know, the other kind of feelings."

"But you didn't return them, Tony. In fact, I didn't even think you knew I had them, you know, way back in the 'stoned' age. You only had eyes for Victoria. And your heart was hers, too. That's okay; but that is the way it was."

"Partially, okay, more than partially, you're right. But there's more. I did fall head over Nikes for her. Beautiful cheerleader; every guy wanted her; she wanted me. Isn't that enough reason for any high school kid to be smitten?"

Smitten, I thought. What an old-fashioned word. I probably would have torn it to shreds had it emanated from Alan, or thought it incongruous coming from Cody, but this was Tony, talking about the past. Surely I could let "smitten" slide. Then I remembered Hannah's words when she met Matthew: "I'm a smitten kitten." I decided the word was somewhat back in vogue and that I was a complete idiot for having even given it a passing thought.

"You look distracted," Tony said.

I was embarrassed. "Sorry."

"After Vicky and I were together through most of high school, it started to occur to me, rather, I let myself acknowledge what was there all the time, that maybe she wasn't the best choice for me. Maybe there was someone else who I had much more in common with … my true soul mate in the form of my best friend."

I was dumbfounded. I just stared at him.

"I started to think that we should break it off before graduation."

"So you married her instead?" I found myself reliving the pain and rejection I'd felt in high school. Sudden, sharp pangs of jealousy began stabbing me again. What was happening?

"I'll just come out and say this!" Tony said. "She got pregnant. Or should I say I got her pregnant. Semantics be damned; that was the situation."

"I had no idea!" I said, stunned.

"We wanted to keep it that way, especially Vicky's parents. But we were pushed into marriage that July, and early that November, she miscarried."

"Oh, my God, Tony! I can't believe you never shared any of this with me."

"Molly, when you marry the wrong girl for what you think is the right reason, you aren't always comfortable going to the *right* girl and asking her to commiserate with you."

"I guess not," I said, trying to absorb what he had just said to me. I couldn't help but relive the damage that Tony's lack of interest in me as a girlfriend had done to my fragile self-esteem and how we are all the sum of our experiences. I believed that I had all of my demons neatly lined up like laundry, each one held up by a clothespin, basking on a line in the afternoon sun. And now, Tony, in the role of windstorm, had blown everything off the line, across splintered fences and into the neighbors' yards, where everything I thought I knew lay twisted and unrecognizable on soiled grass. It wasn't a pretty picture.

"The thing is," Tony continued, "by the time she lost the baby, we'd both grown very attached to it and a lot more comfortable with the idea of becoming parents, even though we were way too young. The miscarriage devastated us and brought us closer. So we stayed together, and despite our grief over the loss, we decided to do what we should have done in the first place and that was to use reliable birth control. We both finished college, and, well, you know when Noah was born, nine years ago."

"You did wait quite a while," I said.

"We did," Tony said. "One of the smarter decisions we've made."

"So what went wrong?"

"Molly, that kid is the light of my life. Nothing could ever make me regret his being born. But Vicky and I had become so complacent that we didn't realize that we weren't in love; we probably never were. We both had our degrees, good jobs, a social life, and everything had a place. Our friends were all having children, some on their second or third, and, well, it was just time to try. It was as if we were mindlessly following some cosmic timetable."

"So what happened? You never let on to me that you were feeling any of this. I guess if I think about it, in hindsight, I can probably see things I didn't notice at the time, but you seemed so happy ... or at least content."

"We were both thrilled to be parents. We were a real family, and that sustained us for several more years. As much as it could. But we weren't happy with one another. I would have stayed in denial a lot longer had I not found out about her affair. And although I tried like hell to keep our family together and to honor the vows I made in front of God, I wanted you. Being with you has always been exciting and comfortable at the same time. I hate using the word 'comfortable' because it sounds like a pair of old shoes, but I mean that you always understand me. I never have to stand on my head to be noticed or for my opinions or feelings to be heard and respected.

"You made me laugh. You *do* make me laugh. I feel like we're two pieces of a big jigsaw puzzle that fell between two sofa cushions and were lost for a very long time. But now, I feel it's time to put them back together. Molly, I love you. I want a future with you. There's never been another woman I've felt this way about. I know a lot has happened ... "

Tony's words fell off abruptly. Anything more would have been superfluous at that moment. I couldn't help but think about the dozens of notebooks I'd once filled up with "Mrs. Tony Lostanza," "Molly Rose Lostanza," "Molly Hacker-Lostanza," "Tony and Molly Lostanza," and various other versions of my desire for new nomenclature.

"Molly, say something. Please."

"I'm not sure what to say."

"How could you not have something to say after everything I've just told you?"

"I'm in shock. Do you get that? Do you expect me to just fly into your arms saying, 'Darling, at long last!' or something to that effect?"

He looked embarrassed, as if that were exactly what he had wanted me to do.

At that moment, Captain Jack could feel my distress and lifted his head. He spurned my attempt to pet him, hissed at Tony as he sprang from my lap, and went running into my bedroom. By the look on Tony's face, I could tell he took the hiss personally.

"Tony, I don't blame you for choosing Victoria way back when, but you were my first love, and being rejected didn't exactly help build a foundation for strong self-esteem. In some ways it taught me that I'm strong and that one's self-esteem shouldn't be based solely on another person ... oh, this is so confusing."

"Molly, I *do* love you."

"You just petitioned for divorce a few days ago. Yeah, I know the marriage was 'long over,' but maybe you're telling me this now because you're feeling the sting of being alone for the first time in your life."

"You can be with someone and still feel alone. I've been 'alone' for years."

"Oh, Tony, I know that. But still, being physically alone feels different. Sometimes better, much better. Just different."

"You think I'm just trying to fill an emptiness in my heart so I'm coming to you? Do you think this is some kind of rebound thing I've got going down?"

"Honestly, I don't know."

"You know me better than that." He looked away from me and muttered to himself, "This is not what I expected."

I suddenly felt angry. Was I supposed to be thrilled with the crumbs he was throwing me God-only-knows how many years later? The feelings I'd felt for him had long evolved into something different. I felt as if he wanted me to don my high school duds and go back to school. Was I supposed to immediately conform, like an octopus to a wall of coral, the moment he spilled his guts?

There was the part of me that had loved this man for so many years. Was I allowing stupid pride to stand in the way of my happiness? Or perhaps destiny was attempting to correct itself, and I was standing in its way. How could I not understand my own feelings? And why couldn't I shake the terrible notion that I was Tony's consolation prize? After all, he did explain that he had loved me … didn't he?

Tony knew me well enough to read my face, or at least part of it. "You're angry! #$%&! I can't believe you're angry! I'm stunned, Molly. I'm just stunned. I'm speechless!"

"Speechlessly," he continued nonstop for another ten minutes, telling me that his revelation was the hardest thing he'd ever done, and that his silence over the years was due to respect for me and respect for his marriage. He said so much that most of it remains a blur.

I was so confused: by him, by his emotions, by my emotions, by my inability to trust my emotions, and by the ever-present question, Was I being too picky?

Tony finally gave up and left. I was drained and didn't even get up to walk him to the door. I had been sucker shot by Cupid's arrow and had no idea how to pull it out of my heart. I only knew that it hurt.

Five minutes after Tony left, my cell rang. I didn't know if I could take any more, but it would be wrong to ignore him.

"Molly?"

"Yes?" I said, wondering why I hadn't checked the caller ID.

"It's Cody. How are you?"

"Oh, Cody! Well, I'm a bit frazzled at the moment, but I plan to survive."

"Nothing serious, I hope."

"Well, you know, life happens."

"Doesn't it, though!" he empathized. "You sure I can't help you?"

"I'm fine. Just hearing from you is nice."

"Listen, I just had this urge to go bowling. We're playing on Tuesday night at the opening of this supercool alley, and I've been given passes for a night of bowling on Wednesday. I can't think of anyone who would be more fun to go with than you. Afterward, I'll take you to eat. Any place you like. No greasy bowling alley."

My head was in a different place, and it was hard to focus.

"How about it?"

"Sure," I said. "Bowling sounds right up my alley."

"Awesome!" he exclaimed. "We'll have a blast."

Chapter 11: MY BRAIN FILES FOR BANKRUPTCY

I slept until nearly noon that Sunday. I honestly don't remember being that depressed since Leo and I broke up. It had taken me so many years to get my brain functioning in a way that gave *me* control, and suddenly, I was more confused than I'd been back in high school. At least then I knew where I stood. Now I was simply emotionally and intellectually bankrupt.

I couldn't help but repeat the scenario over and over in my head: my first love and dear friend told me he loved me and had loved me for years. Maybe I could have handled a surprise revelation, but Tony clearly expected me to respond in kind. How? To what? I wasn't so sure that he knew what he was feeling. I just knew he thought he did.

Maybe you're wondering why my ego wasn't bursting wide open with so much male attention in my midst. For one, I had labeled Tony "FRIEND ONLY" some fourteen years ago, and it wasn't so easy to shift gears. I had a hard time with the fact that he knew he loved me as far back as high school, but I was only now being told. He was a moral, noble man, and as long as he had a wife, he would never profess his love to another woman. Logically and rationally, I got it, but part of me didn't understand at all.

This was my confidant: I could tell him anything. Suddenly, he had taken that away from me—from us. I could no longer share my romantic quandaries, delusions, and ideals with him. I felt as if I had to choose: accept Tony as the man in my life or lose his friendship. I hated that notion; I hated being boxed into a corner with no warning. I was angry.

And then there was that part of me that did love him, that did remember how it felt to lust after this hunky man. He had all of the qualities I loved. He could be "the one." What was wrong with me?

I turned my cell off. I didn't want to hear from anyone. Around one o'clock the house phone rang once and then rang again a minute later. That was Hannah's signal. Despite the advent of caller ID, she knew that if I was too down to pick up the phone, I couldn't see the ID window from whatever piece of furniture I was moping upon. She wanted to see me. She was right; it had been a while. Hannah was probably the only person I would've allowed to come by. Except Randy, but he was spending the day with Kyle, and I didn't want to interfere. I was happy that my sister was on her way over.

Hannah is very smart and very sweet. She instinctively understands things and doesn't overanalyze the way I do. She doesn't beat life's nuances into the ground or pulverize every disconcerting thought until it enervates her. She's a patient and caring listener who doesn't expect others to think as she does.

She accepts me for exactly who I am.

Captain Jack adores my sister. The moment she came in and sat down in the overstuffed armchair, Jack nuzzled up to her leg, rubbing his precious scent all over her. He hopped up to give her hand a kiss (that gentle feeling of sandpaper scraping skin) and settled down into her lap instead of his discombobulated mother's lap.

"So," I said, after telling her the entire story, "is it just me, or can you understand why I feel so out of sync, whack—whatever!"

"When it rains in your life, Molly, it pours," she said sweetly. "I know I couldn't juggle all of those emotions."

"All of those men, you mean," I said, noting her diplomacy. "You're lucky you're young and engaged. I wish I were more like you."

"Oh, I don't," Hannah said adamantly. "You're a fascinating woman. Having you for a big sister is just the best. You see things from angles that I would never even notice. I can see how that might be exhausting, but isn't it exhilarating, too?"

"I'm not feeling so exhilarated," I told her.

"Sis, I don't have the answer for you, but I do understand why you're in such a state of turmoil. I know I was just a kid when you were in high school, but I remember how in love you were with Tony. I think my own notions of romantic love came right from you. You are one of the reasons I found Matthew."

I was humbled. "You give me too much credit."

"No, it's true. Now, listen. I know you're freaked out by the timing, and how could you not wonder about the timing, you know, Tony just filing for divorce and all. But look at it this way: it sounds like he's been busting a gut to tell you all of these years, so, hey, naturally he wouldn't waste any more time."

"That's a good point," I said.

"He was your first love. Don't you want to at least explore the possibility of a life with him? I don't mean tomorrow or the next day, but why ixnay the whole idea just because the timing upset you?"

"I should give it more thought from that perspective," I said.

"Just relax; it'll be fine," Hannah said, stroking a very compliant Jack's neck. "Just one more thing I need to mention. Gee, maybe this isn't

67

the best time."

"Hannah, you know you've got to tell me now."

"Yeah, I know," she said. "It's just that when Matthew and I were out shopping yesterday, we ran into Claudia, Dina, and Ellie. They said Candy has overextended herself with too much 'giving' on Halloween night, so she was still chilling."

"TMI," I said, laughing.

"Yeah, I thought so, too," Hannah said. "And Matthew excused himself and went browsing in the closest video store."

"So what did they say about me?"

"Claudia said that she had a great lunch with you recently, but they all kind of hinted that you were being rather secretive about your life. I was tempted to tell them that maybe you wanted it that way, and that it was your life to be secretive about, but it wasn't my place. I told them you weren't hiding anything that I knew about and that you were just busy."

"And … "

"And they just kept trying to get information from me. Dina kept rephrasing the same questions as if she thought she could trick me into answering one of them. I know they love you and are genuinely concerned, but I felt like I was hooked up to a network or something. Are you still friendly with them all?"

I explained to Hannah that I was still nursing my wounds from the outpouring of love I received that served as the catalyst in my breakup with Leo. Hannah understood that I didn't blame them, but even more, she understood my need to duck for cover when unwanted advice was hurled in my direction.

"Gee, Molly, with all of those women and *all* of these men, I can see why you'd want to limit the cerebral input."

We both laughed.

"All of these men, huh?"

"Well, yeah … if the glass slipper fits!"

After two hours with Hannah, I felt greatly unburdened and ready to face the chaos again. She had such a beautiful way of defusing my anxiety while still respecting it. With just a half hour of sunlight left, Hannah left for home, and by the time darkness fell, I was back in Chapter 11.

★ ★ ★

By Monday morning, I was nearly paralyzed by depression. My brain was so bankrupt that I couldn't even think of a reason to call in sick, and I knew that if I did so, I would attract more attention to myself rather than deflecting it. I "vanted to be alone" more than Garbo had, and God help the person(s) who stood in my way.

Waiting for me at work were two obituaries and more information on a local government corruption story. Another politician caught taking a bribe. A source I had vehemently sought had come through for me. Was I happy? Zzzzzzzzzzzz! I could've broken the equivalent of Watergate and couldn't have cared less.

Everything sucked. I closed my door, which in my office is akin to putting up a sign that reads TRESSPASSERS WILL BE SHOT ON SIGHT and proceeded to focus simultaneously on my misery and my work. And to think I once doubted my ability to successfully multitask.

I wasn't alone for ten minutes when I heard a quick knock, followed by Randy bursting in. Putting his chin in the palm of one hand and holding up his elbow with the palm of the other, he stood there looking at me quizzically, as if I were an abstract sculpture in a museum that he was trying to understand. Even without words, he was always dramatic.

I stared at him, wondering how long we were going to play this game, when finally he decided to speak.

"Okay, my little cavewoman," he said, dropping the pose, "we're shut away in here today because ... "

I just stared at him, noticing his face had a strange orange glow to it. "And your face is orange because ... ?"

"Okay. Self-tanner. Put on too much for too long. Tried to impress. What a mess. I confess. Now I digress. What's up with you, or should I guess?"

"Give it a rest," I chimed in.

"Bastard rhyme!" Randy said sharply, like Alex Trebek's evil twin naysaying a contestant's response. "Doesn't count, but God bless."

I saw the corners of his mouth turn ever so slightly upward. I knew he was pleased with his perceived übercleverness and I was *not* going to rubber stamp it. Instead, I was frothing that he told me the truth about his silly self-tanner and put the onus back on me to tell my much more serious truth.

Did he have to pick now to be so forthright? No Randy games? How quickly he paid the price to hear my story. Now I owed him. But I didn't want to owe him or any man anything.

"I hate men," I said, glaring at him. "ALL of them."

"Molly Rose, how irrational of you. What has gotten into you? Why so blue?"

"If you can be orange, I can be blue!" I said.

"Such colorful banter," he said, now pulling up a chair as close to my desk as he could. "I'll admit, I've suffered through my own 'I hate men' days, too, but, girlfriend, you are in a grand funk."

"This is a newspaper. People who write for newspapers have deadlines. Ever heard of one?"

Randy snickered. "All right, Molly Rose. I do have a scathing review to finish. Happy hour after work then."

"Happy hour?" I said with disgust.

"Okay, then, miserable-flippin'-nasty-bitch-of-an-hour! After work. Deal?"

"Deal," I said. "And close the door behind you."

Randy glared at me.

"Please," I said with a forced smile.

"Now, that wasn't so hard, was it?" he said. "Later, child. And be prepared to spill."

THE BLUE, THE ORANGE, AND THE RED

"Honey, when I said, 'Be prepared to spill,' I didn't mean you should knock over your glass of Pinot Noir."

I was a wreck. The bartender had barely rested the glass of red wine on the bar when I spilled it. Between my nerves and the hand lotion I'd just put on, my hand slipped on the stem of the glass. Yeah, I know, that's lame. Who puts on hand lotion before they drink? I do. Being so involved in the local community, I like to have smooth hands should I have to shake someone else's. Sue me for quirkiness.

Luckily, none of the wine spilled on Randy, or I might have been sued. He's not litigiously minded, but it wouldn't have been a pretty sight. Randy is fastidious about his appearance, and red wine ... oh, the horror. He would have run home with a paper bag on his head, without even stopping to cut out eyeholes.

With the help of a fresh glass of wine (I chose Chardonnay just to play it safe), I told Randy the whole painful saga of Tony's Sunday revelation. He listened without interrupting, though I must say his repertoire of facial expressions are a reaction in their own right. Were one to observe us, Randy's bug eyes, twisted lips, flaring nostrils, knit brows, and puffy cheeks would certainly elicit more attention than my pathetic tale of woe.

"And was that the last time you two communicated? When you emitted forth vibes of anger after his proclamation of true love?"

"That sounds like you're siding with *him*," I said.

"Molly Rose, listen to yourself. I didn't know there were any sides to take. Goodness, child, the man pours out his heart, and you erupt like Mount Vesuvius. I'm only asking a question. I certainly hope you aren't at war with this man. Are you forgetting that you love him?"

"No. If I didn't love him, I wouldn't be so damn upset ... and confused. But I spent years loving him, wanting him, and getting over that pain, and now it feels like I'm a consolation prize. And even if I get past that, is he still the man I want to spend forever with?"

Randy sighed. "And to think I was stressing all morning if Kyle would be the man I would spend all of next weekend with."

"Oh, Randy, I'm sorry. I'm monopolizing the conversation. I do want to hear about Kyle."

"You will," he assured me. "But right now, you're in distress, and we have to fix that. Now, answer my question. Was that the last time you talked with him?"

"I'm a coward," I said. "I left my cell phone off all day. I never do that. He called twice but didn't leave a message. "Oh, God, I'm horrible. I can't imagine if I were in his shoes and he was avoiding *me* like this! I'd be so freakin' hurt."

"Well, when he hooked up with and then married Victoria, maybe you *did* feel a bit 'avoided.' You shouldn't be so hard on yourself. This is a human reaction."

"Oh," I said. "And if that weren't enough, there was a message from Alan on my cell phone—two of them. He wanted to tell me he was back from his weekend—whoopee—and he wanted to hear the sound of my voice! Ugh. What is it with that guy and my voice? Anyway, I know I should have emailed him and thanked him for the plant, but I just couldn't bring myself to do it. Not today."

"Are you still keeping your date with him for this weekend?"

"Yeah, I'm keeping it. This is my chance to teach him and Naomi-Hall Benchley a lesson. Her 'plant' is going to have a rude awakening. I was going to do some scheming last night, but Tony's unscheduled roadwork sent me on a big detour, and I got lost. Oh, Randy, I'm still so lost."

Suddenly, I burst out crying, feeling the enormity of what had happened between Tony and me. Luckily, the bar was so crowded (and loud by this point) that I don't think anyone noticed my tears or Randy putting his arms around me for comfort.

"I don't want to hurt Tony," I cried. "I'm just so confused."

"Then tell him that," Randy said. "Just tell him you need time to sort things out before you talk again. Just don't avoid him. It'll only make it worse. As for Alan, well, go for it, girlfriend. Give him an evening to remember."

"Thank you," I said, still sobbing. "Oh, and did I mention that I have a bowling-slash-dinner date with Cody this week?"

Randy laughed. "Good for you. And don't look now, Molly Rose, but the bartender definitely has a thing for you. A lot of women would love to have your problems."

In the midst of my agony and despair, I couldn't help but check out the bartender to see if Randy was telling the truth. Sure enough, I no more than glanced in his direction than he winked at me.

"Oh, God," I said, and crept back into my comfort zone of misery. "My line of credit in the romance department is just a tad overextended at the moment. Why don't we just leave it at that?"

Randy smiled. "Just had to point him out, Molly Rose. As Fats Waller said, "One never knows, do one?"

Chapter 12: I SLOWLY BEGIN CLIMBING OUT OF CHAPTER 11

I said goodnight to Randy at approximately 7:15 and made my way home to take care of some essential chores. To save myself from the many demons that taunted and haunted me, I filled my mind with more pressing matters. First and foremost, I needed to regenerate my skin with the latest in moisturizing madness that Claudia and I had picked up on our recent shopping trip. Horrors: I had purchased this miracle cream and forgotten all about it. An email earlier in the day from Claudia, asking for my perceptions on the product (an excuse to segue into the state of my love life), had me dutifully planning to start my new facial regime that evening—anything to avoid facing my problems. Instead I would concentrate on any problems *on* my face.

Next on my list of priorities was to test the eye shadow samples that had come "free" with the outrageously priced regenerating cream (a must-have for anyone over thirty, or so we were told). My big dilemma for the evening would be to decide if I preferred the Sassy Bordeaux or the Desert Brown Desire, and then, I would make the momentous decision regarding what color shadow to wear on my date with Cody, taking extra care to be sure that I had perfectly coordinating blush and lip gloss.

Cody would notice these details (and care about them) as much as I cared about what guitar chords he had used in his second number or how many pieces of frayed denim were on the hem of his jeans. (Yes, I'm a frayed I'm that pathetic.) But nonetheless, I was determined to focus on my face, down to bleaching above my lip and plucking my eyebrows into a heart-pounding arch. Surely, Cody would be enthralled to see me freshly plucked.

As I pondered these beautifying rituals, I couldn't help but formulate a reverse plan. Whatever looked good for Cody, the opposite would do just fine for Alan. I remembered that I had a pair of false eyelashes that Dina had given me as a gag when I first met Leo. (The idea was to bat them like crazy to win his heart.) At the time, I had told Dina that these faux centipedes would more likely have sent him running into the closest brick wall. And so, I thought, how perfect; if I could just figure out how to glue them on, I would wear them for Alan.

It then occurred to me, as I walked leisurely past Millie's Vintage House of Treasure, the tackiest thrift shop in town (thankfully closed), that somewhere in my closet, probably to the far left, was this trendy goat-hair animal print vest that Claudia had bestowed on me. Her reason for parting with this $1200 in*vest*ment was the fact that Colin hated it. Despite its designer label and having had some lanky model wear it (or a reasonable facsimile thereof) on a Milan runway, it was rather frightening. The most frightening thing about it was what Claudia paid for it and what Colin might have done had he known.

If you're wondering, as I did, why she didn't just return it, it's because she was determined to wear it to certain prestigious events related to business when her husband would not be present. And what better place to house the monstrosity but in my closet, where I was welcome to wear it whenever I needed to "dress to impress." I never thought such an occasion would occur.

I had successfully filled my head with all of the matters I've just mentioned, and many more. However trite and ridiculous they seem, they were like etymological Klonopin to me. Amazingly, just the transformation of certain words into pathetic plans had destressed me to the point where I managed to stop emoting long enough to avoid a meltdown and get through that evening and the next day with a similar goal in mind.

IF ONLY TONY HADN'T DECIDED TO BEGIN A YOGIC LIFESTYLE AT MY DOOR

I live on the sixth floor. From the elevator, my front door is three doors down to the right, at the end of the hallway. Most of the other apartments on my floor are to the left of the elevator. I hoped this small fact, which I had never given a second thought, would be a factor in *not* having to explain why a handsome six-foot-two man in a sweat suit was sitting in a lotus position at my door with his eyes closed and breathing deeply in a presumably meditative state.

I walked toward him cautiously, fully expecting him to hear my approach and open his eyes. But he didn't. He just continued to breathe and enjoy inner peace, while I stood there awkwardly in my Jimmy Choos with a heavy briefcase in one hand and a bottle of spring water in the other.

My sympathetic side kicked in, and although I couldn't think of any alternative to disturbing his tranquility, I felt bad about doing so. But the cynic in me began to wonder if he knew damn well I was standing there and was somehow playing with me or testing me. I didn't want to allow him to get away with that, but I felt it important to err on the side of believing in the probity of my dear friend.

Clearing my throat was a bust. Clearing it a second time was an even bigger bust, and my B.S. radar began sending me all of the normal warning signs. Still, I was not going to misbehave. I decided I would simply say his name gently.

"Tony," I whispered.

No response. Not even an "om."

"Tony," I said a bit more audibly.

I saw him take several calming breaths, and I knew by now he was fully aware of my presence. Quite frankly, at that precise moment, I wanted to kick his ass.

"Tony, even the great masters bring themselves back to the present. Now would be an excellent time to emulate them."

His eyes opened wide, but his body did not move. He just stared at me.

"How long have you been here doing, um, this?" I asked awkwardly.

He took a long time (by my standards) to respond. "Since 5:30. I expected you would come straight home from work."

"Randy asked me to join him for a drink after work."

"No doubt to talk about me," he said. "I'm sure *Randy* knows all about it."

I think I neglected to mention that Tony was a wee bit jealous of my close relationship with Randy. As he had always fancied himself to be my closest male confidant, he didn't like the idea that, in all likelihood, that title went to Randy.

"Tony, we talked about a lot of things."

"Molly, don't bullshit me here," he said, rising to a standing position.

"Do you happen to know if any of my neighbors saw you here? Did you hear anyone?"

"Don't change the subject," he barked at me. "And please don't tell me that's all you care about: being embarrassed in front of your neighbors. And, no, for the record, I'm not aware of anyone seeing me. And I don't give a damn if anyone did. So, divulge. Did you tell Randy everything? I know you did. You probably emailed that quartet of gal pals you have, too."

"No, I did not do that!" I said adamantly. I started to add that I wanted them out of my love life, but that might clue him into the fact that I was dealing with more men than just him.

"You told Claudia then," he said.

"If you want to know, the only female who knows anything is Hannah, because she came to visit me on Sunday and saw that I was upset. She thinks you're wonderful, just like I do, and stop thinking anyone, not me, not Randy, nor anyone else, was trash talking you."

He relented a bit. "It's just so embarrassing."

We were still standing in the hall. I felt like half of a circus sideshow. "Could you hold my briefcase?" I asked. "Let me open the door so we can take this inside."

Tony obliged, and we made ourselves comfortable in the living room.

"You have nothing to be embarrassed about," I said. "*I* feel embarrassed."

"Why you?" Tony asked.

"Because I should be more in touch with my feelings. I should know how to react when my oldest friend tells me he loves me, even if it's fourteen years since I first loved him."

"Molly, I'll admit, when I poured my heart out to you, I half-expected you to fall into my arms. When you didn't, I was hurt. And when I sensed you were angry, I was just overwhelmed. But I talked to my buddy Andy, and I realized that your reaction was perfectly normal under the circumstances."

"I'm sorry," I said. "My hearing is a bit off. Did you say that you discussed this with *Andy*?"

"Okay, you got me." he said.

I smiled.

"Andy suggested that I put myself in your position. He asked me how I would've felt if you had married another guy and everything had happened in reverse. I couldn't begin to answer him. I probably would have been just as confused, and, yes, somewhat angry, just as you were."

I wanted to cry. "Thank you, Tony. Thank you *so* much for telling me that."

I jumped up from the armchair I was sitting in and sat down next to him on the couch. I touched his face gently and stroked his hair. "You mean so much to me; I just can't reconcile this in a day." I buried my head into his chest and hugged him. He hugged back.

"Take all the time you need," he said. "I mean that."

Tony looked into my eyes and stroked my face, ever so gently. "All of these years I've been with someone else. Happy or not, it isn't the point. I haven't been with you. To expect you to change course because you've suddenly learned that things were not as they appeared to be, well, that's kind of ugly on my part. And arrogant. I'm sorry."

He gave me a gentle kiss on the lips, and don't ask me how I know, but I know that was all he meant it to be, considering the circumstances. But chemistry has a mind of its own, and I suddenly found myself enjoying the deep, romantic, no-holds-barred kiss that I had dreamed of ever since I was sweet sixteen. Ten minutes later, we were still going strong.

Chapter 13: MY HORMONES WAKE UP FROM THEIR NAP

That kiss stirred the passionate beast in me. No matter what I was doing—taking off makeup, putting it on, petting Captain Jack, washing my hair, writing an obituary, pointing the finger at corrupt government officials—I was thinking about "the kiss." My hormones were wide awake and looking at me almost in the same fashion Captain Jack does when I'm late with his dinner. "Hey, Mom, aren't you going to *feed* me? NOW!"

I had assumed that if you wait fourteen years for one man to kiss you, you're likely to be disappointed. Tony's lips on mine provided all of the pleasure I'd always imagined. I wondered if Cody would kiss me on our bowling/dinner date. He was the sensitive type. Surely his kiss would reflect that. As for Alan, the wretched plant, his lips would never touch mine, but I still wondered if indeed he had any kissing ability worth noting. I was not curious enough to consider finding out. And then there were thoughts of Leo.

Leo and I had wanted to fix what had been broken. I sometimes think that we had deluded ourselves into thinking our union was so exceptional that nothing could hurt us. Were we so swept away by the dream we thought we were living that we neglected to be on the lookout for real life?

No matter how I looked at the situation, no matter how much culpability I accepted for my lack of faith, trust, or whatever I should've had but didn't, I could not get past the fact that something so enormous was going on in his life, and he kept every bit of it a secret from me. Conversely, Leo couldn't reconcile that under such tragic circumstances, I didn't understand that he did what he thought best for everyone. He had planned to tell me everything when it was over, so why was I so obstinate and unforgiving? At one point, he told me it was so agonizing to watch Luciana die that to add even the tiniest extra bit of stress to the mix might render him useless.

I didn't buy that. One extra "bit of stress" (did he mean *me?*) would sap all of his strength and leave him with no more potency than a Raggedy Andy doll on Unisom?

The heartbreaking thing was that when it came down to it, we were pretty much in sync on everything except the issue of trust. Why didn't he trust me? Why couldn't I trust that he made a decision under enormous stress and that sometimes we all need to veer off the path most taken? Life is not one straightforward road.

We came to understand each other's point of view; we just were never able to get back to where we were. When we were together, we often found ourselves just staring blankly at each other. It was foolish to think we had resolved anything. There was a brief period when all seemed well again, but it was as if a thick fog had enshrouded us. We could no longer see one another: the color (and the life) had simply drained from our relationship.

When we decided to call it quits and break off our engagement, it was the most excruciating thing I had ever been through, and from what I intuited from Leo, it was the same for him. I think we both kept hoping that the other one would pull some kind of rabbit out of the hat at the last minute, but that never came to pass. Our parting was quiet, but my sobs were plentiful and loud in the solitude of my own space. I had always imagined it was the same way for Leo.

Cody called me twice before our bowling/dinner date. I became so comfortable with him that I had no problem having him pick me up at my apartment. He showed up with a teddy bear in a brown leather jacket, a red T-shirt, and a bandana around his neck. In its paw was an adorable plastic guitar.

"This is *too* cute!" I exclaimed. "I love it."

"Look at the tag," he said excitedly. "See what his name is!"

"I turned over the collectible tag and read, "Cody the Rocker Bear."

I squeezed the bear. "I love him. Thank you so much."

I squeezed Cody, too. (A hug; just a hug!)

"I just found him today," Cody explained. "I was in a floral shop to buy you some flowers, and I saw these bears in the gift section. When I found my namesake, well, he was too good to pass up. I hope you don't think it's too much for a second date."

"No, not at all," I told him.

"Good," he said, looking around. "It seems like you've already fulfilled your quota from the florist shop this week, anyway."

I was about to get pissed off, but he was so good-natured that I let it pass.

Instead, I was disgusted with myself. In the split second that I had to cogitate, instead of continuing to bask in the warmth of this cuddly gesture, I wondered if there had been a run of Cody bears over the years. I was shameful, especially when he said he had just found the bear today.

Listen, we all need to be careful out there. It takes a lot to know one another. I wondered, though: did my thoughts of multiple Cody bears stem from anything that Cody had done, or had my painful breakup with Leo left me unable to trust anyone?

Well, there was the fact that Cody was a rocker, but that's not necessarily a bad thing. Edgy is sexy, and music is passionate, but I've never known any girl, ever, to fantasize about growing up to marry an accountant or insurance agent to subsequently give birth to a tribe of little baby bean counters or statisticians. (My apologies to all of the swashbuckling, scintillating members of these very respectable professions.)

Then, there was "Barbarino." I had a problem with the fact that anyone who liked me could have her had her for a girlfriend. Cody had told me that she changed a great deal since he first met her. I pondered this. Perhaps, without the attitude and her current outstanding warrant for arrest by the fashion police, who knew what lay beneath the insecure wart-nosed band whore who had needlessly attacked me that night at the Rolling Beetle.

All I knew was that I was never going to enjoy another moment of my life if I continued with these insane thoughts. Nothing wrong with being picky, I concluded, but what, indeed, constitutes crossing the line?

"Wow!" Cody said. "Three strikes, and you're hot."

I laughed. "I can't believe my luck. I've never bowled three strikes in a row in my life. Figuratively, I have bowled three strikes and been *out* many times, but never like this. You're my good luck charm, Cody."

"Oh, me, too. Big time. But bowling three strikes is not luck, Molly; it's called skill."

"You're not so bad at this yourself," I told him, deflecting the compliment.

"Ah, but you're beating me," he noted with a grin.

"You know," I said, "a lot of men couldn't say that with a smile."

Cody picked up his ball and proceeded to take his turn. "I've got all the testosterone I need. I don't need to win at bowling to keep my supply cabinet filled up. Besides, the game's not over yet! Ha ha."

He rolled the ball down the lane, quickly knocking over nine pins as the tenth wobbled precariously.

"Down with you!" he said, pointing at it as if his finger had magical powers. "I command you to fall!"

As the pin fell and my revitalized hormones insisted on making their presence known, I couldn't help thinking about Cody's magic finger.

We bowled three games, and it was the most fun I'd had in ages. Cody made me feel so comfortable, and I loved watching his hunky body as he threw the ball. He was so cool and so sexy at the same time.

I ended up winning the first game by three points, and Cody won the second two with only a margin of ten to twenty points. We were very compatible bowling partners; that had to mean something.

After bowling, Cody offered me the choice of three lovely restaurants. The first one happened to be a place Leo and I had often gone, so I nixed that. The second was an upscale BBQ place, but I loved the food there so much that I imagined myself growing a size before the date was over. Instead, I chose a Mediterranean restaurant with a warm ambience and amber candles on every table.

"I was hoping you'd pick this place," he said. "I've always wanted to try it, and I can't think of a more beautiful date than you."

Well, Cody had answered the first question swirling around in my head: had he ever been here with anyone else? For some reason unknown to even me, I decided to be forthright with him.

"Thank you for telling me that, " I said. "I was hoping that this wasn't a favorite place with anyone else."

"As a matter of fact," Cody said, "during the final daze, and that's spelled D A Z E, of my doomed relationship with Barbarino, she wanted me to bring her here. Having been here with her would have tainted the place forever. I know a lot of dudes who have certain places they go, and the people who work in those joints know all of their business. Not me. I'm not interested in shining a spotlight on my private life. It's one thing to get up on stage and let it all hang loose for your audience, but I'm not real keen on living my life like that."

"Well, I sort of figured that," I said. "You're also an artist, and painting is a very solitary art, unlike rock 'n' roll."

"Exactly," he said. "Balance, Molly. It's all about balance."

"But honestly, Cody," I asked, "I relate to what you're saying, but isn't it kind of an ego trip to have all of those people swarming the stage or waiting for you after a concert?"

"If nobody waits for you," he said, "then you've probably done a suck-ass job. And, yeah, everyone's ego likes a boost. I know it's tough to have your cake and eat it, too, but I do like getting away from all of that. Let's just put it this way, Molly, some of the other dudes in the biz are far more amenable than I am to living a certain lifestyle. To each his own, I suppose. I sometimes feel bad for the girls who put themselves out there, well, you know, but after a while, I figure they know what they're getting into, and I'd rather worry about global warming or world hunger."

"Than groupies?" I asked.

He looked embarrassed. "Well, yeah. Than groupies."

The more I talked to Cody, the more sides of him I saw. He was much more of a mixed bag than I'd imagined. I didn't know too many people who used "suck-ass" in one sentence and expressed deep concern for world hunger in the next. I was going to enjoy getting to know him.

The date ended with a powerhouse kiss at my front door. I wanted to ask him inside, but it was a weeknight, and with my hormones standing at attention, I was afraid that before I knew it, Cody would be "standing at attention," too, and I just wasn't quite ready for that.

Chapter 14: THE SHE-DEVIL INVADES MY OFFICE

When my assistant, Ana, told me that there were two women in the reception area waiting to see me, she had barely finished her sentence when in barged Naomi Hall-Benchley and a friend of hers, one with a clear addiction to plastic surgery. I had grown up thinking "plastic" meant Visa, MasterCard, and American Express, not the material composition of someone's face.

Naomi, on the other hand, although she'd had "work" done, was addicted to tanning and toning, and no matter what the thermometer said, even in the dead of winter she was famous for wearing sleeveless dresses and tops to show off the fruits of her daily labor in the gym and in the tanning beds.

To complicate my ever-complicated life, *nothing* ever got past Randy, who had taken from his desk drawer a Scream mask (derived from the famous Edvard Munch painting), put it on his face, and proceeded to stand three feet away from the threshold of my office door, mocking every move Naomi and her friend made behind their backs. He rolled up his tight short-sleeved shirt to make it appear sleeveless, then continued to point at the Scream mask to indicate his horror.

Although Randy is king when it comes to gesturing, he knows he is doing it, and it's part of his shtick, whereas Naomi poses as if each move she makes is a potential shot for a magazine cover. She has virtually no sense of humor about herself at all.

"Molly, meet my new best friend, Ginger Wentworth," Naomi said. "She's a real doll."

She said it so loudly that Randy heard it, and I could see him clutching his stomach, doubling over, as my rubbernecking coworkers gathered behind him.

"My suspicions exactly," I said. I just couldn't help myself. A real doll, indeed. Barbie's face looked more lifelike than Ginger's.

"What?" Naomi said.

"I just figured she was your best friend," I said innocently. "It's obvious you two have a lot in common."

"Okay, Molly," Naomi said, recognizing my thinly veiled dig. But not being able to prove it, she bit her lip.

"Naomi, why are you here?" I was getting nervous about my work.

"Aren't you going to even offer us a seat? Where are your manners?"

"This isn't my home. It's my office. I'm on a deadline. Newspapers have deadlines. You can't come here unannounced and expect me to play hostess."

"I was just delivering something for Art," she said. "You do know he's on the board of this paper."

"Yes, I know. Okay, pull up those chairs if you want. Two minutes. That's it."

"Molly, I'm here to appeal to your senses, trusting that you have some. In a couple of weeks, the fundraiser ball for the hospital is coming up. I'm sure you know they're building a new children's wing. I would appreciate it if you would attend, as a personal favor to me, if you won't do it for yourself, as a date for Art's new colleague."

"Oh, God," I said. "Not *this* again." She obviously knew that Alan and I had a date for that coming Saturday night. This charade of hers was bigger than I had originally thought. Alan was more than just a plant to get grist for her gossip mill; she wanted to extract all the information from him that she could about how I behaved on dates. She wanted me to attend this hospital gala, and being the control freak she is, she wanted to know all about me so as to iron out any potential kinks that might be detrimental to her beloved status symbol of a husband.

"Not interested," I told her.

Ginger decided to chime in and help her new BFF. "I've met him, Molly. He's charming and *so* funny. He had me in stitches."

I'm surprised you didn't pop a few, I thought to myself.

"Well, gosh, here's a thought. Why don't you go out with him, Ginger?"

She stuck out her left hand to show off a stone to put Plymouth rock to shame. "I'm engaged, to a doctor. A superstar from Los Angeles. A plastic surgeon."

"No!" I said in mock surprise, as Naomi glared at me.

"Naomi," I said. "Once again, in a word, no! In two words, NO WAY! In three words, NO FREAKIN' WAY. And if he's *that* much of a catch, I'm sure he can find his own dates."

Naomi stiffened in her chair. "He *is* that much of a catch; he's just been working too hard assimilating himself in a new environment to develop much of a social life. Listen to me, my husband is on this board and pulls weight here. Don't forget that. I need you to do this for me."

"I just don't get this. You have a ton of friends, don't you? You're just Swansea's favorite socialite. Surely you must have address books filled with BFFs who can fill the bill."

"Oh, but I do, Molly," she said, "have address books filled with 'BFFs.' But unlike you, they're all married or in serious relationships. You're the most single person I know."

She smiled, knowing she'd punctured me with her pitchfork.

"No," I said defiantly. "I won't do it."

"Oh, yes you will," she said, as if she knew something I didn't. "You'll come to your senses. This ball is just too fantastic to miss."

"You already tried to set me up with this loser at Susan Decker's wedding. Last August, remember? The answer is still the same."

"Oh, Molly, you're thinking of Chris Baker from Dallas. Art's marketing VP. He's been long snatched up by Samantha Duckworth. And I introduced them. No, this is yet another fine specimen you're going to leave by the wayside. I hear he's quite handsome. Don't repeat your prior foolishness. Just give me a yes, and I'm out of here."

"I do have to ask you to leave *now*," I said.

"See you at the fundraiser," she said cheerfully. "TTFN."

"*Ciao!*" Ginger said. "*Piacere.*"

As they walked out of my office and toward the elevator, Randy, who had remasked himself, followed several paces behind them imitating Naomi's runway walk with grand precision. He had the office staff laughing so hard that Naomi and Ginger turned around, only to find an unmasked Randy looking doe-eyed at them as if to say, "Who, me?"

I didn't know what devious plan Naomi was concocting, but one thing was for sure: I would be stepping up my plans for Alan. No way, after I was through with him, would she ever want me dating anyone she knew—ever again.

Randy rushed into my office to take a bow for his performance.

"I do not have the time to rake you over the coals, " I said, "but stick yourself with a fork, Randy, because you are so done."

"Oh, Molly Rose, stop the dramatics, girlfriend. All I can say is that it's one thing that the Constitution gives people like Naomi the right to 'bare' arms, but what piece of documentation gives that friend of hers the right to 'bare' face? Goodness! I hope she doesn't do tanning beds, too. The poor thing would melt. We could call her 'Puddles.' "

He did have a way of making me laugh, even when I was furious with him.

"Well, I'm behind now," I told him. "I guess the rundown of my date with Cody will have to wait until tomorrow."

Randy was horrified. "No way!"

"Yes, way!" I said.

"*Tomorrow?*" he gasped.

"Tomorrow."

BEING A DUDE MAGNET IS HARD WORK!

I just made my deadline that day, and I was drained. The only positive thing about Naomi and Ginger's visit is that it gave me a great idea for a Lifestyle feature: an in-depth probe on the lengths women will go to for vanity. I'd begin with plastic surgery and tanning addicts.

Alan called me at 5:25 that evening. It was fortuitous timing for me because I was on the elevator in my building, thereby blocking the signal and sending his message right to voice mail. I would have liked to send it somewhere else, but I didn't know how to reroute calls to hell. I made a mental note to check the manual.

"Hi, Molly. Alan. I know how busy you are at work, so please, just know that if I'm not calling it's only because I respect your time limitations. My brain, however, has other ideas. All it does is think of you. You are pretty, witty, and, hey, I'm writing a ditty. Well, sorry to have missed you, but at least I got to hear the sound of your voice. I wonder if you know how sexy you are. I can't wait until Saturday to see you; you are the most exciting woman I've met in years. Call me if you'd like. I'll leave my cell on."

As the doors of the elevator opened, I repeated the words I had just heard in my head: you are pretty, witty, and, hey, I'm writing a ditty. "GAG ME!" I said aloud.

I was ashamed of myself. To think I had questioned Cody's use of the word "blast," a word that people use all the time, when there are men out there who say things like, "You are pretty, witty, and, hey, I'm writing a ditty."

"Well, let me tell you, it's #@*TTY!" I continued.

"Molly Rose, wash your mouth out with soap."

I screamed and dropped my briefcase.

"Damn it, Randy," I said, turning around. "Did you freakin' follow me home? How come I didn't hear the elevator open?"

"How do you think I get these fab glutes? I take the stairs."

"And you've followed me home because ... ?"

Randy reached under the back of his shirt and pulled out a file folder. "Because *someone* dropped her *confidential* source material in the hallway by the elevator, where *anyone*, and I mean *anyone*, could have found it. What a lucky break that it was *I* who happened upon it."

I gasped. I couldn't believe I had been that distracted by my personal life to have dropped something so important and not even known it was missing. As soon as he said it, I remembered someone bumping into me with a lame "uh, sorry," but I had forgotten that the file was under my arm and not securely tucked away in my briefcase.

"Come inside," I said, as I opened the door to my apartment. Remembering Tony's performance the other day, the last thing I needed was for my neighbors to be wondering why various men were appearing at my doorstep the moment I arrived home from work. I'd hate for anyone to think I was just "going to work."

"Thank God you found it," I said. "May I have it?"

Randy smiled. "You know, I would just love to hear all about your date with that delicious Cody."

"You're going to blackmail me?" I asked.

"Oh, Molly Rose, what an ugly way to put it."

"Okay, well, you may be sorry you asked," I warned him.

"Truth time," Randy said. "I *am* dying for the scoop on your date, but I do need a friend to talk to about Kyle."

"Well, if you put it that way," I said, "have a seat."

Randy smiled and sat down. I noticed he was still holding my file.

"I'll take that," I said, grabbing it out of his hands.

"Soda water?" I asked. "Or wine?"

"It's been a vino kind of day. Please."

Just as I went to grab the wine and corkscrew, Cody called my cell to tell me that he couldn't stop thinking about our date the other night, and about how well we connected on so many levels. I shared his enthusiasm, and I cryptically told him so, for I could see Randy's ears had become pointier than Dr. Spock's. I felt bad that I couldn't talk to Cody for long, but he was getting ready for a gig, so we agreed to speak the next day.

Before I could even hang up, I saw "Tony Call Waiting" on my screen. I love you, Tony, I thought, but you're taking a trip to voice mail right now.

I finally got the bottle open and sat down to dish with Randy.

As drained as I was, it felt good to unburden myself and hear about someone else's love life besides my own. Randy told me he was in a real "dither" over Kyle. (In case you're wondering, I don't mind strange verbiage from friends; I only overanalyze the vocabulary of potential mates.)

As Randy explained to me, he and Kyle were evolving beautifully. Not only did they have a lot in common, but their communication styles clicked, and both felt as if they'd known one another in a previous life. For Randy, his "dither" came down to the same issue that had decimated my relationship with Leo: trust. Often Kyle would have to cancel plans abruptly for "work reasons." Randy was becoming increasingly dismayed over this. He wanted to trust Kyle, but we are all a summation of our past experiences, and when you've been burned, it makes it much harder to get too close to another flame, even the most alluring and inviting of them.

Coupled with the trust issue was Randy's guilt over *having* a trust issue. Kyle was beginning to pick up on it, and Randy was afraid Kyle would resent his lack of complete faith.

As Randy alternately sipped wine and spoke, I alternately listened and thought about Leo. Some of the parallels in Randy's story brought my own feelings to the fore. The similarities were not lost on Randy. We both agreed that no love is that unconditional, as many romantics would like to think it is. If you care about someone else, you have to care about yourself first, and that means that sometimes you have to kick blind faith to the curb and let the rational side of you stop snoozing long enough to be aware of your emotional environment.

In my great wisdom, I advised Randy not to leap to any grand, all-encompassing conclusions that might pull the trigger on his relationship, but instead, to tread gently and respectfully, taking each day as it came.

Randy said I was at my "sagacious best." However, after covering his love life and moving on to mine, the sage in me began to wither. I was still in the dark regarding Tony.

My feelings about him had run the gamut over the years; I'd probably, in total, used up more brain cells on him than I had on Leo, simply because we went back so much farther in time. I loved him. I hated him. I agreed to love him as a friend but wished I were his wife. I loved him as a friend but still had fantasies. I loved him only as a friend but had moved on. I found him attractive but didn't have fantasies. No matter what my state of mind, in some strange way, although I had no control over the situation, I was in control of my feelings. Now Tony had the *nerve* to bring *his* feelings into it all, and that's one train I never saw coming down the track.

In the middle of all of that, I could see great possibilities for Cody and me. He was new and exciting, and I wanted to see if we had any true potential together. It was way too early in the game to know, but I wasn't going to bow out simply because Tony, after fourteen years, announced that he wanted me. But was it worth losing Tony, someone who I did care for deeply, just to ride the rails with a new man? Then again, who said I had to make up my mind right away? If things were meant to be for Tony and me, his feelings would stick around for a while until mine had time to catch up with them.

Chapter 15: NOT SO FAST, NAOMI!

The next day, I was determined that nobody would interrupt me. Working in the newspaper business is hectic enough without unexpected visitors. There was a message on my cell from Alan, bright and early in the morning. He was disappointed that I hadn't called him back the night before and he was eager to confirm our Saturday night date. Not wanting to arouse suspicion or have him lose interest before I could give him "the experience of a lifetime," I returned the call. I listened while he gleefully told me of his unbounded anticipation of our Saturday night engagement.

As my stomach churned, I interjected some pleasant phrases of little substance. I made certain to keep my voice low in case Randy was lurking about. Keeping my voice down only elicited "Molly, do you know how sexy you sound when you converse in such soft tones? Why, you're positively mellifluous!"

GAAAAAAAAAAAAAAAG ME!!!

"Alan, I'm in my office, and voices carry. I'm just trying to keep this conversation between the two of us. I'm not trying to be sexy."

"I know," he said, elatedly. "That's what makes you even more of a dynamo."

I was a "mellifluous sexy dynamo." I could live with that—at least for the duration of the conversation.

"I don't think so ... "

"No, you have this smoky, kind of come-hither quality to your voice," he said, as if I would be complimented.

"I'll tell you what, Alan. I'll record my voice for you—analog or digital, your choice—and you can take *it* to dinner instead of me. And if you two have a good time, you can have a go at it all over again next week. The honey will still be dripping from my vocal chords."

He thought I was kidding. "You have a sparkling wit," he said. "What you don't understand is that your voice is so sexy because of the magnificent Molly that comes with it. You're bright, witty ... well, you're just the whole package."

I had no idea how to respond to that, so I said nothing.

"I'm sorry," he said. "I think I'm embarrassing you."

"Well, I'm in a close work environment here, Alan, and I need to get to get back to writing. I just wanted to return your call."

He sounded disappointed that I wasn't returning the compliments. I certainly wasn't going to tell him that he was "the whole package," and furthermore, I would never *see* his package to confirm that veracity of that statement, anyway.

"Well, then, I'll call you Saturday afternoon to set the plans in cement."

I was hoping maybe he'd step in wet cement long enough for Naomi to call him on his cell with date instructions, only to find that the cement had dried by the time he tried to move. What a beautiful fantasy.

I had no sooner hung up from Alan than Claudia called me, rather insistent that I see her for dinner. Feeling as if I'd been neglectful toward her, I agreed. I quickly got off the phone and emailed Tony. I told him I hoped maybe to see him on Sunday, if he wasn't busy with Noah. I apologized for not getting back to him and told him I was swamped at the office. I didn't want to let any more time pass without communication from me, and I hoped my email would make him feel better and give me more time to think.

Cody was spending the day in a recording studio laying down tracks for his group's first CD, so I plowed ahead with a workday that resembled what I perceived to be "a normal day."

I'M SO TIRED ...

It was a long, hard workday for both Randy and me, with no time to swap our respective woes (something we both needed a brief respite from, anyway), and the kind of day that takes every working brain cell you have so that you can bring home a paycheck instead of a pink slip.

As I left my office at 6:30, my iPod protecting me from the outside world, I listened to the Beatles singing "I'm So Tired," for no other song better expressed my sheer exhaustion.

"I'm so tired, I haven't slept a wink, I'm so tired, my mind is on the blink. ..." I love that song because it so beautifully expresses how I feel in those dreadful moments of unbridled fatigue, but the song also has a way of increasing that fatigue tenfold.

The moment I got into my apartment (thank God none of my male friends were waiting in the hallway), I called Claudia to ask her if we could postpone our dinner.

"Claude, I'm a walking zombie, and in about thirty seconds, I'll be a passed-out one."

"Oh, Molly, I need to see you, and I'm going out of town tomorrow for that ad conference in Chicago."

"Claude, Ali Baba had forty thieves, and I desperately need forty winks."

"Girlfriend, listen, why don't you catch about twenty winks, then call me when you wake up, and I'll bring dinner over. From whatever restaurant you like. If you don't call me by 8:45, I'm calling you, and if you don't answer the phone, I'm coming over. You know if you zone out now for the rest of the night, you'll screw up your sleep schedule by waking up at 4:00 a.m. Go to sleep at a reasonable hour, get your forty winks, and coupled with the twenty winks you'll take now, you'll have sixty!"

She had a point. I'd made the mistake of going to bed too early in the past, and it always backfired on me. We agreed on twenty winks and Mandarin chicken salads from the trendiest spot in town.

A DOZEN ROSES, NINE WINKS, AND BUBBLES AD INFINITUM

The moment I finished speaking with Claudia, I fed Captain Jack, then flopped onto my bed, and that's all I remember. If I had any bad dreams, I was spared from remembering them. Nine winks into my agreed-upon fifteen, I heard the doorbell ringing and ringing and ringing. I was so disoriented when I woke up that I had no idea what time it was, what day it was, and who might be ringing the bell. As I came out of my bedroom yelling, "Just a moment," I was trying to figure out why Claudia didn't bother calling me on the house phone first. She was always very good about sticking to whatever plan she had made.

A flash of bright red hit me in the face as I opened the door. My stomach turned over about three times, wondering who was behind it, when I saw the same delivery guy who had brought Alan's plant.

"Hello there again, Miss Popularity!" he said with a wide grin. "These are for you."

I took the roses and put them down on the nearest table. "Hold on," I said, going over to my jacket and taking a few crumpled dollar bills out of the pocket. "Sorry, these look as grungy as I do, but they work."

"Hey, no problem. I appreciate it," he said. "Name's Shawn if none of these guys work out."

"And what's your name if one does work out?" I asked.

He burst out laughing. "Outta luck, I guess. You've got a wicked sense of humor. You're a friend to florists everywhere."

"Thanks, Shawn. That's a first. Take care."

My heart was pounding. You may or may not remember, but Leo

had given me a dozen red roses the night he proposed. A rush of adrenaline snapped me out of my semi-fugue state, and I hurried to open the card.

Your email was very heartfelt, and I would love to see you on Sunday. I didn't want to call now; you need some think time. But I send these as a small token of my love and affection. Tony.

I burst into tears as the house phone rang simultaneously. It was Claudia, asking if she could bring the food over.

"The sooner, the better," I said.

As I hung up, I realized that if I told Claudia the roses were from Tony, that would be headline news, and while she would painfully keep it to herself if I asked her to, she would *not* be able to stop hounding me for personal updates, and I just didn't want that. I loved Claudia, but having my girlfriends in the thick of my relationships was Leo all over again.

Who would I tell her the roses were from? I didn't know, but I would figure it out. Meanwhile, I took the card from Tony and ran into my bedroom, sticking it between the mattress and the box spring for safekeeping. I realized a small corner was still showing, and as I went to fix it, I admitted I was becoming paranoid to excessive extremes. I went back into the bathroom to freshen up before Claudia saw me looking like a Halloween leftover.

"Oh—my—God!" Claudia said, practically dropping our dinner on the floor.

Not wanting to litter my carpet with Mandarin chicken salad, I let Claudia's jaw drop to the floor instead while I took the food to the coffee table where I'd already set up plates and wine glasses.

"Are these from—?"

"No, they're not," I said, trying as hard as I could not to tear up again.

"Well, Molly, I don't know who the heck they're from, but you had the same reaction I did, and don't *think* about denying it."

"Can we sit down and eat?" I pleaded with her.

She was inching toward the couch, her mouth still agape and her eyes popping out of her head, when Captain Jack, despite having eaten an hour ago, smelled the chicken and was determined have a go at dinner: round two.

"Oh, no you don't, Jackie," Claudia said. "You're as cute as a button, but that's my dinner."

We sat down and began eating, Jack rubbing against my leg for attention.

"What does 'cute as a button' mean, anyway?" I asked. "I mean, how did buttons ever become the poster children for cuteness? Did you ever wonder about that?"

"No, but I sure am wondering who sent those roses."

Jack was now on his hind legs, his front paws on my knees, looking at my salad, then at me, then at my salad.

"Okay, baby, Mommy gives you one piece of chicken, and that's it. You go away."

I gave Jack a piece of chicken. Cats are always satisfied with one taste, and they will go away if you ask them to. Yeah, right. Jack was now more eager than ever to share *his* dinner with us.

"This salad is incredible," I said. "I love this peanut dressing. Thanks, Claude, this is a real treat."

"You're welcome. Who sent the roses?"

"Damn, Claude, can't you see I'm fending off an emotional breakdown here? I've been at the computer all day, borrowing brain cells from the universe because I ran out of my own at 2:30, I worked almost two hours overtime, I'm famished, and you're haranguing me."

"Sorry," she said, feeding Jack a small piece of chicken. "Get some sustenance so you can tell me everything."

I felt sick inside. I did not want to go through everything with Claudia. I needed time to think on my own. Jack was becoming more and more of a pain (our fault), so I banished him to the bedroom, only to suffer the sounds of his loud, mournful cries.

"Listen to him," I said, "and he's just crying over food. Imagine if he had real problems ... "

"Like what?" Claudia asked, still trying to take me down the road I didn't want to travel.

"Like why don't you tell me what you said I 'desperately needed to know' before you went out of town. That's a good place to start."

"Well, you know Dina's friend Millicent Larkin, who's Naomi's husband's Art's first cousin?"

"Yeah," I said incredulously. "What in the world does she matter to me?"

"Well, the woman wouldn't know a comfortable shoe if you rammed it down her throat. She can't be seen unless she's a foot taller in her Walter Steigers, her Christian Louboutins, her Malandrinos, or whatever. It's one thing if you're going to a party, but for her, they're a wardrobe staple. I heard she even wears them at home, with her designer bathrobes. Well, is it any surprise *whatsoever* that Miss Thing needs back surgery? Not that she isn't fully covered, but Dina told me that the cost of the back surgery is less than the cost of her shoe collection. Can you believe that?"

"Wow, that is rather unbelievable," I said.

"If someone were going to take a knife to my back, I'd be straight flipping into the year two thousand and twenty-five. But Mills is more upset because the docs told her she can *never* wear those shoes again unless she wants to do some permanent damage to her spine."

"I guess she can sell her shoes on eBay or something," I said. "It's not like she wears the same ones over and over."

"Molly, that is not the point. She's hardly going to put on a pair of designer Keds and go merrily about her business. To Mills, this is like receiving a life sentence in fashion hell. I like to be fashionable as much as the next woman, but my posture will beat out my shoes any day of the week. I visualize her becoming some kind of weird hermit over this. Those heels hurt *my* back just to look at them!"

"You're wacky," I said. "But you are sensible, and I couldn't agree more. However, I don't believe you couldn't go out of town to your ad convention without telling me about Millicent's shoe and spine crisis."

Jack's cries, which had stopped for a while, were now revving up again. He had managed to open the closed but not fully shut bedroom door.

"Oh, my God!" Claudia said. "What's that in his mouth?"

I wanted to sink between my sofa cushions when I saw that Jack was walking toward us with Tony's card in his mouth, which he had obviously pried from the mattress. Stuff happens when you hold a cat captive.

"Did you bring Auntie Claudia a love letter?" Claudia asked, holding up a piece of chicken between her fingers.

Before I could do anything to stop it, Jack had gobbled the chicken and dropped the small envelope at Claudia's feet. She picked it up and held it.

"I'm asking you not to read that," I said.

"Just tell me why not," Claudia said.

"Because it's personal. Did I ever pick up anything from Colin and read it without your permission—ever? Did I ever even so much as ask to do so?"

"No," she said sheepishly. "You've always been more respectful in that area than anyone I know."

"Thank you."

"So, let's make a deal," she said. "How about you just tell me who it's from, and we'll leave it at that."

I took the card from her and put it in my pocket. "It's from Shawn."

"Shawn?"

"Yeah, he's some guy I met earlier in the week. He kind of likes me, and he brought me these roses. Right before you came, as a matter of fact. Honestly, Claudia, I don't even know the guy. He just wrote some syrupy stuff that I prefer to keep to myself."

Claudia looked disappointed. "That's it? I'm sorry I was so vigilant about it. It's just that I thought they were from Leo. I was thinking of you and Leo this week. I remember how you always let him make such a big deal out of Halloween, and on the first of every November he'd always celebrate 'Molly Day," doing all kinds of sweet things for you to thank you for being such a good sport and indulging him."

I started to cry. "I can't believe that slipped my mind. I guess I'm just trying to let go. Maybe it's working."

"By the look of those tears, I'm not so sure."

"I'm fine," I said. "Sweet memories can do that to you. You know that. Now, come on, you said you had something urgent to tell me."

"Okay, Molly. The Millicent story sort of has a part two. You see, when Dina was talking to Millicent about the surgery and all, Millicent had just come from having dinner with the Benchleys the night before."

"Oh, no," I said. "Don't tell me that she-devil is part of this story."

" 'Fraid so, kiddo."

"Go on," I told her, "I can take it. I think."

"Well, Naomi was bragging to everyone that she had you set up on a date, and you were none the wiser. From what Dina got from Millicent, Naomi is just sickeningly proud of this bit of mischief, but she swore everyone to secrecy. Millicent is so despondent over the shoe thing and the back surgery that she couldn't care less about Naomi's trite, little scheming. Oh, did I mention that she's freaked about the scar the surgery will leave on her back? Naomi's friend Ginger is engaged to a plastic surgeon, so I guess she'll be paying him a visit. Where was I? Oh, well, apparently Naomi was more jazzed about your date than she was sympathetic toward Millicent's situation, so Mills unloaded to Dina. Lucky for you."

I just sat there with my fist clenched.

"You look superpissed, Molly, but not all that surprised."

"That's because I'd already figured it out, Claude. And let me tell you something, Naomi is going to be in for the surprise of a lifetime."

For the next hour, I told Claudia every detail about Alan T. Cressman, from the first meeting at Starbucks, to the funeral home flowers brought to my office, to the ironic plant arrangement sent to me at home, and to the plethora of phone calls extolling the virtues of my "mellifluous" voice. After I had filled her in, Claudia and I, thick as thieves, spent the evening devising every imaginable scenario for my upcoming date with Alan. I couldn't wait for Saturday night.

Chapter 16: THE FOURTH UTENSIL

Usually, when people sit down to enjoy a meal, a knife, a fork, and a spoon are the only utensils they need, unless of course, they are using chopsticks, but that's another story.

As I sat at my desk that Friday, thinking of all of the ways to enjoy the assortment of criminally delicious meals that Claudia and I had cooked up in our heads for Alan the night before, I realized that none of the standard utensils would work. I needed a "fourth utensil," an implement beyond the realm of knives, forks, and spoons, something that would help me devour an untested recipe and savor the nuance of every ingredient I might decide to throw in the pot. I couldn't plan ahead; after all, I had no idea what Alan may have concocted on his end. I had to be alert and one step ahead of him at every turn.

Alan was Naomi's wild card. His ridiculous proclamations of affection for me were as phony as Ginger's face or Naomi's friendship. I had no way of knowing what Alan might do or say when we were finally out and about together. Indeed, I would have to rely on my improvisational skills to get me through the evening.

If you've ever had a dream in which you realize that you *are* dreaming and can do any crazy thing you like, that is how I was planning to approach our "date." I was already taking bets with myself on how long it would be before Alan excused himself to the men's room to call Naomi on his cell.

I had no idea what might happen, and I'd like to say the uncertainty was more tantalizing than terrorizing, but that would be a lie. I was a mess, and it showed.

Luckily, after Claudia had left the night before, between my elevated adrenaline and the boost I'd gotten from my meager nine winks, I was able to get a great deal of work done. That left me with even more free time to be a wreck in plain sight at the office.

Suddenly, Randy came waltzing in. "I could have danced all night, I could have danced all night, and still have begged for more … "

"I take it things went well for you and Kyle last night," I said.

"Indeed, we had a marvelous time at the Lapin Gallery opening. I was such a wreck all day worrying that Kyle would cancel, but he was determined not to let his boss spoil our grand night … and it *was* indeed grand. Kyle even helped me to write the review. Oh, we are on such an amazing wavelength. But, of course, he was all too happy to help me get that review out of the way and have moi all to himself. Alas, while I am here lapping up the memories of a splendiferous night, my dear friend Molly Rose looks as if she spent the night on the wrong side of the tracks fending off savage beasts."

"No, that'll be tomorrow night," I said. "And I didn't spend last night on the wrong side of the tracks; I am currently *on* the tracks, and a train is running over my head every five minutes."

"Horrors," said Randy. "Pardon me, boy, is that the Chattanooga Choo Choo?"

"No! It's the "Men-Are-a-Headache-Express!""

"I've never heard that one. Can you hum a few bars?"

"No, I'd rather go visit a few bars."

"Oh, dear, you are not going to let me cheer you up!"

Randy knew when it was time to be serious. He could see I wasn't in a laughing mood.

"Can you tell me," I said, "without the use of song titles, how the evening went?"

Randy pulled up a chair. "Well, as you have well ascertained, for Kyle and me, it was fab. The catering was impeccable, and Pendleton's photography drew a crowd as eclectic as his work. The only problem was Lapin's lover, Nelson, who started way too early on the Moët & Chandon, and who, as you know, is flamboyant *sober*. An hour into the reception, he was three Ralph Lauren sheets to the wind. It was ghastly. At one point he almost nose-dived into the red grapes and baked Brie, whereupon Lapin dragged him by the cummerbund and ordered him to drink milk or sleep it off in the back room."

I was beginning to forget my own worries. "And did he take the suggestion to sleep lying down?" I laughed at my own joke.

"Funny Girl," Randy said, grinning because he had slipped his favorite show into the repartee. "No, Molly Rose! It was the suggestion to drink milk that set him off. He began walking frantically around telling anyone who would listen that nobody, not even his beloved Lapin, would turn him into a Dairy Queen."

I laughed loudly. "So then what?"

"Well, with a little help from his friends, Nelson was locked in the back office, and the moment he was dropped on the couch, he was out like a light. Honestly, it could have ended very badly. Lapin wasn't taking any chances. The moment Nelson fell out, the rented tux was stripped from his body and taken away. Truly a train wreck averted."

As soon as he said that, I came crashing back to reality, thinking of all the possible scenarios for my impending train wreck. I filled Randy in on everything and then begged him to tell me why I was so nervous about a bogus date.

"Honey, if I were planning a scheme as wild as yours, I'd be in a lather, too. Just give me first dibs on the movie rights."

Randy laughed, and my cell phone rang. As he left the office, I looked to see who was calling. What a relief; it was Cody.

"Hey, Molly, I hope I didn't catch you at a bad time. I just accepted an emergency gig in D.C. Helping out a friend. Problem is, I don't want to leave for a week without seeing you. Would telling you I want to see you at the last minute be considered offensive?"

I laughed. "No, that's only when men ask you at the last minute because their first, second, and third choices fell through."

"Oh, hell, Molly, that is so not the case! You *are* my first, second, and third choice, all rolled into one."

"You know, Cody, I'd love to see you tonight. But I want to cook you dinner. I'm a bit too tired to do the gourmet thing, but I make a mean spaghetti and meat sauce. How does that sound? With some salad and a nice bottle of wine."

"Rockin'!" he said. "I'll bring the wine. What time?"

"Eightish," I said. "Work for you?"

"Does it ever! See you then."

Suddenly, all of the anxiety I had been feeling drained out of me. I hadn't yet figured out what "fourth utensil" would get me through my "meal" with Alan, but for tonight, I was having dinner with an adorable Copper Spoon.

MOLLY IS ONE HAPPY GIRL

Cody arrived at 8:17, with two bottles of Chianti and a dazzling smile. As soon as he walked in, I saw Jack crouch under a chair, wondering who this male intruder was whom I was so happy to see. Not wanting to frighten Cody off, I gave Jack a look (that always puts cats right in their places … not!) and decided to ignore any show of objection.

"Hey, I've got an orange cat, too. Apple," Cody said, his eyes meeting Jack's. "You a boy or a girl?"

"Boy," I said, "and a jealous one at that."

"I'll let him warm up to me," Cody said with a smile.

"You named yours Apple? That's cute."

100

3

"Well, Orange seemed ridiculous, but I wanted to keep it in the fruit family, and Grapefruit didn't sound so cool. So being a Beatles fan, I opted for Apple. Hey, whatever you've got cooking in the pot" (if he only knew) "smells delicious. I had an energy bar for lunch because I wanted to save room for your spaghetti."

Normally, I seat my guests in the living room and have some sort of chatter before dinner. But Cody and I were both ravenous, everything was ready, and so we sat down at the candlelit dining room table, segueing into delightful dinner conversation.

There was a sliver of a moment when my thoughts raced back to Leo. I suppose it was the lone strand of spaghetti on Cody's fork, but I couldn't help thinking of the night when the lounge lizard sang "Just the Way You Are" as Leo thread the spaghetti out of his nostril. Luckily, Cody was such a pleasure to be with that within seconds he had my full attention again.

"This was magnificent, Molly. And I can't tell you how much I appreciate your cooking for me, last minute, especially after a hard day at the office. How did you know I loved Italian food? Oh, speaking of which, my neighbor is thinking of buying the old Mangiamo restaurant and opening a new Italian hot spot. You remember that place. It's in an old house from the late 1800s."

"Isn't that the building that's supposed to be haunted?" I asked.

"Sure is," he said. "That's why the other guy closed it. He swore there were ghosts chained up in the basement and that one was an old drunk copping feels from the women in the bar area."

"I remember that. I was going to write about it, but then something political happened, and I did something few journalists do."

"You wrote about the news?"

"Exactly!" I said, pleased that Cody and I were connecting so well. "A plus for you."

Cody smiled. I could see I made him feel good. He did exactly the same for me.

"The thing is, Molly, the guy didn't even care about the ghosts in the building, but he closed it because he thought this female ghost was possessing his wife. She was supposedly acting like someone else a good deal of the time, and while I don't know the details, I do know that he was so freaked by it that he wanted to call in the cops. Yeah, like they exorcise ghosts. I mean, can you picture this, 'Hey Bob, finish your damn donut, will ya? We got an exorcism at Fifth and Main. Just came over the dispatch, dude.' "

"That's hilarious," I said.

"His wife told him he'd be a laughingstock if he called in the cops, and she threatened to divorce him if he drew any attention to her. What did he think the cops were going to do, anyway?"

"Yeah," I said. "After all, possession is nine tenths of the law!"

We both burst out laughing, and Cody reached across the table with his left hand and grabbed my right. He squeezed it, his eyes looking right into mine. I felt something. It was undeniable. Captain Jack was so jealous, he had jumped onto my lap. I heard a low growl, and I feared he might attack Cody's hand.

"Down boy," I said, firmly.

Cody pulled his hand back and looked horrified. "Oh, God, I'm sorry, Molly."

I started to laugh. I hadn't stopped to think how that might sound. "No, no, give me that sexy hand back," I said, grabbing for Cody's hand. "I was talking to Jack. He jumped up onto my lap and I heard a little warning growl that I think was meant for you."

"Whew! Thank God," Cody said, then laughed.

Cody and I bonded like Krazy Glue that night. Everything about him felt right and good to me. For me, laughter is the glue that brings people together in the best of times and in the worst of times. No matter how much two people have in common, if they can't laugh or be silly together, it will never work.

As if it were routine with us, he got up and helped me clear the table. As I washed the dishes, he dried, kissing me on the neck every so often. Finally, when we were done, he turned me around and gave me the most magnificent kiss I could imagine. When he took a breather, he looked soulfully into my eyes.

"Talk to me," I said invitingly. "I want to know what you're thinking."

"Are you sure?" he said seductively.

"Very," I said.

"Your cat just bit me on the ankle."

We laughed uproariously and then went back to kissing. That evening, Jack was banished from my bedroom, and Cody was invited in. I still hadn't found the "fourth utensil" to get me through Saturday night, but I had found one for Friday night, and, well, let's just say Molly was a very happy girl.

Chapter 17: OH, WHAT A BEAUTIFUL MORNING ...

It was sheer heaven to wake up in Cody's arms that Saturday morning. Of course, I didn't exactly "wake up" naturally. Captain Jack, still outside the door, was giving his vocal chords a stunning workout, emitting sounds that I had never before heard. Cody opened his eyes, just barely, but he was smiling. I told him I'd be right back, and as I got out of bed, I felt his eyes soaking in the curves of my body. I turned around and saw that his smile had turned into a welcoming grin. I didn't even bother grabbing for my robe as I fully intended to shed it again with minutes. Besides, I wanted Cody to enjoy the view from backstage.

I felt bad having banished Jack from the bedroom, but I had been afraid that he might've attacked Cody while he was sleeping or worse, while he was doing something else. Anyway, like a good mom, I was going to feed him.

If you have animals, you know that they always savor their food so that it lasts longer. Yes, they chew slowly while their taste buds do a happy dance. In other words, Jack had inhaled his morning meal before I could even open the fridge to put the can away. Then he began crying for more, as if to tell me that I owed him seconds for my evil deed doing. Animals always understand that you don't want to overfeed them because it'll only make them sick. Content that Jack understood, I made a quick stop into the powder room, as my insistent boy mewed outside the door, then returned to my bedroom.

Cody, who was coming out of the bathroom, was standing there as I entered the bedroom. Naked, we just stood there for a moment "appreciating" one another, and within minutes we were back in bed for some excruciatingly delicious pleasure. At one point, Cody and I were in such a state of bliss that we didn't realize that our "sounds of passion" were competing with Jack's now-howling discontent. Among the three of us, we sounded like an orchestra warming up, and we broke into laughter. (Cody and me, not Jack.)

When the scratching began on my door, I let Jack in. Cody could now fend for himself (the paint on the door couldn't), and poor Jack had suffered long enough. Cody kept apologizing for having to leave. He had to meet up with his band early in the afternoon to rehearse for the Washington, D.C., gig and then pack up the van, as they were leaving early afternoon (aka "morning for musicians") on Sunday.

Normally, I would have been ultra-disappointed, but then the grotesque reality hit me: I had a "date" with Alan that evening.

BY AFTERNOON, REALITY REARS ITS UGLY HEAD

Like a savage, snarling beast, I realized that I would not be able to savor my newfound bliss without interruption. A part of me considered canceling with Alan, but this wasn't about Alan; it was about my long-running "cold war" with Naomi. I loathed the fact that she was likely relishing her presumptuous triumph and doing victory laps in her head while her body lay frying in a tanning bed.

"What to wear?" took on new meaning for me. I did not want to look my alluring best for Alan. I also didn't want to be seen about town looking as if I'd rolled out of bed (ah, and what a lovely roll it was!) wearing some fashion throwback that might permanently damage my reputation for being as "in style" as my personal coffers would allow.

Then it hit me. Claudia's $1,200 "trendy" animal print goat hair vest was still hanging in my closet. Perfect. It was just strange enough to throw the very preppy Alan into a state of fear. Of course, I could not wear the vest by itself, so I called its owner and insisted she help me "dress to impress." I caught Claudia on her cell, at O'Hare, waiting for a flight home. Being in Chicago made it geographically difficult for her to make it to my closet, but her photographic memory of my wardrobe made my request easy to fulfill.

First, Claudia called one of her clients, a hip shoe store with a shop right in town, and had them send over a pair of classic calf hair and leather pumps. Yes, with an animal print. Though fashionable, they personally made me gag, but they were indeed perfect company for the eye-popping vest. Claudia was a true "mix master," and even over the phone, with flight announcements regularly being called in the background, she zeroed in on my fashion 911. First, she had me don a short black skirt, tight stonewashed red cotton top, and black-and-white polka dot legwear. Claudia explained to me that she was going for the "mosaic look," which would be trendy to those in the know, but might unfurl the cuffs on Alan's Brooks Brothers pants.

I must admit, I was dying to tell her about Cody, but I simply wasn't ready to go there. All that was left to do was to call Alan, tell him that I had to make a detour at a friend's house, and would meet him at the restaurant.

BY EVENING, I'M A SEXY, MELLIFLUOUS, FASHION MOSAIC MESS!

Alan was waiting for me when I entered the restaurant. He stood up immediately, smiled broadly, and motioned to the host that I had arrived. Attired in perfectly pressed gray pants (without cuffs), he wore an elegant light gray dress shirt with a blue, gray, and burgundy tie and a navy blue blazer with a burgundy handkerchief. His light hair was nicely groomed without looking as if it had been gelled into place, and he had dabbed on just the right amount of cologne.

We were incongruous in appearance from hello, but Alan seemed delighted by our differences, as if my fashion statement relieved him from some hell of only being out with a female clone of himself. My intuitions were right on the mark.

"Molly, you look incredible. Your outfit is as clever, as interesting, and as beautiful and sexy as you are."

I saw the host's eyes give me the once over, and he pursed his lips to keep from smiling (or perhaps laughing) as he led us to our table. Alan was too taken with me to notice.

"That's very sweet of you, Alan. Honestly, I didn't know what to wear. I just pulled this outfit together at the last minute. I wanted to look special for you."

"Your outfit is as captivating as your mellifluousness is spellbinding. Your dotted stockings are sensational, but I certainly can't ask you to eat standing up so I can look at your legs."

I just looked at him. I wondered if Naomi had told him to pour it on thick or if this was his own idea. One thing seemed pretty clear: he was seeing me at Naomi's request, but his attraction to me was genuine.

I found Alan to be a sweet guy, if not overly effusive, but then again, it was hard for me to respect a man who dates women just to please a rich client. There are words for men like that, but I won't use them here. Additionally, I reminded myself of the funeral home bouquet he had brought to my office. I had to get myself worked up, or my plan to thwart Naomi's scheme would never come off.

"Oh, God," he said, sitting down. "Molly, I'm acting like a schoolboy out on his first grown-up date. Please forgive me. It's not my intention to make you uncomfortable."

No, I thought. You wouldn't want me to walk before dinner. How would you explain *that* to Mrs. Benchley?

"I know, Alan. It's nice to have a man appreciate you, but you don't need to gush."

"It's unbecoming, isn't it?" he said.

Within seconds, the waiter appeared and asked what we'd like to drink. I needed some liquid courage, and Chardonnay wasn't going to do it. "I'll have a dry Beefeater martini," I said to my own surprise.

I thought that might scare Alan off, but he looked at the waiter with a smile and said, "I'll have what my lady friend is having."

I had never had a man declare his unbecomingness to me before, much less use the word, so I didn't know how to respond. Luckily, he kept talking.

"Molly, do let me explain something about myself."

"Oh, please. Feel free to tell me anything."

"I'm privileged to come from a good family. I've wanted for little, and I've been well educated. Schoolmates and friends have often envied me. People rather assume that a guy like me has it all. But I don't. Quite frankly, every woman I've dated blends into one country club, tennis-playing, Talbot-clothed female, rubber stamped and approved by my family. My recently deceased uncle was the only one to ever suggest to me that there was life outside our family walls, but he was too deeply steeped in professional and personal obligations to challenge himself with the many daydreams that rattled his brain. He never shared his innermost desires with my aunt; she would have thought there was something wrong with her or that she had failed him. And she hadn't. A person can be well traveled and still not have seen much. That is how my uncle perceived his life, and the last time I saw him, he implored me to break the family mold. I don't know if you can understand this, but you are all of the different women I've wanted to meet rolled up into one."

I was feeling empathetic toward him, but his over-the-top compliments were starting to feel like little insects crawling on my skin, and the notion that I could fill his long-lost needs in one fell swoop was quite off-putting. I couldn't have been happier when the drinks arrived.

"To our first date," Alan said, raising his glass. "This is our first date, isn't it? We're not going to count Starbucks, are we?"

Now, there was an impossible question. To celebrate either occasion as "our first date" was not the direction I wanted to travel. All I could think about was all of the sublime traveling Cody and I enjoyed, and even pretending to *think* about a future with Alan was painful. I just smiled at Alan and raised my glass. He appeared to notice that I was avoiding his question, and I presumed that the last thing he wanted to do at that point was to seem any more eager. As if that were possible.

"Alan, I do understand what you're saying. Your uncle was a wise man. There's a reason for that old cliché about life not being a dress rehearsal; it's true. Too many people are complacent, and even unhappy people prefer to stay with the devil they know than to take a chance on the unknown."

"Molly, you do understand."

If the guy fell any harder for me, he would have knocked himself out.

"Alan, you're a great guy. I mean, surely I'm not the first woman you've been attracted to or dated. I mean, that's ridiculous. Did you ever have any long-term relationships?"

"I was engaged," he said, sipping his drink. "To Dolores."

"Dolores." I repeated.

"Dolores. In English the word 'dolorous' means grievous. In Spanish its dolor, meaning pain, or doloroso, meaning painful. In Italian—"

"I get the idea," I said, taking a large sip. God forbid the guy was a closet etymologist just waiting for the right girl who would listen to a comprehensive oration of every word in his vocabulary before tracing it back to its roots.

Alan seemed disgusted with himself. "I'm sorry. What a bore I am. My point was that Dolores was well named. Everything in life was painful to her. If Talbot's didn't have the dress she wanted in her size, she would suffer over it."

"Stores do special order at the customer's request."

"Of course they do. But it was painful for her to wait. It was a personal insult that they didn't have her size. If she wanted to eat at a restaurant at the last minute, and they were booked solid, she would sulk if we weren't given special treatment. To hear her talk about a mosquito bite, you'd think she'd been attacked by a rabid beast."

I laughed. I didn't want to, but I couldn't help it. "So what did you see in her?"

"She's pretty. Very pretty. And, on the outside, she's quite cheerful. My family approved. Our lives appeared to mesh."

"Who broke it off?"

"I did. I couldn't marry her, Molly. I was already miserable. But I made up some story about my own insecurities and how I didn't feel I could make her happy."

"I see."

"You know, I've always been told that one of the worst things one can do to kill a date is to talk about your ex. Mind you, I'm glad to tell you about myself, but I'm just surprised you're interested. I shouldn't be, though. Everything about you is new and refreshing. You're just amazing."

WHEN MARTINIS ATTACK

The compliments flowed ad nauseam for another ten minutes, and when the waiter came, we hadn't even looked at the menus yet. It occurred to me that while Alan's fountain gushed only for me, we mostly talked about him. Under normal circumstances, that would have turned me off, but I wanted to be turned off, and so I was quite content to find something to become embittered about.

"Can you give us a few minutes to look over the menu?" Alan asked.

"Certainly, sir. I have some more orders to fill. I'll be back."

I was starting to feel the effects of the martini, and my courage to act foolish was escalating by the moment. "Marauders to kill?" I asked, feigning shock. "Did that guy say he had marauders to kill?"

Alan laughed. "No, Molly, he said he had MORE ORDERS TO FILL."

"Oh, well, that's a relief!" I said, wondering what to do next. "I pictured a sh*tload, I mean, shipload, of pirates invading the place!"

"You're the only treasure they'd find here," he said. "And I'd have to save you, my beautiful damsel."

GAAAAAAAAAAAAAAAAAAG me! If I stabbed this guy with my butter knife, would he bleed?

"Nothing wrong with pirates. I like a guy with earrings and bandanas," I said, thinking of Cody and how sexy he was. "And if they've got a parrot on their shoulder, hey, cool."

I could see that Alan was visibly envious of my phantom description. Maybe I was onto something.

"I never trust guys who look like pirates," he said. "You know, the ones with ponytails who ride Harleys?"

"How would you know what kind of tail they have? Have you ever seen one without his pants on?" That was sure to disgust him. I was disgusting myself.

Alan was visibly feeling the effects of his martini and didn't know what to make of me, but he chose to see the glass as half full. Speaking of half full, when Alan buried his head into the menu, I poured my martini into my water glass, then poured some of Alan's water into my martini glass. I didn't like getting drunk, especially in public.

"I meant that they wear their HAIR in ponytails," he said, once again raising his voice on the words he assumed I couldn't hear correctly.

"Oh, I'm glad you're only talking about their hair, because from the way you described them, it sounded like you think every guy with a ponytail is a horse's ass."

No wonder this guy and his family lived in a box. He seemed so ignorant about the world. Now he was pissing me off. I was delighted.

Alan ordered for the both of us, never asking me what I wanted, and that scorched me. He chose the broiled chicken with sundried tomatoes and wild mushrooms and roasted red bliss potatoes. That was exactly what I would have ordered, but that hardly mattered. I was beginning to feel Dolores's pain. Our inane conversation continued for an indistinguishable number of minutes.

"You must think I'm a pretty judgmental guy," Alan said, signaling to the waiter for another round of martinis.

"Well, Alan, I'd be lying if—"

"I'm sorry, Molly. I guess maybe I've been screwed over by too many of those types."

"What types?" I asked. "And how did they screw you over?"

"You know, the bad boy type. The long hair, the earrings, the souped-up cars."

"I thought they all drove Harleys," I shot back.

Alan was now drunk and confused. "Well, hell, I don't know. But those kinds of guys always get the girls like you. Maybe I'm a bit jealous. Okay, well, there, I've said it. But I've tried to be friendly with some. You know what they say about keeping your friends close and your enemies closer."

"No," I said, pretending to be as drunk as he was. "What do they say about keeping your enemas close?"

By now, Alan was roaring drunk and didn't have any conception of how loud his voice could get. "NOT ENEMAS, enemies. ENEMAS ARE FOR CONSTIPATION, and your enemies are just people who are so full of it they NEED them, but, oh, whatever."

By now Alan had attracted the attention of at least five other tables and several of the staff. Before he could say anymore, his cell phone rang.

"Oh, hell," he said, fumbling in his pocket. "I thought I'd turned this damn thing off." Flustered, he finally retrieved the phone and immediately dropped it on the table, whereupon it fortuitously slid over to me. And just as I had thought, the name NAOMI BENCHLEY appeared in the window. I slid the phone back to him, and he answered it, sounding out of breath.

"Yeah, it's Alan. Who's this? Oh, yeah. No, I didn't look. I sound what? Hey, this is Saturday night. Isn't a guy allowed a bit of fun? I'm not sure why you're calling."

Oh, like hell he's not! I said to myself. Naomi was probably seething that her plant was potted.

As curious as I was about their conversation, I was still feeling Cody's lips on mine, replaying every moment of our incredible lovemaking in my head. I sat demurely in my seat while Alan bantered back and forth with Naomi, incurring the wrath of both the clientele and management.

It was all quite embarrassing, but I played it well. I looked apologetically at some of the people as if to say, "What's a girl to do?" Oddly, I noticed one woman staring intently at me, as if she knew me. She was sitting with an older couple. I assumed they were her parents, but I just couldn't place her. She, on the other hand, seemed to know exactly who I was, and it unnerved me. Finally, my return stare made *her* uncomfortable, and she averted her eyes.

"I gave you all of the papers at the Black Cat or Le Chat Noir, whatever the name of that place is. I was meticu-wuss, I mean, meticulous, about putting that specific contact in there prior to our lunch."

I couldn't believe how long and how loudly Alan was going on with this ruse. Before he could even finish his conversation, the manager was standing sternly by the table. Alan looked horrified and with a brief "gotta go" hung up on Naomi.

"Sir, we prefer our customers not to use their mobile phones in our restaurant. It creates an unpleasant atmosphere for—"

"I am so very sorry," Alan stated as soberly as he could. "Sir, I am truly embarrassed. I thought I had turned my phone off, and the last thing I expected on a Saturday night was a call from a very difficult client. This kind of behavior is out of character for me. I'm mortified."

I started to feel bad for the guy, but his shame and embarrassment was well deserved.

The manager was very kind. He asked Alan to please keep his voice low, and all would be fine.

"What a fine mess I've made of things," he blubbered. "Are you a

Laurel and Hardy fan? If you are, you'll know what I mean by 'a fine mess.' Abbott and Costello were quite a duo, 'Who's on first' and all, but my loyalty is with Stan and Ollie."

I just stared at him. He was on his own. He didn't seem to even mind that I didn't speak to him, because that way he didn't have to field any questions. I expected him to fully hate me by this point, but after a long diatribe of self-loathing, he found his way back to square one. Not only was he complimenting my physical attributes, he was calling me "quirky and perky" and all sorts of silly pairs of rhyming words. He even had the presence of mind to remember the voice message he left and had the gall to applaud himself for calling me "pretty and witty," reminding me that he had written a "ditty."

We finished our meal, and I did nothing more than nod pleasantly, interjecting phrases like "Oh, that's nice" and "How interesting." By the time the waiter took our plates, Alan appeared to have sobered up a great deal.

"Gee, Molly, I talked all night about my life. I never asked you a thing about yours."

"Oh, it's pretty boring," I said. "Last night, for example, I came home and cooked up an impromptu spaghetti dinner for this awesome rocker dude with long hair and an earring. After dinner, we went into the bedroom and screwed our brains out. Got up in the morning, fed my cat, freshened up in the powder room, and went back into my bedroom, where the long-haired guy and I went at it all over again."

Alan erupted with laughter. "What a marvelous sense of humor you have," he said. "You almost had me going there for a minute. Oh, Molly, I've been a royal screw-up, and you are a total delight! I don't suppose you'd—"

"If you'll excuse me, Alan, I've got to visit the ladies' room."

Alan stood up as I rose from my chair, and sat down again, looking as if he wanted to sink into a black hole. I understand. God only knows I'd been there enough times myself, but he deserved it.

I never expected such a disastrous date to end up with Alan still enamored of my questionable charms, but it didn't matter. I'd thrown a wrench into Naomi's perfect little setup, and that's all I cared about. I had two messages from Cody and called him right back. He said the band had gotten a late start and were still packing up the van. He was wondering why I had turned off my cell and wasn't answering my home phone. I felt terrible. I lied and said I'd been out with Dina, Ellie, and Candy.

When I told Cody that I'd be home in twenty minutes, he told me that they'd be done packing the van in twenty minutes, and since they weren't leaving for D.C. until tomorrow afternoon.

I said goodbye to Alan as politely and quickly as I could. He grabbed me and held me as if we were long-lost lovers, kissing me on the neck. Ugh! When I managed to break free, he looked as dolorous as a person could get. I noticed that woman with a familiar face was watching me again, but I was so excited to be spending another night with Cody, that I rushed out of the restaurant and didn't give Alan, Naomi, or anyone else another thought.

Chapter 18: AND THE TONY GOES TO ...

Basking in the afterglow of sex with a hot guy is a wonderful thing, but it's a bummer when, two days in a row, you've almost forgotten that you have plans later on with another man.

Sunday was the day I had promised to spend with Tony. Thankfully, Cody had to leave town. There was no way I could put Tony off, and I wouldn't have wanted to tell Cody, after two nights together, that I had other plans with another man.

I was exhausted. While part of me felt I deserved a Tony award for my performance at the restaurant, another part of me felt guilty. The part of me that was angry with Alan for succumbing to Naomi's demands was proud of my performance. The part of me that recognized Alan as a sweet man looking for love felt very guilty. And while I was holding the guilty stick, I felt bad that I had lied to Cody and said I'd been with my girlfriends. I consoled myself with the fact that all of this had been arranged *before* things took such a romantic turn with Cody. I was simply honoring previous commitments.

AREN'T SUNDAYS FOR RELAXING?

Cody was just out the door when my home phone rang. I have "bubbles radar," and I knew it was Claudia. She knows never to call me before 11:00 a.m. on Sundays, and she wasn't going to wait one minute longer than necessary to get the details of my "date" with Alan.

"Molly," she began. "Didn't I solve your fashion 911 last night?"

"Yeah," I said suspiciously.

"Okay, well, then you must tell me everything. In person. Have you had any kind of food yet? I'll bring over brunch, lunch, or whatever."

"No, I haven't eaten but I do have plans to see Tony this afternoon."

"I'm not going to take up your entire day. But I want to hear it all, and I need to *see* it all."

"Sorry, Claude, hate to break it to you, but I didn't record it."

"Smart ass," Claudia said. "The outfit I put together on the phone. Put it on for me, okay?"

"Oh, jeez. Tell me you're kidding!"

"Molly, while you were out on your date, I was waiting at O'Hare for four hours for a delayed flight back home. It was ghastly. And I sat there with all of these people and screaming kids and pissed-off adults

113

thinking that my reward for all of this would be to see your outfit and hear about your date."

"What time did you get home?" I asked.

"Around 3:30 in the morning!" she exclaimed. "It was horrible, and Colin was a wreck! I'm *still* a wreck!"

"So then you'll want to stay home and relax," I said cheerfully.

"How lame. I am *so* coming over. I'll bring melon and whole grain muffins with raisins and walnuts. My curiosity is taking a bigger toll on me than the O'Hare ordeal. I'll see you in forty-five. And be wearing the duds!"

There was no stopping Claudia, and I did owe her. It was easier to give into her demands than to fight her. Besides, I still didn't know what time Tony and I would be getting together.

I put on my outfit exactly as I had worn it for Alan. Seeing my getup in the light of day was horrifying. I couldn't believe I'd gone out on the town looking so bizarre. My polka-dotted legs seemed to scare Jack, and he kept sniffing the shoes and then looking up at me as if to say, "Why, Mom?" When you are dressed so freakily that your cat notices, you might just have issues. Serious ones.

I was dressed and waiting for the always punctual Claudia (except when her flights are delayed) when Tony called. He sounded distressed. Anxiously, he asked what time we could get together. I told him that I had promised to help Claudia with a work project and would be free around one o'clock. He said that was fine with him, but I could tell he wanted to come over way sooner than later.

"Oh, my God!" Claudia shrieked as I let her in exactly on time. "Girlfriend, you are a trendsetter, and I am the brains behind it all. Are we a team, or are we a team? Rock and ROLL!"

If you only knew, I thought.

"Claude, Jack is staring at me," I said, trying to sober her up.

"Because male cats know hot chicks when they see them."

"And they also know when people look stupid."

Claudia looked aghast. I had hurt her feelings. I picked up my invisible guilty stick and smacked myself with it. "Claude, I mean, it's a darling outfit for someone a bit younger than me, and it was perfect for the occasion, but come on, you can't tell me *you* would wear exactly *this* out in public, would you?"

Claudia looked me over as she took the muffins out of the bag and placed them on the plates I'd laid out on the coffee table. "Okay, I guess

114

you're right. But it is a cool outfit for someone."

"And you're still the best mix master I know!" I said.

She seemed to brighten, and the bubbles began filling the air again.

"Well, I'm waiting to hear all about it. Don't leave *anything* out," she warned me.

For the next thirty-five minutes, I regaled her with every detail I could remember, watching her as she sat simultaneously delighted and stupefied. I couldn't help but think that I would have to replay all of this for Randy (sans the fashion show), and I would have the added challenge of trying to stay focused while he gestured and posed.

Then the doorbell rang. I won't spell out the expletives that filled my head, but I was angry that Tony had arrived before our agreed-upon time. Only it wasn't Tony. It was Shawn, out of his florist jacket and bringing me an enormous bouquet of flowers. I had no idea who would send them, but I suspected they might be from Tony again, as a preamble to whatever he had to say to me.

Claudia was fixated on the door, crooking her neck to see who it was.

"Shawn," I whispered. "What are you doing here again?"

"Are we whispering?" he whispered.

"Yes, we are."

I could see he was trying to see who was in my apartment as much as Claudia was trying to see who was outside my door. "I was doing some work in the shop. My cousin owns it; did you know that?"

"No, I had no idea," I whispered impatiently.

"Well, anyway, when the call came in for a delivery to you, I just had to take it. He says you're a real boon to his business, and I can see why. Except I don't know what a 'boon' is." He stepped back, still holding the bouquet, and looked at my outfit. "Wow and double wow!"

"Thanks," I whispered. My voice quickly took a serious tone. "Shawn, just give me the card and real quick, okay?"

He took the card from the stick and handed it to me. I stuck it under the waist of my miniskirt as I didn't want Claudia reading any declarations of love from Tony. As you'll recall, I barely escaped that fate just days before.

"I'm going to pretend that you're just a friend bringing these to me, so play along," I said.

"Sure," he whispered, and then he and Claudia got a glimpse of one another.

"Ms. Porter-Bellman!"

"Claudia. Call me Claudia, Shawn."

#@$%!

"Molly, is *this* the Shawn that you mentioned the other day?"

She had me. I didn't bother answering her.

"Shawn's cousin Mark is one of our best clients in town. We do all of their advertising. Shawn's interested in doing an internship with us during his senior year in college."

I was mortified. I had no idea he was *that* young, and I was so busted.

I went to reach for my purse to get a tip for Shawn.

"No, no, I'm not allowed to take a tip. It's been very generously taken care of," he said.

"So, Shawn," Claudia said. "We still have to do lunch. I'll tell you all about the ad biz. Call me, okay?"

"Awesome," Shawn said. "Thanks. I will. And Molly, you look kickass!"

"She's a trendsetter," Claudia said wickedly. "Don't you think?"

"The bomb," Shawn marveled, bursting with youth. "Epic!"

As soon as I had politely bid farewell to Shawn, I noticed Claudia was in hysterics, simultaneously examining the flowers and formulating a thousand questions in her head.

"Not a word from you," I warned her.

Jack was disturbed by all of the activity in the room. "Meow," he said.

"Or from you!" I said.

"MEOW!" he repeated, letting me know who was boss.

"Okay, Molly, it's time to share."

Oh, God, I thought. I knew this was coming. She doesn't miss a beat.

"Very obviously, that card you wouldn't let me see, the one Jack found hidden in your bedroom, was not from this Shawn or any other Shawn, which begs the question ... "

Just as she was about to finish her sentence, the little envelope I'd stuck under the waist of my skirt fell alongside my polka-dotted legs onto the floor. Jack raced to check it out and began batting it around with his paw. Claudia looked at me and rolled her eyes. Then she turned her attention to Jack.

"Here, Jackie. Come to Auntie Claude."

"Claudia," I said.

"I'm sorry, Molly, but you lied to me the last time, so I'm reading *this* card."

My heart was pounding.

Despite a smack and a hiss from Jack, who still wanted to bat the card around some more, Claudia grabbed it before I could.

"That's MY card!" I said. "At the very least, let me read it first!"

Claudia looked at the card and then at me. "Okay, but you had better let me see it," she said, begrudgingly giving me the card. I figured if it were from Tony, I could just eat it or stick it somewhere she'd never be able get to. As it turned out, none of that was necessary. I read the card and handed it to Claudia.

Dear Sweet Molly: I am deeply embarrassed by my behavior last night. I regret my actions more than I can say. Would you consider giving me just one more chance to show you the real me? I am devastated by the turn of events brought on by my shameful indulgence. One more chance? Pretty please? With great fondness, Alan.

I could see that he had written it himself. No doubt, it wasn't exactly a message one would want to "call in."

"So who was the other card from?" Claudia asked. "The one that came with the roses?"

"That was from Alan, too. It was just syrupy, and I wasn't up for any jokes. Sorry I didn't share." I picked up the "guilty stick" and lobbed myself on the head for telling yet another lie despite the fact that it was done for self-preservation. I just wasn't ready to be my own tabloid reporter and deliver breaking news on the state of my love life. Besides, I hadn't quite figured out what the state of my love life was. Then again, if I were playing tabloid reporter, the truth wouldn't be a factor, anyway.

"Sounds like the poor guy had it bad for you," Claudia said. "I think he's for real. Maybe Naomi did you a favor."

"I don't think so," I said.

"Well, I know he acted like a dork, but you sort of did push the guy. It's not like you're seeing anyone else. Maybe you should give him a try."

I looked at my watch and saw it was nearing one o'clock. Despite the fact that Claudia and Tony knew each other, and there was nothing out of the norm about Tony and me getting together, I knew Claudia would pick up on the "changes," and I wasn't ready for that. I gently reminded her that Tony was coming and told her that I had something to do before he arrived.

Her ordeal at the airport was catching up with her, and now that her adrenaline rush was over, she was all too happy to go home and sleep.

I shut the door behind her and sighed. It was ten minutes to one. Just enough time to change clothes. There was a knock on the door. I stood frozen.

"Molly, it's me," Tony said. "Sorry I'm ten minutes early. Hope that's okay."

THE TONY GOES TO ME

"#@%&!" Tony said, as I opened the door to find him standing there with a bouquet of sunflowers. "This is like bringing coals to Newcastle or snow to Alaska ... damn. Plants, roses, bouquets ... who in the world are these from?"

"Tony, it's not what it looks like," I said, thinking to myself that he wasn't my boyfriend, and I didn't need to defend myself.

"Either you're setting up shop, or the entire town's in love with you."

"Don't be silly."

"I've never seen this many flowers at a funeral."

"You're exaggerating," I said, "and you're right on the money. "First of all, *you* sent me the roses, remember? And don't forget that lovely bouquet you brought me the day after Halloween. These others are from someone whose uncle died. I went out of my way to write a special obituary. The family was grateful, and the nephew just sort of went a little crazy thanking me. And Claudia was just here. She has this client who's a florist, and he sent her this luscious bouquet, but since she's going out of town ... "

I was a mess. I was blathering on and couldn't even keep my own story straight. I didn't know why I was making up so many white lies and telling half-truths, but Tony would not want to hear the real story any more than I wanted to tell it.

"I love the sunflowers," I told him. "You know I do."

Content that I had satisfied his curiosity, he suddenly noticed (and I suddenly remembered) what I was wearing. He just stared at me, dumbfounded.

"I told you that I had to help Claudia with a work project," I said, thinking on my feet. "Well, Claudia had some ideas for ads targeting young women, and she needed me to model them for her. What can I say?"

He continued to stare, looking at me from my neck down to my shoes. "I love it," he said. "You've always been a great sport, Molly. I think Claudia knows her stuff. I've seen a lot of teenagers dressed like this."

Suddenly, I felt a bit defensive. The strange outfit was growing on me. Alan had liked it, and so had Claudia, until I pushed her into admitting she wouldn't wear it.

"It's kind of cool," I said. "This vest alone is $1,200 and comes from an Italian designer. Trust me, this is rather 'in,' but it's not me."

"It's different," he said.

Playfully, I stuck my tongue out at him. "I'm going to change. It's a jeans and sweatshirt kind of day for me." I wanted to make a joke about "slipping into something more comfortable," but under the circumstances, I restrained.

"By all means, Molly, be comfortable."

"Would you like anything—"

"We've been friends for how long?" he interrupted. "Don't worry; I'll just grab something to drink. I had breakfast with Noah."

I smiled and went into the bedroom to change my clothing.

★ ★ ★

Captain Jack had snuggled up next to Tony on the couch and gone to sleep. When I came out of the bedroom, Jack opened one eye as if to let me know he was watching and that he had some definite opinions about who the man in my life should be.

Tony stroked Jack's neck. "We've been buddies a long time, haven't we?"

Jack purred and snuggled closer. I couldn't believe Tony was sucking up to my cat, but I was happy to see Tony had gotten over the hiss Jack had given him on his previous visit.

"There's something to be said for old friendships, you know. Going back that far with a person, or a cat," he said and smiled, "you don't have to explain your history or why you like one thing and don't like another. You can just be yourself. One thing I learned a long time ago, Molly ... "

"What's that?" I asked, settling onto the opposite end of the couch.

"We always love the persons most with whom we can be our true selves."

"You're right," I said. "We've talked about this before. Putting on airs or acts never does lead to the real thing."

Tony's usual wry grimace had lost its "ace." Only the "grim" was left. I hated seeing him look so sad. I cared about him so deeply, and my heart began to ache. But I wasn't sure what I could do for him, especially in keeping with the theme of being oneself. I was worn out from my performance with Alan the night before, and I had no desire whatsoever to be anything less than me when it came to my dear friend Tony.

"Molly, I haven't been able to stop thinking about you, nor have I been able to get rid of this sick feeling that I made a huge mistake in revealing my feelings. The thing is, when I go over it in my head, I can't think of any other way I *should* have done it. I *had* to tell you. I realize that to you, my declaration of love must've seemed sudden and reboundish, but it wasn't. I've had feelings for you, deep feelings, for a very long time."

I knew what he was feeling because I'd been there so many times myself; he was hoping that the passage of time, even one ever so brief, would somehow bring me to my senses. Ironically, my greatest experience in learning that lesson had come from Tony himself. During high school, I had fantasy after fantasy about Tony telling me that Vicky had been a huge mistake. Even after they married, and I had resolved myself to just be his friend, I secretly hoped it would be a short marriage—maybe their parents would even have it annulled. I knew what it was like to hope that everything would be different: THE NEXT TIME! But I recovered and moved on.

Years later, when Leo and I began to slide downward, I fell back into the same old habits. Every time I saw Leo, I had hoped, prior to our meeting, that under the cover of darkness the night before, Cupid, tooth-fairy style, had snuck into our respective homes and left us a gift for our suffering: the ability to forgive and to trust. We both wanted the same thing. Why had we failed? We had loved one another so intensely and with such fire. Did Leo ever think of me anymore? Had he found someone else? Had he married her?

"Did you hear me, Molly? I said I've had feelings for you for a very long time. You look like your mind was doing some time traveling."

"Yeah," I said. "It was."

"I know," he said. "Back to high school. Back to the time when you and I—"

"Leo," I said. "Please!"

Tony's mouth fell open in sync with mine. He spoke first. "Oh, #@$%! I'm dumber than a box of rocks."

"Oh, God. I'm so sorry, Tony. I didn't mean to call you by his name." I tried to recover quickly. "It's just that I was thinking of the painful moments in my life, and Leo being more recent and all … "

"It's more than that," he said. "You were engaged to Leo. You met and fell in love. You didn't have to feel like the guy's best buddy. You still miss him, don't you? You want him back, don't you?"

"I'll always have feelings for him," I said. "But our breakup was quite a while ago. We're not in touch. We didn't stay friends. I have no idea where he is, and I haven't tried to find him. That's over, and I've accepted it. I have no doubt he has moved on, too." I wanted to add that I had dated several men since Leo, and that my relationship with Cody was showing some scintillating potential.

"Are you seeing someone now?" Tony asked, looking directly into my eyes.

I'd told enough white lies in the last few days and had reached my quota. If I lied to Tony now, it wouldn't be a white lie; it would just be a lie. It was all so ironic because I used to share all of my romantic misfortunes with Tony. It suddenly dawned on me that if he'd had feelings for me all of these years, the baring of my soul must have been torture for him. But that was okay; I had been tortured by his love life, too. On that score we were even.

"I've been dating," I said. "I'm not in a steady relationship at the moment, but there is one that shows some promise."

"You're softening the blow, aren't you? You're probably engaged again."

"No, I'm not," I said adamantly. "I've told you the truth. I've met someone, and the relationship is very, very new. We have a lot of fun together, but it's way too soon to know where it will go."

"You should have told me this when I first revealed my feelings for you."

"I barely knew the guy then. I'm telling you, Tony, I wouldn't even call him my boyfriend at this juncture."

Tony exhaled like a defeated man. "Does that mean that you haven't ruled me out?"

"I love you. And I'm attracted to you. Still. I don't know where my feelings might go. But you're pressuring me whether you know it or not, and you cannot pressure someone into falling in love with you or wanting you. You've told me how you feel, and I know that wasn't easy for you. Let's just go on as friends. Maybe my heart will open up to you again. I don't know. You're freaking me out with this. I hate it. You're telling me you love me, and I'm getting upset with you. I don't want to be upset."

"I know you're right. I feel like some lovesick loser has invaded my body. I've kept these feelings hidden for so long; I tried so hard with Vicky because she was my wife and the mother of my son. I held so much in, and now the dam has broken. I'm sorry. I love what we have together. You're right. I need to lighten up, and we'll see where life takes us."

"Let's go up to Stony Mountain," I blurted out. "We can sit on the boulders and talk for hours, or we can take a hike. How does that sound?"

"Great," Tony said, as if new life had been breathed into him. "Now, just to make sure I heard you right, you're not telling *me* to take a hike, right?"

I laughed. This was the man I knew and loved. "Well, I might, but don't worry. I'll go with you. And to show you how nice I am, if you find a nice flat rock, I'll leave you alone to meditate."

"No heavy thinking, and no closing my eyes. Not today. I think I've overmeditated, anyway."

"I think you OD'd."

We shared a laugh, and I felt the presence of my old friend again.

Chapter 19: I'M ZONKED FROM THE WEEKEND TRIFECTA

"Get out of my chair! Now! I'm dangerous on four hours' sleep."

"Molly Rose, I had a feeling that we were going to arrive at work this morning with a smidge of attitude."

"Did we?" I said, dropping my briefcase loudly on my desk. "I've got a lot more than a smidge. And you know what else I've got? The jitters—and a cup of steaming hot coffee in my hand. Not a good combination, if you know what I mean.

Randy's eyes opened wide, and he rolled my chair back from the desk but he remained seated.

"If you don't get out of my chair NOW, I am so going to pour this on your lap! And if you think I'm kidding … "

Randy jumped up and struck a Jack Benny-like pose, with one hand on either side of his face, as if he were aghast. "Molly Rose, the damaging of fine garments is a crime in itself. But to even think of doing harm to the central plumbing of a virile male such as myself is not a thought to even be contrived in jest."

"Who's jesting? Now, contrive this! Move out of my way or—"

"Snippy, too!" he said. "Oh, I'm getting goose bumps! You must have some *fabulous* dish for me. Cannot wait to hear it. I see you didn't bring any lunch with you."

"Like I had time to make lunch on four hours' sleep. Jack's lucky he got breakfast," I said, as I plopped into my chair and wheeled myself back to my desk.

"Lunch, then? My treat?"

"Just get out of here before you start singing soprano."

Randy shivered. "Oh, this is going to be *so* good."

"Before you leave, do you know if anyone died over the weekend?" I asked.

"Oh, dear, I do believe so. A few, God rest their souls. One was a schoolteacher by the name of Mary Lee Barnsteed. Very beloved in the community. A first-grade teacher for forty years. I was just reading the notes while I was waiting for you."

"Thanks," I said. "Now go, walk out the door, don't turn around, you're not welcome anymore … "

"Sing it," Randy said.

"Go!" I shouted.

"Lunch. Twelve-thirty?"

"Lunch!" I growled lovingly. "Now, get out."

Randy closed the door, and I began to laugh. He quickly opened the door again. "Caught you, Molly Rose."

I picked up my cup of coffee and raised my arm. The only gesture Randy had time for was closing my door—and tight.

I JUST *SOUND* LIKE A BITCH SOMETIMES

Please don't judge me too harshly on what you just read. Randy and I have an understanding. He reads my moods better than anyone. He knows that when I'm superbitchy, I'm also chock-full of fascinating rhetoric from hours past. There are so many people I have to be on my best behavior with, so when the bitch in me needs to emerge, Randy is often the first person she meets. And he's just fine with it because he knows he's in for a reward: my personal life on a platter.

My head was bursting from all the events of the weekend. I was confused, exhausted, and totally unprepared for Alan T. Cressman to be calling me at five minutes after nine.

"Alan?" I said, peeved that he was calling me at the office. "I was going to call you later and thank you for the flowers. They were quite exquisite but unnecessary."

"Oh, Molly, I feel like I've been hit over the head with a sledgehammer. One half of my brain remains mortified by my behavior Saturday night, and the other half of my brain is in mourning."

"Who died?" I asked.

"My former next-door neighbor and first-grade teacher, Mary Lee Barnsteed. My cousin Richard just called with the news. He was devastated. He had her twice."

"I see."

"Molly, she made every child feel special. She taught us to believe in ourselves and aim for the sky. Her warmth, her patience, her penchant for turning the meek into the strong … "

"Mother Teresa," I mumbled to myself.

"Did you say something, Molly?"

"I do have the notes here on my desk."

"Molly, that's why I'm calling. Notes, schmotes! I want her to have a beautiful obituary. I want her to have a tribute worthy of all of her contributions to the school, to the community, to so many lives."

I felt bad for Alan, but I didn't have the time (or the stomach) to meet with him again.

"Alan, I'm on a deadline. And I do have quite a bit of information already here."

"Molly, I'm begging you."

"Okay, Alan, listen, I'll put my headphones on, and I'll type while you talk. I'll do my best. I don't have a lot of time. I'm sorry; I *am* on deadline, and I'm not feeling well."

"I'll make a deal with you. We'll do the obituary on the phone if you promise to give me another chance for dinner."

Now he was pissing me off, and I was in no mood for his attempted emotional blackmail.

"Alan! Is this about your teacher, or is this about you and me?"

"It's about Miss Barnsteed." He sounded wounded that I'd even asked.

"Then let's keep this professional, shall we? I am sorry for your loss, and I'm going to go the extra mile for you, but don't push it. And FYI, I'm not a morning person."

"That doesn't make sense at all, Molly. I know you're a very compassionate woman. I don't believe you wouldn't mourn for someone you loved."

Now I felt like Alan must've on Saturday night. Karma was getting some early revenge on me. "I mean MORNING, Alan, as in 'early in the day.' M–O–R–N–I–N–G! A.M. Ante meridiem."

"Oh," he said. "I'm so relieved. If I weren't up to my neck in grief, I'd be roaring with laughter. Miss Barnsteed was a beautiful soul. You remind me of her, Molly. Miss Barnsteed spoke Latin, too. She'd have liked you."

He was headed some place I refused to go.

"Alan, doesn't Mrs. Barnsteed have family I should be talking with? After all, someone who knew her quite well called this information into the paper last night."

"Most likely her caregiver. She has a niece and a nephew, but they live in Iowa. And it's Miss Barnsteed. She never married. The kids used to ask her why, and she'd always just chuckle and say, 'Just picky, I suppose!' "

I raised my right hand to fan the smoke that was coming out of my right ear, then repeated the action with my left.

"Alan, I'm putting my assistant, Ana, on the phone. She'll take the information from you, and I'll write a worthy tribute. Hold, please!"

"But Molly … "

LORD, WHY ARE YOU TESTING ME LIKE THIS?

Okay, so now I sound like a card-carrying bitch, but I assure you, it's only a temporary state of mind. Being compared to Alan's picky spinster schoolteacher was just way more than my bad mood could take.

I could hear Randy outside my office talking with Ana. "Oh, no she didn't. Stop! I'm gasping!"

And then he was gone—back into his office because he, too, wanted to keep his job. About ten seconds later an IM popped up on my screen. "ROTFLMAO! This is getting 2 exciting. I won't make it until 12:30!"

"Can always get a 2nd cup of HOT coffee," I typed back. "That'll take UR mind off my biz."

"OK! I'll B GD. C U L8R! CRAZY M ROZ!"

"Call Me crazy again & UR NUTS!" I warned.

"OUCH. LOL! K. TTYL."

By 11:30, I had finished Miss Barnsteed's obit, along with two others. It was then that it dawned on me that I hadn't heard a word from Cody since he left Sunday morning after our two passionate nights together. At 11:35, an email from Tony popped up on the screen.

"Molly. No mush. Promise. Thanks for yesterday. Stony Mountain did wonders for me, but being with you did much more. We'll talk soon. XOXO, Tony."

Tony's email brought a smile to my face. Just as I closed it, another one popped up, this time from Alan. I considering deleting it but thought better of it. It was long and rambling, and I was not in the mood for his garrulous blather. Is that redundant? I don't care.

Looking at the calendar, I noticed it was Leo's birthday. I burst into tears and cried until my eye pencil, shadow, mascara, and foundation had blended into a mosaic mess. I slipped out of my office before anyone could get a look at my streaks, reapplied my war paint, and was primed and ready for Randy at 12:30 sharp.

Randy never skimped when it came to dining out. He was a man of class, and the more "dish" I had for him, the more expensive the venue he chose to hear it in. I had never eaten at Denny's before (only kidding; just want to make sure you're still with me).

The Water Lily was an exquisite restaurant. A soft waterfall flowed onto some polished rocks, and the sound of a gentle flute played in the background. I felt so relaxed I had to remind myself that I was at a restaurant, not a spa, and that a waiter, not a masseur, would be coming to greet me.

Randy and I clinked our glasses of Sauvignon Blanc together. "Here's to happiness above and beyond all else," he said.

Happy birthday, Leo, I thought. "That's beautiful, Randy," I said.

"Who goes first?" he asked. "Me, who only has *one* man to talk about, or you who has several? Ladies first."

After the waiter gave us our lunch menu, I gave Randy a conversational menu. As neither of us had three hours for lunch, and it would take me about that much time, if not more, to go over *everything*, Randy had to make a choice. I promised I would tell all, but we only had an hour, and he had to choose his poison.

"Okay," he said, not wasting a moment. "Brief teaser about the dinner with Alan T. Film at eleven. Romantic nights with Cody, emotional upheaval with Tony: decide as you see fit. Molly Rose, first and foremost I'm your friend. What do you most need to talk to me about?"

"You are very thoughtful," I said to him. "A very thoughtful pain in the ass."

Randy laughed and raised his wine glass. "Another toast."

"Sure," I said, raising my glass. "To what?"

"Happy birthday, Leo!" he said, almost causing a wine fall to complement the waterfall. "Goodness, Molly Rose. Be careful. It's our first time here."

"How did you know?" I asked, tearing up.

"Honey, the man was going to be my best-friend-in-law. I've never taken him out of my database. Not only that, I remembered because his birthday is between Halloween and Thanksgiving."

"Happy birthday, Leo," I said. "Now, let's change the subject. And don't remind me that the holidays are coming up. The thought of them freaks me out."

"I'm so with you there," Randy said.

I briefly detailed my two nights with Cody, sharing the fact that we had consummated our attraction for one another. Randy emoted wildly with his face as if to simultaneously admire and approve my actions. But he could hear the worried tenor in my voice when I said Tony's name, and he wanted to help me.

"I think you want to talk about Tony . . . or Leo!" he said.

My eyes narrowed and gave him a warning stare. He recoiled with a brief flutter of the eyelids and a locking twist of the lips as if to say, "Never mind." If we wanted, Randy and I could just exchange facial movements and "converse" without interruption for an entire meal.

"I'll tell you about *Tony*," I said.

Randy swept his eyes downward as if to say, "The floor is yours."

"It was all so easy and so hard at the same time," I said. "I had reconciled my feelings for Tony so many years ago. When he told me how he felt, it blew me away. I felt as if our situations had been reversed somehow. I was flattered that he felt that way, but I wished that he didn't. I'd long moved on from thinking of him that way, but because I still adore him, well, it hurt terribly to see him in such pain. And I won't lie, how could my imagination *not* run away with me? How can I *not* consider what we could be together? God, Randy, I'm so confused. At first I just thought my biggest problem was my worry that our friendship would be jeopardized."

"And?" Randy asked. "Is that still how you feel?"

"Let's just say everything is more complicated. When he kissed me that time, I felt something exciting happen, but I chalked it up to being kissed by a man I have loved for years and to the simple pleasure of a beautiful kiss. Then yesterday, when we went up to Stony Mountain, it was as if all of the stress just drained from our bodies. We laughed, joked, and chased each other like children. For the first time in years, I didn't have to worry about crossing the boundaries of a friendship with a married man. We watched the birds, we looked out over the vast panorama of autumn's changing leaves, and we kissed. Again. Then we talked. Then we kissed. It wasn't hot and heavy, you know, it was just natural. Like the simple pleasure of a light rain." I looked to my right. "Or a waterfall."

"Oh my, Molly Rose," Randy said, settling back into his chair with an unconscious hand-under-the-chin gesture. "This is some serious business. And how was the kissing with Cody?"

"Hot and heavy," we said in unison.

"Shut up," I said, then laughed "Were you there?"

"Oh, honey, I was in my own little paradise. Until Sunday came."

"What happened?" I asked, glad to be turning the conversation away from myself.

"Kyle and I had the perfect weekend. Then Sunday, right before noon, his cell rang, and he said he had to go join his boss to entertain some prospective clients."

"You're kidding! Again?"

"Yes! Again. I honestly don't understand it. I have no reason to doubt him because everything else is so right. But the demands of his job—if they *are* indeed such—oh, I hate myself for doubting him, Molly Rose. But Sunday afternoon?"

"Why didn't you just ask him to explain?"

"And have him think I don't trust him, when he's been so upfront and wonderful? That would just kill our relationship."

A waiter brought a square piece of chocolate cake to the next table. A single candle sat atop it. The birthday honoree made a wish and blew out her candle. I looked at Randy.

"Oh, God, Molly Rose. I wasn't thinking. I shouldn't have said that about trust."

"You did nothing wrong, Randy. Trust isn't exactly a unique concept in a relationship. Just because Leo and I let it destroy our relationship ... "

Randy called for the check, and we left. He put his arm around me and held me as we walked back to the office in the brisk November air. After a long dry spell, my love life was offering me all sorts of new possibilities, and I was as miserable as the day Leo and I had said goodbye. At least I had a friend at my side.

Chapter 20: LEAVES, LEAVES, LEAVE ME ALONE!

By the end of the workday, my gloom intensified as I wended my way home. It was dark, but the streets were brightly lit, and I decided to walk over to the park where I had met Leo. As it was a popular gathering place, there were plenty of people (none of whom I wanted to meet) cruising and schmoozing by the kiosk. I felt angry to see them laughing and having a good time.

I turned for home, but something in me wanted to stay. I wanted to be on the hallowed grounds where I had met Leo. I needed to be there. But the fallen autumn leaves that Leo and I had once frolicked in were now just dead, crunchy reminders of the happiest days of my life, and the pain was too deep.

Angrily, I kicked the leaves with big sliding steps all the way out of the park, then hurried home to a very hungry orange cat.

I was not a lot of fun the next three days at work. I tried not to get too upset when Cody didn't call me by Tuesday, but I was wondering if what I thought could be the start of something wonderful was instead the end of something that shouldn't have happened.

"Should I feel used?" I asked Randy, as I shoved a turkey wrap into my mouth. (Believe it or not, I often ate at my desk, despite all the fancy straunts I've told you about.)

"It's only Tuesday, Molly Rose. I would remember that the man's out of town on a gig, and we do presume that to be the truth, *don't we?*" He didn't wait for me to respond. "So give him some time, and give him some trust."

"Oh, that's easy for you to say! You had a great evening with Kyle last night, and you're back on the trust wagon again."

"You're oversimplifying things," Randy admonished me. "Kyle has apologized profusely for the last-minute cancellations. He isn't taking to his new boss all that well, but he needs to play the game for now. He moved here to take this position, and it's a huge stepping-stone in his career. I have to trust him, and if doubts creep in, well, that's okay because I'm human. And you are too … I think."

I picked up the paper my sandwich came wrapped in, made it into a ball, and threw it at Randy's head.

"Stop!" Randy gasped, batting the balled paper away just as Jack does when I make little aluminum foil balls for him. "Don't you know there is grease on that thing? Yikes!"

"Yikes?" I repeated. "Who says 'Yikes' anymore?"

"Substitute language *can* be arranged," Randy said, fanning the area in which the offensive object had whizzed through his airspace. "As I was going to say before I was so rudely interrupted, if you don't hear from him by Thursday or Friday, well, you may have a point there. But I hope it doesn't come to that."

"If it does, I'm taking it all out on YOU!" I said.

"Okay, then," Randy said standing up, "that's my clue to retreat to the quiet of my inner sanctum where my smoked Norwegian salmon and asparagus tips should have been delivered by now."

"Ugh," I said.

"Molly Rose, do not look thy nose down on the much-anticipated repast of others. It doesn't suit you."

"Ask me if I care."

"Don't worry," Randy said lovingly. "My bet is that he'll call."

But Wednesday came, and he still hadn't called. Tony called, and I knew that he had mustered every bit of willpower he had not to call me on Monday. I knew him that well.

Then the self-loathing began. I knew what I was doing, and I hated it. I was playing picky little mind games. If Tony had called me on Monday, I would have thought he was desperate. But he waited and called me on Wednesday, and I still saw him as desperate because I knew he wanted to call me sooner. This was a man I had loved most of my life. He wasn't an unwanted suitor. He was a man I respected, was attracted to, loved being with, and cherished as a dear friend.

Meanwhile, Cody, a newcomer (no pun intended) in my life, hadn't called, and I was freaking over it. And if he had called, I wouldn't have pegged *him* as desperate; I would have just been happy to hear from him. Why was I being so unfair to Tony? I felt like Groucho Marx, who once said he wouldn't want to be a member of any club that would have him as a member. I was being irrational, hypocritical, and downright unfair. But I'm a woman. I'm entitled to all that every once in a while, right? God only knows men are.

As if that weren't bad enough, Tony asked if we could get

together again on Sunday, and I said something akin to "we'll see" because I wanted to hear from Cody first and find out if he wanted to see me over the weekend despite the fact I was feeling used and rejected by him. Of course, I didn't tell Tony that; I simply said I may have to work over the weekend, and I'd know more by week's end. He accepted that, and I felt crummy about the whole thing.

PICKY TO THE MAX

By Thursday I could have easily been mistaken for the poster woman for PMS. Even Randy steered clear of me, and Jack didn't even vocalize his desire for breakfast. My boss, Ray, gave me a new assignment via email to avoid coming into my office.

I was most assuredly going most exceptionally mad. I'd even had a dream the night before that consisted of nothing but Barbarino the Barbarian laughing hysterically at me as she clutched Cody around the waist. But in the dream, Cody was just a blur to me. She was in high-def and loving every miserable moment of it. And they say we don't remember most of our dreams.

Robotically, I worked through lunch and got my preliminary notes to Ray way before he expected them. He IMed me around three o'clock and told me to take off early; I'd earned it. I emailed my notes to myself so I wouldn't have to carry a briefcase home that night and left within five minutes of his message.

Randy, who had left me alone but *never* "leaves me alone," followed me out to the elevator when he saw me heading out. Without saying a word, he gave me a great big hug and kissed me on the cheek. I managed a weak smile, then got on the elevator.

Once outside, the bright blue fall sky beckoned me to the park. Daylight savings time had ended two weeks earlier, and so the blue sky was an even more precious commodity than usual. As it was still early, I didn't have to worry about the after-work crowd that gathers there every day. I would find peace. I would be able to sort through the yin and yang in my mind and never a paradoxical thought should darken my brain again. Yeah, right.

There were several people in the park, but all of disparate backgrounds. Everyone seemed to be enjoying the beauty of the day, and I didn't feel like an outsider as I had a few days before. Little details of my first and subsequent park dates with Leo came back to me, like the time he told me to meet him by the "Muffy Darling" bench. All of the benches in the park had brass plaques commemorating someone's life, birthday, achievement, or whatever. We loved the bench because the name was so silly, and it was way back from where the crowds gathered.

One day I was to meet Leo at four o'clock. The leaves were in heaps and piles and every other formation possible. Leo was almost always punctual, so I was beginning to worry after sitting on the bench for fifteen minutes with no sign of him. Suddenly, I heard my name being called, in a very muffled, high-pitched voice.

"Molly Hacker, where are you? I love you, Molly Hacker."

I froze. I heard the voice again. "Molly, I love you."

I managed to thaw slightly so that I could move my head to the right, then to the left. Nothing. No sign of anyone except in the distance. I summed up the courage to look behind me. Still nobody.

"Molly Hacker! Are you ignoring me?" the muffled voice squeaked as I sat there mute on the Muffy bench. "You look beautiful today."

I stood up and scoped the open area with a 360-degree sweep of my eyes. Nobody. And there was nothing anyone could hide behind, either. The nearest tree was several yards away from me, and it would be impossible for me to hear anyone if he or she were behind the tree.

"If you don't talk to me," the voice began.

"You'll WHAT?" I said, speaking back for the first time.

"I'll have to kiss you and hug you forever and ever," said Leo, springing wildly from what I thought was simply a large pile of leaves in front of me.

I screamed so loud that people in the distance looked over, but when they saw a lovers' embrace, they went back to their own business. Leo had arrived at the park in plenty of time to make several piles of leaves, so that his hiding place would not stand out. And then he waited. He waited for fifteen minutes or more just to make his surprise all the more of, well, a surprise.

Thinking about that day made me cry. My memories of Leo had no business being so painful. I had dealt with our breakup. I had moved on. So why the tears? Perhaps it was the park, the time of year, the fact that Leo's birthday had just passed. It was all of that and nothing more. Of course I would remember him with such love. But that was *all* I was doing—remembering him.

I let my tears turn to anger. I didn't dare walk over to the Muffy bench. Instead I began looking for heaps of leaves to crush, listening to them crackle as I tried to step on my pain.

"It's like walking on potato chips, isn't it?" a voice said.

For a moment my heart stopped, but I realized it was a voice I didn't recognize. I turned around to find a tall, well-built, extremely well-dressed man in his midforties. Every hair was perfectly in place, and he wore a white silk scarf around his neck.

"If I ever decide to walk on potato chips, I'll let you know."

He laughed heartily.

"If you'll excuse me," I said, attempting to pass him.

"You didn't look like you were in a hurry a moment ago," he said.

"Well, I sure am now!" I said with emphasis.

"You're not going to make anything easy for me, are you?"

He was pissing me off. "Look, buddy, do I freakin' look like I'm in the mood to talk to you? No, I don't, and if you think differently, that's on you. Now, let me pass." I had never been so harsh with anyone so good looking in my entire life.

He put his hands up, palms facing me, to show that he meant no harm. I was still pissed.

"I'm sorry," he said. "I was just trying to be friendly. I couldn't help notice how naturally beautiful you are. The last of the sun was hitting your hair at just the right angle, and my heart did a little happy dance."

"Oh, puh-leeze!" *My heart did a little HAPPY DANCE? Is this Alan's cousin?*

"Really," he said. "I mean it."

"And I can't help but notice how your smug, arrogant demeanor makes the leaves fall to the ground with a thud and how that big oak over there looks like it wants to kick your ass."

His smile morphed into a huge grin. He had the most beautiful white teeth and his eyes were filled with laughter.

How dare he look even the least bit appealing to me, I thought, determined not to let him get to me.

"I'm Maximilian," he said. "It means 'supreme quality' in Latin."

"Maybe someday you'll live up to that," I said, missing his tongue-in-cheek delivery.

He looked hurt, and suddenly I felt horrible.

"Sorry," I said. "Just please let me pass."

"You can just call me Max. It means, 'puts foot in mouth once too often.' "

"I'm Molly. It means, 'please get out of my way.' "

He looked hurt again. I didn't have time for him or his games.

"You may want to take my head off, but I'll chance it. Are you single?" he asked.

"Why, would it matter?"

"Of course," he said. "Why would I want to meet a married woman?"

"Well, you know, just because someone is single doesn't mean they're unattached, either."

"Very true," he said. "I'm divorced. Two years. I've yet to find someone that wasn't interested in me for all the wrong reasons."

He looked like money; I assumed that's what he meant, but I didn't care.

"I hope you find her," I said, softening my tone.

"Maybe I just have," he said. "You know, the more I talk to you, uh … "

"Molly," I reminded him.

"Molly. Molly Hacker?"

Oh, God, I thought. How does he know who I am? He's obviously rich, so he's probably some awful friend of Naomi's.

"Colin Bellman works for me. I saw you at Colin and Claudia's wedding. I thought you were beautiful, but I was married then. Ever since, I've been reading your features. You have a lot of integrity and wisdom. And you don't let people off the hook, as I now have learned firsthand. I can see where your feisty personality would work well in getting a story."

I was relieved that he didn't know me through Naomi, but I suddenly hated being in a small town. Did everyone know me? If I ever decide I want to write another memoir, remind me to live the second half of my life in a big city where nobody knows my name.

"Thanks," I said. "I'm humbled. I don't know what to say."

"Well, nice meeting you, Molly," he said, turning to go.

What? He wasn't going to stay and flatter me some more? That was it? He was just going to walk away and give up?

"Nice meeting you, too . . . uh, Max."

He smiled that beautiful smile of his, whipped his scarf around his neck, and walked off like Rhett Butler on his way back to Charleston.

I watched him go. I didn't even know the guy. I hadn't even liked the guy … at first. And now he was walking out on me. Maybe I was too picky … to the Max.

Chapter 21: NO LONGER "OFF MY ROCKER"

Friday morning began with a call from my mom, telling me she was in town unexpectedly and wanted to take me to lunch. I was still in a foul mood, but I missed my mom.

Usually, when I go to lunch, I lay my cell phone discreetly on the top of my bag or put it on vibrate if I'm wearing something with pockets, so as not to disturb anyone around me. I never leave it on the table. Well, almost never.

Obsessed with the fact that Cody hadn't called, I laid my phone down meticulously to the right of my knife and spoon. I could feel my mom's eyes burning a hole through the tablecloth.

She smiled. "Is that the latest in place settings?"

"Uh, no ...

"You always know what's in vogue. Is this some new form of cellular cutlery?"

She was messing with my head. "Mom, I'm waiting for a call from a source. It could make or break my current investigation."

"I see. What's the topic?"

She was *so* messing with me. "Plastic surgery and tanning salons," I muttered.

"And you have a secret source?"

"There are a lot of doctors who perform unnecessary or damaging surgery on patients who shouldn't have it—all for the money. It's a serious issue."

"And you're doing a crackdown of sorts?"

"Mom, if you want to grill something, I'm sure the chef will let you flip a hamburger or maybe even a crab cake."

She laughed her distinctive and delightful laugh. "I'll behave. So, tell me what you've been up to."

"Just working like crazy."

"Seeing anyone?"

"Oh, not really."

"Not really. Is that like being sort of pregnant?"

Did she have to use the word "pregnant" to make her point? "I've been on a couple of dates, and from time to time I hang out with Tony. How are you and Dad?"

"Your father and I are great. He just had his annual checkup and he's as fit as a fiddle. I've never seen any fit fiddles, but cellos are rather plump, so I suppose that makes sense. Every morning we power walk three miles together, and Daddy plays golf twice a month. I still go to the gym three times a week, and I'm still volunteering at the hospital. Life is good. I wish I saw my daughters more often, but life is good."

"I'm sorry, Mom," I said, glancing at my phone to make sure I hadn't turned the ringer off and Cody's name wasn't glowing in neon lights in the window.

"No need for apologies, honey. I've seen Hannah more often only because I'm helping her with wedding plans. Both of my girls have busy lives. Anyway, Thanksgiving will be here, and I want to make sure you're coming."

"That's great, Mom. You know I'll be there."

"You're welcome to bring Randy again. I don't know if he's seeing anyone, but they'd both be welcome."

"Thanks. I'll tell him. Randy *is* seeing someone. His name is Kyle. He's new in town and doesn't have any family here."

"Then by all means, invite Randy and Kyle."

"Okay," I said, burying my head in the menu.

"And perhaps *you* would like to bring someone, Molly."

I looked up at her. "Gee, thanks, but you know that Tony will be spending the day with Noah so he won't be free. I guess you didn't know, but he and Vicky are getting a divorce."

"I'm sorry to hear that, Molly. However, I wasn't thinking Tony," she said. "I was thinking about *him*."

"Him?"

Her eyes rolled and landed on my cell phone. "Him."

"And what can I get you ladies?" the waiter said.

My mom smiled and winked at me. I pretended not to notice. I was never so happy to give a lunch order in all of my life.

★ ★ ★

I walked sulkily back to the office. My phone rang, but it was the "I'm Forever Blowing Bubbles" ringtone, so I didn't get my hopes up.

"Hey, Claude, what's up?" I asked morosely.

"Who's *down* is more the question. What's wrong with you, Molly?"

"Nothing. Do I have to be in a constant state of euphoria all the time?"

"Now I *know* something's wrong," Claudia said emphatically.

"Anger makes you sarcastic. What gives?"

Before I could respond, Claudia pushed on. "Molly, I cannot believe what you did."

"Which was?" I said, walking along the street at a brisk pace.

"You gave Max Ballarin the brush-off in the park!"

"Oh, puh-leeze. He was hitting on me when I was in the worst mood ever. Then he apparently runs to you and Colin and outs me. How lame is that?"

"He did not do that, Molly. Colin and I had lunch with him today, and it was just natural that your name came up. You're very lucky that he's so taken with you. He's tired of the hussies who throw themselves at him. He wants to call you, but only if you want him to. My God, Molly, this guy is the catch of the century. Did you not notice how freaking gorgeous he is? And rich? And just plain ol' nice?"

I was about to issue a flat-out refusal, when I realized that it was Friday, and the man I'd had sex with last weekend had still not called me. I owed Cody nothing. "Okay, give him my number. I'm almost back at the office. Gotta, go, Claude. Later, girlfriend."

"But, Molly ... "

I felt bad that I'd clicked Claude off in midsentence. And I had probably ticked her off, too, but at least she left our conversation victorious. I had given her the green light to exercise her matchmaking prowess. I didn't care if the "catch of the century" wanted to call me. I wanted to know why Cody hadn't called. And furthermore, I mused, why wasn't *I* the "catch of the century"? It always seems that men are referred to in such terms, not women. However, knowing me, if someone did refer to me that way, I'd feel insulted and want to take the giant hook out of my mouth and be cast back in the sea.

I had no more finished my thought and was headed toward the front door of my office building than my cell rang again. I didn't even pay attention to the ringtone; I just assumed it was Claudia.

"Sorry, I cut you off, Claude. I didn't realize you were still talking."

"Who's Claude?"

"Huh?"

"I was just wondering who Claude was."

"Cody?"

"Of course. How are you, Molly?"

"I'm, uh, I'm fine. Claude is my best girlfriend, Claudia Porter-

Bellman. I've told you about her. The bubbly one who works in advertising."

"Oh, yeah," Cody said, his voice brightening. "I don't know why I thought you were ... well, never mind!"

"Are you back?"

"Sure am. We stayed an extra day because this cat invited us to play a private party the next day. Some senator's birthday bash. Damn, those people are trippy. I'll give you the lowdown later."

"Sounds fascinating," I said, wondering why Cody couldn't have at least called or texted during the week to say hi or to let me know that he was staying longer.

"I wanted to call you before now," Cody said, "but I was never alone. Felt like I had copper spoons ... well, let's just say that I'm on my way to the hospital now to have these dudes surgically detached from me." He laughed. "Only kidding, but seriously, I had zero privacy. And we didn't get to bed until the wee small hours."

Get to bed. Suddenly, the word "groupies" popped into my head, but I expelled it quickly.

"Molly, I'd like to take you out to dinner tonight. If you're free, it being last minute and all."

There was something in Cody's voice that was different. It was almost as if he didn't expect me to be free. "Sure, Cody, I'd love to have dinner with you."

"Excellent!" he said. "I'm going to my place and crash for a few hours. There's this seafood place I've been anxious to try, but if you prefer something else, I'm cool with that."

"No, I love seafood," I said. I was just happy that he was "dying to try it," which meant that it hadn't been a favorite haunt with Barbarino or anyone else. And I loved the fact that despite his rocker persona, Cody wasn't content to just "hang out." He was a quirky mixture of everything that I loved in a man. Still, I felt insecure about our relationship, and I hated that. And, naturally, I blamed myself.

MY HE-MAIL IS BULGING AT THE SEAMS

When I got back to the office, Randy was standing across the main room, waving a white flag, much to the amusement of our other colleagues. He saw that my face had relaxed, my furrowed brow was no more, and knew that Cody had called. But Randy knew I never recovered *that* quickly, and that it would be in his best interest to give me space. He also knew that simply because I was "okay" didn't mean I was in the mood to spill my guts. He smiled and went back to his office. I would give him the Thanksgiving invitation later, and when I felt like it, I would add the sordid details of my love life.

My he-mail was bulging. There were two emails from Tony with the subject lines "This Saturday?" and "Maybe Sunday?" Alan had sent me four emails, two of which were inane, arcane urban legends I'd read over a decade ago—one about a Neiman Marcus cookie recipe and the other about Bill Gates giving out money. Then there was a rather unfunny joke, and the fourth, an intense plea to see me again and let me get to know the man behind the faux pas. As I was reading, a fifth email from Alan popped up.

> *Dear Molly,*
> *Just as I had written to you, asking you to overlook les faux pas of a weary man, I learn from my secretary that the Bill Gates story and the cookie recipe story are archaic scams that have been infiltrating the Internet for years. You must think me terribly naïve and quite unhip. I have been hanging out with the wrong people. I need a friend like you to enlighten me. I feel as if I've passed my expiration date, and I don't like feeling so outmoded. I promise not to be overbearing or ask too much. May I see you again? I do believe I have some good qualities you might appreciate were they not obfuscated by my frequent blunders. Please give me another chance, and I promise not to use my middle initial.*
> *Your humble friend,*
> *Alan*

Why did he have to write me such a sweet note and make everything more difficult? Despite having been lured into Naomi's trap, his fondness for me was real, and he was a likeable guy. How could I say no? But how could I say yes? He had only asked to be friends, but all men say that when you turn them down on the romantic level. He *had* to say that. And he was a bit too old-fashioned and goofy, but a few lessons from me could help the old-fashioned part and the goofy part; well, it was rather endearing. Leo was goofy. I like goofy. I couldn't believe I was giving Alan T. Cressman this much thought.

Next, an email popped up with the subject line "Hello from Max Ballarin from the Park." Wow, I thought, neither he nor Claudia wasted any time. I wasn't ready to read anything from Max.

My he-mail had overwhelmed me. I sent a quick response to Tony to tell him we could get together on Sunday and went back to work.

DO YOU LIKE SEAFOOD?

As Cody and I entered the softly lit restaurant with the sawdust floors, he gave me an affectionate squeeze and said, "You do like seafood, right?"

It was on our third date when Leo cooked a to-die-for Italian meal at my place and first asked me if I liked seafood. As I savored the first course, penne arriabiata, I envisioned Leo dreaming up seafood feasts to cook for me in the future. Boy, did I call that one wrong. Before I knew it, Leo was opening his mouth to reveal the masticated food inside.

I didn't know what to say. Then it hit me: seafood. See food.

"Oh, you are *so* gross," I admonished him, unable to hide my amusement.

His eyes twinkled, and he closed his mouth and went on chewing. "I just knew we were right for each other," he said.

"Molly, did you hear me?" Cody said, as we took our seats. "I was just saying that I hope you do like seafood."

"I love it," I said, trying to recover. "Deciding what to order is always my biggest problem."

He smiled and then looked very serious. "You know, Molly, every time we performed this week, I was wishing I could just zap you into the audience. I could see you in my mind: your hot naked body and everything you are that makes you such a powerhouse of a woman."

I was rather awestruck, though I couldn't help but notice that my "hot naked body" appeared to be Cody's priority. He must've read my mind.

"I don't think that came out exactly as I meant it. Your hot naked body is so exciting to me because of the woman it belongs to. I just couldn't help but visualize you ... oh damn, there I go again."

"Well," I said, turning a light shade of red, "you have some attributes that I can't get out of my mind's eye, either. So I'll cut you a break. And nobody has ever called me a 'powerhouse of a woman' before, so you get points for that."

We laughed, getting very hot for one another all over again.

The server came over to us and told us the specials. "Tonight, we have grouper. It's done Mediterranean style ... "

Grouper? Once again, the word "groupies" popped into my head, and I expelled it again, this time with a mental slap to my brain for having trust issues.

"I love crabs," Cody said.

Oh, my God, I thought. Groupies and crabs. Please, God, tell me that I have a very twisted mind playing tricks on me. I couldn't help but remember what Randy always told me, that my sharp mind was my best friend and my worst enemy rolled into one. I wasn't about to let trust ruin another love affair before it got started.

It turned out to be an amazing evening followed by an all-nighter of even greater magnitude. Was I finally on the path to finding true love again?

AN ODE TO THAT WHICH LINGERS ...

I must, I must, I must begin to trust.

Cody and I had a long, lingering Saturday morning together. I felt so comfortable with him and didn't want him to go, but we both had things to do. He suggested Sunday.

But I had plans with Tony, and despite my passion for Cody, I needed to see Tony. I needed the warmth and security of someone who had been in my life a long time and who I could trust. (Not that I had reason *not* to trust Cody.)

So why did I have lingering doubts about having had great sex with Cody, especially when a lovely evening and a beautiful morning preceded and succeeded it? I was convinced that not only was everyone right about my pickiness, it had escalated into mind-numbing neurosis. I tried naming it: pickiphobia, pickyitis, trustopickomania, and staysingleforeverobia. Oh, and then there was one that I didn't make up: paranoia.

Right before Cody left, I came *thisclose* to inviting him to join me for Thanksgiving. But I knew that if I did so, I would be introducing Cody to my family, thereby opening up my love life for scrutiny. I didn't want to do that, but I *did* want to invite him. I tortured myself for a good while, then I called Randy and extended my mother's invitation to him and Kyle. Kyle happened to be at Randy's when I called and got on the phone to tell me how pleased he was to be invited. Randy jokingly assured me that Kyle would have no impromptu business meetings. They sounded happy together, and that made me feel good.

I was looking forward to a much-needed night alone. In my head, I wrote replies to Alan and Max but decided I needed more time to think things over. I couldn't help but remember how very handsome Max was, and how humble and endearing Alan had been in his last communication. I had to stop. I was already on circuit overload. Issues of trust lingered in my head; I couldn't think straight and had no clue who or what I wanted. I decided that "circus overload" was more fitting. My life was a five-ring circus, and I was desperate for just one ring; I just didn't know which one it was.

I did the only logical thing a woman in my situation could do. I took a nap.

Chapter 22: WHERE HAVE ALL THE FLOWERS GONE?

Captain Jack and I spent all Saturday night lazing on the couch. Jack shared my passion for Hitchcock films, and we watched my three favorites in a row: *Rear Window*, *Shadow of a Doubt*, and *Vertigo*. I told Jack that I was suffering from a case of vertigo myself—I had all of these men swirling around me and didn't know "vere to go." Jack was not amused and started whining for treats.

After losing myself in film for six-plus hours, I turned off the TV. I looked around the room. I wondered if Shawn and the floral shop missed me. All of my flowers had wilted and had to be thrown out, but the one remaining arrangement was the beautiful plant that Alan had sent me the day after Halloween from out of town. I wondered if there was some mystic symbolism that I was missing. Did the last arrangement standing belong to the last man standing? Should I take a closer look at Alan? Should I get to know this sweet soul?

Around midnight, I decided to give myself a French manicure. I had no sooner gotten a base coat on my nails than my cell rang. It startled me so much that I nearly jumped out of my skin and destroyed three nails in the process.

"Hello?"

"Molly Rose, you sound agitated, too."

"My wet nails just collided with my face. What's wrong?"

"Oh, I'm so sorry. Listen, I called on your cell because I figured if you had company and were turned on, your phone would be turned off."

"How crude you are. Totally TMI. Just tell me why you're so upset."

"It looks like I'll be flying solo on Thanksgiving after all. Kyle just got a call from his brother. They've been estranged, but his brother and wife just had a baby, and they decided this would be the time to lay their issues to rest and join together to celebrate the bounty of the season. Heartwarming, wouldn't you say?"

"I'm sorry, Randy."

"I'm happy for him, but he had plans with me. His brother hadn't spoken with him for two years because he didn't like what he perceived as Kyle's 'lifestyle choices.' Now the guy has a change of heart. Well and good, but does Kyle need to jump when he says jump? Come to Thanksgiving when his brother says, 'Come to Thanksgiving?' Forgo his plans avec moi?"

"I'm not bringing anyone to my parents' house. We'll go together."

"Oh, Molly Rose, I don't think I'll be in the mood ... "

"Oh, yes you will, but I won't press you now; I know you're upset. Where's Kyle?"

"He slammed out of here. He was angry that I wasn't happy for him. I asked him why he couldn't reunite at a time when he didn't already have plans, but he said Thanksgiving weekend is the only time he could get a break and that he needs to reconnect with his family."

"Is that unreasonable?"

"That is so not the issue. Reasonable or not, I just feel pushed aside. I certainly hope this isn't a death knell for us. Everything has been going so swimmingly."

"You'll swim again," I reassured him. "Sometimes you just have to tread water for a while."

"You're right. I'm a spoiled brat, I suppose, but it's part of my charm. But I don't have to like it, and you can't make me."

I laughed. "I wouldn't dare try."

"So, no men for *you* this weekend."

"I'm having brunch with Tony tomorrow. And if I have any vim or verve left in me, I'm going to meet Claudia's friend Max for dinner."

"Full day. And what about that poor Alan Cressman?"

"Lunch. Next week," I said hesitantly.

"Is he getting to you?" Randy asked, finding delight again with the joy of goading me.

"I wouldn't say that."

"Falling for his charms, are we? What, no hunky rocker?"

"He's recording. We're going to talk on Monday."

"Did I miss anyone?"

"Okay, you're becoming obnoxious. I don't need to hold your hand anymore."

"Not if your nails are wet. I don't want any of that gook getting on me."

"No, we both know how you feel about gook. Listen, one last piece of advice."

"Listening, Molly Rose. Do spill ... "

"Make up with Kyle. It's not that you don't have a point, Randy. I do get it. But he wants and needs to feel whole with his family again. So what do you want? Do you want to be right, or do you want your man?"

"Those words will come back to haunt you, Molly Rose."

Lisette Brodey

"I know, Randy. I know."

I HAVE HOT FLASHBACKS

Please read carefully: I said "hot flashbacks," not "hot flashes." (I'll deal with that some day—in another life.) I'm talking about Tony. When he came to my door to pick me up for Sunday brunch, he was wearing his gold L.L. Bean field coat and faded jeans. He looked ever so rugged and manly, like he'd just stepped out of the Bean catalog, which was exactly how I remembered him in high school. You've seen those gorgeous guys who are always posing with golden labrador retrievers, right? Both are so cute you don't know who you'd want to hug first, but since Tony was dogless, the choice was clear.

"Hi!" I said, throwing my arms around him.

"Wow!" he said, squeezing me as hard as he could. "Is it my aftershave?"

"No, it' just you. You look exactly like I remember you when we first met."

"Before I hurt you … "

"Let's not go there. Let's just have an amazing brunch."

He smiled and kissed me on the forehead, then on the lips. "I'm always into 'amazing,' especially if it's with you."

I don't know what had come over me. Maybe the commonsense fairy had knocked me on the head with a magic wand; maybe Cupid had finally learned to shoot straight (at me!), but I was feeling the love. No, I wasn't suddenly madly in love with Tony, but I was accepting the possibility that it could happen … again.

Our brunch was magical, and what I loved most is that I had hot flashbacks of the past while simultaneously feeling elated about the present. Without wanting to do so, I realized that I had been punishing Tony for having married Victoria, therefore stepping on any potential warm feelings for him like an unwanted cockroach. Hmmm, interesting choice of insects … I never realized it before, but based on the name alone, I guess cockroaches must be men. Well, that can't be right, because if that were the case, they couldn't multiply, and Naomi wouldn't exist. Sometimes I think aloud; please bear with me. You already know I'm a bit kooky, and you've read this far … and don't ask me why I said "unwanted cockroach" as I've never known any wanted cockroaches, except for those whose photos hang in the post office. And, yes, I do have an "off switch," but it frequently malfunctions.

It was only a two-hour get together (Tony had plans with Noah that afternoon), but I was happy. And surprisingly enough, I was able to feel happy without feeling guilty that I had dates with three other men lined up. I knew the euphoria probably wouldn't last, but I was going for it with gusto.

DO I WANT TO BRING MAX INTO THE MIX?

It took me over an hour to get ready for my dinner with Max. When I'd finally put myself together, I took one look in the mirror and screamed. My "day dress" made me look as if I'd stepped out of a conference room. I had a hot liquid silver number in my closet, but that went way too far in the opposite direction. I opted for a simple tobacco brown dress with some crazy long beads to funk it up and set out to meet Max at Thai Gardens. (Don't even get me started on how difficult it was to choose a restaurant where I hadn't already been seen with another guy.)

The man looked drop-dead elegant. I suddenly wanted to go home and change into my liquid silver, but he seemed so pleased with me as I stood before him that I suddenly forgot all about my clothing. Wait, I don't think that quite came out the way I meant it …

He told me that I looked beautiful, but he said it simply and gracefully and didn't overwhelm me with words. (Sorry, Alan.) As we were seated in close proximity to the ornate fountain that served as the restaurant's centerpiece, I felt like royalty.

Now it was my turn to fumble. "I'm so glad to be here," I said nervously. "I'm not sure that I deserve to be in your company considering the way that I treated you in the park."

"You weren't in a good place; you had some heavy things weighing on your mind, and a total stranger came up to you with an unfortunate choice of words that didn't suit you at the moment. I don't blame you."

But you're so gorgeous, I thought. Thou shalt not be rude to gorgeous men.

"I should have been nicer," I said.

He flashed his amazing smile. "Here we are sitting across the table from one another. Now I'll ask you: do you think you turned me off?"

I had no clue how to respond, so I chose to simply smile and turn six shades of red.

A waiter came by and handed us two menus, but I didn't want to

further the awkwardness by sticking my head into it, so I forged ahead.
"You know, Max, you surprised me by remembering me from Claudia and
Colin's wedding."

"I always notice a beautiful woman, Molly, but I was married
then."

"Claudia told me. May I ask what happened? Or don't you want to
talk about it?"

"Isn't it the kiss of death to talk about your ex on the first date?" (I
couldn't help but remember that Alan had made a similar comment to me
as he spoke about Dolores. But that was different—fake date that it was.)

"Well, considering the circumstances, I don't know a thing about
you. I think there's a difference in knowing a little bit about a man's
history than being with one who doesn't want to talk about anything *but*
his ex. So, consider yourself asked. Occupational hazard; I'm a reporter."

He smiled. "You sure?"

"You tell me about your ex; I'll tell you about mine. Would that
make you feel better?"

"I would like you to know more about me. I am a big believer in
knowing where a person comes from; gives me a much better idea on
where they're going—or want to go."

Despite Max's eagerness to tell me about his past, the gentleman
in him insisted on learning more about me. By the time we had finished
the yam bai cha phlu tod krawp, he was ready to spill on his ex-wife.

"Phyllis's dad was one of the most respected ophthalmologists in
Manhattan and a very good friend of my father's. We weren't set up per
se, but we were invited to so many of the same events that we couldn't
help but gravitate toward one another. I think we hit if off so well because
we had similar backgrounds and similar thoughts about the ups and downs
of a privileged life. I'm sorry. I shouldn't have said that. Most people get
offended by hearing about things that trouble anyone of privilege."

"We're all human beings," I said. "Money solves a lot, but there
are a lot of miserable people with money in this world. Everyone's entitled
to have problems."

"Thank you for that," he said. "Phyllis was a philosophy major in
college. She had always planned on going for a doctorate and teaching, but
she's a people person, and the longer she thought about the intense and
lonesome study involved, the less it appealed to her."

The waiter cleared away our plates and introduced us to mee phat
raat naa puu, Max interrupted himself to serve me and then continued with

his story.

"So, with her family background, she decided to open up an optical boutique. She called it Phyllisoptical. Get it? Sort of a tie-in of everything she knew: philosophy, eyewear and—"

"Her own name," I interjected.

"Right you are." He laughed. "Her own name."

"So what happened?"

"Well, Molly, without running the risk of boring you to death, the store in New York became such a success that she opened one in Fort Lauderdale and another one in Miami Beach. This is rather embarrassing to explain, but up north there were some women who didn't care that I was married and some men in Florida who didn't give a second thought to the ring on her finger."

"Okay," I said. "But it sounds like you were committed to one another. Did it matter that there were people out there who didn't respect your marriage?"

Max hung his head as if he were getting ready to kiss the mee phat raat naa puu. "The New York store was running smoothly, and Phyllis needed to be in Florida most of the time to jump-start the other two. I went down to join her as often as I could, but the nature of my work at that time didn't afford me a lot of flexibility."

"You drifted apart?" I asked.

"Rumors," he said softly.

"Rumors?" I repeated, as if the word could only be spoken in a whisper.

"Rumors from the north reached her; rumors from the south reached me. I know that sounds simplistic and ridiculous, like we were two fools who let idle gossip destroy us, but the fact is, everything had always been so wonderful between us, and we just weren't prepared for the fallout. It all came down to one thing, Molly."

"Don't tell me," I said, trying to delicately swallow a mouthful of fried vermicelli. "Trust."

Max looked surprised. "That's right. How did you know? Did Claudia tell you?"

"Claudia didn't tell me anything," I said. "The same thing happened to me."

At that moment, Max and I bonded. Yeah, believe it or not, we bonded over our lost loves, over our anger at ourselves, over lessons learned too late, and over a desire to never repeat that same mistake.

In principle, I agree with Max. Talking about your ex on a first date is not the cool thing to do, but we weren't kids. We were both products of our past experiences, as are we all. Max was genuinely interested in knowing about Leo, and we somehow managed to make one another feel better.

By the time the waiter brought our khanom fak thawng for dessert, we had moved from the past into the present. When we left the restaurant three and a half hours later, I felt as if I'd known Max forever. His winning smile had attracted me, but his savoir faire intrigued me. I knew I had to see him again.

BUBBLES BEFORE COFFEE

Bubbles before my morning coffee: not a good thing. I need to wake up gradually; I need time for the caffeine to work its magic. And these were not surprise bubbles; these were expected bubbles. Did that make it any easier for me? Of course not. But when Ana told me who was on the phone, I knew I'd no choice than to get it over with.

"Oh, my God, Molly. Were you out all freaking night? Or were you freaking out all night? Or maybe I should ask if you were *up* all freaking night because I didn't hear anything from you. Are you trying to make me suffer or what? I left my cell phone on because I was so sure you'd at least send me a friendly little text-a-roonie to let me know how it went with that total hunk of a man that you steamrolled in the park and still lived to go on a date with. Doesn't he have the most killer smile? Are you going to see him again? Did you like him? Do you think he liked you? I am so dying to know."

"Have you come up for air yet?" I asked nonchalantly.

"How can you sound *so* nonplussed after a date with the most eligible bachelor in town?"

"It's early," I said groggily.

"Wake up, girlfriend. Life is knocking on your noggin. It's freaking 9:00 a.m."

"I know. That's the problem. It's only 9:00 a.m."

"Molly, I'm sorry, I get up at 5:45 and this is like the middle of the day for me. It should be for you, too. Get a grip."

My office door opened slowly, and Randy cautiously walked in. He knew exactly who I was speaking with, and he'd come for the show—and the dirt. He quietly took a seat, placing his coffee and bran muffin on the edge of my desk.

"Molly, talk to me! I already know the freaking time! It's on the wall; it's on my cell phone. Where did he take you? Did he ask you out again? Did he kiss you goodnight? Did he do more than that? He is so hot, but I hope you didn't let him, not yet. I'll get to that later. Molly, wake yourself up and talk."

"Claude, I'm sorry, I don't mean to burst your bubbles … "

Randy began gesturing wildly, beating his chest with the "stop, you're too funny" movement, which I knew all too well.

"Oh, go ahead, make your bubbles jokes. I'll let you get away with it because I want to know about your date."

"Inquiring minds," I said.

"I can have you arrested for inhumanity," she said, sounding serious.

"Could you repeat that, please?" I said as I hit the speakerphone button.

"I *said*, I could have you arrested for inhumanity."

Randy and I couldn't even look at each other. He knew he couldn't utter a sound or she'd know he was in there.

I wasn't trying to be inhumane with my best girlfriend, but I had passed through that stage where I wanted to share every little detail of my romantic life—especially before I'd even had time to think. I didn't like being verbally pounded, and I was grateful that I'd chosen to keep Cody a secret. I love Claude, but she can wear me out. It wasn't her fault that Leo and I ended as we did, but I hadn't been able to reconcile the fact that if she hadn't put ideas into my head, we might still be together. I messed up, not Claudia, but the situation changed me nonetheless.

"You're being inhumane to *me*!" I exclaimed. "Can't we talk later?"

"You're out of your mind if you think I'm going to let you go with 'can we talk later.' I was *so* there for you when you needed my help with that crazy fashion 911 and now you're trying to blow me off because it's too early."

Randy twisted his face as if to say, "Guess she's telling you, Molly Rose."

"Okay, I'll give you the short version because you know this isn't my time of day. I met him at Thai Gardens. He looked totally gorgeous and was a gracious date."

"Gracious date? That's all you can say?"

"Excuse me for not talking at the speed of light. Unlike you, Claude, I sometimes *pause* between words."

Randy made cat claws with his hands and threw in a scratching gesture before I narrowed my eyes to make him stop.

"Just *talk*, Molly."

"As I was saying, he was very gracious and wonderful to be with. We both talked about our past a little bit ... "

"Oh, tell me you didn't slime him with Leo stories."

"Claudia, we wanted to know a little bit about each other, and that's the conversation *we* chose to have. We're two adult people, and we have that right. I told him about me, and he told me about his marriage. It was totally cool, and we moved on to other things."

"What did you move on to? Don't tell me you slept with him on the first date. That would be disastrous!"

Randy widened his eyes as he took a bite of his bran muffin and washed it down with coffee.

"Why don't you just tell me what you want to hear? Is something wrong? You sound wound up—even for you!"

I took a sip of my coffee. I was starting to come alive.

"Molly, I shouldn't be revealing this," Claude began.

And I shouldn't have you on speakerphone, I thought, but I told myself that I needed Randy's support.

"I'm wound up because I have been going at it with Candy since eight o'clock this morning. You know she used to be hot and heavy with some guy at the brokerage firm where she works, right?" She didn't wait for me to respond. "Okay, not cool to date coworkers, but brokerage firms are full of hunky guys, and who could blame her?"

"I know it ended," I said. "Candy told me herself. I'm not getting the news flash here."

"Molly, *everyone* found out they had been dating, and yeah, other people do the office romance thing, too, so no big deal. But then this new guy comes there from Lynch yesterday, and he and Candy are drawn to each other like supermagnets."

"Okay," I said, drinking my coffee.

"And this is why I was hoping you and Max didn't consummate your attractiveness for one another right away, because Candy and this new guy went out last night, and he spent the night at her place. She had way too much to drink, but I think she would have gone for it sober. Okay, well, that's totally her call, but when she got to work this morning, bright and early at 7:45, what does she find on her desk but a Staples EASY button!"

With that, I lost all control, and my mouthful of coffee went spritzing all over my desk and right toward Randy. In an attempt to dodge my spritz, he dove for the floor, screaming, while his cup flew out of his hands, over my desk, and landed square in my face. We were both screaming, and Claudia, who immediately figured out that she had been on speakerphone, began screaming at me, demanding to know what was happening. The three of us became so uncontrollably loud that Ray, Ana, and two other coworkers came in to find Randy lying on the floor, me and my *white* chiffon top soaked with coffee, and a woman screaming at both of us on the phone. As if that weren't bad enough, our coworkers began snapping photos and taking videos of us with their cell phones. I was beside myself with visions of ending up on the Internet and wondering how I would wend my way back home without having the entire town see me in my new caffeinated fashion statement.

Is it any wonder I don't like to dish with girlfriends the way I once did?

Chapter 23: FROM BAD TO WORSE

I was a wreck. My coworkers, doubled over with laughter, had finally left my office, and I was alone trying to blot myself dry with anything I could find, while simultaneously threatening anyone who might even be *thinking* of broadcasting my misfortunes. I turned my cell phone off. While I was eager to hear from Cody, I didn't want to talk to anyone until I had showered and redressed. My hair was sopping wet, and my mascara was embarrassed to be on my face.

My only solace was that it was morning, and most people had just come to work. Maybe I'd be lucky enough not to meet the entire world on my way home. It was fairly mild for a November day, and for that fact I was grateful, as I didn't want to ruin my jacket by putting it on over coffee-soaked clothing. Still, it was too chilly to be without it, but I decided to brave the elements.

A mere one block from my office, in front of Starbucks, what fiend should dishonor my presence than Barbarino. She came rushing out of the front door, wearing, of all things, a Starbucks uniform.

"Molly! Didn't anyone tell you that you're supposed to *drink* coffee?" She flung her hair back and laughed herself silly.

"You work here?" I asked incredulously.

"I guess maybe I do, genius. You don't think I'd be sportin' these duds without a paycheck to go along with them, do you?"

"Honestly, I have no idea what you would do or not do. I never give you any thought," I said, trying to move past her. "Ever."

She angled herself to block me from moving on.

"Don't even *think* about casting aspirations on me. And don't try to dismiss me, either," she said. "I'm royalty. Don't let the uniform fool you. I rock! I'm the greatest. I'm the queen."

"Excuse me, your heinous," I said. "I need to be going."

"Nah, don't think so," Barbarino said, putting on her street 'tude. "I need to set you straight on something."

"Oh, I think *not!*"

"I don't know what you think you've got going on with Cody, if anything, but it will never last. He could never be into a chick like you for more than ten minutes."

"Well, if that's the case, my ten minutes should be up, and you shouldn't be so worried."

She looked angry. "Just because I read magazines instead of those boring old books like *Madame Ovary* doesn't mean I'm stupid or unworthy!"

"Where did that come from?" I asked. "Do you think I care what you read ... or don't read?" (I couldn't wait to tell Randy about *Madame Ovary*.)

"You know what I'm saying. People like you look down on people like me. I am the essence, baby. I've got bitch fire. I'm pure woman and men like Cody dig that. You're like a rented tuxedo. Dudes put you on, look cool for a while, then take you off and return your ass to the store. And you're never as clean as when they first put you on."

I'd never been compared to a rented tuxedo before, especially in such a disgusting way, and didn't want to stoop to her level and tell her what I might like to compare her to. Maybe if I hadn't been standing on a corner in broad daylight, soaked in coffee with a deadline to meet back at the office, I would have been more into exchanging barbs with the Barbarino. But I knew that if I did, she'd twist my words, and I didn't want anything getting back to Cody.

"I need to go. Move out of my way."

"No comeback, writer chick? Well, try this one on for size: Cody is spending Thanksgiving with me. Not you. With me."

My heart skipped a beat. I had come so close to inviting Cody to my parents' house. I didn't know if she was lying or just trying to find out if he was going to be with me. But she sounded so sure of herself, and I was becoming increasingly agitated.

"I've *got* to go!" I said, pushing past her.

"Oh, wait, I'll help you. Sorry, can't; used up my bottle of Freak Be Gone this morning."

Without stopping, I turned to her. I didn't want to respond, but I couldn't help myself. "Didn't I just see the Swansea Pest Control truck pass by? How did they ever miss you?"

I continued walking toward home at a brisk pace.

"YOU COFFEE-STAINED FREAK COWARD!" she yelled after me! "YOU CAN RUN, BUT THE TRUTH WILL FIND YOU!"

I saw a clock in a store window with the little hand on the nine and the big hand on the six. I was drained and couldn't believe what "truths" had been bestowed upon me in a single half hour.

DOES KARMA WORK THAT QUICKLY?

Somewhere along the road of life, I had gotten the idea that karma takes a while to come full circle. You know, you do something a little iffy, and maybe twenty years or more down the line, something a little iffy happens back. And if you do something awful, something horrific will come back to bite you big time, and you'll spend the rest of this life (and the next) paying top dollar for your evil ways. I finally understood what John Lennon meant by "Instant Karma." I was a living, breathing example of it.

At 10:15, I had showered, redressed, reapplied my makeup, rekissed Captain Jack goodbye a second time, and headed back to the office. I was five minutes from the office when the sky began to look a bit ominous. I didn't pay all that much attention to it; I was almost there. Then, just prior to passing the now-dreaded Starbucks, the skies opened up with the fierceness of a warrior betrayed. Even if I'd had an umbrella, I would have been sopping wet before I could even open the darn thing, and quite possibly, the rage of the storm would have swept it right out of my hands. That was the good news: no lost or damaged umbrellas. I guess the other good news might be that I was only soaked with water, not coffee. But the bad news is that once again, I was sopping wet, and there was Barbarino, standing in the doorway, laughing her head off.

But wait, more good news: I managed to make a run for it before she could stick her head out and throw more verbal daggers at me face to face. But a loathsome barb made chase and managed to gain entry into my auditory canal before I was out of earshot: "I HOPE YOU CATCH AMMONIA IN THE RAIN! DIE, BITCH!"

As I continued to race down the street, I heard my cell ring, but I could not pull it out in the rain for fear of destroying it. I was already a lost, wet cause, but I did care about my phone.

As I entered the office, a sea of agape faces stared at me. I didn't have the time or inclination to make individual threats, so I simply announced that I was poised to kill anyone who even *thought* about laughing at me or taking any more photos or videos with their cell phones. Nobody moved as I dashed into my office and shut the door. I collapsed into my swivel chair with such velocity (and such wet, slippery clothing) that I was immediately, and quite unwillingly, propelled onto the floor.

My office door flung open and quickly shut.

"Oh, Molly Rose, this is so not your day! Your parade is being rained on big time, girlfriend."

"YOU THINK?" I said angrily.

"Now, now," Randy said, helping me up. "I am your friend, remember that. Oh, no, you've got a nice big smudge of dirt on this lovely coat."

I growled at him.

"Don't worry, Molly Rose, I'll Shout it out for you, lickety-split. And if I can't, I'll just nickname you Spot."

"I would so stop now if I were you," I said as Randy helped me off with my coat and eased me slowly and gently back into my chair. "Not unless you want to be called by your given name, *Harry*, and that's only for starters."

Randy beat his chest with his standard "gasping" gesture. "I am on my best behavior. Don't even *jest* about such things."

"Jest? Who's jesting?"

"Oh my," Randy said, fanning the air. "Well, I just wanted to make sure you were all right. I've got a deadline to meet, and goodness knows you're going to have to work at warp speed to meet yours."

I looked at the clock. I was already an hour and a half behind, and my mind was on everything but my article. Then, to top it off, two obituaries were sitting on my desk. Grateful that the deceased were not loved ones of Alan T. Cressman's, I turned off my cell phone, shut out the world, and went to work.

DRIED, DRAINED, AND DEPLETED

And depressed. Don't let me forget that.

When I left the office at 6:30, my work was complete, but there was nothing left of me. I had dried off, Randy had removed the dirt smudge from my coat, and I left the office wearing the jacket I'd worn in and carrying the coat, along with my briefcase and my bag, as I made my way home.

It wasn't until I got home and Jack began rubbing up against my leg, that I realized I'd never even checked my cell phone (or thought about it) all day. My horror turned quickly to relief as I realized that I had been in way too precarious of a state to deal with any more drama whatsoever. But then I remembered that Cody was going to call me. How could I have forgotten that?

I had ten voicemail messages; three from Cody, one from Alan, one from Max, two from Tony, one from my mother, one from my sister, and one from Randy, reminding me that life as I knew it was not over.

The first message was Cody's: "Hey, sweet Molly, I'm just calling to let you know that I have to go out of town. A friend of mine in New York needs me in a recording session. His guitarist is having restorative

157

rhinoplasty or something like that. Some dude punched his lights out in a club fight. I told him I wanted to see my girl before I left, so I was wondering if you could sneak out for lunch with me before I make tracks to the Big Apple, or should I say make tracks *in* the Big Apple. Call me ASAP, will you? I hope to see you because I'll only be back in town for a second before I head to White Plains for Thanksgiving weekend. Family obligations, you know." (No, I did *not* know.) "Anyway, I'll be waiting to hear from you. Big kisses—and I'm still thinking about last Friday night. You rock my world, baby."

Okay, you get the gist of it. He wanted to see me before he left town for the first time. For lunch. That was the call that came in while I was dodging raindrops. The next call came in about a half hour later, and the third one sometime after that—the one where he wondered why I wasn't picking up my messages, why I had left instructions for no personal calls to be put through at work, why I hadn't checked my email, wondering if I was angry with him, and saying he had to go. Oh, yeah, and he said he would call me *after* Thanksgiving weekend. Do I mind being in a sexual relationship with a guy who will probably be too busy to call me for two weeks? Not in the least … and you'll give me HOW much for that bridge to Brooklyn?

Needless to tell you, Cody's messages left me plunging into the depths of despair (okay, so allow me a bit of melodrama), and although I left a loving message explaining my day (minus the Barbarino encounters), I felt no better. I wondered if she would be joining him for Thanksgiving, and maybe, just maybe, I *did* have something to worry about. Denmark wasn't the only state with something rotten in it.

Max's message explained that he would be working overtime in the coming week so that he could take off Thanksgiving week without any worries. He said he would like to see me *after* the holiday. Just like Cody, he didn't even mention calling from wherever he was going. I was too upset to take into account that I had only known Max a bit more than a week. I was bummed and pissed, but mostly with Cody. I hoped the local florist wasn't counting on me to boost his holiday business; I was suddenly persona non grata.

Alan was downright bizarre. Unlike Cody and Max, he seemed to have plenty of time for me, but there was something odd in his voice. I played his message back twice to make sure I heard "Yo, baby" right. However, "What's shakin' in mellifluous Mollyland?" came through loud and clear. Like a croupier who has worked a twenty-four-hour shift, I was way too tired to deal.

I knew Tony would be spending Thanksgiving week with Noah, but at least *he* wanted to see me in the meantime. However, he seemed a bit preoccupied with discovering the identity of Victoria's secret lover. He kept insisting his intense curiosity raged only in the form of protecting his son from unsavory characters, but I couldn't help but wonder if he was having second thoughts about his divorce—and about his feelings for me. Clearly, as I've been saying all along, it isn't easy to allow yourself to be in love with the same guy who, after years of desiring madly, you were finally content to love only as a friend. Time (and Leo) helped me over that one, but I was afraid to go back. But then I wondered: was it only *my* fears or was I sensing that Tony didn't love me the way he said he did. Perhaps he had only convinced himself of that because he was tired of being alone. I would be a very easy (and safe) way for him to move on. He wouldn't have to go through the hideous ritual of dating: he would simply have the trustworthy and loving Molly Hacker on standby for everlasting, eternal love.

Meantime, my old feelings for Tony were peeking around corners and creeping back in very subtle ways despite my intense attraction to Cody, curious interest in Alan, and burgeoning fascination with Max. Leo was long gone, so I tried to keep him out of every equation, especially since I was so bad at math.

I CALL MY OWN TIME-OUT

I decided that I was going to take control. If anyone was going to slip under the radar for two weeks, it would be me. I would not communicate with any "men of interest" until I was good and ready. I was officially incommunicado. I would go to work, and I would attend my parents' Thanksgiving the following week with Randy. I would attend to my cat's every other whim. I would nonchalantly tell my girlfriends that I was taking a little me-time. Maybe, in that two weeks time, with Thanksgiving behind me (and the dreaded December holidays in front of me), I would have figured everything out. There would be world peace, and I would live happily ever after.

After recording twelve messages on my cell, I went with lucky thirteen: "Hello, you've attempted to reach Molly. She is taking a brief respite from life as she knows it and will be in a self-imposed exile until Monday, December the second. If you feel that you have a true emergency, leave her a message. If you abuse the privilege just granted to you, Molly will be a very unhappy girl and will likely banish you from her life forever. Do not take this personally; Molly simply wishes to spend her holiday, and the week preceding it, lost in her own land of make-believe and fairy tales. Give the girl a break and have a happy Thanksgiving."

I realized that, for the most part, if Cody, Tony, Alan, or Max called, each man would very likely think the message was left just for him. That was a good thing and a bad thing. I knew there would be four unique interpretations of what I was saying. And if I mattered to any of them, they would accept me as I was trying to accept each and every one of them. I also realized that I was risking each and every potential relationship.

But my favorite quote of all time, by Anonymous, came back to save me: *If you love something, let it go. If it comes back to you, it's yours forever. If it doesn't, then it was never meant to be.*

Millions of men and women throughout time had likely found solace in those words, just as I had when Leo and I broke up. They were good words. They were true words. They would serve me well, despite the fact that the quote is, "If you love some*thing*, let it go." It does not say, "If you want the real deal on all of the guys you're dating, dump them for two weeks and see which fools are left standing."

But upon further introspection, I realized that Cody and Max were both blowing *me* off for two weeks. Did I care enough about either one of them to be left standing when they returned? True, Cody had asked to see me before he left town, but for all I knew, he wanted no more than a pre-turkey roll in the hay. And he had asked to see me for lunch. I rarely GET lunch. And if I do … oh, don't even let me go there.

I don't think it was unnatural for me to be a tad perturbed with Cody: our relationship had progressed to the infamous "next level," and with that comes some kind of accountability, right? As for Max, despite the incredible connection we made over dinner, I had only known him a little over a week, and he certainly didn't owe me any explanations. I wanted to know about his plans only because such knowledge might have clued me into whether or not there was any true romantic potential (or another woman in the picture). And just because Tony and Alan were still available to me, that didn't mean that I took either one of them for granted, especially Tony.

I was once again a confused mess. No sooner had I recorded my message and turned off my cell, than I was wondering what "missed calls" would show up later. I would then know who had tried to reach me, and I could torture myself imagining their reaction. I was being foolish and ridiculous, but at least I was in control.

Chapter 24: I SNAP ONCE TOO OFTEN

That evening, the first thing I did when I got home was to feed Captain Jack, change into my sweats, and slip a thick rubber band onto my left wrist. Any thoughts of men for whom I had the slightest romantic notions would result in a loud snap of the band on my delicate, ladylike wrist. I am not one to inflict physical torture on myself, but knowing my enormous capabilities for mental self-torture, the rubber band method was by far the best choice of action for self-preservation. I was very sure that after only a couple of snaps, I would quickly learn the art of temporarily banishing men from my brain.

I was awakened the following morning by an unapologetic clock radio playing "What Kind Of Fool Am I?" Foggy and dazed, I was alarmed by the sight of several large welts on my reddened left wrist. Perhaps I had miscalculated the number of snaps it would take to banish the male species from my brain.

Showered and dressed within thirty-five minutes, I became overwhelmed with a burning desire to turn on my cell phone. If you'll recall, I had turned it off the day before, after recording my I-Vant-To-Be-Alone message, and I was dying to see who had tried to call me and who, if anyone, dared defy my warning to back off. And, yeah, a part of me wanted to know if anyone cared enough to defy my warning while simultaneously professing his undying love for me. Yes, I can be lame and hypocritical with a propensity to contradict myself at any given moment. Sue me.

BY LUNCH TIME, I HAVE SELLER'S REMORSE

As Randy and I sat at my desk, our respective "brown bags" before us, the enormity of what I had done began to dawn on me. I had made a bold declaration to shut out most of the world for almost two weeks. I had sold myself a sad bill of goods, and now I was paying the price.

"Can I go through with this?"

"Yes, you can, Molly Rose. You must. You can't make such a brazen pronouncement and then let it die. You have to keep your word, or those men will never respect you."

"I know you're right, Randy, but—"

"But nothing. Cody offered to see you for lunch and nothing but lunch before he bolts for two weeks, spending his Thanksgiving with mystery people. And excuse moi for being brazen, but who knows what that man wanted to *do* for lunch. He must know that most days you don't even *get* a lunch hour! Maybe he just wanted a—"

"Randy, please."

"Well, it's not such an unpleasant thought if you think about it."

"Randy!"

"I know, I know, we're not talking pleasure; we're talking about this man's respect for you. That is certainly most paramount to anything else. A Boy Like That wants one thing only, and when he's done he'll leave you lonely—"

Randy appeared lost in delicious thought (as well as in lyrics from *West Side Story*). I pulled my pita bread sandwich out of the foil I had wrapped it in and watched helplessly as alfalfa sprouts fell like fairy dust onto my desk. Just as I was about to bite into my sandwich, two huge pieces of avocado and a slice of tomato fell out and landed on top of the sprouts. Within seconds, my soynaise began to drip from the pita like a leaky faucet.

"Oh, great; oh, freakin' great."

Placing his turkey on trimmed wheat bread to the side, Randy looked at me sympathetically. "What an appetizing repast we have here. And, goodness, what are those ghastly red marks on your wrist? Tell me who did that to you, and I'll send someone to beat him up."

"I did it to myself. You know, the ol' rubber band technique. I thought snapping it would keep me from thinking about men."

Randy cringed. "Self-mutilation is never the answer, Molly Rose. Gasp."

"I know. I'm not doing anything right. I can't think. I can't even eat a sandwich. According to you, Cody is only interested in sex, Max is headed off to God-knows-where, Tony is moping over Vicky's lover, and Alan is—"

"Alan," we said in unison.

"I wonder if anyone heard my inane message. If nobody has tried to call me, I can just erase it and go back to my regularly scheduled suffering."

Randy looked at the clock. "Oh, Molly Rose. I don't like that song. It's time to change the station. I guarantee you *someone* has heard that message. What stamina you have. It's one o'clock, and you haven't even checked your phone yet. Believe me, if you have that kind of willpower, you can make it through these two weeks."

"You THINK?" I asked, stuffing a piece of slimy avocado back into my pita sandwich, leaving a sticky green coating on my fingers.

"Everything will be fine. Now, put that concoction back together and get some sustenance. Just try to be neat about it," Randy said, delicately handing me a napkin.

"Is that all you care about? Neatness?" I picked up the piece of avocado with my right hand and squashed it between my fingers before Randy's eyes. As the gooey green substance oozed repulsively, I watched with delight as Randy turned several shades of green himself.

When I was all done, he took several deep breaths to restore his delicate composure, then looked at me. "Feel better now?"

"Much," I said triumphantly.

"Don't lie to Randy. You're a wreck. A hungry wreck. Now that the show is over, I'm going to order lunch for you. One must *eat* food, not wear it or use it to de-whet the appetite of others."

I put my guilty face on, and Randy recognized it as such. "Everything will be okay, Molly Rose. You'll see."

I PAY HOMAGE TO RANDY

First, let me graciously thank Randy for getting me through the day. He is one man I would never want to be without. He has saved my life and my sanity more times than I can count.

When I got home that evening, before I resumed any moping I may have done, I counted my blessings, and Randy was at the top of the list. I vowed right then that I would always do everything in my power to be there for him, too. It had always been that way between us in the many years we'd known one another, but on that particular day, the power of our friendship shone more brightly than ever.

I realized that Randy was going through his own insecurities where Kyle was concerned, especially as Kyle had made the decision to go home for Thanksgiving to reconcile with his family at their convenience. At least, that's how Randy saw it. I knew that all sorts of doubts were eating away at him, but I also felt that Kyle had the potential to be Randy's true soul mate. If they were meant to be, I wanted everything to work out. I wanted everything to work out for me, too. I just had no idea who things were meant to work out with.

At seven minutes after eight, Randy called. He knew I was dying to check my messages and my missed calls. He knew I would be the biggest mess on the planet if I didn't. He knew I would be hell to work with if I kept myself in the dark any longer. I thanked him for his selflessness and told him I'd fill him in the next morning. I was immediately admonished that if I didn't call him back with the dirt, life as I knew it would be over. I love my friend.

YOU'RE SO VAIN, YOU PROBABLY THINK THAT MESSAGE WAS ABOUT YOU ... DONTCHA, DONTCHA ...

"Oh, baby ... I heard your message. I listened twice. Damn, I'm sorry. Believe me, I'm not happy about not seeing you for two weeks. When I tell you I'll be laying down tracks in the Big Apple, that's all I'll be lay ... I mean doing. That's all. Trust me, studio time doesn't come cheap, and I can't eff it up if I want to keep getting gigs like this. I would have suggested that you join me for the weekend, but I'll be working straight through it. Frickin' A, Molly, I wanted to see you to say goodbye. I don't mean to disrespect what you asked on your message, but, hell, you knowing how I feel about you *is* a true emergency. You rock my world, baby ... "

Cody's voice trailed off as I heard a man speaking in the background. One thing was for sure, he did sound upset. But I couldn't help wondering if there had been any truth to Barbarino's claim that she and Cody were spending Thanksgiving together. It did not fail to escape my notice that he had nothing whatsoever to say about that.

"Molly, it's me. Listen, I know I'm not the only man in your life. I wish I were, but short of gambling away Noah's college fund, I would guess I am not. But I do know that message was meant for me. My latently revealed feelings for you are every bit as real as I told you they were. But I still need to know the identity of Vicky's lover. My son's welfare is at stake. Those two things are not mutually exclusive. You need to understand that. Don't misunderstand me. We have a connection; we have a history; we have chemistry. Whatever is bothering you—whatever is running through that beautiful mind of yours—please don't forget that. I won't leave any more messages; I promise. But I had to leave this one. I had to. I can't help but think that I've upset you, and I can't let you languish in agony for two weeks. I care; God knows I care. Later, sweetie."

I could tell Tony was getting choked up and was near tears. I didn't know whether to feel guilty or uplifted for allowing myself (and the men) some time apart. I decided to check my missed calls. Cody had called three times but had left only the one message. Tony had called once,

Alan had called three times, and Max had not called at all.

After calling the Associated Press and Randy (okay, so I'm telling the half-truth—I only called AP) with an update on my love life, I decided that a frozen eggplant parmesan, some mixed field greens, and a glass of Zinfandel would at the very least sustain me body and soul.

Adequately nourished and appropriately mellowed, I started rehashing the madness I had set in motion. I started thinking about my own personal philosophy. I had always told myself that the only true failure is quitting and that even if things don't turn out the way I hope or intend, I should at least follow through with whatever I start. What I had never quite sorted out to my liking is how one determines when to hold 'em and when to fold 'em. If one sets a stupid ball rolling, should one continue to let said ball roll until it is a royal ball of confusion?

Should not one quit a harebrained scheme? Yes, one should, but my plan was not necessarily such at all—I was just feeling lonely and frightened. And Randy, whom I trusted more than anyone in my life, had told me to stay the course. His sanction was enough for me. I would finish what I had started.

I always finish almost everything that I start. Except for a bottle of nail polish. I have never finished a bottle of nail polish in my life, nor do I know anyone who has. Nail polish seems to thicken when you get to the end of it. Unlike Maxwell House coffee, it is never "good 'til the last drop." When one buys a bottle of nail polish, one is buying only three quarters of that bottle at best. Do we *ever* get what we pay for?

Life is a conundrum. That's all I know.

Chapter 25: I SURVIVE FIVE DAYS WITHOUT A LOVE INTEREST

I made it through the entire week without cracking. I was a good egg after all.

By Friday afternoon, I was convinced I could make it through the upcoming weekend and subsequent holiday week with minimal trauma. If you're wondering what activity my cell phone enjoyed that first week, here is the breakdown:

Cody called four more times and left one unintentional message. I'm quite sure he thought he had clicked off. I heard nothing but a rash of expletives exchanged with another male voice about how he had likely screwed up with the best girl he'd met in years. Instinctively, I wanted to call him back and tell him that he still had every chance in the world with me. If you must know, I was still wearing a rubber band on my wrist, not so much because I needed it, but because it horrified Randy, and I loved the faces he made when he caught sight of it. I know; I'm terrible.

Tony called one more time and left one more message. "Molly, I don't want to disrespect your wishes, and trust me, I've been meditating on this one. It's just that I've never known you to slip under the radar for so long. I'm starting to worry. Damn, I wish you knew how @$#%ing much I care about you." I wondered if it was a good thing or a bad thing that I had driven both Cody and Tony to emote with expletives. Randy told me I think too much and that I should care only *if* they emoted. He was right.

Alan's number showed up on three different days, and on Thursday, he left a bizarre message: "What's shakin', baby? This is Alan. I'm achin' to hear your voice, but it is apparent that you are serious about requiring some time alone. All bears need to hibernate, especially the cuddly ones like you. Listen, sugar dumpling, turns out that I'll be heading outta Dodge on Friday. Last-minute decision—the Cressman clan is going to congregate in New England at the home of friends. You have a beautiful Thanksgiving and remember who loves ya, baby!"

Say what? I honestly couldn't figure out what had happened to Alan. It was as if he were trying on different personalities the way one might try on clothes only to end up with one horribly mismatched outfit—and in the wrong size to boot. I felt bad for him, but I didn't want to dwell on it.

I saw that Max had tried to reach me on Thursday as well but was the only one to leave no message. On Friday, there was one number I didn't recognize that showed up twice. I was very sure that someone, not realizing my cell was off, was calling from a number I wouldn't recognize in hopes that I'd pick up. The identity of the culprit piqued my curiosity, but instinct told me it was Cody, so I tried not to dwell on that, either.

I was a ridiculous mixed bag of emotions. All four men had called, but only Max respected my wishes and left no message. And he only called once. Cody, Tony, and Alan not only all called multiple times, but left messages despite my asking for none to be left. I didn't know whether to be happy that they were fighting for me or to feel angry that they paid no attention to what I had asked them to do—or not do. I didn't know whether to be happy that Max, the consummate gentleman, had done exactly as I wished or to conclude that he didn't care that much. And why should he care? We had just met.

As I prepared to leave the office on Friday, I felt a burning desire to see Max.

A STRANGE ENCOUNTER OF THE PRETEEN KIND

I almost went to the park on my way home from work, but I didn't know if I could handle seeing the happy people mingling at the kiosk. All kinds of emotions, involving all the men in my life were hitting me hard, and I didn't want to have a public breakdown.

As I approached the front of my apartment building, a preteen girl I didn't recognize was sitting on the steps. She was tall for her age, with long blond hair, and looked to be about eleven or twelve.

"Are you okay?" I said to her. "Are you waiting for someone?"

"Um ... " she said.

Her "um" bore a strange resemblance to Tony's "om."

"Are you meditating?" I asked.

"I don't take medications," she said. "Those are for old people."

I shook my head, hoping that every bit of incredulity would fall away, but I didn't think that it would.

"Never mind," I asked. "Where's your mom?"

"She's working. She's an aunt trap." I then thought I heard her say "manure."

"Did you say 'manure'?" I asked.

"Huh? You mean like cow sh*t?"

"Yeah, that's what I mean."

"No, lady," she corrected me firmly. "I didn't say 'manure.' I said 'aunt trap but newer.' "

Oh, gotcha, I thought. But newer. Silly me for not hearing that correctly the first time. I turned my head to the right and then to the left to see where she may have parked her spaceship.

"Did you just say your mom was an aunt trap?"

"Yeah. A newer one."

I didn't know whether to be amused or alarmed. "Well," I said, playing along, "if someone is going to be an aunt trap, it's certainly better to be a newer one than an old one."

"Whatever," she said, rolling her eyes.

"Oh, maybe you meant ant, as in insects, and not aunt, as in the mate of an uncle."

She burst out laughing. "Lady, you are psycho."

This was decidedly the strangest conversation I had ever had in my life, and it wasn't even with a man. I felt as if I were playing "What's My Line?" with an alien preteen. "Does your mom make ant farms?"

She began laughing hilariously. "Lady, cows and pigs and goats live on farms. And farmers. Not ants. Get a clue."

I'll admit, I could see how ridiculous my conversation must have seemed to her, but hers seemed equally as ridiculous to me. "Have we met before?" I asked.

"Um ... "

"Have we?"

"Sort of. I think. Are you the lady who gave out the goldfish?"

I wanted to laugh, but it would be wrong to laugh at a child, especially not knowing the circumstances. But the bizarre conversation was killing me. "I don't have any fish to give out. I don't keep them in my apartment because I'm afraid my cat would go after them."

"No!" she corrected me. "The kind you eat."

"I don't eat gold ... oh, you mean Pepperidge Farm Goldfish!"

"Yeah, lady, what do you think I meant? Real ones? Ewwww gross. You gave me some on Halloween."

"Donatella Versace!" I said elatedly. At least something was starting to make sense. I recognized the girl as being the same one who had dressed up like the fashion maven on Halloween. I figured she probably lived in my building or a neighboring one.

"You came to my door. With Tigger and Eeyore. And I guess that was your mom. Dressed up like a witch."

"Yeah, I guess. Do you have a clock?"

It dawned on me that the girl might be very worried about her

169

mom or dad not being home yet, and I looked at my phone, only to realize that it was, of course, turned off. "Wait a minute, I have to turn my phone on to get the time."

She reached in her pocket and pulled out her own cell phone. "It's twenty after five." She paused for a moment. "No, do you have a clock? A biodegradable one?"

"I'm not familiar with biodegradable clocks. Did you study biodegradable materials in school?"

"Yeah, we did. In environmental studies, but whatever."

Whatever, I repeated to myself silently.

"So, do you have one? You know, the kind that ticks loudly?"

Now she was suddenly making sense, and her words were ticking me OFF. "Are you talking about a biological clock?"

"Whatever. Yeah, I guess. The kind that tells you when it's time to have a baby."

"That's not an appropriate thing to ask someone. Where's your mom?"

"She's working. She's an aunt trap but newer. Where's your mom?"

I was going to mutter a response, but she continued. "Are you Molly?"

"Yes, I am. And how do you know that?"

"Some dude just delivered flowers to you."

"How do you know they were for me?"

" 'Cause I saw the name on the card, and now I remember you telling me your name on Halloween."

"And your name is?"

"I told you on Halloween," she said. "Donatella." She burst out laughing. "I gotta go."

"That would probably be a good idea," I said. "But wait, did you see what the guy looked like who delivered the flowers?"

"Like a dude in a uniform carrying flowers. Whatever."

"Shawn," I mumbled to myself. "So he delivered them and then came back out again."

"Well, yeah. I guess. Unless it was his evil twin that came out and drove away in the van. That was the hugest thing of flowers I ever saw. That must have cost, like, twenty bucks or something."

Her naïveté amused me. "Yeah, could be as much as twenty bucks," I said, wondering if the flower arrangement was as large as she perceived it to be.

"Peace, lady," she said as she ran off down the street.

"May the force be with you," I shouted after her for no reason at all. And then, like a child myself, I raced inside the building to see what floral magnificence awaited me—and from whom.

HOLY FLORAL ARRANGEMENT, BATMAN!

When I reached the front desk, I could not believe my eyes when I was handed what were the most exquisite flowers I had ever seen. Sitting in an ornate green vase were the most stunning lilac roses, ornamental cabbage, green chrysanthemums, and other flowers I could not even name, accented by tiny hummingbirds hand-painted in the most glorious detail.

My heart was racing madly, and I couldn't wait to get upstairs and into my apartment where I could read the card.

Molly:
I heard your message. We all need space from the world. I won't try to call you again. I'll just say I love you and I miss you—with flowers. And I'll deny that I sent these until you say that you love me, too. I'll be waiting.

I had no idea who sent them. I just knew I had to call Randy.

RANDY RUSHES OVER

Despite the fact that I had just said goodbye to Randy less than forty-five minutes ago and wished him a nice weekend, when I called to tell him about the unexpected delivery, he insisted on coming right over. Not only was he dying to see the flowers, he also needed a friend. Kyle had just informed him that he had to work late because he was taking an extra day off the following week to visit his family. Randy was as weary of his unsteady love life as I was of mine. I knew he needed a diversion.

"Be still my heart. Porter Williams," Randy exclaimed, as we sat on the couch admiring the grand bouquet before us on my coffee table.

"What are you talking about?"

"Oh, Molly Rose, did I ever tell you about Porter Williams? He's that delicious black man who I had a two-year relationship with several years ago. He's a floral designer in New York now. My God, I learned *so* much from that man."

171

"Oh, I see. It never occurred to me that you were so good with flowers because you'd had professional training," I told him.

"Oh, well, that, too. But that's not what I—"

"Moving right along," I said.

"I can't believe the timing of this delivery," Randy went on excitedly. "I'm betting these were delivered at precisely the same time Kyle was bailing on me for tonight. You know there's no such thing as coincidence, don't you? What a sublime arrangement. It's as if Porter knew I would be feasting my eyes upon these, recalling what it was like to feast my eyes upon him."

"You do know these flowers were sent to *me*, don't you?"

"Let's not quibble about details. Porter Williams. Chocolate bliss."

"What happened? Why did you two break up?"

Randy looked a bit shaky as he picked up the glass of wine he had poured. "Short version: when we got together, Porter was just starting to become known. It was an exciting time. We went to lots of parties and spent weekends in New York and the Hamptons. But then … "

"Then what?" I asked, noticing that he was feeling a bit more than sentimental. He was in pain.

"Porter became a superstar. I was doing well with my drama critiquing, and I certainly knew a lot of people, too, but I suddenly felt overshadowed by everything that was happening for him."

"Did you feel jealous?"

"Not so much that," Randy explained. "But I didn't feel special. I felt as if I were just one of his many fans or admirers. It wasn't Porter and me anymore. It was Porter, the rest of the world, and me. Everything we had built together started to crumble. Eventually, he went to New York, permanently, and I moved to Swansea."

"So why don't I remember you telling me about him?"

"I did," Randy told me. "But not by name. Generically. Porter was hard for me to talk about without getting apoplectic."

"Do you still have feelings for him? Do you think these flowers are a sign that you and Kyle aren't meant to be?"

"Molly Rose, as much as I had an insatiable appetite for Porter, there is a depth with Kyle that I've never had with another man. I've told you before: he gets me. I don't have to be in the center ring with Kyle. I know the man is building his business now, and these are the sacrifices we must make. I want to feel secure. I'm *not* saying these flowers are a sign that I should go back to Porter; maybe they're just saying that I should be wary about Kyle. But I do trust him. Look at me. Wouldn't it be divine if I could figure out which side of my mouth I want to talk with?"

I took a sip of my wine. "You know what? I'm not the only confused mess here. Tonight I've got company."

Randy and I clinked our glasses together as we sighed in unison.

Believe it or not, I was in no hurry to get to the mystery of who sent me the flowers. As much as my brain was overflowing (and I had yet to tell Randy about the young girl on the steps), I owed him my ear for as long as he needed it, which turned out to be for about two hours.

Around 8:45, as we were dining on the shrimp scampi dinners we had ordered, Randy became profusely apologetic for having taken over my "emergency."

"Don't even think twice about that," I told him. "I've been in emergency mode for way too long. I'm tired of it. But I would like to know who sent me these flowers."

"Well, whatever hunky man sent you these, this note says that he's not going to admit anything until you tell him you love him," Randy reminded me. "Do you love any of them?"

"I don't know," I said wistfully. "The potential is there … but love … I just don't know."

I TURN AN IMPORTANT CORNER

After that evening, having received the flowers and spent so much uninterrupted time with Randy (if you don't count Captain Jack's mewing for attention), something in me changed. I was suddenly able to breathe again. I realized that I had wound myself into such a state of frenzy over men that I was losing sight of myself. I didn't need a man to define me. I wanted a man to share my life with, and as eager as I was for that to happen, attaining something so important at warp speed wasn't the answer.

My life wasn't a reality show. I didn't have to give a rose to the eligible bachelors in my life each week and send one or two home. I did consider that a reality show might be easier in the sense that I wouldn't have to hide my various love interests from one another. If I were dating in front of millions, everything would be out in the open. Banish the thought.

I wasn't lying to any of the men, but I wasn't being honest, either. And I *was* having sex with Cody, who had referred to me several times as his "girl." Did I consider Cody "my guy"? Yes and no. Although I was having meals with other men and trying to figure out my feelings, I didn't believe in sleeping with more than one guy at a time. I couldn't help but wonder if I should have waited longer to be with Cody, but being with him was as rockin' hot as his music, and I had every right to enjoy all that he had to offer.

Someone loved me. Whether it was someone I would find myself loving as well, I didn't know. But I was lovable. The wonderful men I had met and the attention they were showing me had proven that. I needed to calm down. I needed to find my center again. I suddenly understood why Tony found peace in meditation.

Slowing down one's quest for eternal love isn't that much different from rushing to get out of the house on time. I know that the more I rush, the far greater chance there is that I will forget something: my keys, my briefcase, or my mind. There is an even greater danger of going out into the world mismatched: God forbid I should be seen in public wearing a navy dress with black shoes or even more ghastly, with mismatched shoes. But you know what, even that doesn't sound so bad: almost everything is in vogue at least once. If that ever happens to me, maybe I'll get lucky, and mistaking black for navy will be all the rage.

I passed through that weekend in relative harmony with myself. I had been worried about how Claudia might react to my message, but she left a brief voicemail simply saying that she wished she had the same luxury of slipping under the radar for a bit. Then, immediately after bestowing such a kindness on me, she promised to make my life a living hell if I tried to extend my respite one day longer.

Randy and Kyle ended up spending a great weekend together, so thankfully, he was in a chipper mood the following week. On Thursday, Thanksgiving, we enjoyed a lovely meal at my parents' home, and on the following Monday, I took a deep breath as I prepared to go back into the real world again.

Remember, I said I turned a corner. That doesn't mean I wasn't the same picky Molly Hacker.

Chapter 26: I REEENTER THE EARTH'S ATMOSPHERE

Thanksgiving weekend was now behind me, and I only had the dreaded Christmas holidaze to worry about. Holiday shopping was something that Claudia and I traditionally enjoyed together, but I was feeling some distance from her. It was my fault (and Leo's) that we broke up, but I could never stop wondering what might have happened had Claudia and the girls not tried so hard to help—especially when I never asked them to do so. That was a real sticking point for me.

But to be fair, it was a way of life for girlfriends to have each other's backs, and who was I to blame them if doing what came naturally turned out to be the catalyst for the demise of my relationship. I took the responsibility, but I couldn't help but believe that if Claudia and I became too close again, history might repeat itself. I love my friends, especially Claude, and I didn't like the feelings I was having, but they were real nonetheless.

I longed for days of yore that I had never known. I loved the idyll depicted on vintage holiday cards. As I walked to work, feeling the December chill, I imagined passing men and women in Victorian clothing. They would nod their heads ever so slightly and smile. I would admire these dapper men and the elegant women, and I would ask the lady in the pink skirt where she got her muffler, while I would compliment the lady in the sage skirt on the beautiful flowers that wove so charmingly through her pompadour.

My mind would wander as I enjoyed the simple pleasure of mulling cider and making my great-grandmother's eggnog. I would dream of petting the family terriers by the glow of the fireplace as my husband hung the mistletoe. The old-fashioned toys on the Christmas tree would tickle my imagination. As I continued my walk to work, still thinking of such a bountiful and beautiful life, it occurred to me: am I freakin' crazy?

Let's begin with the basics. I would never put my hands in a freakin' muffler because it would be too hard to answer my cell, for starters, much less to text anyone. If I wore a long skirt, I'd probably trip over it, and if I had to wear lace-up boots every day, I would be absurdly late for work. Let me restate: if I lived in those times, I wouldn't even have a paying job.

I would have been married off in my teens to the first suitable boy (pickiness be damned!), and like other women of my time, I would rouse at daybreak to fire up my great cast-iron stove, then with the aid of my trusty treadle sewing machine I would sew my child's coats (instead of "sowing my wild oats"), and with my washboard, I would scrub the household laundry clean. I wouldn't have my beloved Captain Jack, and if I did, he'd be wearing whimsical little outfits with matching hats and posing for postcards.

Now, while I do appreciate a cup of mulled cider on a winter's day, do you know how many freakin' calories there are in eggnog? And how about those little fruitcakes people pass around? One helping alone will bust your buttons. This is precisely the reason you never see a half-eaten fruitcake. Nobody ever opens them. They exist to be regifted.

As for my great-grandmother, while I inherited some of her genes, I don't even know the poor woman's name, and if she ever made eggnog, I sure as heck don't have the recipe.

While it is true that nowadays the holiday season virtually begins in September (or earlier), the Monday following Black Friday is always a frenzied mess. Every retail establishment I was passing in the quaint and charming town of Swansea was working at warp speed to advertise their specials, discounts, and promotions, to tout the latest merchandise, to pipe Christmas music through the store, to redress their windows, and to smile brightly at passersby.

I return momentarily to the subject of fruitcakes. While these are usually delightful little cakes soaked in booze and loaded up with fruits, nuts, and spices, often iced and decorated, there exist some fruitcakes of the subhuman genus. You may, for example, even find one working for your local Starbucks. Said fruitcakes do not smile at passersby; they torture them with their very existence.

Barbarino had *so* been hoping to see me. She was clearing off a table when I made the fatal mistake of peeping in the window, and she waved her long, sinewy arm while snapping her fingers multiple times to form a half circle as a nauseating smile formed on the lower part of her sadistic puss. Then, raising both arms in the air, she made matching victory signs with the first two fingers on each hand. She then threw her head back and laughed riotously. I knew it. There was no other explanation: she had spent Thanksgiving with Cody.

AND THE VERY LAST THING I NEED FIRST THING IN THE MORNING ...

I decided not to check my cell phone until I had made it safely to the office and had my first cup of coffee. It all seemed so simple at the time.

Half asleep, I arrived at work five minutes before I was due, and I had just gotten off the elevator when I found Randy waiting for me.

"Oh, Molly Rose. Only a true blue friend who has a critical review to write and needs to be working on it would wait by the elevator to issue an emergency alert."

"Please tell me nobody sent flowers to me here at the office."

"Oh, don't you so wish, girl."

"Please tell me Alan isn't in my office."

"Don't you so wish … again."

And just as I was about to forgo another guess and *ask*, Ray came gunning for Randy.

"Randy Goodrich, I AM going to have a review from you by 10:00 a.m., am I not?"

"It's writing itself as we speak," Randy said frantically.

"Well, good, then. I can let it continue to write itself and save the paper a bundle by firing you."

"A bundle?" Randy whispered under his breath. "Don't I wish."

"It will seem like a very large bundle when you no longer have it," Ray snarled. "And I won't have to worry so much about having our grant renewed."

"Leaving the scene as I speak," Randy replied. And turning his head back to me for one last second, he yelled, "Enter with caution, Molly Rose; the she—"

I stood there pondering the last words I was able to hear. "The she—"

Ray looked at me nervously. I fully expected him to issue a follow-up threat to the one he'd just given Randy, but he almost looked apologetic, and then he was gone.

UGLY RETURNS FOR ROUND TWO

My office door was partially open as I approached. I tapped it lightly to open it farther, only to find the reason for Randy's dire warning sitting impatiently in the chair in front of my desk. The she-devil, Naomi Hall-Benchley, had returned. And clearly, Ray knew she was there and seemed to approve of her untimely visit.

I was fuming, but I was not going to give her the pleasure of witnessing my discontent. I put my coffee and my bag on my desk, hung up my coat, and sat down.

"Good morning to you, too, Molly."

I glared at her.

"Okay, let's shelve the small talk along with any obligatory pretense there might be."

I continued to glare, but I wanted to spit. Nails. I watched as Naomi brushed back a wisp of her frosted hair and swept something only she could see from her black skirt. Naomi, who lived her life for social appearances and photo ops, was always primed and ready for her unbearable likeness to be shot. (What a pleasant idea!) I knew that some staff photographers were probably itching to take her photo, but a visit to my office was neither newsworthy nor for public consumption.

"Molly, the last time I came to see you, with my friend Ginger, you may remember I asked you with the utmost respect to please attend a hospital fundraiser as a date for Art's colleague. To my chagrin, and to Ginger's, who was cohosting the event, you flatly turned me down."

"And I'll do it again, if that's why you're here."

"No, you won't, and yes, I am," she said.

"Yes, I will, and this conversation is over."

"Think again, and no, it's not."

If you recall how hard I had to clamp down on my tongue to avoid mixing it up with Barbarino, trust me, this was far worse.

"Molly," she continued, "the annual holiday dinner for Art's foundation is coming up soon. It is one of, if not *the* most important event of the season. And as you know, the foundation provides a sizeable grant to this paper every year. That sizeable grant is one of the reasons you and your friend Randy have jobs, especially in these tough times. Now, all I need you to do is to serve as a date for Art's colleague. The two companies have close ties, and it's important for Art's career."

"I'm not interested. And I hope you're not threatening my job."

"Molly, did it ever occur to you that your obstinacy and misguided pride might keep you walking single file for the rest of your picky life?"

She made me sick. And what if she had a point? What if I had been avoiding the greatest man alive—just because he worked for some company that did business with Art Benchley? I would have to risk never meeting him. Besides, before having recorded such a dire message on my cell phone, I had four very interested men. And I didn't know which one he was, but one of them loved me.

"Naomi, the answer is no. The answer will always *be* no."

"No is not a suitable response. I'm asking a personal favor, and furthermore, I have never threatened anyone's livelihood. I'm a philanthropist who is asking you to be philanthropic in a more personal way. That's all."

As she nervously began rattling the gold bracelets on her wrist, I let loose on her in the most restrained way that I could. "I don't know what your game is, but I'm tired of you trying to pimp me out—"

She shuttered. "Ugh! What an ugly and unnecessary word."

"It is what it is. And that *is* what you're trying to do. You're also threatening me. And, for the last time, I am not the only single woman in Swansea who might be suitable for this man. As I stated on your last unscheduled visit, he can't be much of a catch if he needs you to fix him up. I don't care how new he is in town or how hard he works. Besides, who needs a colleague at another company to find him a woman?"

Naomi began nervously pushing the cuticles on her right hand with her thumb. "He's not *asking* to meet a woman, but he clearly *wants* to meet one. I'd like to be the one to introduce him to someone. If you must know, it's in Art's very best interest that this man is happy and stays in his current position. He's been more valuable to Art than anyone else has in a long time. I'm here to do right by my husband, and if you're as smart as I think, for your own good, you'll stop your whimpering recalcitrance and say yes."

"Do I sense trouble in Benchley Paradise?" I asked.

Naomi stood up and glowered at me. The door was open, and over her shoulder, in the main room, I could see Ray nervously pacing. It unsettled me. I was angry. I had always been the type of employee to go above and beyond the job description, but I was beginning to wonder what my job description was: reporter or prostitute. Sorry if that sounds harsh. It's exactly what I was feeling. I was also feeling hurt that Ray appeared to be condoning Naomi's breach of moral ethics.

"I have the kind of marriage that most women can only dream about!" she retorted. "You should be so lucky."

"Love on the rocks? Spousal arousal gone AWOL?"

"You are vile. And my marriage is perfect," she said loudly, as a few people in the outer office began to whisper among themselves.

I didn't like lowering myself to her level, but the position that she and probably Ray were putting me in was worse.

Ray, upon hearing her raised voice, came quickly into my office. By this time, everyone was sneaking peeks in our direction.

"Molly, I think you have a deadline," Ray said diplomatically, smiling at Naomi.

"But ... "

Ray took her gently by the arm and led her out of my office. "Molly does have a deadline," I heard him say, his voice trailing off.

I couldn't believe what had just happened. Words like "sexual harassment" started coming into my head, and I began wondering if I should sue my employer. There was nothing funny about it. It had turned ugly.

"I'm terribly sorry, Molly," Ray said, reappearing in my office. "I'm under a lot of pressure from that woman. I just thought maybe this once you wouldn't mind, and maybe there'd be something in it for you. But I was wrong to ask. I'm very sorry."

He looked so forlorn that I wanted to console him. But I couldn't. I was far too angry.

I PARTAKE IN SOME AFTERNOON T AND CODE D

I was determined not to let Naomi ruin my day. I returned to work with a vengeance and finished my latest feature before deadline. Even with a last-minute obituary thrown in, I managed to stay ahead of the game. Randy and I were both so busy that we didn't even get to swap war stories at lunch.

At 4:20 that afternoon, I finally turned on my cell phone. There was a text from Alan, asking if I was free to take his call. I texted him back in the affirmative, and my phone was ringing only seconds after hitting SEND.

Alan's voice sounded deeper than usual. "Hello, bay-bee," he said, his voice dipping and rising all within four syllables. I was surprised when he didn't continue with, "This is the Big Bopper speaking," as he burst into some odd rendition of "Chantilly Lace."

"Alan?"

"Afternoon T, as sweet as can be, when shared with the mellifluous-voiced Molly."

"Alan T. Cressman," I said, at a loss for words.

"It is me. Alan T. Not grammatically correct, but 'I' doesn't rhyme with 'T.' "

"Uh ... no, it doesn't."

"I'm just having a little fun, Molly. How have you been? Is everything okay?"

Noticing his strange, personality-changing behavior had not subsided, I asked him the same question. "I'm okay, Alan, but I'm wondering about you. You seem different. Very different."

"I'm going through a personal metamorphosis, Molly. Stagnation hasn't exactly been my friend. I'm just a man trying to break free and find himself. Listen, I know you've been craving space, and I don't want to crowd you. I would love to take you to dinner, though. Perhaps this Saturday night. Believe it or not, I'd like to go back to the same restaurant we visited before. I'd like to return to the scene of the crime and see if I can get it right this time. Kind of like a do-over so I can move on. I promise, I'll take you some place even more exquisite on our third date. I just don't want to cringe every time I think of us together there. Will you indulge me?"

"Oh, Alan, you shouldn't be so hard on yourself."

"Is it a date then?"

In a strange way, I related to him. After all, I was in the process of trying to reinvent myself as well. I didn't do it by changing the cadence of my voice or plucking new vocabulary out of someone else's jargon, but I was trying to find my "true essence" all the same.

"Sure, Alan, I'd love to see you on Saturday."

"I'm delighted," he said, sounding like his old self. "I'll confirm toward the end of the week."

And just as I was saying goodbye to Alan, my caller ID indicated that Cody was calling.

"Hey, Cody," I said, clicking him in.

"Am I glad to hear your voice. Molly, I wasn't sure we'd ever speak again. Freakin' A, I'm so sorry. I didn't know that my going away would unravel you like that, baby. I was just laying down tracks, and you can take that to the bank. Except for dinner with the family on Thanksgiving, I've been living in a padded room. It was hard to concentrate at times—"

"Whoa," I said. "Just slow down, will you?" I couldn't believe that he was making it all about him. "Cody, I was taking some time for me. What makes you think it was all about you?"

"I just thought—"

"You thought wrong, then, Cody," I admonished him. "It wasn't about you. Either you're going to take my word for that or not."

"#@%*! Well, I feel like an ass," he relented. "Damn, I'm sorry, sweetie. It's just that the timing of your hiatus from the world seemed to happen right after I told you I was going to New York."

As presumptuous as Cody may have sounded, he was partially right. But I couldn't tell him that Max, Alan, and Tony had also played a part in my decision to abscond. I couldn't very well chastise the guy for not taking the other men in my life into consideration when we *were* having a sexual, and presumably exclusive, relationship.

"Let's just chill," I suggested. "And start from scratch."

"I'm down with that."

"So, how was your Thanksgiving?" I said, asking him the loaded question.

"My folks live in White Plains. I descended on them for two days and headed back to New York. I don't see my family nearly enough. I'm glad I made the time to be there. It was important. How about you?"

Visions of Barbarino flashing the victory sign unsettled my brain. I didn't think Cody was lying about his whereabouts, but how well did I know him? Besides, how was I to know what those bizarre victory signs translated to in Barbarino's deluded mind? Maybe she thought Cody's absence for two weeks meant we had broken up. That alone would be a victory for her. Once again, I was getting ahead of myself.

"Randy and I had dinner at my parents' house. My sister, Hannah, and her fiancé, Matthew, were there, and a few extended family members. It was a lovely day."

"Maybe next year, we'll celebrate together," he said.

My heart skipped a few beats. Cody appeared to be looking farther down the road than I was. I couldn't help but wonder if the Porter Williams bouquet had come from Cody. After all, Cody had been in New York at the time, so it was very likely that any one of numerous New York florists might have recommended Porter's work. Was Cody the one so in love with me?

"I like that thought," I said.

"I've been thinking a lot of thoughts that I like," Cody said, and went directly from speaking casually about Thanksgiving dinner with his parents into an X-rated scenario that had me inappropriately and wildly overstimulated in my office chair.

"You're killing me," I said.

"Damn, baby, I keep forgetting you're at the office. "It's just that I'm lying here in bed and I'm so damn—"

"HARD to talk here," I told him.

He laughed seductively, and I wondered if I could take a cold shower under the office water cooler without being noticed.

"What do you say to continuing this tonight at your place?"

"What time can you be there?"

"Let's get an early start," he said. "How about seven? Want me to bring dinner?"

"I'll take care of that," I told him. "Just a bottle of wine and your hunky self."

"Can't wait to see you, baby. You rock my world."

I clicked off the phone, lay back in my chair, closed my eyes, and took a deep breath. "Wow," I said softly, replaying the erotic repartee in my head.

"Oh, Molly Rose!"

I opened my eyes with a start. "I didn't hear you come in here. Did you just beam yourself here from your office? You have this way of just materializing at the worst possible moments."

"Molly Rose, you are way too flushed for this time of day! Please don't tell me you were just having phone sex at the office."

"I have no intention of telling you."

"Oh, certainly you can share with Randy."

"And certainly Randy can mind his own business."

"Come on now," Randy said playfully. "What's the story, morning glory; what's the word, hummingbird?"

"You can sing the entire soundtrack to *Bye, Bye Birdie* if you wish; I'm not talking."

Randy closed the door and sat down in one of the visitor's chairs. "I know you too well. It had to be Cody. When are you seeing him? How about the others? Who else called?"

"I have an obituary to write," I told him. "Yours!"

"Oh, puh-leeze! Who risked life and limb to warn you about the she-devil this morning? Who has been your number one confidant in the whole wide world?"

"You know it was Cody," I told him. "And I don't want to get *you* all hot and bothered, but I'm thinking it had to have been Cody who sent me the Porter Williams bouquet. After all, he was in New York at the time."

"That makes perfect sense. I just wish you could have told me that without mentioning the P name."

"Porter?"

"Hush."

"I thought you loved talking about that 'delicious' man. What did you call him? 'Chocolate bliss?' "

"Oh, Molly Rose, ever since that bouquet came I haven't stopped thinking about him. I couldn't help but make some subtle inquiries, either!"

"I'll bet," I interjected.

"It's a very good thing that we broke up when we did. That man's ego is bigger than his ... well, from what I hear, no one man has been good enough for Porter."

"Maybe he never found anyone as special as you," I suggested.

"I wish that were the case," Randy went on, "but I know him. Quite frankly, I just think he's too in love with himself to give to any one person. From what I hear of his activities, he might as well just change his name to Ben Dover!"

"Who's Ben Dover?" I asked. "Oh," I said, answering my own question, my face slightly reddened.

"That's as up close and personal as I'll get right now, but suffice it to say I haven't liked what I've been hearing."

"I guess not," I said, trying not to laugh.

"We need to change the subject. Who else called?"

"Alan," I told him.

"And how is Mr. Alan T. Cressman? Still doing the *Sybil* thing?"

"I'm afraid so," I said. "He called it a 'personal metamorphosis.' "

"How euphemistic of him."

"You know, Randy, there's something very adorable and intriguing about Alan. But I still have to wonder if Naomi isn't behind all of this."

"You're hallucinating again, Molly Rose."

"No, seriously. I mean, maybe she's having him try out different personalities to see what kind of man I'm more likely to go for. Did you know that Ellie once overheard Naomi bet someone that she would be the one to set up 'Picky Molly Hacker'? I think she's doing all of this for no other reason than to win a bet with another socialite."

"You do have a point, but—"

"Randy, it's flattering, even coming from her, that she thinks I'm the perfect woman for Art's colleague. But seriously, there are *plenty* of good-looking single women in town. It doesn't have to be me."

"Who knows? Maybe you're the only one she's had time to vet."

"God, I hate it when you make sense. Listen, it's almost five, and I'm so out of here."

"Anything for you," Randy said.

I hated the fact that he looked so sad. I understood where he was coming from. He was crazy about the new man in his life, but hearing about the old one brought feelings to the surface that should have died a long time ago. But life doesn't work that way. When you love someone and it doesn't work out, the relationship may die, but the feelings may linger forever. One just moves on. That's all. One must.

Chapter 27: I'M RUNNING ON FUMES … LITERALLY!

Exhausted, but in the best possible way, I was running so late getting out of my apartment the next morning that I put on my running shoes and sprinted to the office. My generator had long run out of fuel, but it wouldn't be the first time I had muddled through a day of work on fumes alone, and if my luck held up, it wouldn't be the last.

Cody wasn't a fan of mornings anymore than I was, but despite having spent yet another wild night with him, I still wasn't comfortable enough letting him stay in my apartment while I went off to work, the way I always had done with Leo.

I don't want to sell my respectability short. Cody and I did have a terrific precoital meal. Originally, in my fog of a brain, I imagined we might have some kind of dialogue about how the two weeks apart had affected us, and that might have happened (or not) had I not asked him if he was okay with the sundried tomato pasta I prepared in my haste to get ready.

"Molly, I'm up for whatever you've got planned: potluck, clambake, blue plate special … whatever."

"Wienie roast?" I asked.

"Not so fast," Cody said in mock alarm.

And it was all "downhill" from there. We made a thousand jokes and laughed until our stomachs hurt. I wasn't the least bit upset that our conversation hadn't taken a more serious turn. There was time for all of that. One thing I knew for sure: I never wanted to fall in love with any man who couldn't make me laugh or laugh with me.

You'll have to use your imagination if you want to know about our night together, but I did want to mention the Porter Williams bouquet. When Cody saw it sitting on my coffee table, he didn't so much as blink. I couldn't figure out if he simply had a fantastic poker face or just wasn't the kind of guy who picked up on things like that. But it was such a magnificent work of art, and it was hard to believe Cody, if he hadn't sent it, wouldn't have wondered who did.

I didn't know if he was the one who loved me or not. I wasn't interested in a one-way love affair. Until I fell in love, I was better off not knowing who loved me back.

I AM VERY TEMPTED…BUT I BEHAVE

By the time I reached Starbucks, my sprint had slowed considerably. As I passed the window, I debated whether or not to look in and decided that doing so was not worthy of me. But how the hell could I help myself? I *had* to see if she was waiting for me, and I *had* to know if she was still feeling as jubilant and victorious as she had the morning before.

Barbarino was clearing off a table when I passed. The moment she looked up, every fiber of my being wanted to flash her a few hand signals of my own. I restrained myself. I am a lady. I am a class act. I do not stoop to that level. Besides, the look on her face told me all I needed to know. She wasn't happy, but her sour look could have been due to anything. I wasn't going to give her another thought or dignify her crass behavior with any kind of rebuttal, as well deserved as it might be.

CAFFEINE TAKES OVER WHERE FUMES LEAVE OFF

Fumes had helped me reach the office, and caffeine did its job in helping me to get through the day. Despite the fatigue, I was elated by thoughts of my prior night of bliss, but I was also saddened by one of the obituaries. I saw that a very dear friend of my mom's had died suddenly, and I wasn't prepared for the feelings it stirred in me.

For one, I don't know why I hadn't considered the fact that eventually I was going to have to prepare an obituary for someone I knew and that it might be unsettling. I felt keenly more aware of my own mortality than ever before, and I felt sad about my mom's friend. Suddenly, I felt guilty thinking about my happiness with Cody, but it also occurred to me exactly how important it was to seize the moment.

In the meantime, Randy refilled my coffee mug every time he went to refill his own. It was his way of saying that he also had had great night and that we both needed to stay awake on the job. Believe it or not, he does have his quiet moments. They are rare, but I am thankful for them.

THE MAX FACTOR

When I left the office, the sun was going down, but there was a beautiful freshness in the air that made me want to stay outside. I decided to head over to the park. I reached into my purse, put on some lipstick, and arrived just as the after-work crowd was forming.

As I walked toward the kiosk window to buy a bottle of spring water, a rather large guy in an Eskimo-like down jacket blocked my passage, pointing finger guns at me.

187

"I'm gunning for YOU, perty lady," he said. "Yer a sight fer sore eyes. Dang it."

I smiled politely and tried to move around him.

"Aw, c'mon. Humor me, perty lady."

"I just want a bottle of water," I told him.

"One bottle of water coming up."

"No, no," I told him. "I'll buy my own water. But thank you."

"Okay, so my opening line was lame," he said. "Forgive a guy. My name is Cal Leighton. Who do I have the pleasure of unsuccessfully trying to pick up?"

"My wife," the male voice said. Startled, I turned to find Max standing by my side with a huge grin on his face. I had never been so happy to see anyone.

"Darling," I cried. "I wasn't expecting you so early. Rough day? Are the kids with your mother?"

Cal looked crushed and put his fur-lined hood on his head as a chilly breeze blew past. As Max and I embraced, Cal sneered at the handsome stranger in my arms and immediately pointed his finger guns at another unsuspecting female. "I'm under the gun to find me a wife. What are you doing for the rest of *your* life?"

"Save your breath, dude," the woman retorted. "You'll need it to blow up your date."

Max and I shared a laugh.

"Maybe I shouldn't be laughing," he said. "I'm afraid I didn't do much better the first time we met."

I couldn't help notice, yet again, how gorgeous Max was. I shuddered to recall my initial reaction to him. "I wasn't in the best frame of mind that day. I take full responsibility. Believe me, there is no resemblance between you and that man in any way, shape, or form."

"Glad to know that," he said. (As if he didn't know what a fine specimen of a man he was, capable of picking up any woman he wanted.) "You still want that bottle of water, or would you like to share a glass of wine with me?"

"They have a terrific Sauvignon Blanc here," I told him.

"My favorite," he said, the light in his eyes dancing. "My, what good taste you have."

I don't know where my hot memories of Cody had run off to, but Max mesmerized me. I was sure his "good taste" comment referred to my appreciation for him as well as the wine, but I didn't care. The proper measure of cockiness in a man was quite appealing to me.

We were lucky to find a table set away from the center of activity. Max held out the chair for me, then took his own seat. "I wanted to call you, Molly, but your message asked for solitude, and giving you anything less would be unthinkable."

"Thank you for respecting me," I said. "Those two weeks did me a lot of good."

"I took a similar hiatus," he said. "In Bermuda. By my lonesome. You know, Molly, there are worse things than being single. It can be nice to steer your own ship and not have to worry about someone else becoming seasick. I'm just not sure about this dating thing."

My heart sank. Was Max saying he had no interest in seeing me again?

"Don't misunderstand; looking at our friend 'Eskimo Man' over there," he said, nodding in Cal's direction, "all I can say is 'there but for the grace of God go I.' " Max pointed finger guns at me at laughed. "Know what I mean, you perty lil thang?"

"How in the world do you manage to do the exact same absurd gesture and look so damn good doing it?" I said, surprising myself.

"I have my dashing good looks to camouflage any faux pas I might make. Isn't that how I got you to go to dinner with me?"

I blushed. "That may have had something to do with it," I said. "That and your ridiculous charm."

He smiled broadly and winked.

I couldn't believe I was flirting so absurdly with this man. I hadn't behaved this way on our date (neither had he, for that matter), and now I was acting like a bitch in heat.

"As I was saying," Max said, bringing me back to earth, "after a whole lot of thought and a few serious hangovers from thinking and drinking so much, it occurred me that I vastly prefer the idea of friendship than that of dating."

"It *can* be wearisome," I said, a bit too knowingly. I could tell Max picked up on it. I hoped he couldn't tell from my tone that I was dating *four* men at once.

"Molly, that dinner I had with you was one of the nicest meals I've had in a long time. Technically, it may have been a first date of sorts, but it felt more like getting together with an old friend. That doesn't usually happen for me. Almost every woman I have asked out is planning our wedding by the time dinner is finished."

I didn't know what Max's previous dates had done to turn him off;

189

I wanted to make sure I wasn't doing the same thing. "I'm curious; what exactly is it that they say or do to give you that impression?"

"What don't they do: tell me their ring size, ask me if I want children, make inappropriate remarks about my finances, talk our 'our future,' plan vacations, suggest meeting one another's families, make lewd remarks, and serve themselves up like chateaubriand on a silver platter. It's not about me. They don't try to get to know me. They only want to know what I can offer them. You're the first woman in quite a while who had an interest in me. I'm not itching to belabor my past, but it is what makes me who I am today."

"It was only natural to want to know about you," I said. "And your life. Our past is always a part of our present … in one way or another."

"Thank you for that, my dear," he said, reaching for my hand. "You are lovely."

I blushed again, unsure of what to say next.

"Molly, I'm not going to 'date' anymore. I'm only going to see friends, and I do consider you to be a friend. Can we leave it at that? I have a sneaking suspicion that the dating scene has been rough for you, too."

"You're a wise man, Max Ballarin."

"There are a lot of benefits to having friends," Max said, winking again.

I rather liked the idea of "friends with benefits," which is what I assumed he was telling me. But I felt greatly relieved to have Max as a friend rather than a suitor. I wasn't sure what kind of impact the change in terminology would have on my feelings, but I was now dating one less man, and such a splendid one at that.

Several dogs began barking, and we both turned toward the park to see what the commotion was about. An American bulldog was sniffing the butt of a greyhound, and the owner, a petite redhead with a southern accent, was screaming, "Spensah, stop that!" Spencer wasn't listening, nor did he care about the Airedale terrier and the pitbull who were also admonishing him to stop.

"They're barking because they're jealous," Max said. "And because they've got stronger owners who won't let them near that sweet hound."

In that instant, I heard Leo singing, just as he had one day at the park as we witnessed a very similar scene. "Getting to know you, getting to know all about you … "

Leo had always liked the way Randy wove show lyrics into his dialogue and once in a while, just for kicks, he would do it, too. "Getting to like you; getting to hope you like me."

"Don't you agree, Molly?"

"Oh, Max, yeah. For sure. Those other dogs are green with envy."

"Looks like you drifted off for a moment," Max said.

Before I could answer, Max, as if he knew I had gone to a place too private to share, changed the subject, and we chatted with ease for another half hour.

We had been together nearly an hour and a half, and as we had both come directly from our respective offices, we were tired. Max insisted on walking me home. As we neared the hub of activity, we saw Cal Leighton going strong. Finishing off what was likely one of many gin and tonics, he approached a cute blonde who had just entered the fray.

Pointing his finger guns at her, he said, "I'm sticking to my guns; you're the hottest cowgirl in this here rodeo."

"Bite me," she said.

Max laughed, draped his arm around my shoulder, and we walked like that all the way back to my front steps.

I went up to my apartment, fed Captain Jack, and slept straight through until the next morning.

I'M AWAKENED BY BUBBLES

If I hadn't gone to sleep at eight o'clock the night before, I would have not been happy to be awakened by bubbles at 6:30 in the morning. I was nocturnal, and Claudia was diurnal, which means "coming out during the day." I'd never even heard the word until my early-rising friend often described herself as such. I'm digressing.

Claudia made good on her promise not to let my hiatus (from most of the world) extend past Thanksgiving weekend. There weren't a lot of convenient times for us to get together, but 7:30 a.m. was perfect for Claudia. I agreed, but when she suggested the Starbucks close to my office, I had to think fast to come up with a reason why that was out of the question. I told her that too many of my coworkers had breakfast there, and I didn't want to see their faces any sooner than necessary.

She bought my excuse, and I offered to buy breakfast.

At 7:35, we met a few blocks away at Swansea's most historic diner.

"Molly, maybe it's a good thing you wanted to meet here instead.

They can fill a soup bowl with coffee for you. Wake up, Little Snoozy."

I wanted so bad to tell her how lucky she was that she hadn't called the day before, but the last thing I wanted to talk about was Cody.

"I don't need a soup bowl," I told her. "But I would have rather met you *after* work."

"Oh, Molly, I know, but I do like to get home to my husband whenever I can."

I felt embarrassed, and Claudia picked up on it.

"Sorry, girlfriend. I didn't mean anything—"

"No apology necessary," I said.

"I hope we're going to do our annual Christmas shopping together," she said enthusiastically. "I can't traipse through all those stores without my BFF along for at least one excursion."

"Of course we will," I said, suddenly wondering if I should buy gifts for any of the men in my life.

"This is a trip," she said, as the waitress put two large diner cups of coffee before us, followed by two blueberry muffins. "Maybe you won't need a soup bowl after all. These are huge. Will you look at these muffins! I'm going to have a muffin top myself if I eat the whole thing. Speaking of which … "

"What?" I asked.

"Oh, nothing," she went on. "Molly, you had me worried when I heard your message. Of course, there was a huge part of me that envied you for being able to just evaporate into the ozone, although I know you still went to work because I checked, so I assume that Randy wasn't one of the friends that you put on hold, but nonetheless I hope that you weren't going through any kind of crisis because I would feel terrible if our relationship has gotten to a point where you wouldn't come directly to me without passing go. Do you know what I'm saying?"

Although she was the one who had just spoken one heck of a run-on sentence, I felt like it was me who needed to come up for air.

"Claude, I just wanted a break from the world. Why don't you tell me what you've been up to. What hot advertising campaign have you got in the works?"

"Just snagged a new client. They're a lean, green, ecological machine. But I don't think you want to hear all about biodegradable packaging over your morning coffee."

"Speaking of biodegradable," I said, happy to have something to offer that wasn't about the men in my life, "I had the weirdest encounter with this young girl recently. She was just sitting on the steps of my apartment house when I got home. We had this very bizarre conversation, but right in the middle of it, she asked me if I have a biodegradable clock."

I thought Claudia might ask me what that meant or burst out laughing, but instead, she looked painfully guilty.

"What do you know that I don't know?" I asked, picking up her unusual reaction immediately.

"Oh, about that girl, I know nothing. But I'm assuming she meant biological clock, which clearly, at her age she would know nothing about unless someone had spoon-fed her the information, and why she would ask a total stranger that is way beyond my comprehension, but, God, what a rude little thing. I hope you told her that it was none of her beeswax, Molly."

"Agreed on all points, Claude, and I did tell her, but you looked funny when I told you about her. What's up?"

"Nothing, girlfriend," she said. "Oh, my God, look, they have a crank phone on the wall here. Did you ever use one of those?"

"No, but I used to make crank phone calls when I was very young, and you are totally changing the subject."

"I have some news," Claudia said. "I was just afraid it would make you feel bad."

"What are you talking about?" I asked.

"Colin and I have decided to try for a baby."

At that moment, my "biodegradable clock" began to tick very loudly, but I felt bad that my best girlfriend thought she needed to withhold that kind of news from me. "Claude, why couldn't you just tell me that? I am thrilled for you. I mean that."

"I'm sorry, Molly. I was just hoping that by the time I got pregnant, which may not be for quite a while, who knows, that you would have found someone."

I just looked at her and shook my head. I had no words.

"Enough about me. Why don't you tell me the real reason you took that hiatus," she said. "It had to do with a man or men, didn't it? Was it Max? What is going on between you and that hunky-dunky masterpiece of a male?"

"I saw him last night," I said. "We agreed to be friends."

"FRIENDS?" Claudia said loudly, capturing the attention of half the diner. "Are you nuts? Why would you only want to be *friends* with someone who looked like that?"

Suddenly, she sounded as shallow as the women Max had

described to me, but I let that pass. "It was his idea. He just hates the concept of dating. So do I. So, we're just going to refer to ourselves as 'friends who get together.' "

"Thank God, Molly. I thought you had gone bonkers. But you know, I'm thinking you might take advantage of this friend thing. When do you get your next vacation? Maybe you two could go away on a friendly little vacation together. I've got the best idea."

"Whoa. Stop!" I said. I didn't want to tell her everything Max had said about women who plan vacations for him (and everything else), but I suddenly felt that I had been doing the very right thing in trying to keep her out of my love life. She always meant well, but I didn't want to lose the possibility of a relationship with Max due to her good intentions.

"What did I say?" Claudia said. "Are you seeing other men? Is that it?"

I didn't want to lie, but I wasn't going to give her the scoop, either. "I'm keeping my eyes open. Believe it or not, I have a second date with Alan this Saturday night."

"For real?" Claudia asked. "You're going out again with that Alan T. Cressman guy? The one we put that phantasmagorical outfit together for? The guy who got drunk at dinner, fell into the glassworks, and made a spectacle of himself? Naomi's plant? Are you serious? You're going out with him *again*? It just so happens, I saw him Monday night at a cocktail party at Chuffy's, that chic new restaurant in town that is also my client extraordinaire, and I will say he is very easy on the eyes, but Molly, why would you make yourself vulnerable to those kinds of machinations again? I have to be a Blunt Betty here; have you lost your mind?"

Once again, I was exhausted by the time her bubbly, run-on monologue came to an end. "There's something about him that I find appealing," I told her. "It's not that I don't still have my suspicions, because I do, but believe it or not, the she-devil herself came to my office Monday morning."

"For real?"

"She wants me to be a date for some colleague of Art's for his foundation's holiday party."

"We'll be there," Claudia said. "So will most of Swansea society. Colin does some work with them, but that's unimportant. Let's get back to you and Alan."

"My point," I said, diligently trying to make one, "is that while I have my suspicions about Alan's motives, Naomi's visit on Monday clearly reminded me that she isn't shy about following her ridiculous matchmaking agenda all on her loathsome."

Claudia laughed. "Oh, you think?" she said, clearly in possession of information I was not. "Think again, Molly!"

"What?" I said. "If you know something, tell me?"

"Well, had I realized the significance on Monday night of what I heard, I would have speed dialed you on the spot. But you need to know that Naomi was at that Chuffy's cocktail party, too, and she was conversationally quite cozy with Alan. I thought that whole thing with you had passed its expiration date, but apparently not. I was just walking past them when I heard Alan say, 'I've got it covered, Naomi. Trust me. It will be all wrapped up by the weekend.' Clearly, he was talking about you, girlfriend."

I was horrified. Perhaps there was a benefit to sharing some things with my girlfriend. My gut had told me that Alan was up to something, but I had been planning to ignore it. I told Claudia about all of Alan's recent personality changes and how he had explained them to me as a "personal metamorphosis."

"Molly, do you not know the biggest crock in the world when you hear it? That guy is so desperate to please the town socialite that he's trying on personalities at breakneck speed until he finds one that you'll be attracted to. Do I need to remind you that Ellie overheard Naomi betting a friend that *she* would be the one responsible for setting you up?"

"I know," I said. "I was just telling Randy about that."

"Well, your brain must have had a leak after you shared it with him because you clearly have forgotten."

"But why would she want to set me up with Art's colleague *and* Alan?"

"Who knows why? Maybe she's tired of trying to introduce you to one guy at a time. You're so picky; maybe she's just trying to increase her odds. So, are you going to cancel your date with Alan T. Cresssman?

"Hell, no!" I said emphatically.

Claudia smiled devilishly. "If you need a mix master, girlfriend, you've got my number! Wow, look at the time. It's 8:40. We both need to make a dash for it."

We hugged goodbye outside the diner, and as we went our separate ways, I couldn't believe that yet again, I had turned another corner—right back into the land of ridiculous and absurd. Alan would be sorry he messed with me.

I AM WIRED AT WORK

I came barreling into the office looking as if I had been plugged into a dynamo. My eyes were wide open, and I was moving rapidly, like a recording in fast-forward mode. Randy, who was used to seeing me sluggish before coffee and rarely at full throttle until noon, almost dropped *his* coffee seeing me fully dosed with mine (not to mention the effervescent effect being with Claudia usually has on me). Once in my office, I quickly filled Randy in on the latest, caught his update, and went to work.

While it was a plus to be so awake, it was not a plus to have every thought in my brain on active status simultaneously. My thoughts kept shifting back and forth from the article I was writing on historic landmark preservation to the preservation of my love life (and my sanity).

While it was indeed pleasurable to relive my all-night romp with Cody, having such a lucid replay on continuous loop mode was not only exhausting but incongruous with a brain that needed to focus on subjects far less stimulating lest have its owner lose her job. And, on a higher plane of thought, while recalling the many pleasures we shared delighted my libido, I did not want our relationship to be only a sexual one and vowed that our next date would entail a more respectable amount of substantive conversation before we "rocked one another's worlds."

All of this brain activity prompted me to remember the time Leo and I had taken hemispheric brain dominance tests on the Internet, to see if we were right- or left-brain thinkers. I don't even remember the results; I only remember it being another vastly scintillating moment in our history.

Then, I had Naomi and Alan to seethe about, and as I pondered how to best handle the two of them, it occurred to me that Tony had not called at all. I was starting to worry about him.

I worked straight through lunch, and by three o'clock, I had admirably finished all deadline material and rewarded myself by turning on my cell phone. Cody had left a message saying that he was headed back to New York the following morning and hoped to see me that night. I was all for it, because I needed to confirm our compatibility beyond the bedroom. There was no word from Tony, and to top it all off, I was having all kinds of succulent thoughts about my friend Max.

I wondered if I had turned any freakin' corners at all. As flattering as having so many men in my life felt at given moments, I felt more and more angst-ridden about whittling it down to that one special man.

Chapter 28: A LITTLE MORE CONVERSATION, A LITTLE LESS ACTION, PLEASE!

In respectful disagreement with Elvis Presley, a little *less* action was just what Cody and I needed. I was indeed grateful when Cody suggested that we spend a bit more quality time together, offering me the choice of having him bring dinner over or take me to a local Italian straunt. Had the place not been owned by Tony's uncle, I would have opted to go out, but I was just as happy to have Cody bring over a meal.

Cody's choice of a Caprese salad, followed by linguine with white clam sauce, was perfect. To my delight, he brought over some gourmet cat treats for Captain Jack.

"Thank you for bringing dinner over," I said as we began our meal. "This fresh mozzarella is fabuloso."

"The best Caprese salad in town," he said. "I hope Jack likes the treats."

"Oh, he will," I said, nodding my head to indicate Jack, who was impatiently sitting by Cody's right leg. "But right now he wants what we're having."

"Guess I'd better pony up with the mozzarella," Cody said, feeding a piece to Jack.

"A wise idea," I told him.

"Hey, I'm not a dummy; I don't want my ankles bitten again."

I laughed. "Jack never bites in the same place twice. He always aims higher."

Cody laughed. "Aiming higher as in my shin, yes? He wouldn't go any higher than that, right?"

"You just be good to my boy, and you'll never have to find out."

Cody put his fork down, leaned back ever so slightly, and looked at me with a huge grin on his face. "Have I told you how much I dig being with you? I'm sorry I've had to be away so much. It's tough enough taking care of Copper Spoons business, but this studio work came up in New York, and it's too great an opportunity to pass up. I'm playing guitar for a cat with a big name, and there's no telling where it might lead."

I couldn't help but wonder if Cody's potential success might lead him right out of town for good. As much as I enjoyed our time together, I was past the age of just wanting a bed buddy.

"I need to say something," Cody continued. "I'm reading your face, Molly, and I can't help but think you might be wondering if I'm gonna book on this town if things start to gel."

197

Captain Jack was now rubbing against my leg for some of my mozzarella. I broke off a small piece and fed it to him. "You read me too well. I don't know if I should be flattered or frightened."

"Be flattered, baby. It means I'm paying attention to you. I've got to say, Monday night with you was outta-this-world awesome, but that's all because you mean so much to me. It *does* matter to me who I'm with. Big time. We won't talk about my youthful sexcapades because I had a slightly different take on all of that once upon a time, but I'm asking you to look past my rocker life form and see that there's a guy sitting here before you who wants a little more permanence in his life than most people would imagine."

"I'm intrigued," I said, refilling both of our wine glasses with some French Sauterne from my collection.

"Did I ever tell you that I'm looking to co-own an art gallery here in Swansea down the road?"

"No, you didn't," I said, suddenly wondering if I'd fit in working there alongside him. "How far down the road are we talking?"

"A couple of years, maybe," Cody said. "Believe it or not, my art is every bit as important to me as my music. I'm keeping my options open, but that's something that I want. Molly, I promise you, if I couldn't see the possibilities for us, I wouldn't be wasting your time or mine. New York is only a small commute away. I don't have to evaporate into the ether to do my thing. Are you hearing me?"

"Yeah, I think so," I said, as I twirled a strand of linguine around my fork, suddenly remembering Leo stringing a piece comically through his nose.

"What are you smiling at?" Cody said. "Why do I suddenly think it's not about me?"

Cody was even more perceptive than I'd given him credit for. I had to think quickly.

"Oh, I was just remembering an amusing incident that happened a few days ago I forgot to tell you about. I got home some time after five, and there was this girl sitting on my front steps, probably about eleven or so. I had no clue who she was, so I asked her where her mom was … "

"Uh huh. Go on."

"She told me her mom was an 'aunt trap but newer.' I have no clue what she was trying to say."

"Say that again," Cody told me.

"Aunt trap but newer."

"Entrepreneur," Cody said.

"Whoa, how did you know that?"

"You just said it, Molly, but you couldn't hear yourself saying it."

"Aunt trap but newer. Entrepreneur. Oh, of course. You know, it turns out I had met her before. She'd been here with her mom and a few other kids on Halloween."

"Huh. Really? That's something," Cody said.

He looked momentarily lost. I figured I was boring him, so I changed the subject and found his attention again. We talked for another four hours. There were moments when Cody seemed to retreat ever so briefly from the conversation, but as was my habit to do the same, I couldn't complain. Not only was he interested in how I envisioned my future, but he couched his inquiries in such a manner that clearly indicated he had given our possible life together a great deal of thought.

Ever so drained, we got into bed around 12:30, exchanged some sweet nothings, and drifted off to sleep in each other's arms. It was beautiful and exactly what I had needed.

TONY RESURFACES

I awoke in Cody's arms almost the same way I had gone to sleep in them. It felt good, so good that I told him that he was free to linger in my apartment after I left for work. Cody said he was touched by the gesture but was rushing to get back to New York and had an important errand to run before he could leave.

As soon as he drove off, I began my daily walk to work. If you're wondering why he didn't offer me a ride, my morning perambulation to the office is a very important part of my day. It's a good way for me to wake up and breathe in some fresh air. Being only ten minutes away by foot, even when the elements require braving, as I have previously illustrated, the moving of my legs and the inhalations of fresh air are naturally healthy ways for me to greet the day. Once I get to the office and pour my first cup of coffee, the less-than-stellar methods of falling into tune with the world thus begin.

Tony called about four minutes after I had turned on my cell phone. I don't think I mentioned it before, but Tony is an athletic trainer at the local university. He's also a man of many other talents. To make extra money, he often tutors students in several core subjects, does odd jobs, and is a masterful landscaper. His schedule keeps him busy but also allows him flexibility in taking care of his son.

"I'm so glad you finally resurfaced," I said, happy to hear his voice.

"Yeah, Vicky said the same thing."

"What are you talking about, Tony? You haven't gone anywhere, have you?"

"No, Molly. I resurfaced the driveway. With all of this crap going on, I hadn't gotten around to it, and it's getting ridiculously close to winter. If you don't plug the long cracks and the areas where it's eroded, water can get in there. And if that happens, and the weather turns cold, that water will freeze and make everything worse. It was an unexpected sixty-five degrees yesterday, so I thought that would probably be my last chance, especially in December, to get it done."

The tale of Tony resurfacing a driveway was almost as unexpected as his proclamation of love for me, though vastly less interesting. But it left behind some questions that did interest me.

"Okay, I get that. But you say that Vicky wanted you to do this. Does this mean you're back together? She gets the house? What? So when she tells you to hit the road it's freshly paved?"

Tony was humorless. (I'm leaving out the possibility that I wasn't the least bit amusing.) "It means Vicky wants to cover all of her bases as well as the driveway. Hell no we're not back together. Damn, Molly, it's pissing me off that you can't hear a thing I've said to you all along."

"Sorry, Tony. I think I just spent too many years training myself *not* to hear the wrong thing and reminding myself that you belonged to someone else. It's a hard habit to break."

"Well, break it," Tony said, sounding almost annoyed. "Listen, I'm assuming you're headed to the paper."

I couldn't help but notice that I was headed right toward Starbucks, but I was too caught up in my conversation to care at that point, much less to bother looking in the window. Tony's raw edge was unsettling me. "Yeah, I'm almost there."

"Please tell me you're not tied up with some other guy tonight."

"No, he's just going tie *me* up this time. We already did the 'together' thing last night."

There was a long pause on the other end. "If that's supposed to be funny, I'm not laughing. And if you believed me when I told you how much I care, you wouldn't even make a joke like that. You're pissing me off."

"Tony, I'm sorry. Lighten up. What is wrong with you?"

"Molly, can you see me tonight?"

I had hoped to have a night without a man (yes, I did!), but he sounded very eager to see me and as if he *needed* to see me. I didn't like the edge to his voice and was concerned about him.

"Sure, Tony."

"I can't eat dinner with you. I'm picking Noah up from his grandmother's. I'll be there around nine if that's not too late for you."

I GET MORE THAN I'M EXPECTING

I was hoping that Tony would meditate himself out of his bad mood, but when he arrived at my apartment at nine o'clock that evening, he wore his displeasure like an ill-fitting suit. The fury in his dark brown eyes flickered, and I had no idea what to expect.

He kissed me on the cheek and came into the apartment, immediately looking at the bouquet on the coffee table but showing no outward reaction. Standing in the middle of my living room, he looked as if he was lost in a forest and was trying to decide which way to turn.

"Tony, sit down."

"I'm too antsy to sit," he said, walking from across the living room and back again.

"Oh, great, so you're going to pace like an expectant father in the delivery room?"

"What the hell made you say THAT?" he barked at me, forcing Jack to go under a chair and let out a low growl.

I'd been through a lot with Tony over the years, but never before had I felt like I was the object of his scorn, and I didn't like it one bit.

"Tony, if you're angry with me, say so. If you're angry with someone else, then talk to me about it. And don't tell me you're too pissed to talk about it, because if that's the case, you shouldn't be here. And don't upset my cat!"

"Like an expectant father pacing in the delivery room? That's what you said, isn't it?"

"WHATEVER! It's an expression!"

He just stared at me.

"Have a seat. We'll talk. Or leave and I'll give you a rain check. But I'm not going to dance cheek to cheek with your rage and indignation—especially since I have no clue what it's all about. I've had a long day and wasn't counting on company tonight. If you need me, I'm here, but enough is—"

"Sorry," he said, as if I had just knocked the wind out of him. "Sorry, sorry, sorry." He walked over to the couch and sat down. "Sorry." "Can I get you anything?"

"Just a bottle of water. I don't think I should have any alcohol."

I walked to the kitchen, grabbed two bottles of spring water, and joined Tony on the couch. "Agreed. Look, let's get something out of the way. First, if you're upset with me, tell me."

"It's not you, Molly," he said, taking the plastic cover off the sports cap and squeezing it so hard that it shot upward toward the ceiling and landed right smack in the middle of the Porter Williams bouquet.

We exchanged blank stares in place of the laughter that eluded us.

"I know what I said this morning," he continued, "about being pissed off with you for not believing that I love you. I can't blame you, but I *do* love you. And what I have to tell you will probably make you believe me even less, not more, but lying is the worst #@$%ing thing I could do."

"You know all too well how I feel about trust."

"I know I've been telling you that Vicky and I were over a long time ago. And we are. We're sharing a house until arrangements can be made."

"You told me all of this. And I know you're upset because you don't know who she's been seeing all of this time."

"Yeah, that."

"Any clue?"

"None. Molly, I wouldn't care if Noah weren't involved. You do know that, right?"

"So why do you seem angrier than you have in a very long time?"

"Why did you make that crack about me pacing like an expectant father?"

"I told you, it was just an expression. An expre ... Oh, my God! Is Vicky pregnant?"

He stared blankly at me.

"Is she pregnant?" I repeated.

"Fourteen weeks."

"Are you the father?" I asked incredulously.

"I don't know."

"Say, WHAT? You don't know? Tony, you told me—"

"I know exactly what I told you, Molly, and I meant every—"

"You're a walking contradiction. Or maybe a sitting one. Or better yet, a pacing one! All I know is that you haven't been honest."

"There was this one night," Tony said. "We both had a lot to drink, and we were arguing over her lover. She said they weren't together anymore. Mystery man had a pang of conscience and had left her for all of twenty-four hours. And in that short time period, she wanted to get back at him. If he was going back to his wife, then she was going back to her husband. I'd gone without for so long, and I'm only human. I made it easy for her."

I couldn't believe what I was hearing. "Oh, and so Vicky wanted you, and that's all it took. She snapped her fingers, and you unzipped your fly and sprang to attention. That was a turn-on to you? Are you freakin' kidding me?"

"That's not exactly how it happened, and I highly doubt you want details."

"It's your business. I'm not doing the jealous girlfriend thing here because I'm *not* your girlfriend. But if that's all it took for Vicky to get you back into bed, long after you supposedly accepted that your marriage was over, then maybe it's not so over."

"It is *very* over, no matter whose baby it turns out to be."

"Swell, just swell! And what are the chances that it's yours?"

"All I know is that she's been with him on a regular basis, and there was just that one night with me."

"That's all it takes. One night. Does the guy know she's pregnant?"

"Not yet. She's not showing, and she's definitely not talking."

"But she confided in you?"

"Not exactly. I overheard her on the phone with the doctor's office one day when she thought I had left. She had no choice but to tell me. Molly, believe me, this is a complication I wasn't expecting, no #@$%ing pun intended. I don't think the baby is mine, but Vicky's pregnancy affects Noah's life, and that affects me. I'll deal with it the best I know how. What I can't deal with is having you bolt because of this. I just found out last week, and I had to tell you. You've got to believe that I love you."

"Tony, you know how many years I would have given anything to hear that? My feelings for you run so deep. You *know* how hard I've worked to think of you as my friend. And now, on top of asking me to undo all of that, I have to deal with the fact that you not only slept with the woman you claim not to love anymore, but she could be carrying your child."

"Molly, come on. I'm not stupid. I know damn well you're seeing other guys. For all I know you're sleeping with someone. I'm not letting that stop me from loving you."

Tony was fishing, and I wasn't attaching myself to his hook. I looked at him as blankly as he looked at the Porter Williams bouquet. He had the perfect opportunity to use the bouquet to enhance the argument that I had other men in my life, but he didn't. I had to wonder why. The card had said that the sender wouldn't express his love until I loved him back, but men change their minds every bit as much as women do.

"I know I've just put a lot on you. I'm not asking you to make any life-altering decisions. Just keep me in your life, and let's see what happens when the dust settles. Can you do that?"

I looked into his beautiful brown eyes. A gentle soulfulness had replaced the fury, and I felt myself being pulled back into my old feelings. He could sense my vulnerability, and I knew it.

"I can do that," I said.

"I just have one request. December eighteenth is my birthday. I know you know that. I've had so many crummy birthdays in the past several years, and I want this one to be meaningful. There's this country inn just outside Swansea, in Wellington. I'm sure you know it. I'd like to reserve a corner table. I want you to celebrate with me. That's almost two weeks away. Will you do that? It would mean *everything* to me, Molly."

I couldn't believe the effect he was having on me, especially after the news I'd just heard. I didn't want to kiss him back when he ever-so-softly put his lips to mine, but I couldn't help myself. Once again, I kissed him deeply and passionately for a long time. I agreed to share his birthday with him. But I was still very upset.

THE WIZARD OF OZZIE AND HARRIET

I needed Randy's ear the next morning more than I needed my silly ol' caffeine. He agreed to meet me at the office early so we could talk. I had gone to bed and awakened feeling the same way: angry and jealous that Tony had been intimate with Vicky. One need not remind me of the double, triple, or quadruple standards found within my feelings, but they were my feelings all the same.

" … yet he's been insisting that he freakin' loves me," I told Randy. "But look how easily she was able to lure him to bed."

"Let us suppress this distasteful a.m. rancor, Molly Rose. It is unnecessary to examine the issue at hand."

"Please, Randy. If he cared for me, he would not have—"

"Oh, yes he would have," Randy interrupted me. "Loving you and needing to keep his plumbing in working condition are not mutually exclusive. Use it or lose it. Not to mention basic human need. It's not that I can't understand why you've chosen to make fireworks with that scrumptious Cody Cervantes, but you spent so many pre-Leonardo years wishing for domestic bliss with Mr. Lostanza, and now that he's available, you're unsure. Perhaps now you ought to follow the yellow brick road, Dorothy."

"And where will it lead me, Randy? To the Wizard of Ozzie and Harriet?"

Randy applauded lightly, but with enthusiasm. "So spry and full of wit at such an early hour. Such a dated reference, though. And *so* before your time. Perhaps Ozzy and Sharon? Even though they also are rather—"

"Whatever. I need more coffee," I interrupted, looking disdainfully at my empty mug.

"Most days, I would agree. Today is not one of them. In fact, it's the last thing you need. You're like an iron left on for too long. You need to be unplugged so you can cool down."

I picked up the stapler on my desk and began stapling nothing.

Randy put his coffee down, stood up, brushed the wasted staples on my desk into his right hand with his left, then walked to the side of my desk to dispose of them. "Waste not, want not."

I pulled some rubber bands from my desk and began playing with them. "I hope these won't offend you."

"If you neither shoot them nor make a mess, I shall tolerate them."

I never understood how Randy could say half the things he did without breaking out into laughter, but that was part of the show. I was very grateful that he had come in early to talk to me.

"Shall we return to the matters of consequence?"

"I know I'm sleeping with Cody. And I'm not going to apologize for it. I have real feelings for him. It's *because* I loved Tony for so long that I'm being careful. I already know what it's like to fall that hard for him, and I know that I'm capable of doing so. And, yeah, I wanted to be the Harriet to his Ozzie, once upon a time. Of course, that show was before my time, but my grandmother spoke so fondly of it, and of how life should be."

"And what about your, ahem, *friend*, Max Ballarin?"

"I'm intrigued by him. There's something about him that lures me in a little bit more each time."

"And Alan T. Cressman?"

"Naomi's plant. I'm having dinner with him tomorrow."

"Such a cute plant, too."

"There's nothing cute about what he and Naomi are up to."

"But you are still looking forward to seeing him, are you not?"

"Why are you asking me about all of the men? I wanted to talk about Tony."

"Precisely! And you get my point, Molly Rose. You need to cut that man some slack while you figure out your feelings. But under the circumstances, I hope that child does not turn out to be his. So, how did you leave it with Tony?"

"Well, for one, I promised to have dinner with him on his birthday—the eighteenth. He wants to go to the Wellington Inn for a special dinner. I agreed."

"It amazes me how in sync our lives are," Randy said. "That's Kyle's birthday, too. Just last night, I made him promise to keep the night open for an evening to remember. I want to take him somewhere exquisite. I had been considering the Wellington Inn, but now that you and I have 'discussed amongst ourselves,' I will choose an alternate venue since you clearly have first dibs. Wouldn't that have been something?"

I laughed. "Yeah, it would have. It's not as bad as some scenarios I could imagine, but for sure, the last thing we all need is to end up at the same place. But I *would* like to meet Kyle, though."

"Molly Rose, if he hadn't bailed on me over Thanksgiving, it would have happened then. Soon, I promise. Things are progressing between us, and naturally I want my best friend to meet him. You will."

"I look forward to it," I said, a bit calmer. "Thanks for letting me chew off your ear."

"I'll never have Van Gogh's talent," Randy said, laughing. "But at least now I'll look a bit more like him."

I looked at the clock, and it was five minutes to nine. I got out of my chair and walked around to give Randy a hug. "You're the best. And look, we're both still early for work."

T.G.I.F.

It had been a long week, and there was only one man who I had any intention of spending my Friday night with, Captain Jack. He deserved my full attention: a night of snuggling on the couch watching old movies.

On the way home from work, I was momentarily tempted to stop at the park, but thoughts of Leo began creeping back into my consciousness, compounding my anxiety to the max. Yes, Max, I couldn't help but note that I had met him in the same place I had met Leo. Maybe that's why I had been so mean to him that first day. Perhaps there was a part of me that felt that no man had a right to charm me in the great outdoors the way Leo had. Or perhaps something about meeting a man in the park made me feel disloyal to the man with whom I had long parted company.

I didn't know. I didn't want to think, and I didn't want to run into any jerks likes Cal Leighton zealously pointing finger guns at me.

Claudia had called just as I was leaving work and wanted to know if I was free for our annual Christmas shopping the next day. Spending Saturday with my girlfriend seemed like the perfect thing to do, especially as I'd been feeling guilty about keeping my distance from her. I still had no intention of sharing more than I had to, but with Claudia I could at least prepare for my evening with Alan in wicked company.

Chapter 29: SPEAK SOFTLY AND CARRY A BIG SCHTICK

By the end of a day's shopping with Claudia, we had gone through every possible scenario/schtick that I could possibly pull on my "date" with Alan. By seven o'clock that evening, I felt as if I'd been on fifteen dates with Alan, and none of them had worked out. It probably didn't do me much good to play out all the scenes in advance with Claudia, but I felt so bad for keeping her out of the loop where Tony and Cody were concerned, that I overcompensated in letting her direct the rehearsals for that night's show. It was all rather moot because I knew that whatever was going to happen with Alan would probably be worlds away from whatever I had prepared for in advance. I was willing and able to let the chips fall where they may, as long as they were made of steel and landed on Naomi's head. I was tired of being used as a pawn in her silly society bets or as a magic carrot to put her in good favor with her loving husband. I didn't want to be a part of anyone's machinations or ruses. Whatever was going on, and I had no clue, I was going to end it. That's all I knew.

I insisted on meeting Alan at the restaurant. There was no way I was letting him pick me up, much less take me home.

Traipsing through myriad stores all day long and fantasizing about the appropriate costume in which to play out the final act had been great fun. In the end, however, I decided there was nothing better than the LBD (little black dress) to retain the intrigue and preserve my power. Besides, I had escaped public notice wearing that wild outfit the first time around, and I wasn't going to press my luck.

My hair was a mess from trying on clothes all day, so I swept it up onto my head with a pearl-encrusted tortoise-shell clip, then chose simple but long pearl-drop earrings and a classic strand of pearls for my neck.

Alan was waiting for me with the biggest smile I'd ever seen him wear, a single red rose in his hand, and looking like someone who looked *like* Alan but who wasn't him. Huh? Did that make any sense? Okay, for one, his hair was longer than it had been and definitely not standard financial institution length. He was wearing jeans that looked very close to being brand new, a green shirt, and a woven taupe tie. I hated that he looked so happy to see me.

"Molly, you are steaming hot! All over the country, every *Vogue* magazine in existence is bemoaning a blank cover because you just walked right off it."

Oh, fiddle dee dee, Alan, how you do flatter a girl! Notice, there are no quote marks around that sentence, which means I did not say it. I only thought it. Besides, I didn't think Scarlett O'Hara was the right woman to destroy Alan's scheme with Naomi. She was too hotheaded and would only make things worse.

"You're too kind, Alan. And I must say, you look quite different from the other times we've met."

"I hope so," he said, as the host seated us, and the same waiter we'd had before eyed us curiously.

"I think I told you, Molly. I'm undergoing a personal metamorphosis."

When the waiter interrupted to ask for our drink order, I opted to start with some San Pellegrino with lime until I could figure out what I wanted with my dinner.

"This is a do-over date, Molly, so I know that what I don't want is another Beefeater martini. Perhaps I should just stick to iced tea."

"Iced tea. Not Long Island iced tea," I said, confirming the obvious.

"Long Island iced tea is our house specialty," our distracted waiter interjected, as he eyed a shapely brunette passing.

"Then that's what I'll have," Alan said without hesitation.

He leaned closer to me after the waiter had left. "Molly, it's all about a new slant on life. No more same old same old for me. I'm looking for adventure. I've had Swansea iced tea from the time I was a child. If what they are drinking in Long Island is exciting enough to be the specialty of the house here, it's just what I need. I'm tweaking as I'm speaking."

I didn't think that Alan realized that Long Island iced tea was made with rum, tequila, vodka, gin, triple sec, and more, but I wasn't going to stand in the way of his adventure. I would, however, call him a cab if he needed one.

"Your hair is longish," I told him.

"I'm letting it grow even longer," Alan said with wicked defiance. "Damn what they all think. I got the idea from you."

"To grow your hair longer?"

"On our last date, you made a joke about having wild sex with a long-haired rocker dude. I want to *be* that dude. No more of the staid, afraid ... "

Overpaid.

"... mentally grayed ... "

Longing to be la—

"Sparkling water with lime for the lady; Long Island iced tea for the gentleman," the waiter said, putting our drinks in front of us. "I'll return shortly to take your order."

"Cheers!" Alan said gleefully, raising his glass. "Here's to a do-over date. It's worth the wait; won't it be great? Call it fate, but don't hesitate to be my mate."

I looked at him, suddenly remembering his very annoying rhyming habit. "I see you're still rhyming, just like the old Alan." I knew that would get him.

He looked horrified and downed a swill of drink. He was playing this personal metamorphosis thing to the hilt, but I still couldn't ignore that it was very likely an excuse to try on different personalities in hopes of attracting me to one of them.

"Wasn't that tiresome and embarrassing," he said. "It's no wonder I can't date outside my species. No other reptiles will have me."

I couldn't think of an acceptable response, and when the waiter returned, I recalled that on our first date, Alan had ordered my meal for me. He started to do so again, but he caught me glaring at him.

"Holy Toledo, Ohio. You'd like to order your own dinner!" Alan said, as if a long-awaited ton of bricks had fallen on his head.

"You think?" I said irascibly. I couldn't help it if I sounded mean. The idea of someone ordering for me, as I've already told you, scorches me to the core.

"Please, Molly, anything you'd like."

"Stuffed shrimp," I told the waiter. "Balsamic vinaigrette on my salad."

"Marinated salmon with mango-kiwi relish," Alan said. "Honey mustard on my salad. And that's an order!"

Alan burst out laughing while the waiter politely chuckled. I emitted a slight guffaw, and it occurred to me that we were all amused for different reasons, though an analysis of such is not high priority at this time. I'm sure you can figure it all out. I'm not about to go all doctoral dissertation on you. I'll just get back to the action.

"Molly, I feel I need to explain. My father has always ordered for my mother. It makes her feel 'taken care of.' Dolores, my mournful ex-girlfriend, also saw it the same way, and it became a very unfortunate habit of mine. To even think that an independent, forward-thinking, sexy, mellifluous-voiced creature like you would want otherwise is Neanderthal of me. I'm so sorry."

"It's forgotten. But it's hard to imagine that having a man order for me would ever make me feel loved. Quite frankly, it makes me feel *controlled*, and that's not a good feeling."

The Long Island iced tea beckoned Alan to drink it. After a healthy gulp, he looked at me. "Is it not painfully obvious why I need to transform myself? I'm a Cressman cutout. I need a 'T' in my name to distinguish myself from my father. And even then, we're two peas in a pod. Only I'm not the second pea, Molly. I'm an artichoke. A perennial thistle. I am a man of profoundly lobed and gleaming-green leaves with a beautiful heart underneath. I'm not a pea in a pod. Perhaps I should change my name legally to Artie Choke! Or Art T. Choke! Same initials. HA!"

I saw the man at the next table look over at us and roll his eyes. I made a gentle motion with my hand for my overly effusive artichoke (who was also my date—a fruit from the date palm) to lower his voice.

"Alan," I said, stopping momentarily as the waiter placed our salads in front of us. "I understand your frustration. But you know, you don't run *from* something, you go *to* something. You can't just run from being Alan T. Cressman if you don't know who you want to be."

"I want to be someone you might care about."

"It's not about me. It's about you. I don't have a blueprint for the perfect man. Besides, even if I did, that would only be 'on paper.' Chemistry is everything. Everything else is superficial in the end. There are indefinable things that attract us to people, sometimes defying all logic. Stop trying on personalities in hopes of finding one I'll like. I don't care what kind of deal you've got going with Naomi."

Alan looked alarmed. "What do you know about—"

He hesitated, then said, "I'll admit it, that meddlesome, spotlight-grabbing philanthrobitch, excuse my French, suggested I meet you a long time ago. She was quite adamant about it, so much so that I didn't even want to make your acquaintance. When Shakespeare said that all the world's a stage and the men and women in it merely players, he neglected to mention Naomi Hall-Benchley is the master puppeteer, director, if you will. My interest in you began when I saw your photo at the newspaper and only increased after we met. Right now, that respect-encroaching upper cruster has me working on a financial portfolio for a cousin of hers." Alan looked agitated and took another large gulp of his drink. "I'm doing a job for her, and I'm doing it well. But Naomi doesn't see it that way. She'll want a reward for bringing business my way. I think she has another cousin she wants me to escort to some function. Oh, and there's one little thing I'm sure she wants me to do after that: marry the woman. I'm fed up with the whole lot of those vapid socialites, including the ones in my own family. Mrs. Hall-Benchley can expect anything she likes, but all she'll get from me is a sound financial plan."

It was starting to dawn on me that I'd made a huge mistake about Alan's intentions, but I didn't want to dismiss the fact that he also was a very clever man and may have recovered from my accusation far more adeptly than I may have given him credit. I noticed the Long Island iced tea was starting to affect him.

"Molly, the SheEO of my company suggested to me today that I get a haircut."

"What did you say? Is your CEO female?"

"Huh? Yes, she is. How did you know? Anyway, I asked her if she were suggesting that I get another job because I quite liked my hair longer."

"And what did she say?"

"She immediately began backpedaling and told me that I was not someone she'd ever want to replace."

"Wow."

"I'm staying put for now, but I won't be at that job outside of a year. I don't know what I'll do. A part of me wants to get a Harley and hit the mopin' toad!"

"The mopin' toad? What's that? A frog in a bad mood?"

"Huh?"

"You said 'mopin' toad.' Now, there's a reptile outside of your species!"

"HA! I meant OPEN ROAD! I'D LIKE TO HIT THE OPEN ROAD!"

"No time like the present, bud!" a man's voice from the next table boomed, followed by a swell of laughter from nearby tables.

Alan looked embarrassed. I felt bad for him, but he hadn't convinced me. To my astonishment, he pulled back his hair over his right ear to reveal a piercing. "Look, Molly, my first stud. And I'll show you something else."

I couldn't imagine what else he had brought to "show and tell" in a public restaurant. Alan unbuttoned his cuff and rolled up his sleeve to reveal a small blue-and-white dove tattooed right on the side of his arm, a few inches above his elbow. At that moment, I realized that Alan's "personal metamorphosis" was real and had nothing to do with Naomi.

"It's a dove. It means freedom. That's what I want, Molly. I want

212

to reinvent myself. I'm going about it rather clumsilly, I mean clumsly, I mean clumsily, but I'm not going to live out my life for my family. I'm not going to live differently just for the sake of it, either, but I'm going to seek adventure just like my uncle told me to do. Don't you understand that's why I find you so intriguing? YOU'RE NOT ALL MOLDY LIKE OTHER WOMEN!"

"You're not talking about *my* wife, are you, bud?" boomed the male patron again. "Because if you are—"

"No, he's not," I said. "Don't drink anymore of that, Alan. It's got five different kinds of booze in it."

"Oh, cripes," Alan said. "And I meant to say, um, that you don't fit into a mold. I didn't mean moldy—"

"I know what you meant. It's okay."

The waiter took away our empty salad plates and served our entrees. Alan ordered a bottle of San Pellegrino for himself, and suddenly seemed at peace. I looked around the restaurant, ever so briefly, to make sure Alan hadn't made any lasting enemies. Everyone had gone back to his or her own business, but I did notice the same woman who I'd seen last time. She was staring at me and quickly looked down when our eyes met. If I did know her, she was no one of significance to me, so I turned around to face Alan again.

He was smiling at me, and his eyes were dancing. He had brushed his hair aside in such a way that his diamond earring stud sparkled. I noticed the delightful way his hair almost touched his shoulders. He reached across the table for my hand, and I instinctively reached for his. It was the last thing I expected, but a connection was made. And it was real.

I AM MY OWN REALITY SHOW

It was inevitable that bubbles would awaken me late Sunday morning. And only fair. After all, Claudia had spent the good part of her Saturday helping to prepare me for a date that turned out to be different from what we had both anticipated. I couldn't tell her that Alan had suddenly become a "person of interest." Instead, I simply told her that I had been wrong about him, and that very possibly, he liked Naomi even less than I did. Naturally, that mini-exposé begged the question of whether or not I had any sparks for Alan, but luckily for me, Claudia's mother-in-law was due for lunch, and she had to "skedaddle."

Every time I watch my favorite reality dating show, I always pay attention when the bachelor or the bachelorette reveals that he or she didn't expect to have true feelings for so many people at once, often noting that it was not thought possible. I'm here to tell you: it is.

Although Tony had escorted me to Susan Decker's wedding, I had no idea at the time that he had any feelings for me. I was a single, picky woman trying to pick up the pieces of a broken engagement and soul mate gone forever. Perhaps it was watching Susan marry that reminded me: I, too, could find eternal love again. Perhaps it was my sister Hannah's upcoming August nuptials that made me feel pressured to do so. Maybe it was simply being accosted at Susan's wedding by the likes of my aunt Pauline and Naomi Hall-Benchley that put me on the path to finding love all by myself. But now I had four men in my life that I cared about. There was no prescribed amount of time in which I had to let one go. (I always thought that a bit harsh on TV, but perhaps there was a real blessing in there.)

Another blessing the TV bachelorette has over me is that everyone knows about everyone else. I was seeing four men in the small burb of Swansea, and there were just so many places to hide. My apartment would do as long as the neighbors stayed out of my business, and despite the trendy, upwardly mobile town I lived in, eventually I would run out of restaurants.

However, I was not a reality show contestant, and therefore I was going to take my time, in the real world, to figure out which man, if any, was right for me.

SOMETHING SPECIAL? FOR ME?

About an hour after Claudia called, Cody phoned to let me know that he was on his way home. He had finished in New York late Saturday afternoon but had gone to White Plains for a short visit with his parents. He planned to return to Swansea later in the afternoon. Cody said he had something special for me but had a couple of errands to take care of before he could come over. For one, he needed to coordinate rehearsal schedules with Burt, the Copper Spoons drummer, and I was happy that he was focusing on a few local gigs again.

Around 7:30 that Sunday night, Cody arrived at my front door, looking gorgeously bedraggled but seeming a bit distant, too.

"Hey, Molly," he said, throwing his arms around me. "Did you miss me?"

"Of course I did. How was New York?"

214

"Oh, baby," he said, walking toward my kitchen to help himself to a bottle of water, "I can't wait for you to hear what we've been doing. We recorded and mixed some kick-ass tracks. Wow, I'm just so pumped."

I felt bad, but it was hard for me to focus on "kick-ass tracks" when Cody seemed to have forgotten about having "something special" for me. I did consider that perhaps one of those "kick-ass tracks" was a song written for me, but as Cody was working on another musician's CD, that didn't seem the least bit probable. Had he forgotten my surprise?

We gabbed about everything and nothing for an hour and change, when Cody suggested we order in for pizza. That was fine with me; I was feeling rather mellow and all for keeping our togetherness under the radar.

"Baby," Cody said, his mouth crammed with pepperoni and mushroom pizza, "I need to ask you something."

"I'm all yours, Cody."

"Are you?" His mouth was so full I was surprised that even those two words had managed to snake their way around the masticated pizza to exit the orifice known as the mouth.

"Am I what, Cody?"

"Molly," Cody said, wiping tomato sauce from his lips, finally swallowing his food. "You know you rock my world, baby. How many times have I told you that?"

"Several," I replied, feeling hot thinking about all the ways he rocked mine.

"I told you, baby, I've had a lot of youthful indiscretions, and I'm not going to lie and say that playing rock guitar doesn't offer a cat like me the opportunity to continue those indiscretions beyond his prime. Not that I'm over the hill, but—"

"What are you trying to say?"

"Forgive me, Molly, but you're not rocking anyone else's world, are you?"

I was flabbergasted. I didn't quite know how to respond. If I were "rocking any other worlds," it certainly wasn't sexually, which is exactly what he was asking me.

My appetite for pizza had waned; I was full after only two slices. Cody, despite the seriousness of his question, wasn't going to let whatever answer I gave interfere with his appetite. He picked up his fourth slice and bit into it with gusto.

"You're the only man I've been with since I broke up with my fiancé, Leo. I'm not into bed hopping. I can promise you that. Why are you asking?"

215

"Do I have mozzarella on my chin?"

"You might want to check your nose for sauce," I said, handing him a napkin. "Your chin is cheese-free. And Jack just slurped a globule of mozzarella from your wrist."

He looked at Captain Jack, who was sitting right below him, happily licking his chops. Cody seemed distracted, then remembered the delicate subject matter he had initiated. "Sorry. I just thought I should ask. Full disclosure and all that."

I was starting to feel sick. While I wasn't sexually active with any of the other men, I certainly had imagined how pleasurable it might be to be with each and every one of them.

"I'm glad you asked," I said. I began to think of all of the other women vying for Cody, especially Barbarino, who would gladly accept my throne should I choose to abdicate. My competitive side made an appearance. "I want to be the only one rockin' your world, Cody. Haven't I shown you that? So, where's the something special you have for me?"

Cody hesitated, and for a split second I thought I saw his face go blank. "You *have* shown me, Molly. Oh, baby, I salute you and your many talents. Let me digest this pizza for a bit, and if you'll allow me into your boudoir again, I'll be glad to give you something very special."

At that moment, Captain Jack looked up at Cody and hissed. Whatever Cody had in mind, I knew the earth was about to move. For another blissful night, he would be the only man on my mind. But I couldn't shake the feeling he was holding something back.

RANDY WRITES MY OBITUARY

It's not as bad as it sounds. Randy woke up in a dither and having nothing at home to occupy him, went straight to the office, arriving at the ungodly hour of 7:20. Ahead of schedule, he finished his column and to ensure that I would have a few minutes to chat with him, wrote an obituary that had been called in that morning. Not mine. Only mine to write. Sue me; I was being dramatic again.

Always the respectful one, Randy texted me, asking if I could possibly come in a few minutes early. Cody had left before me, and so I was easily able to make it in by 8:40.

"Writing obituaries is depressing," Randy informed me.

"Writing about weddings is more depressing," I shot back. "Besides, you know that's only a small part of my job."

"Whatever," Randy said, squirming to find a comfortable position in his chair. "Sit down, Molly Rose."

"May I take my coat off first?" I asked.

"Hannah Leigh called," Randy said, as if he were playing secretary. "She wants to know if you want to get your parents' Christmas gift together this year."

"I wish I knew what to get for Hannah," I said.

"She'll be getting a new husband this August. You can cross that off the list. What else might she need?"

"Besides a new last name? Not much. Honestly, Randy, what were my parents thinking naming her Hannah Hacker? Maybe they knew she'd get married first, and it wouldn't matter. They gave me a name that flowed better knowing I'd be holding onto it longer."

"Oh, please. And your sister's name is Hannah *Leigh* Hacker! Middle names are so much prettier, Molly Rose."

"Are they, Harry *Foxville* Goodrich?"

Randy self-ejected from the guest chair and lunging forward slammed my office door shut. "Hush!"

"I thought you liked Foxville."

"On alternate Thursdays," Randy said. "But other names are meant to be changed—and forgotten!"

"Calm down," I said, sipping my coffee and glancing at the online edition of the *Herald*. "What was on your mind when you texted me earlier?"

"Well, I wanted to tell you about some plans I made for our big night on the eighteenth, but that will have to wait. I hate to bring this up so early in the morning, but Ana told me that the she-devil, Ms. Benchley, called Ray bright and early this a.m. From what Ana reports, Ray's conversation became so animated, read *agitated*, Molly Rose, that he got up and closed his door in the middle of it. Ana said he came out of the office at 8:15 looking like he'd been trampled on by a pack of spike-heeled socialites. Or maybe just one. Far be it from me to foment a stir here, but why do I think that my best friend, Molly Rose, was the main course of whatever conversational fare was had? And since she didn't call me yesterday, I remain in the dark about whatever might have happened on Saturday night with Alan T. Cressman. Therefore, I'm stuck with an inquiring mind and can't help wondering: how in the world does this all tie together? Hmmm."

After spewing several expletives in reaction to Naomi's latest intrusion, I filled the compliant-eared Randy in on the latest with Alan.

"I'm very glad to know that Mr. Cressman isn't entrenched in the enemy camp. Am I to understand that you might have some newfound interest in the man?"

"It could be possible," I said, scanning my email as we were speaking. "As a matter of fact, here's an email from him." I paused a few moments to read Alan's message. "Holy she-devil, Randy! This is unbelievable!"

"What? Spill, woman."

"Alan wrote to tell me what a wonderful time he had on Saturday. It turns out that someone who knew the two of us, at least by sight, reported back to Naomi that we'd had dinner together. Naomi had the she-cojones to call Alan on Sunday and tell him that I was off the market and *not* to date me again! Are you freakin' kidding me? I'll say it again: 'ARE YOU FREAKIN' KIDDING ME?' That woman needs to be stopped. Who does she think she is trying to run my love life one way or the other! I wonder who it was who saw us. Wait, I know. It must've been that woman I saw staring at me. Whoever she is, she was there both times I had dates with Alan. I can't believe there was a tail on me."

"Oh my," Randy said, giddy with amusement over my furor.

"Call the dog patrol. If there's a bitch missing her tail in Swansea, it belongs to Naomi. How dare she have me followed?"

"Wait, wait," Randy said. "I thought it was her goal to set you up and win some bet. Why would she tell the handsome Mr. Cressman *not* to see you?"

"First of all, Alan and I hooked up on our own. When she tried to put us together a good while back, he rejected her. Second, she still wants me to go to that foundation Christmas party with Art's colleague. She's banking on that working out so that she can please her husband and win her bet at the same time. *And* she's aiming to hook Alan up with some cousin of hers. So it's no longer an advantage to her for Alan and me to get together. I'll bet she called Ray about that Christmas party. No doubt she's twisting his arm to get him to twist mine. I am *not* going. I told her that. GET A LIFE, NAOMI! Do you see a pillow anywhere?"

"Why?" Randy asked. "Are you going back to sleep?"

"No!" I barked. "I need something to muffle my scream."

"Or maybe you want to smother someone," Randy said, looking around the room as if someone else had made the tempting suggestion.

"I'll be gone for several hours," I said, standing up and grabbing my coat.

"Molly Rose, you just got here. Goodness gracious, St. Ignatius. Don't go gunning for that woman. She's not worth it. Besides, I'm very loath to visit friends in prison. And orange is quite an unbecoming color on you. Well, on most people, truth be told."

"Oh, stop. I also had an email from a confidential informant who's willing to meet me on that feature I'm doing. I've got to meet said person at ten o'clock or lose the opportunity. I have to go home and get my car."

Randy stood up. "Okay. But promise me you won't pay a visit to Ms. Hall-Benchley when you're through."

"I'd love to, Randy, but I wouldn't give her the satisfaction. Besides, I would have no idea where she's lollygagging the day away."

"Okay, then, I'll take you at your word," Randy chided me as I opened my office door to leave. "I don't want to have to write *your* obituary. Be careful out there."

DON'T ASK, DON'T TELL

I was with my confidential informant until 11:30. She was "confidential" but not the "informant" I had hoped she would be. Having heard through the grapevine that I was considering a feature on the dark side of plastic surgery, she had called me.

Asking to be known only as "the source," she was bursting a freakin' gut to give me the lowdown on a plastic surgery scandal that she claimed would "rock the town." But when we met, she was incognito, far from chatalicious, and anything but forthcoming. I sensed that she had very mixed feelings about the doctor she had wanted to expose, and in hindsight, I realized that what I thought was a slight speech impediment on the phone was instead a drunken slur, as it ceased to exist when we met.

Still, with the little bit of information I did have, I was determined to see what else I could find on my own about Dr. William Miller, Swansea's new plastic surgeon. I called Ray, with much trepidation, to tell him I was going to grab some lunch, then head over to the library to invade their archives. When he told me to take a leisurely lunch, to put it on my expense account, *and* to work from home if there was time left on the clock afterward, I felt sick.

Ray is a nice guy, but he's a busy editor, often tightly wound, with a job that never ends and two out of four kids in college. He is easily stressed and doesn't have time for superfluous niceties. I knew something wicked my way was coming, and I didn't like it.

I found a diner outside town and made myself comfortable in a

219

corner booth. I just needed time to think about my life: my love life.

I was confounded by my situation. I wanted *one* man, yet I had four amazing prospects. I was having hot sex with one of them, and I suspected that my circus days would be ending soon because I was lousy at juggling.

I knew that if I'd met Cody ten years ago, we would have been disastrous together. But Cody seemed to have a good grip on where he'd been and where he was going, and I appreciated the fact that he was not only diversifying, but was looking down the road a bit. Oh, and did I mention HOT AS HELL!

Max intrigued me. He had told me openly about his marriage and divorce, but I sensed a complex man, closer to Leo, who would take some time to know yet be well worth the effort. He was the oldest of the four, well established, and, and did I mention FREAKIN' GORGEOUS!

Alan was both "together "and confused at the same time, but he knew it. I found his openness endearing. I loved that he wasn't willing to settle for the status quo, that he stood up to Naomi, and wanted more than the life of privilege that was his birthright. Charmed by his nascent desire to "color outside the lines," I wanted to know more … and more. And did I mention he was ADORABLE?

And then there was Tony. You know all about him by now. In some ways, he was the one I was most afraid to love because I already had. I knew what it meant to love him, and I knew what it felt to be rejected by him. I also had to consider the fact that he might have a second child on the way with his future ex-wife. I was also worried about him. He hadn't sounded right. I decided to call him from my cozy corner of the diner.

"Molly, I was just going to call you."

"I was worried about you. I just wanted to—"

"Great news! Vicky's OB/GYN just called. She wasn't here, and as I'm still her husband, the nurse didn't flinch at giving me the news."

"She's not pregnant?"

"Oh, she's pregnant all right, but she's a month further along than she led me to believe. No way I'm the father!"

"Thank God! Are you sure, Tony? Why did she let you think it could be yours?"

"You're a reporter, Molly. What do you think? Isn't it obvious? She wanted a backup daddy if the real one didn't pan out. I'm no closer to finding out who he is. He never calls the house phone, and she keeps her cell phone guarded twenty-four/seven. I do know this: he can start stockpiling cigars. She's having twins."

"Holy #@$!%!"

"Molly, I wish I'd known this the other night. If she hadn't tried to deceive me, I never would have—"

"What? Told me that the two of you had sex?"

There was a pause. "Well, yeah. You know, kind of a 'don't ask, don't tell' sort of thing. No, I wouldn't have told you."

"Thank you for your honesty."

"We discussed this, didn't we? I'm not interrogating *you*, am I? How's that for fair play?"

Tony and his three rhetorical questions had me. "Right. Don't ask; don't tell. Well, I'm just thankful it's, I mean *they* are not your babies. Listen, I'm in the middle of a working lunch, by my lonesome, and I just felt the need to check on you. Can we talk again soon?"

"Sure. And listen, I'm ecstatic that you're sharing my birthday with me. I just called earlier to make the reservations and found out that my favorite jazz combo will be playing there. I've reserved the best table in the house. Looking forward to this evening has been getting me through this hell of late. Know that, honey."

DON'T ASK DONATELLA

I wrapped things up at the library around 3:45 and arrived home about fifteen minutes later. Following up on the story had led me to a virtual dead end, and I wasn't in the best frame of mind. Lost in thought, I was taken aback to see my preteen friend sitting on the front steps of my building again. It seemed almost as if she were waiting for me.

"You're coming from the wrong direction," she blurted out.

"That's because I drove home tonight," I told her.

"Whatever," came the unenthused reply. "How come you're so early?"

I put my briefcase down on the steps and looked at her. She was wearing faded jeans, a couple layers of shirts with a khaki Henley on top, and a bright purple sleeveless down vest on top of that. She had well-worn purple Converse sneakers and some sort of fanny pack. Faux strands of purple hair were woven into her long blond tresses, and although I was quite certain she lived in the neighborhood, she looked lost. Forlorn.

"Maybe I should be asking you some questions, yo—"

"Oh, God. You're not gonna call me 'young lady,' are you?

'Cause you look like you were gonna call me that. Only *really* old people get to call me that."

I was grateful to have escaped such a classification. "Why is it that you get to ask *me* all the questions?"

"You asked me *my* name. You asked me where my mother was. You asked me who delivered your flowers. You asked me if I came by for Halloween. Sheesh, lady, you have a short memory for a huge question asker."

"And yours is way too long," I said, sitting next to her. "And I'm going to tell you something. When you're an adult, and you see a girl your age all by herself, you'll want to know where her parents are, too."

"Ask me if I care. Besides, they're working, I guess. It's only four o'clock. I ain't breakin' no curfew. I'm allowed to be here."

"Do you know someone in this building?" I asked gently.

"Just you," she said.

"Are you here to see me?" I asked. "That seems kind of funny since you seem to know that I don't normally come home this early. And we don't know—"

"I'm just hanging, lady. It's a free country."

My confidential informant had been easier to tap into than this girl. She wasn't budging, but neither was I.

"You like music?" I asked.

"I'm a Dead Head."

"You're a Grateful Dead fan? Aren't you a bit young? I'm surprised you've even heard of them."

"I like lots of old people's music. Like Led Zep, T-Rex, the Stones, and Deep Purple. I like what's cool. You know, whatever. I like new stuff. I'm not deaf, lady."

I was happy to have found a subject that interested her.

"Do you and your friends listen to a lot of music?"

"Whatever," she said, drifting away from me.

My suspicions that she didn't have many friends in the area seemed all the more real. I wasn't sure what to say without upsetting her.

"My friends are all where I used to live. Kids around here are so uncool. Their moms all give them cookies and stuff when they come home from school. How bogus is that?"

I wondered who her mother was and if she knew how badly her daughter wanted her home to dole out afterschool treats.

"Where did you used to live?" I asked.

"Near Grandmom and Grandpop. I miss them."

"When's the last time you saw your grandparents?"

"Thanksgiving. Whatever, lady."

"You remember that my name is Molly, right?"

"Yeah. So?"

"What's your name?"

"I told you, Donatella."

"I remember you dressed up like Donatella Versace for Halloween, but I was wondering what your *real* name was.

She looked agitated. "DONATELLA, lady. That *is* my real name. Like 'Dona Ask; Dona Tella.' "

The universe was definitely sending me a quote for the day, but I had no time to contemplate it. "Sorry, Donatella. And I'm sorry you miss your grandparents so much. Will you see them again soon?"

"Christmas."

"Do they live far?"

"In White Plains."

"Did you say 'White Plains'? Is your daddy— "

"Oh man, I messed up," she said, rising frantically from the steps. "Donatella, wait!"

"Peace, lady," she said, and tore off down the street.

I stood up and watched her turn into a splash of color and disappear around a corner. I couldn't believe that I was crying, but I felt so betrayed.

"Damn you, Cody," I said to no one at all. "Why didn't you tell me?"

Chapter 30: I AM DEVASTATED!

After Donatella disappeared into the fading afternoon light, I stood there on the steps as the tears fell liberally from my eyes. Everything was clear; nothing was clear. I had never, not in all of the musings of my mind, imagined that Cody and Barbarino had a daughter together. It had never occurred to me that the "mother" who escorted three children to my door on Halloween night was Barbarino, checking me out. Were "Tigger "and "Eeyore" also their children? Was I getting ahead of myself? How ironic that I felt such a swell of relief to learn that Tony was not becoming a father again only to realize that Cody had been one all along.

Thanksgiving suddenly made sense. Cody had to have been with Barbarino because of their child—or perhaps children. I understood why she threw that in my face and why she was so depressed afterward. Probably she hoped that every family holiday would bring forth reconciliation with Cody. Why hadn't he told me? Was he ever planning to do so? How many more "hot nights" did we have to have for me to qualify as a recipient of such information? Or perhaps was it because we had had so many lusty adventures that he didn't take me seriously. How could I have misread him?

Maybe you're thinking that I don't deserve any sympathy—after all, I've got eyes for other men and haven't made up my mind about any of them yet. But I respect each and every one of them. I'm not trying to play anyone. Why didn't he tell me?

I had no sooner sobbed my way up the elevator to my floor, entered my apartment, and flung myself onto my couch, weeping, when there was a knock at my door. A mascara-stained face is not a pretty one, and I neither wanted to inflict it on anyone nor answer any questions. And if it was Cody at the door, I wasn't ready to have "the conversation" yet.

Captain Jack looked at me and then at the door. He wanted to know why I didn't answer it, but I could tell my heavy sobs were unsettling him. His tail puffed out, and he began slowly stalking around in a circle.

"Molly Rose, I saw you go into the building. Open up!"

I jumped up, ran to the door, and opened it for the only person I wanted to see. I threw my arms around Randy, hysterical, but mindful not to get mascara on his coat.

Captain Jack walked up to Randy, nuzzled against his leg, almost as if he were thanking him for being there, then walked back to his bed in the corner of the room and went to sleep.

"What in the world! What happened to you since this morning? Oh, please tell me you didn't mix it up with the she-devil!"

"I told you; I wasn't going anywhere near her. This has nothing to do with her."

"Let's sit down," Randy said, leading me to the couch. "I haven't seen you cry like this since Leo."

"I know, Randy, all of this has taken me right back to our breakup, and it's so painful."

"Molly Rose, roll back the tape. I missed the last episode. What happened?"

I filled him in on everything that had just happened, everything I surmised to be the situation with Cody, and asked Randy, myself, and the universe if the trust demon that doomed Leo and me was coming back to wreak havoc all over again.

"Calm down. You're in hysterics. Let's not cross any state lines to incoherence."

"I'm already in a state of shock."

"You're going to have to have a talk with the man, but I'm admonishing you not to do it now. Wait until you are calm. Okay, so maybe 'calm' is to dream the impossible dream, but a relative calm would be acceptable."

I shot him a look.

"Don't turn this into a calamity, Molly Rose. Don't jump to unnecessary conclusions."

"Oh, Randy, why wouldn't Cody tell me that he had children with that woman? I don't expect to know everything and I wouldn't *want* to know everything … but this? And why has she been hanging out on my steps? I think I scared her off asking about her daddy. That makes me feel *sick* inside: upsetting a child. She seems like kind of a sad kid, you know? There's something rather endearing about her, though I can't say the same for her mother."

"Everything will work out the way it is supposed to," Randy said.

"I'm not so sure about that. Once the trust is gone, what do you have left?"

Randy pulled a Kleenex from his pocket and wiped my tears. "Sometimes, it just seems like we've lost everything, when in reality, we've gained perspective, making it easier for us to get everything back when the time is right."

I stopped crying and looked at him.

225

"I know it's one of the oldest clichés in the world, but things *do* happen for a reason. Sometimes we have to have our world shaken up before we can learn to appreciate how beautiful it is. Sometimes it's a blessing to think we have lost what we treasure most."

"Can I quote you on this next time you're in freak-out mode over Kyle?"

"Oh, trepidant one! Doubt not the sage who sits before you! Threaten not the compadre who soothes your weary soul."

"I feel like my entire world has been rocked. And not in the way Cody means it."

"Do tell!"

"No, I won't tell. I'm miserable. And not that I'm not happy to see you, oh sagacious one, but was there any special reason for your visit? I'm sure you're anxious to get home after the long day you've put in."

Reaching into his pocket and pulling out an envelope, Randy said, "This is why I came over. I would have forgotten had you not asked."

I took the envelope from him with my name on it. I didn't recognize the writing.

Molly, may I interest you in dinner with a friend? A drink and a taste of whatever fare might delight your palate? I thoroughly enjoyed our last meeting in the park, but I dare not rely on serendipitous encounters by their lonesome. Would love to see you one night this week. Please let me know, sweet friend. Max.

"Well, isn't this nice," I said, handing Randy the note. "He had this hand-delivered?"

"Indeed he did. Straight out of a Jane Austen novel. I had no idea who it could be from, but my mind went crazy with possibilities, and I didn't know if it was time-sensitive or what, so I brought it over."

"Thank you, Randy. And don't leave out the part about how you were dying of curiosity, too."

"Molly Rose! Don't look a gift courier in the mouth. Speaking of serendipitous, I would say my timely arrival is thy very same beast."

I laughed. Then, after a few seconds, I thought about my situation and burst into tears all over again. "I can't go through this another time. I can't. It will kill me."

"What can't you go through again, Molly Rose?"

"Huh?"

"I asked you what you cannot go through again. Breaking up with another man over trust, or resurrecting your love for Leo only to watch it die all over again?"

Tears fell from my eyes, smudging the words "sweet friend" on Max's card.

"I don't know, Randy. I don't know."

EVEN A STOPPED CLOCK IS RIGHT TWICE A DAY

That was the last thing Leo said to me before "goodbye, my love." After conversing, crying, and talking in circles, we could never get to the core of what went wrong.

Several months after our breakup, there was a bad thunderstorm in Swansea, and the large lamppost clock in the center of town, a block from my office, was damaged. For five weeks, the clock read 12:30. Not only was it a painful reminder of Leo's last words to me, but it was devastating in that I saw him for the last time at 12:30, on a Thursday night, when we had tried for the last time to make things right.

The Swansea City Council finally had the clock fixed, but no matter what the time of day it read thereafter, I always thought about Leo when I looked at it. I know this isn't much of a revelation. I thought of Leo when I looked at anything and everything.

Two days had passed since my encounter with Donatella. I wondered if Cody knew that we had met. I almost called him five times. But I restrained myself. I didn't know what to say, and I was so afraid of losing him. I wondered if this was the universe's way of telling me to appreciate the man I had and stop looking. I engaged myself in a plethora of theories, and nothing made sense. I wasn't even right once a day, much less twice.

I had made a date with Max for Thursday night, but I didn't want to go until I knew where things stood with Cody. Max deserved my full attention. And so, Wednesday afternoon, I called Cody and asked him if we could meet at my apartment that evening. A man with Cody's voice, but sounding nothing like the energetic man I knew, agreed to see me around eightish.

CODY, I HARDLY KNEW YE!

At 8:25, the man who had sounded like Cody on the phone and who looked like Cody in person entered my apartment. He looked at me, then

227

cast his eyes downward. I couldn't figure out if he was upset with me or afraid I was upset with him. The tension was thick like London fog, and my four-legged feline radar machine picked up on it.

Instead of taking a seat on the couch next to me, Cody sat alone in the stuffed chair next to it. Captain Jack, picking up on Cody's self-imposed "isolation," began ominously circling the legs of the coffee table, one at a time. He would stop momentarily to sniff the dying leaves from the Porter Williams bouquet that had fallen, bat them with his paw, then circle another leg. Cody became fixated with Jack's routine, and it was obvious that doing so was easier than focusing on me. When Jack had finished with the coffee table's legs and approached the agitated rocker's legs, Cody's nerves got the better of him. He stood up momentarily to ward off whatever he thought my furry bodyguard might do. Jack hissed, then hissed again. Finally, appearing satisfied that he had sufficiently neutralized any threat, Jack slunk back underneath the coffee table, where he crouched facing Cody. Staring.

Except for the "Hello, Molly" Cody had muttered at the door, this wordless scene went on for a good five minutes but felt like an interminably long bad movie. I wanted to start a dialogue and end the collective misery, but I wasn't sure what to say.

"You have any beer?" Cody choked out.

"I think I have a six-pack of Sam Adams in the fridge. Want one?"

"Yeah. Thanks. No glass."

I went to the kitchen to grab Cody's beer and decided to pour myself a glass of white wine. I saw no good reason for Cody to be the only one to benefit from libation.

Cody took the bottle from me, downed a swig, and waited until I had sat down to begin speaking. "Well, Molly, I guess we have some things to talk about."

Successfully, I fought off the tears that I knew would well up in my eyes if I let them. There was a huge wall between us, but it was transparent, and I could still see Cody's beautiful brown eyes, and I wished we could just forget everything and do some "world rocking."

"You met Donatella."

"Yes."

"But it wasn't until this past Monday that you figured out who she is. Or at least that's what I'm surmising."

"You're surmising correctly."

Cody guzzled such an enormous amount of beer at once that I

thought it prudent to get him a second bottle so as to not interrupt whatever he was going to tell me. What disturbed me was that while at first it seemed that he was nervous telling me the truth, whatever it was, he also seemed angry with me. I didn't know what I had done.

"I think this will be easiest for us both if you don't interrupt me just yet."

"Sure," I said, "but how about something to eat with your beer?"

"I've eaten. Just let me talk, Molly."

"Sorry," I said, slinking back in my seat.

"Remember last week, when you told me that you met a young girl who said her mom was an … I can't remember the words … "

"Aunt trap but newer."

"Right," he said. "And I recognized those words as meaning 'entrepreneur.' I knew at that moment the young girl must've been Donatella. Her mother, as you might know, isn't exactly thrilled with her Starbucks gig … "

I swallowed the lump in my throat as Cody confirmed that Barbarino was the mother.

" … and so she tells people that she's an entrepreneur. You probably don't know this, but she makes this funky jewelry that she's always trying to sell, and 'entrepreneur' is her favorite self-description." (I wanted to contribute some descriptive words of my own but thought better of it.)

I nodded to let Cody know I was listening, but that I respected his wish not to be interrupted.

"The next morning you offered to let me stay and sleep in. I wanted to, believe me, but all I could think to do was to run over to Starbucks to ask Barb what was going on. In fact, you walked right by the window, and I was so sure you were going to look in, but you seemed absorbed in whoever you were talking to on your cell."

As soon as Cody said that, I remembered everything perfectly. Tony had called that morning in a bad mood, and I'd lost all interest in Starbucks as I passed.

"Molly, that funky little girl you met is mine: the result of being a young guitarist who chose to forget that actions have consequences. But that doesn't mean I'm sorry she's here. She's the light of my life. I just wish the circumstances were different. Some eleven plus years ago, I met Barb backstage after a concert. Quite frankly, I barely remember her from that night. Weed, booze, and too many women can confuse the mind. Anyway, I traveled a lot in those days and didn't see Barb again for three years. When we met again, she quickly reminded me who she was and told me that I had a daughter."

I gasped.

"Yeah, that was my reaction, too." He paused. "If you're wondering if I just took her at her word, hell no. I had a paternity test. Two of them. Donatella is definitely my little girl. I fell in love with her on the spot, Molly, and by that time, I would have been devastated not to be her father. Quite frankly, Donie is the real reason that I stayed with her mother for as long as I did. I wanted to explain that to you when we met, but it was TMI for the moment. You know?"

I nodded in agreement.

"Donie doesn't even remember me *not* being in her life. Things were tough, so we moved to White Plains for several years and rented my parents' guesthouse. It was good at first, but I was also younger and didn't have my priorities in the same order they're in now. I tried to make it work. But more and more, Barb wanted to control everything in my life. Remember the way she tried to chase you off that night you first came to my gig? Well, she pretty much spewed the same kind of venom toward my entire fan base, not to mention every female friend I have. Or had. I was so angry with myself for having let it go on for so long. Not only that, I knew that it was my daughter, not her mother, who I was in love with, and extricating myself from the misery was way overdue. I'm not going to get into my life story, but I spent a whole lot of miserable years going nowhere fast. Every time I'd move forward, Barb's jealousy and interference would push me back. Something had to give, so, I decided to move back to Swansea. That wasn't working; I didn't see enough of my little girl. So, after a little while, Barb and Donie moved here, too."

"So you all live together again?" I broke in, realizing that I'd never been to Cody's apartment and feeling stupid for having been so dense. "That's some breakup!"

"No," Cody said firmly. "We *don't* live together. We *did* break up. At least, I broke up with her; I'm hoping she'll break up with me and move on. Whatever. We do live close to one another, and Donie lives with us both. I hadn't invited you over yet because I didn't want you to see her things before I could tell you about her."

I figured I had let Cody talk long enough without interruption, so I threw in a question.

"Why was your daughter hanging out on the front steps of my building?"

230

"You think I didn't want to know the same thing? Barb found out where you live, and as I guess you know, she brought Donie and two neighbor kids by on Halloween." (I was grateful that "Tigger" and "Eeyore" were not Cody's.) "I'm pissed about it, Molly, but not only did Barb do that, but she told Donie you were the lady who wanted to take Daddy away from them."

"Oh, my God," I said.

"Donie is a smart kid. She knows that her mother is difficult *and* a jealous person. She's seen Barb in action—way too many times for my taste. So, while she's loyal to her mother, she will always check things out for herself. Believe it or not, she knows to take Mommy with a big grain of salt. That's something I'm grateful for and pissed off about all at the same time. I don't like my daughter being used as a pawn in Barb's games. I'm going to sue for full custody, Molly, and that's one of the reasons I was thinking about opening an art gallery. To put down roots. Do you think I was happy to find out that Donie was hanging around this building? Barb is supposed to be supervising her afterschool activities but apparently thought spying on you and me should be one of them. I'm furious." Cody took another swig of beer. "Damn, I'm pissed!"

As much as I wanted to hear everything Cody had to stay, I didn't want him to stray too far from the most important part of our conversation: our relationship. (This might be a good place for me to remind anyone reading this to be careful what you wish for.)

"After you saw Barbarino that morning and figured out what was going on, why didn't you tell me when you got back from New York? You know, that night you said you had something special for me."

Halfway through his second beer, Cody checked to make sure Jack, who was still crouching, hadn't come any closer or raised his hackles, then continued to speak. "I bought something for you in New York. A necklace. With a heart on it. I was looking forward to giving it to you."

"So what happened?"

"Remember I told you that I had to stop by Burt's before coming over that night?"

"Yeah, and ... "

"Well, I was so excited about the necklace, I showed it to Burt's wife, Aubrey. I don't think you ever met her, but she was at the Rolling Beetle the same night you were. She didn't know you by name, so I described you."

"Okay," I said, feeling something evil about to encroach on my

231

space.

"She remembered you, Molly. She remembered Barb attacking you. Only she was surprised that you were and the same girl I'd been seeing. Wanna know why?"

"I guess you're going to tell me," I said, not liking his tone.

"Aubrey told me she'd seen you on two different Saturday nights at the same restaurant where she goes with her folks."

I blanched. I suddenly realized who had been staring at me on my dates with Alan.

"She said that the first time she saw you with the guy, she couldn't tell what your relationship was, but said she only noticed you because you had some kind of crazy outfit on that got the attention of everyone at her table. And apparently half of the restaurant."

I was horrified. I had made far more of a public fashion statement than I'd realized, and now it was going to doom my relationship with Cody.

Cody, who was now lit up, went on. "Molly, she said she had seen you just this past Saturday night, and you were holding hands with the guy, looking as cozy as cozy can be. Is that true?"

I was busted. I could see how bad it looked, and I didn't know what to say.

"That guy I was with, that was Alan T. Cressman. Remember him? The guy I was with the night you met me at the other Starbucks?"

"So? Okay, thanks for the ID. But how does that change anything?"

"There's this socialite in town, Naomi Hall-Benchley, who is always trying to set me up and run slash ruin my life. I'm not even going to get into it with you, because it's simultaneously complicated and stupid, but I went out with Alan both times because I thought he was part of her evil plan, so to speak, and I wanted to make them both pay."

"Huh?"

"Just listen. I went out with him pretending to be interested just to throw a wrench into whatever plans I thought the two of them had cooked up. But at the last dinner, I realized that Alan hated her every bit as much as I did. So, when Aubrey saw us holding hands, it was because I was just being sympathetic to some things going on in his life that he had told me about."

Cody finished the second Sam Adams and put the bottle down. Without asking, he got up, walked to the fridge, and took another bottle.

232

He popped off the top with the wall opener and came back to his chair.

"Molly, that's lame. That's #@$*ing lame!"

"It's the truth!"

"The whole truth, Molly? Do you have any interest in that guy at all?"

"Maybe a little. But not so much."

Cody began angrily pounding the arm of the chair as Jack's tail puffed out and his furry backside began to twitch in anticipation of an attack.

"Maybe a little, but not so much," Cody repeated. "MAYBE A LITTLE, BUT NOT SO MUCH? *#@% THAT, MOLLY!"

"Cody, please!"

"Anyone else you're seeing?"

I was dead in the water. "Cody, I told you the other night. I'm only having one sexual relationship, and it's with you. There hasn't been anyone else. I have some male friends who I see, but they're just friends. Tony is a friend from high school, and Max is just a friend. We're not dating."

Technically, I had told the truth.

"Oh, so there are four of us! Gee, maybe we can start a weekly poker game and give you a night off. What do you say, Molly?"

"Cody, stop!"

"No, I'm pissed! I thought we were a duo, a couple. You and me! I was going to tell you about Donatella on Sunday night. And give you the necklace. That's what I had planned until I learned what you'd been up to with, what's his name, Alan?"

I didn't know what to say but it suddenly dawned on me that Cody had things to own up to as well. "Wait, you were coming over on Sunday night to tell me the truth and bring me a gift. Right?"

"Right."

"And before you came you talked to this Aubrey person" (bitch!) "who told you I'd been out with Alan, holding hands, and you were pissed, right?"

"Right!"

"So you neither gave me the necklace nor told me about your daughter. Right?"

"Right."

"So you asked me if anyone else was rockin' my world, and when I said no, you were still pissed. Way pissed. But you took me to BED anyway. Are you freakin' kidding ME?"

Now it was Cody's turn to falter. But he quickly recovered. "Molly, sorry if this sounds bad, but if things were over between us, damn it, I wanted one more night to remember you by. I just couldn't give that up. I have needs."

"How sexcapadish of you, Cody! Maybe your early-rocker days aren't as over as you'd like to believe."

"Whatever," Cody said, sounding a bit like Donatella. "If you're so mature and responsible, tell me this. When you figured out that young girl was my daughter, and she was hanging out where she had no business being, why didn't you put her welfare first and give me a call?"

"You're gonna blame *me* for Barbarino's shameful lack of parenting skills?"

"A kid roaming the streets is a kid roaming the streets. Maybe you're not fit to be a mother!"

At that stinging remark, I burst into tears, but that didn't stop Cody.

"Oh, Molly, word to the wise. Next time you don't want to be seen, don't go to that place you went with what's-his-name. From what Aubrey tells me, the maître d' has a bad rep for ratting people out. In fact, he gets paid to do so. A little side business. Sweet, huh? I thought you might want to know that when you cheat on your next boyfriend."

Naomi, I thought. That's how she knew we were there. The rat in the tuxedo told her—for cash!

"Cody, please … "

"I can't trust you. I thought I had found someone special. I thought you were so different from Barb."

"I am nothing like that woman," I said through my tears. "And you need to remember that trust is a two-way street. I told you, I haven't been with any other men. I don't know what you do when you're out of town. Don't you hang out with women that you know? It's not like we ever got together and set ground rules that I went and broke. This is a very new relationship—"

"That got old fast!" Cody snapped, as Jack lurched for his right leg, sinking his teeth into Cody.

"OUCH!" he said, downing the last of the third beer. "I'm so outta here, Molly, it's not funny. Tell your bodyguard to chill."

Before I could say another word, Jack hissed, Cody was gone, and I had only three empty beer bottles and a broken heart to prove he had been there.

234

MORNING SLUDGE AND VIOLINS ... VIOLINS?

I think you know enough about me by now to figure out what kind of night I had after Cody left, so, I'll go light on the details. Just know that I didn't call a soul and alternately sobbed and dozed my way to morning. To say that I was exhausted by the time day broke would be a vast understatement of fact. I was wrecked: like a slain monster dragged from the crypt and injected with some kind of life serum, I attempted to transport myself to the office, my day crypt, running solely on toxic fumes. It was not a pretty sight.

I made it in just under the wire and was kind of surprised not to see Randy anywhere in sight. Half asleep, I poured myself a cup of black sludge. By sheer luck, it went into the cup. Once in my office, I took several sips, hung up my coat, sat in my chair, and without even knowing I was doing so, laid my head on my arms and drifted off. (I've been *very* tired at work before, but not like this!)

My first thought upon hearing a violin concerto was that I had been feeling *so* sorry for myself that I was dreaming of violins as a musical accompaniment to my misery. To add to this delusion, when I lifted my head and opened my eyes, I saw a tuxedo-clad violinist standing before my desk, playing. Not knowing whether closing my eyes or fully opening them would make the apparition (though pleasant) dissipate, I opened my eyes and sat up. By this point, two other violinists had joined him, and there I was, wrecked at my desk, being serenaded by three dark-haired men at five minutes after nine.

It could have been a dream: even the part where I saw Randy eagerly watching for my response. But it was not. It was, however, the most bizarre start to a day in the office I had ever experienced. For the brief minute or two that they played, several coworkers had meandered over toward my door.

Luckily, as soon as Randy came into my office, noticing the red swelling under my eyes and the Pillsbury puffiness of my eyelids, he silenced the bowed string instrument men with a smile. They nodded graciously and turned to leave. Randy whispered something to them, shook the right hand of each one, then shut the door for a couple minutes of alone time with me.

"Randy, you're never going to believe this," I told him, "but I'm so out of my mind that I'm thinking I just saw and heard three violinists here in my office. You're here to confirm my delusion, right?"

"Oh, Molly Rose. I hired those delightful men to play for Kyle and my special dinner on the eighteenth. They have such an interesting story, I have learned, so I have decided to feature them in an upcoming column. That's why they were here. I thought it would be a treat for you to begin your day with some culture, but apparently, from the looks of things, you have yet to end the previous day."

"I'm so sorry I couldn't fully appreciate them, but I know Kyle will. I'm sure it will be a very memorable night for you both."

"As I take it last night was for you, but not of the good kind."

I began to weep. As much as I would have preferred to replay the scene in its entirety, I was well versed in the art of quick recap. Randy, in respect of our mutual time pressures, responded with various facial and eye movements rather than speech until I got to the part where Cody said that perhaps I wasn't fit to be a mother. Knowing how much I did want children, Randy felt my pain.

"Oh, Molly Rose! That is untrue and uncalled for!"

"He was just hurting," I said.

"Do not defend!" Randy admonished me. "Clearly, he was hurting. But you were both in pain, and you did not hurl any nastiness at him, did you?"

"No."

"Good. Now listen to Randy. There is nothing here that cannot be sorted out. Give him time, and give yourself time. If indeed it is Cody that you want."

"All I know, Randy, is that losing him this way has hit me hard. I'm feeling a tremendous loss and an unsettling sense of déjà vu." Randy walked around the desk, gave me a hug, and went back to work. Somehow, I managed to do the same.

Around noon, Max called to confirm our date for the evening. In all of the madness, I had forgotten about him. Before I even had a chance to tell him I wasn't up for dinner, he suggested that we just meet in the park after work and schedule dinner another night when I was feeling better. I nearly declined but decided that a short diversion with my handsome friend might be the perfect antidote to my wretched state of being.

NOT IN THE MOOD FOR PICK-UP SCHTICKS!

Just as I arrived at the park, Max apologetically texted me that he was running a few minutes late. I didn't mind. It had been a beautiful day, and once again, the breathing of fresh air was just what I needed. Being at one with nature was always healing; being hit on was not.

Wearing the same Eskimo jacket, now with a broad silk scarf looped under his chin, Cal Leighton and his gin and tonic approached me. This time, he was speaking with a ghastly British accent. "I do say, my dear woman, perhaps you can be of assistance. I seem to have gotten my ascot around my neck. I do say, it makes it terribly difficult to sit down."

"Then I do say you should continue standing. I would just appreciate it if you would do so anywhere but in front of me."

I had inadvertently spurred him on. "So you won't mind if I follow behind you, then?"

"That's usually what asses do," a woman next to me said. I nodded my thanks to her and slipped out of Cal's view and ran right into Max.

"Exquisite timing!" I told him as we hugged.

"Not the finger-gun guy again?"

"I'm afraid so. Except tonight he's British and has his ascot around his neck."

Max laughed. "Poor guy. I wonder if he ever thought to simply say hello to a woman."

"Doubtful," I said. "That would be too obvious."

Max looked at me and smiled. "Some of the best things in our lives are hiding in plain sight."

"Maybe they are."

"You okay, Molly? You look tired. Beautiful, but tired. Do you want to get a drink and sit?"

"Sure. But no wine for me this time. Sparkling water will do just fine."

I grabbed the last empty table, by a beautiful oak tree, as Max went off to get our drinks.

"Here you go," Max said, placing my drink before me, as he brushed a few dead leaves from the table. "I'm so glad you could meet me tonight, Molly. When we spoke, you sounded out of sorts. Quite selfishly, I was afraid you would cancel our dinner plans, so I asked you to meet me here instead. I do hope you'll give me a rain check for dinner, though. I'd like to treat you to something special."

"Thanks, Max. You're right; I just wasn't up for much tonight."

"You look upset, Molly. Did something happen?"

I didn't know how to answer him.

"If it has to do with a man, and I'm pretty sure that it does, please feel free to share it with me, *if* you wish."

I had already spilled my guts to Randy over lunch (sounds appetizing, yes?), but as I had no intention of sharing my woes with another soul, but still being in need of doing so, I thought Max was probably the perfect person. As delicately as I could, I told him about my fizzled romance with Cody.

"I don't think it's over," Max said when I had finished speaking. "Not unless you want it to be. But no, I don't."

"He was *so* angry with me."

"He'll cool down. Didn't you tell your friend Randy that he was 'just hurting'? I think that was a wise assessment of fact. I'm sorry if our friendship in any way contributed to this blow-up. I don't suppose it would help if I told him we're just friends."

"Oh, no, Max. He'd take one look at you and go ballistic."

Max smiled. Realizing that I had inadvertently just told Max how gorgeous I found him to be, I wasn't sure where to go next.

"It sounds as if Cody has a lot on his plate. Raising a child isn't easy, and being attached to a crazy ex who doesn't want to be an ex can be very stressful. It sounds as if there are a lot of pressures in his life, and you were his port in a storm, of sorts. I agree with your friend Randy, the remark about you not making a fit mother was vastly uncalled for, but I don't believe he meant it for a moment. I think right about now he's probably feeling a lot worse than you are. You were right when you said he was hurting. I know you are, too, but give it a bit of time, my friend. No matter what happens between the two of you, end it civilly. End as friends. I don't know if he's the man for you, and quite frankly, it sounds as though you don't either. But it's very clear you do care about him."

"Thank you for listening, Max. I'm very glad to call you my friend."

We talked for another half hour, but Max, who saw I was fading fast, suggested we call it a night. As we passed through the hub of activity by the kiosk, Cal Leighton was still going great guns. His ascot had now been manipulated (as best as one could do) to resemble an eighteenth-century jabot—you know, that lacy-looking tie that gave Austin Powers such memorable flair.

We watched in amusement as Cal descended on a new target. "Crikey, baby! You look shagalicious!"

"Go shag yourself, douche bag," came the animated response.

238

"Oh, behave!" Cal responded cheerfully.

"Amazing, Molly. He's not a bad-looking guy. I wonder why in the world he needs to make himself such a laughingstock?"

"Who knows? Low self-esteem, maybe. It affects people in strange ways."

"That it does. Well, I have a feeling good ol' Cal will find his perfect match. Every pot has a lid, you know. Cal just may have flipped his, but I'm sure he'll find another one."

Max and I laughed all the way back to my apartment building, where we said our goodnight on the front steps. My friend had made me feel worlds better. Captain Jack and I had an early dinner, and by 8:30, I was fast asleep.

I SUBSIST UNDER THE RADAR

For the next five days, I stayed on the down low. I was simultaneously missing Cody and feeling angry with him. It occurred to me had I not called *him* that night, I may have never heard from him again. Would he have called *me* or just taken Aubrey's word for it that I was some kind of two-timing slut and simply disappeared from my life? Did it even matter? Bottom line: he was gone, and nothing I said had made an iota of difference.

At the risk of sounding pathetic, I will confess that I altered my route to the office, adding another three minutes onto my walk, just to avoid walking past Starbucks. I had no idea if Barbarino knew of our breakup, but I was not going to give her any reason to gloat.

That weekend, Alan called to let me know that Naomi was stepping up the pressure to force him to take her cousin Muriel to the foundation Christmas party. I sympathized, and thought it prudent (and only right) to let him know that the maître d' at "our restaurant" was a spy. He didn't ask how I found out, and I didn't offer. Alan, like me, seemed quite consumed with the pressures in his own life. The absence of rhymes, effusive compliments, and changing personalities suggested that his "personal metamorphosis" was on temporary hold while he dealt with myriad stressors at work.

Max called regularly to check on me, giving me an opportunity to be a friend in return, and Tony, still worse for the wear, called to let me know that no matter what was going on in his life, he would be wearing a smile and his best suit of clothes for our special date on the eighteenth, his birthday.

239

Lisette Brodey

I did venture out into civilization once. That Sunday, I went shopping with Hannah, but at my request, we drove to a place about an hour outside Swansea. In addition to buying our parents' gift, I wanted to find Tony something special for his birthday and finish my other holiday shopping. I filled Hannah in on everything that was going on. My little sister is just a great listener who manages to offer uplifting thoughts minus the crazy ideas. And she never judges or berates me for not having told her such-and-such sooner. She's thoughtful to a fault. One caveat: I felt terrible when, once again, she kept her wedding plans to a ridiculous minimum to avoid hurting me. I'm a big girl. I can take it. If nothing else, that Sunday gave me a chance to let my sister know that she had every right to crow about her happiness without fear of sending her older sister into a state of permanent disrepair.

That Sunday evening, Claudia called. She was assuming that Max had asked me to the foundation Christmas party and was primed with advice on how to explain Alan to Max and vice versa. I reminded her that Max and I were just friends, and she reminded me that friends can escort friends to functions. I reminded her that I did not want to go to any society functions, especially one where the she-devil would be in attendance and would likely do something drastic to discredit me in front of Max while simultaneously shoving me into the loving arms of Art's dateless associate. I did not want to tell her that I had a special date with Tony that same evening, nor did I want to explain my despondency over the dissolution of a relationship that she never even knew existed.

She sounded almost disappointed that there were no schemes to be planned, no outfits to put together, and no advice to give. I felt guilty for shutting her out but couldn't forget what "helping hands" had done for my relationship with Leo. And yes, I pointed out to myself that I had lost Cody all by my lonesome.

Claudia reminded me that friends talk to friends, and I reminded her that friends don't push friends to talk and that sometimes we all need a bit of alone time. After a string of "reminders" back and forth, we said goodbye. I felt sad about withholding parts of my life but reminded myself that I had every right to make personal choices, and no doubt, Claudia had secrets of her own.

By the evening of December seventeenth, I was tired of feeling low and looking forward to my date the next evening with Tony. I was shoving Cody under a sofa cushion to snuggle up the spare change, and somehow, I would return to the land of the living.

Chapter 31: THE NIGHT THEY DROVE OLD SWANSEA DOWN

It was a dark and stormy night. No, it wasn't. It was a gray December day, and there was no rain in the forecast at all. Once in a while, the sun would peek through the clouds to wink at the small burb of Swansea, as if to say, "I know something you don't know." If my description of a semi-gloating sun sounds a bit over the top, perhaps after you hear what happened that night, you'll understand.

That morning, I woke up feeling better than I had in days. While I was far from copacetic about my current status with Cody, I was excited about Tony's birthday. I had splurged and bought him a terrific sports watch I knew he'd been eyeing and was looking forward to giving it to him during our cozy, fireside dinner at the Wellington Inn.

When I got to the office that morning, I was eager to share my enthusiasm with Randy and to see if he had solidified all of his plans for the violin-serenaded dinner he had planned in honor of Kyle's birthday. With all of the interruptions in their relationship, I knew Randy was dotting every "i" and crossing every "t" in the celebration.

Randy, my perpetual rock, was not in the office when I arrived. My first thought was that he had stopped off somewhere before work to make some last-minute arrangement, but when I saw Ray, who refused to look at me, my stomach flipped, then flopped, and I knew something was wrong.

Without making any eye contact at all, Ray followed me into my office and shut the door.

"Please, Molly, have a seat."

"Those must be some great shoes you're wearing," I said, sitting down behind my desk.

"What do you mean?"

"Well, you've been staring at them since I came in the door, and you've yet to look at me."

Startled, Ray looked up.

"Where's Randy?" I asked.

"Randy had a last-minute opportunity to interview a member of the New York Philharmonic. Fascinating story. I'm sure he'll tell you all about it. He caught an early train to New York. I expect him back in the office this afternoon."

"Oh," I said, hoping that all of the traveling wouldn't tucker Randy out for his big night.

"Look, Molly," Ray said, fidgeting with the frayed left cuff of his shirt. "This is about the most awkward thing I've ever had to say to an employee. Please don't interrupt me, or I'll never get it out. And before I say anything, I just need you to know that I despise the words that are going to come out of my mouth."

You're fired, Molly, I thought. What else could there be? You're fired. You're fired. You're fired. Right before Christmas. You're fired.

"I'm disgusted by what I'm about to say," he repeated, "but I am between a rock and a hard place. I hope you'll see that and take pity on me."

My rock was in New York, and the first "hard place" that came to mind was Naomi. Not only had she recently paid me a visit, but I remembered Randy telling me that her last call to Ray had frazzled him to the core.

"Please tell me Naomi Hall-Benchley has nothing to do with this."

Ray let his head fall into the open palm of his hands. I had my answer.

Finally, he looked up, took a deep breath to fortify himself, and began speaking. "Molly, as you well know, Naomi is eager for you to attend this foundation party tonight as a date for Art's colleague."

"Not THAT again! I told her my attendance was out of the question, Ray. I was under the impression that I worked for a newspaper, not an escort service. No! And that's my final answer."

"You see, Molly, grants from that foundation pay some of the salaries around here, and Naomi, along with her husband, sit on the board. I find it repugnant that I've been given this ultimatum, much less that I'm passing it on to you, but—"

"Fire me, then!" I blurted out. "Freakin' fire me, Ray. I won't be pimped out by the she-devil, even if it costs me my job."

Ray's head fell over into his sweating palms again. Once again, he took a few seconds, then looked up at me.

"*Your* job is not on the chopping block, Molly. Randy's is."

My jaw fell to the floor.

"You know that the Arts and Entertainment position has always been a soft-money—"

"Are you telling me that if I don't keep company with that guy at the party, *Randy* will lose his job?"

Ray nodded shamefully.

Tears fell liberally from my eyes. For the moment, there were no options. I was livid. I felt betrayed, manipulated, defeated, and dirtied. But

242

I knew the present moment was not the optimal time to deal with all of that. I looked at my distraught boss, who seemed to be mirroring my emotions. "What time do my mascara-streaked face and I have to be there?"

"Seven forty-five," came the barely audible response. "Swansea Court Hotel. Main ballroom."

MY GLORIOUS DAY CONTINUES

When Randy called me a half hour later, the grim tone in his voice told me that he already knew what had happened. I was scared to death that he was going to tell me that he had quit and was never coming back again.

"Where are you?" I asked.

"I'm at Avery Fisher Hall at Lincoln Center waiting to meet a brilliant cellist. I'll be interviewing him, and then I shall be lunching with him and his wife. I am slated to return home afterward, but I ought to just stay here and let the city swallow me whole. I knew this was going to happen. I told myself it was going to happen, and I chastised myself for having such thoughts."

"I'm surprised you didn't warn me," I said, finding his choice of words odd.

"Warn you?" Randy said. "That's an odd choice of words, Molly Rose. What are you talking about?"

"What are *you* talking about?"

"Kyle. Who else? The man called last night. He was said he was profusely apologetic and saddened, but with 'profound regret' he had to cancel our evening together. 'Profound regret.' Is that not a sweet kiss-off line? Every time I have allowed myself to think we were forging ahead, the man has bailed on me. On Thanksgiving he chose his brother, who had previously shunned him, over me."

"Oh, Randy, we talked about Thanksgiving so many times. I know it wasn't fair, but he wanted to reunite with his family. If he hadn't done so and remained estranged, Kyle might have resented you. You have to let that part of it go and be happy it worked out for him."

"If only that were all. He's clearly commitment-phobic, and quite frankly, I'm not so sure there's not someone else. I'm not only devastated, but I'm mortified, not to mention outraged and embarrassed that I now have to cancel all of my arrangements."

"Tony!" I shrieked. "Oh, my, God, Tony!"

"Not following you. How does Tony fit into my grave plight?"

243

"I have to cancel *my* dinner with Tony."

"Whatever for, Molly Rose? You can't do that to the poor man!"

"I have to. The she-devil is behind it. Our poor, mortified boss delivered the ultimatum this morning: accompany Art's dateless colleague to the foundation's annual holiday party or the foundation will cut funds and, um ... "

"What?" Randy asked angrily. "Tell me what will happen!"

"... um ... Ana will lose her job."

"How brutal! That sweet woman is working her way through college and trying to help her family at the same time."

"Exactly," I exclaimed. I hated lying to Randy. I *never* lie to Randy, but I was scared to death that in his distraught state, he would quit his job and simply tell Ray, Kyle, Naomi, and the entire foundation to go to hell, leaving himself without a salary and leaving me without my closest friend.

"I wish I were there," Randy said.

"Me, too," I said, thanking God that he wasn't. (Lying to Randy over the phone is one thing; in person: next to impossible.)

"Molly Rose, you're doing the right thing. But what you're being asked to do is beyond reprehensible, and something must be done about it. Just let Tony know that you had little choice and that you will reschedule. He'll be upset, but I'm sure he'll be fine with it."

"Oh, like you're fine with Kyle's cancellation?"

"Different situation. Mine is an ongoing occurrence; yours is not. A charming young woman is waving at me. I believe she is associated with my cellist. We will talk when I get back."

"I'm probably stepping out soon," I said. "Ray just emailed me to tell me to leave as early as I need to get ready, as long as my deadline is met. Wasn't that nice of the coward? And just as I was thinking of volunteering for night shift."

"Malfeasance shall have its just desserts," Randy said, as I could hear a chatty female voice addressing him. "Must go."

I clicked off from Randy and speed-dialed Tony while I still had my nerve.

THE PROS AND CONS OF VOICEMAIL

Who reading this hasn't been vastly relieved to reach someone's voicemail when bad news was to be delivered? Or perhaps when needing to return a phone call but not wanting to speak to the person, as I am guilty of doing as described in this very tome. That said, I was devastated to reach Tony's voicemail. To make matters worse, he had left a special message saying that he was unavailable for the day and would be checking his messages early that evening. I didn't know what to do. I called Tony's office at the university, hoping to catch him there. The student who picked up the phone told me that Tony was at a birthday lunch with some colleagues and then was heading off to see his son before a very important evening engagement. She said that I was welcome to leave a message, but he wouldn't get it until the next day. I left a message anyway.

I was a wreck. (Yes, I know, that's preposterous to conceive.) I called Tony's cell again and left a message asking him to please call me immediately. Hours passed. Not a peep. As it turned out, I wasn't able to leave work a moment before four o'clock, and thankfully, I missed Randy, who texted me to say he'd be in right around that time. He was so miserable about Kyle but had made an intelligent decision to write his piece about the cellist ahead of schedule, in the office, rather than go home and mope.

The only good thing about the wretched day, if one can call it that, is that I already had a hair appointment scheduled on the nose at five o'clock and had picked out a fabulous outfit ready to be worn. Having a little extra time, I decided to go home and feed Captain Jack, grab my outfit and accessories, then drive to the salon so that I could head to the dreaded soirée from there.

As I reached the front door of the hair salon, I had no choice: I had to leave my bad news on Tony's voicemail.

"Hi, Tony. It's Molly. As you know, I called several hours earlier and have been frantic to talk to you personally. I hate leaving bad news like this. I hate *having* bad news. I can't make our dinner tonight. I'll explain it to you when we talk, but I am being virtually forced to do something for work tonight or see a coworker laid off if I refuse. Tony, sharing this evening with you means everything to me; I just can't do it at the expense of someone's job. Please understand and reschedule. Any other night you want. Please don't be angry. I know you are, but please don't be. I'm so sorry."

I felt horrible. I wanted to tell him that it was Randy's job in question, but I was too afraid in his anger he might tell Randy, who then might resign before I had time to do damage control. Worse, I couldn't even wish Tony a happy birthday. Who leaves a message like I left with "Happy birthday" stuck to the end of it? One might as well be saying …

245

well, you know.

To magnify the muddle of my misfortune, my hair salon has a major dead zone beyond the reception area, and Tony wouldn't be able to call me back. Even with no dead zone, it's not a good idea to use a cell phone against hair dye or to have a personal conversation on speakerphone in a public place.

When my hairdresser, Nancy, saw me in tears, I was tempted to tell her to give me a Mohawk or to weave purple strands into my hair like Donatella's. I would have loved sticking it to Naomi Hall-Benchley, but not with the entire town looking on, not with Randy's job at stake and for that matter, my own.

I ARRIVE AT THE GATES OF HELL

My shimmering plum-colored dress and I arrived at the gates of, I mean the reception table outside the main ballroom at two minutes to eight.

Appropriately clad in a fiery red dress, the she-devil invaded my airspace only moments after I had checked my coat. She eyed me up and down like meat she was taking to market. Patting her braided updo, she fluttered her eyelids and smiled broadly at a passing photographer whose camera was pointed at a stunning young woman in a skintight black dress. Realizing that I had witnessed the photographer's snub, she glowered ever so quickly before resuming her standard posturing.

"Well, you do clean up nicely, Molly," she said. "The earrings are a bit too shimmery for my taste, but I suppose they match your purple party frock."

"And what a devilishly red frock you're sporting, Naomi. Something's missing! Oh, I know, it's your pitchfork. Perhaps you checked it by mistake."

She bit her tongue. "I'm just glad you showed. It wouldn't have been pretty had you not."

"Randy's job?"

"Whatever you're babbling about, I'm sure I have no idea."

"You won't get away with this, Naomi."

"You're here, are you not? Enough said. If you wouldn't spend so much time fighting me, you'd realize that I'm about to introduce you to an incredibly eligible and handsome man."

"Incredibly eligible and handsome men are known for getting dates all by their lonesome."

"You know, I wish I *had* a pitchfork right now. I'd stab you with it just to shut you up. To answer your ongoing lunacy, I have explained that *very busy* handsome, eligible men, new to a geographic region, often do require introductions to the right ... "

I had to laugh. She was about to compliment me and caught herself in the nick of time.

"Molly, just come with me already!"

She slapped a smile on her fake-tanned face, looped her arm through mine, and walked me through the dapper crowd toward Art Benchley and the man I'd come to think of as his "dateless colleague." From a distance, he appeared rather stiff and nervous, as if he were dreading the introduction as much as I was.

"This is Molly Hacker, a features reporter from the *Swansea Herald*," she said to the tall, handsome, and impeccably dressed man before me. "Molly, this is your date for the evening, Kyle Tillman. Kyle is new in town, from New York, and works for Bennett & Shane Limited, a fine company that works closely with the Benchley World Foundation."

Kyle and I just looked at each other. We both wanted to burst out laughing, but as if we'd known one another for years and already had a plan of action, we suppressed our laughter and chose another route.

"Molly Hacker," Kyle said. "Had I known you were so ravishingly beautiful, I would have never waited so long to meet you. I think I would have beat down your door like the big bad wolf. Wait, did he beat down the door or huff and puff? I can't remember!"

"Kyle, I'm blushing. I feel so *randy* just standing next to you!"

Naomi didn't know whether to be pleased or horrified, and Art just chuckled to himself as if he couldn't care less what was going on.

With the tension gone from his body, Kyle looked like an entirely different man. I could see that he was warm and loving and every bit the caring soul who had been described to me.

"Excuse us, Naomi," Kyle said, putting his arm around me, "I'm taking this enchanting creature to a more private spot where we can get to know one another. Drinks, dining, or dancing, Molly?"

"I love men who alliterate," I told him. "All three sound good to me!"

He let out a huge laugh that I knew didn't belong to him. As we walked away, I heard the she-devil say to her husband, "I told you they'd be a match made in heaven."

"I spend way too much time in hell, Naomi. I must have missed the news flash."

"I did this for you … " I heard her begin as we walked away.

Kyle and I grabbed a few hot hors d'oeuvres as we made our way to the bar. While we were waiting to get our drinks, I noticed Max in the throng, smiling longingly at me, as three women attempted to vie for his attention with their simpering smiles and small talk. So many men would have lapped up the attention, whereas Max seemed dismayed by it, and I understood why. It was all so phony. None of them could see beyond his looks, wealth, and social status.

Once having gotten our drinks, Kyle and I found our way to a more secluded part of the room and took a seat on a satin-covered mahogany bench.

"Can you believe this, Molly? How's Randy? I'm sick with worry over him."

"He's a wreck. He was in New York today. He told me he might as well stay and let the city swallow him whole, but I'm sure he's back by now. He's at the office working. I had a text from him when I left the hairdresser. Kyle, what happened? Why did you have to cancel at the last minute?"

"These people are unbelievable. I don't even work *for* the Benchleys; I just do business *with* them. That woman is the most controlling, conniving, neurotic mess I've had the displeasure to encounter in ages. Underneath the spit and polish, the coiffed hair and the designer clothes, is an insecure harridan. I'd like to blame her for this upheaval in my relationship with Randy, but it's my fault for not coming out to them. Or at the very least, just saying no."

I just looked at him, feeling lost for words.

"Molly … I feel like I should call you 'Molly Rose' … it's not that I'm in the closet; I just don't think my personal status, whether I'm seeing a man or a woman, is any of their business. I know I've let Randy down once too often. A couple of times I had to work late. It honestly couldn't be helped. Other times, I was roped into a last-minute social obligation and didn't want to tell them I was leaving my lover behind. I didn't want to open up a can of worms. It's none of their damn business."

"I understand, Kyle."

"But will Randy? He would've handled this entirely different because that's who he is. It's easier for him. I don't know how to explain myself to you. I can tell you that I'm very proud of who I am and proud of the man I love, who at this moment, I'm afraid, has anything but love for me."

"He's devastated. I think he'll come around, but you have to tell him what you've been going through because he does not understand. Can you blame him? Trying to keep it all to yourself hasn't been working. But I understand why you did it. I do."

"It was my fight," Kyle said. "I should have handled it much better. I should have given Randy more of an explanation. After Naomi pulled me aside to threaten me last night, I went right into a meeting. There was no chance for me to grab more than a moment of privacy beforehand. It wasn't my intention to be cryptic about anything. Still, I feel like a sniveling coward."

"I didn't receive *my* threat until this morning," I explained. "Naomi told my boss that the foundation would pull the grant for Randy's job if I didn't show. I had a date with my friend Tony. It's his birthday. Oh, and it's yours, too. Happy birthday, Kyle. For what it's worth."

"Thanks, Molly. Are you telling me that you came here tonight to save Randy's job?"

"The only reason."

"You're ever so much the best friend he told me you were. By the way, I was invited to this frolicking festivity weeks ago, but I declined. Last night Naomi told me that Art's father, Keaton Benchley, would take my snub personally if I were a no-show. Keaton Benchley's cousin, Walter Bennett, is the CEO of my company. Just as I was making my peace with that not-so-veiled threat, she not only insisted that I come, but told me I was to escort a very eligible bachelorette. Please don't take this the wrong way, but I couldn't help wonder why, if you were as gorgeous as you are and as she described, you would need to be set up on a blind date."

I laughed. "I had the exact same question about you. She's positively unreal. But what I *don't* get is why she does it. I hear bits and pieces from different people, but I can't say I understand."

"I spend a lot of time with Art Benchley. He tolerates his wife, at best. I think she's scared to death of losing him and everything that comes with being Mrs. Benchley. He doesn't care about my personal life, but his father does. Word has it that his father cares about every nuance of every person associated with the Benchley name. Quite frankly, she and her father-in-law would have made a better couple. From what I have surmised, if she can please the senior Benchley, she's in for the long haul because Art's financial interests, his position at the company, and his name in his father's will mean everything. She hooked us up to please the old man. If Art won't play matchmaker to appease his father, she will. To her, she's doing it for her husband, but we both know she's doing it for herself. That much aside, I sense it's a huge game to her, not to mention the control freak in her."

"She makes bets with other socialites."

"So I've heard. Playing with other people's lives is mere folly for her. What am I going to do? I'm a wreck about Randy. I can't lose him."

"If you're as truthful with him as you've just been with me, I think he will understand. Maybe not immediately, but I believe he will. He doesn't want to lose you either."

Kyle looked uneasy. He stuck out his chin as he bit his upper lip, contemplatively.

"Is there something else?"

"I'm afraid so, Molly. You know that Randy's ex is Porter Williams, right?"

I looked at him. "Please don't tell me you dated him, too!"

"Worse," Kyle said. "I dated his sister, Sylvie."

"Oh, wow!"

"In fact, I originally met both Keaton Benchley and Walter Bennett at an affair in New York with Sylvie. So you see, Molly, they know me as a straight man. If you're wondering why Naomi and company never considered the alternative, that may be one reason why. Sylvie and I are still the best of friends. She helped me to be who I am today. I come from a rather rigid family. It just wasn't easy to embrace my sexuality. When I finally came out to my family two years ago, my parents weren't happy, but my brother disowned me."

"And Randy knows nothing about your former life with Sylvie?"

Kyle shook his head dejectedly. "Only the part about my brother."

"Oh, God, Kyle."

"Canceling our date will seem like nothing when he finds this out." Kyle looked pleadingly into my eyes. He wanted so desperately for me to tell him Randy would be just fine with all of it. I couldn't. I put my hand on top of his. Two defeated spirits, we just stared ahead, our respective thoughts burning in our brains through the loud clinking of glasses, the holiday music, and the laughter of the local aristocracy.

DECK THE HALLS

"Well, Molly, I think we ought to mingle before we attract too much attention here by our lonesome. Let's try to blend in as best we can."

"Agreed," I said to Kyle, who had stood up and offered me his hand.

As we began walking toward the crowd, I saw Alan by the bar waiting for a drink. His hair was still longer, but he was dressed in a beautiful gray but very traditional suit and was not wearing his stud earring. By his side was a tall, heavyset woman with her dark brown hair pulled back into a braided bun. Minimally made up, she seemed very self-conscious in her lace-trimmed, green velour dress, as if the dress and Alan were incongruous with every part of her.

Looking very sullen, I saw Alan attempt a smile as he handed her a drink and took his own. Then, as he saw me, he brightened considerably, while his date remained expressionless.

"Molly, how nice to see you," Alan said, looking enviously at Kyle. "I'd like you to meet Muriel Hall. She's Naomi's cousin."

"Oh," I said, exchanging brief glances with Alan, then with Kyle.

"Muriel, this is Molly Hacker."

"Nice to meet you," I said.

I turned to Kyle. "This is my friend Alan Cressman. Alan, Muriel, this is Kyle Tillman. He does a lot of business with Art Benchley."

"Oh!" Alan said, his eyes widening. "I see."

Just as I gave myself credit for communicating our respective situations without saying anything directly, Muriel surprised us all by speaking.

"So, Molly, did my cousin Naomi con you two into banding together for the evening?"

Alan, Kyle, and I shared a look.

"Well, did she?" Muriel turned to Alan. "Come on, we all know she twisted *your* arm to bring me. You're not interested in a galumphing gal like me. Not in this lifetime. I saw the way your eyes caught on fire when you looked at Molly. You've got as much interest in me as you do in a clogged toilet."

"Oh, Muriel ... " Alan said. "Don't say that."

"It's true. So what did she threaten you with? The spreading of vicious lies? The loss of the Benchley account? What?"

"The latter," Alan mumbled.

"Chin up," Muriel said to him as Kyle and I listened in horror. "It's not your fault. I just don't understand why my cousin insists on putting people in these agonizing situations. You think I'm not demoralized going out with man after man who shrinks in horror when he sees me?"

"I promise you I didn't shrink in horror," Alan said. "I can surely attest to that, Muriel."

"Sure you did. I'm not the social butterfly a man like you would care about," Muriel said. "For starters, I'm too big to flutter off the ground."

There was something rather charming about her, and we all laughed.

"You're just lovely," Kyle told her.

"And you're probably gay," she shot back.

Kyle and I didn't dare look at one another, and Alan just stood there, feeling a shame that was not his to own.

"Muriel, may I ask you something?"

"Shoot, Molly!"

"If you know what Naomi's up to, why did you agree to come out with Alan?"

"Why? Why? Why? Believe it or not, I have offered a flat refusal many a time. But sometimes it just gets too lonely sitting at home. Especially during the holidays. Deck the halls and all that. I'm sure there's one Hall we'd all like to deck."

We all laughed. Muriel continued speaking. "And, well, because I keep hoping *he* is out there. He's probably not going to be the guy I came with, but if there's a love connection, even a *like* connection, who cares? A shot in the dark is better than no shot at all. I might be married now had Naomi not interfered, you know."

"How's that?" Alan asked.

"Well, about two years ago, I met a wonderful man. Fred Homer. He's in the HVAC field. Heating ventilating and air conditioning. He was fixing central air at my office. Instant chemistry, just like in the movies. Things heated up just as he was cooling things down. Can you guess what happened?"

"What did *she* do?" Alan said, feeling her pain.

"A month into our relationship, I made the fatal error of introducing Fred to my family. Presto! He had a job offer in Chicago as a high-level supervisor for an HVAC company out there. How could I tell the guy that my cousin had arranged it all just to erase any chance that he might one day tarnish the Hall coat of arms? Bought and paid for or not, it was a life-changing opportunity for him. And he deserved it. So, at least indirectly I made his life better. The man had more class and compassion than my hollow-hearted cousin will ever have. Six months out there, Fred met a woman in his apartment building. Doing laundry. They're married with a baby on the way. Just got the news today. In a Christmas card. So, yes, I could have stayed home tonight and moped by the television, but here I am with Alan T. Cressman, the latest swashbuckler that Naomi has blackmailed into dating her oafish cousin."

"I'm sorry," Alan said. "What are oat fish?"

"OAFISH," Muriel said. "Clumsy, awkward, like an oaf."

"Ah!" said Alan. "That would describe many of my own foibles. Like the verbal one I just perpetrated upon the three of you. Molly can bear witness to my myriad blunders in this area. Molly and the Beefeater Man."

"You're a gentle soul," Muriel said to Alan. "But you still don't have one iota of attraction for me."

Just as Alan was about to stumble over a response, Max showed up. He said hello to all of us, then turned to Muriel with a dazzling smile. "Would you do me the honor of dancing with me?"

"You can't be ser—"

"I would love to have this dance," Max repeated firmly to a stunned Muriel.

I looked over Max's shoulder and saw the collective horror of the three women who, swathed in insincerity, had been battling for Max's attention. Max's choice for a dance partner clearly insulted their dignity, as each pouted in her own respective huff.

Muriel handed Alan her drink. "Be a love and hold this for me." She turned to me with an excited whisper. "He's just being nice, I know that. But I'm going to feel like Cinderella, even if I do turn into a pumpkin when it's all over."

HAVE YOURSELF A BUBBLY LITTLE CHRISTMAS

Max spent a good fifteen minutes whirling Muriel around the dance floor, while Kyle and I chatted with Alan. By the time Muriel returned to Alan, ego boosted, she seemed happy to spend some time in his good company. Kyle and I had walked through the crowd, stopping to talk to many people that we each knew. Peripherally, I caught several glimpses of the gloating she-devil, reveling in her perceived victory.

Kyle and I, despite our vast relief at realizing we were one another's blind date, became increasingly worried about Randy and Tony, and the pain our respective cancellations had had on them. I had no clue what Tony might be feeling or thinking. I hoped he had heard my voicemail and had not come to my door only to find me not at home. I wanted to call him, but there was no place I could talk privately and thought it was better to wait until I had both the time and privacy to sort things out. Kyle felt exactly the same about Randy but was scared to death that the she-devil may have served as a catalyst in ruining what Kyle described as "the best relationship of my life." And, of course, I was also a wreck over Randy, especially knowing he was suffering far more than he needed to be.

"Molly!" came the excited greeting behind me.

I turned to find Claudia, gorgeously attired in a salmon-colored dress, sipping a glass of champagne and staring wide-eyed at Kyle and me.

"Claude!"

"Don't act so surprised to see me, Molly. I told you Colin and I would be here. Who's this dashing hombre by your side?"

"This is Kyle Tillman. Kyle, this is my very good friend Claudia Porter-Bellman."

"Nice to meet you, Claudia."

"You, too, Kyle. So, you're Molly's best-kept secret."

"No," we said in unison, but Claudia didn't hear us.

"Why didn't you just tell me you were seeing someone?" Claudia asked. "It would explain a lot, you know?" She sidled up against me and spoke quietly through clenched teeth. "Like why Max came stag and Alan is with someone else but keeps looking over at you."

Poor Kyle tried to look nonchalant as he looked at Claudia with a fixed smile on his face.

"Best friends share the important things in their lives," Claudia said, her mouth resuming full function. "Don't you think so, Kyle? Friends don't keep things from those closest to them."

Kyle looked like he wanted to evaporate into the ether. Finally, Claudia noticed our mutual discomfort.

"What? What am I missing?"

"Claude, Kyle has been dating *Randy*. It's a long story, but the she-devil and her machinations are what brought us here together tonight—as each other's blind date."

"Oh, my God! I'm so sorry. And here I'm running off at the mouth like a fool. I'm so sorry."

Kyle smiled and looked at her now-empty champagne glass. "No problem. Blame it on the bubbles."

"What?" Claudia said suspiciously. "You just met Molly tonight, yet you know about 'bubbles'?"

"I've been acquainted with champagne for many years," Kyle said diplomatically through his confusion.

"Oh, of course," Claudia said. "So sorry. You're right. Molly can explain that inane bubbles thing to you later. Right after she explains why she didn't fill me in on any of this. Yes, yes, Molly will have a lot to jabber on about, don't you think?"

"Perhaps," Kyle said. "If you'd let her."

Claudia looked mortified. "I'm so sorry. I had a horrid day working on the lean, green ecological machine's campaign. The details are a snooze, trust me, but I'm afraid I relied a little too much on the Piper-Heidsieck to derattle my nerves. I probably didn't need three glasses of *bubbles*."

"A little like bringing coals to Newcastle," I said.

"That is so not funny. Don't embarrass yourself in front of Randy's handsome friend. If you two have just met, you'll want to preserve your dignity. Kyle, did you know that Molly and Randy are super-duper close friends? They share everything. So much so, that I think Molly forgets she has a best girlfriend. But we won't talk about that now, as I can see you've both got heaping spoonfuls of stress on your plate. Oh my, what do you know, my husband is waving at me. I'm sure he wants me to nourish myself with some of the spectacular dishes on the buffet table. Have you two feasted your eyes on the food yet? Or better yet, feasted *on* the food? Try the artichoke, leek, and potato gratin. Must skedaddle. For now. Kyle, I'm charmed. Molly, we'll talk. I mean, we'll talk!"

And as I stood there looking after her, wondering how everything had turned into such a mess, I had no clue that the real "festivities" had yet to begin.

A FAMILIAR FACE

Food, especially of the gourmet kind, sounded like a good idea. Except for the hors d'oeuvres we'd plucked off the trays of the catering staff, Kyle and I were quite hungry despite everything that had happened to kill our appetites. Everyone had been too busy cocktailing and conversing upon arrival to fully appreciate the temptations of the long, gourmet-dished table. Suddenly, a preponderant number of the guests were holding court by the food. Aside from Claudia and Colin, Alan and Muriel, Max, and me, the she-devil and Art were nearby, too. Oh, and one other familiar

255

face.

"I see you've changed husbands, little lady. You're quite the square dancer. You do-si-do'd and changed your partner," Cal said, eyeing me, then looking at Kyle. "How 'bout you give it one more go and end up with me? Trust me, I'll swing you, little lady, like you've never been swung before. As you can see, I've no longer got my ascot around my neck."

Believe it or not, I was surprised he remembered me, considering the number of women I'd seen him hit on within a short time. Aside from being shocked by his presence, while numerous responses danced in my head, I couldn't think of an appropriate one befitting of the environment. Kyle looked a bit bewildered and amused at the same time. I was greatly relieved when Alan and Muriel came to save me.

"Who are you torturing now, Cal?" Muriel said, patting him on the back and almost dislodging the gin and tonic from his hand.

"Ah," Cal said, spinning around to greet her. "The one that got away. My lovely Hall monitor. The Hallmark card that wouldn't let me send her. Take Hall of Me; Why Not Take Hall of Me? I know I don't have Hall-a-tosis!"

"I don't want any of you, Cal," Muriel said boldly, to the amusement of those in immediate proximity. "Look at all of this good food. Why don't you go have some of it? Give the gin a rest. It's not your friend."

"It sure wasn't mine," Alan interjected, winking at me.

"Muriel," Cal said curiously eyeing Alan, "who's this guy?" Then, indicating me, he continued. "And why were you dancing with this one's husband who's over there fighting off the ladies?"

I was uncomfortable with Cal referring to Max as my husband, despite the little show we'd put on for him in the park, but luckily he was quickly distracted by Muriel's attention to him.

"Food, Cal," Muriel said. "There's a virtual world buffet here. Did you see the chef with the big knife standing by the roast beef? Real men need sustenance. Go on now. Off with you."

"You're the most incorrigible woman I know. Wit and tenacity are my favorite aphrodisiacs."

I was instantly grateful I had kept every one of my smart comebacks to myself, and I suddenly understood why Cal was every bit as incorrigible as he thought Muriel to be.

"I'm off," Cal said to Muriel. "But I'll be back with brand new mojo, so watch out!"

"So … you know Cal Leighton," I said to Muriel.

"Apparently you do, too, Molly."

"I never expected to see him here."

"Are you kidding?" Muriel said. "Of course he'd be here. He's a scion of Leighton Technologies. His old man and Naomi's father-in-law, Keaton, were prep school *and* college roommates."

"It sure is a small world," Kyle said. "Perhaps a bit too small. He seems quite taken with you, Muriel."

"I kind of feel for the guy," Muriel said. "He's always been a square peg in a round hole, and being around all of this old cobwebby money has never done a darn thing for him except make him painfully aware of his shortcomings. So he uses the gin to cure his shyness. As you can see, it doesn't work. Even the money-hungry ones seem to bypass poor Cal."

"How sad," Alan said. "I do understand feeling like you don't fit in, though."

"Oh, honey," Muriel said. "You don't know the half of it. Cal was the first guy Naomi ever set me up with. You can only imagine that when Cal Senior bemoaned the tragic fate of his square-pegged son's inability to find a woman, my cousin swooped in and offered me up. One square peg with another. What a perfect match. Oh yeah. Na-oms bet everyone in town we'd be married in six months. I'm a big gal. That doesn't mean I want or deserve a buffoon. Even if he has a good heart and is easy on the eyes. I have every right to be as turned on by my man as the next gal. My cousin is still trying to hook him up, though. She never stops trying. But even she's run low on prospects."

I remembered what Max had said that night when he walked me home. Every pot has a lid.

"There must someone for Cal."

"Of course there is," Muriel said. "Especially when he lays off the booze. Over the years, he's found a couple good prospects. But guess what? They've all gone bye-bye like my Fred. Money stays with money, Molly. Cal and I might have been happily married by now, God forbid NOT to each other, but the powers that be saw to that! Speak of the devil …"

"The she-devil," I said to Kyle, as the four of us looked up to see Naomi and Art approaching us, the she-devil wearing a smile that I wanted to rip from her face with my bare hands.

CRASH! CRASH! CRASH! CRASH!

"Well, isn't everyone getting along splendiferously," Naomi gloated, turning to Art for the approval she so desperately wanted but wasn't getting.

"Molly and I were just on our way to taste the cuisine," Kyle said, taking me by the arm and out of striking distance. I could see how distraught he was. His panic over Randy was reaching a near crescendo, and my worry over Tony and Randy wasn't far behind.

From our vantage point, as we sampled the various delicacies (we were too upset to have a full meal), Kyle and I could see Alan and Muriel tolerating conversation with the she-devil. I had no idea that within seconds, the foundation's idyllic party would be crashed, and life for many of Swansea's finest, including myself, would be changed forever.

Dressed to bedazzle, but with the look of a hound out for blood, Tony walked briskly through the crowd toward Art and Naomi. "Benchley! How #@$&ing dare you!"

I didn't know how, but I knew Tony had found out that Naomi was behind the destruction of the date he had lovingly planned for weeks. The she-devil, who had no idea why he was there, was horrified by his disruptive presence, but it was Art who cowered at the sight of him.

"Oh, my God! That's my friend Tony," I told Kyle. "He's going right for Naomi, too."

"Maybe Art will just let him rip her to shreds," Kyle said. "I'm a very nonviolent man, Molly, but someone in a red dress needs to learn a lesson."

As Tony approached the two, everyone in close proximity went silent as Art tried to reason with Tony.

"Look, Tony, let's take this outside. This is just between the two of us."

"The hell it is!" Tony shouted.

"It has nothing to do with my wife or anyone in this room," Art said nervously. "Nothing. You and I will work it out."

"It has *everything* to do with your wife," Tony snapped back at him.

Nervously, I grabbed Kyle by the hand, and we started walking around the buffet table toward Tony, who was now face to face with the Benchleys on the other side. As much as I wanted to see Naomi's public beheading, I was scared to death of the anger in Tony's eyes.

"Be rational, man," Art said. "Leave my wife out of this."

"Naomi *almost* looks happy," Kyle whispered to me. "She's so hungry for attention from her husband. Do you think this public display is to her liking?"

"Tony," Naomi said. "I have no idea what I could possibly have done to put you into such an unbecoming tailspin." At that moment, Naomi got a peripheral glance at me as I wended my way toward the action. The look on her face told me a sudden lightbulb had suddenly gone off. Having seen Tony and me together at Susan Decker's wedding the previous August, she had figured out that she must have interfered in ways she had not foreseen. Still, she appeared riveted by the scene and grossly unapologetic. "Oh, please, don't tell me you and Molly are an item."

"You're going out with Tony?" I heard Claudia's voice erupt from the crowd.

"See, man," Art said desperately, "you've got a new woman now, and Vic ... "

Tony stopped suddenly. He knew I was standing by but he was fixated on the Benchleys. Naomi was no longer his primary target; Art was.

"Holy @%#*ing %^@$!" Tony said. "It's YOU! You're the one!"

"I thought you knew," Art said, trembling.

"Buddy, I had NO idea! But thanks for filling me in! Happy Birthday to me!"

"What is he talking about?" Naomi asked her husband insistently. "Art, WHAT is he talking about?"

Tony suddenly looked relaxed. He had come gunning for Naomi but had claimed her spouse for a trophy instead and was about to pay Naomi back in a way he had never intended. "So it's you, Benchley. You're the mystery man."

"Outside, now!" Art said, trying to intimidate Tony with his authority. "Now!"

Tony burst out laughing. "No such luck, Benchley!"

The crowd began murmuring as all of Swansea had gathered in a circle to watch the action. Even the band had stopped playing. I saw Naomi's BFF Ginger rush toward the action. Keaton Benchley, standing stoically with his wife, watched in horror-filled but rapt attention, as their son's life was made public.

"It's not what you think," Art told him.

Tony laughed again. "Oh, no, dear boy, it's not what *you* think."

"What the hell is he talking about?" Naomi demanded to know.

"She's not so happy anymore," Kyle whispered to me.

"Oh, my God, I know what's coming," I whispered back, as I was only seconds behind Tony in unmasking Vicky's lover.

"If I were you," Tony told Art, "I'd start stockpiling cigars."

"What the—"

"Oh, you didn't know?" Tony said. "She didn't tell you? I guess it was Victoria's secret."

Naomi turned ferociously to her husband. "What do you have to do with Victoria's Secret?"

"Maybe he's got a lingerie fetish," someone from the crowd said a bit too loudly. Laughter ensued, but it was a dark and stormy night in Benchleyland.

Naomi was now as panicked as her husband. "Tony, if my husband was spotted in Victoria's Secret buying lingerie, I promise you he was shopping for me." She turned to him and spat under her breath. "I'm right, am I not?"

"Naomi, you poor uninformed, meddlesome shrew," Tony began, as the excited crowd began to buzz. "Let me be the first to give you and Art the good news. My wife, Victoria, and your husband have been seeing one another for quite a while now. And what do you know! She's pregnant."

The black hole that Art Benchley wanted to swallow him up was malfunctioning, and he stood on the floor, speechless, as the crowd now began loudly chattering. "And guess what? It's a double blessing: she's having twins. So when you leave your control freak of a wife for mine, don't even think about playing daddy to my son. Do you hear me?"

It was precisely at the moment Naomi screamed that Kyle and I saw Randy running toward us. I knew he had come with an urgent message, but when he saw Kyle and me standing cozily together, he had no idea what to think. But he was angry.

"Well, what am I seeing here!" Randy exclaimed. "This isn't what I—"

"Of course not," Kyle said. "You know it's not, Randy. Naomi pulled the same thing on both Molly and me. Neither of us had a clue we were to be one another's dates. The only reason Molly came was to save your job."

"My job?" Randy said, looking at me, stupefied. "It was *my* job she threatened, not Ana's?"

"That's right, Randy," I said, as Naomi and Art's words took the attention off our situation. "I know you're angry at me for lying, but I was so afraid you'd quit."

"We'll discuss later, Molly Rose." Randy glowered at Kyle. "And you, Mister Profound Regret, you couldn't tell me the truth last night because … ?"

As Kyle stammered to find the right words, Randy silenced him. "Don't answer me now. There's no time to waste. Molly Rose, I'm going to quickly synopsize this for you, so pay attention. Ray asked me to tell you that it was fine if you wanted to work from home tomorrow. As you had left your briefcase at work, I decided to take it to your apartment house to leave with the concierge. Of course, I wanted to spare you from having to even set foot in the office. Well, when I entered the lobby of your apartment building, Tony had just come off the elevator. Poor distraught man had gone looking for you, and when I saw him looking as emotionally bruised and battered as myself, I told him exactly what had happened. Unbeknownst to me, someone else had come looking for you, too, and heard me disclose your whereabouts. I came here to warn, and here's your number two man now."

"Molly! There you are!" Cody yelled through the now-boisterous crowd.

Cody, unlike Tony, was discordant with the finely dressed assemblage. As he came barreling toward me in his jeans, black knit shirt, and patched denim jacket, Naomi, despite being up to her scrawny neck in a nightmare, was craning it in my direction. Tony, who had said his piece to the Benchleys, was also coming toward me. Meantime, Claudia, angered by my lack of disclosure about Tony, had moved through the crowd to get a front-row seat on my interaction with the long-haired man she had never seen before. Cody, ebullient at seeing me, was oblivious to it all.

"Molly, I heard Randy tell that man why you were here. I couldn't wait any longer to tell you how sorry I am. I don't want to lose you. I was very unfair to you, and I've been a #@$*ing wreck since our breakup!"

"Your breakup?" Claudia screeched.

Tony, for a moment victorious, was angry again. "Your breakup? You've been seeing this guy, Molly?"

"Cody," Randy said diplomatically. "It's such a pleasure to see you again. Perhaps this wouldn't be the best time to talk with Molly Rose."

"Hey, dude, how are you?" Cody said. "I can't help it. I've got to make things right."

261

"Maybe you could make things right *tomorrow*," Randy suggested.

Cody started to protest but eyed someone in the crowd he was not happy to see. "Oh, holy @$@%!"

As I came to later learn, Barbarino, who had been tailing Cody, put on quite a show for my concierge, who stupidly repeated my whereabouts to her as Randy had described them to Tony. Got that? Well, just as Barbarino, clad in her winter-white organza minidress, piled heavily with funky, clunky jewelry, came stomping in spiked boots toward Cody and me, someone graced her path.

Finger guns loaded, Cal aimed them right at Barbarino. "I'm zeroing in on a vision of snowy loveliness."

"Get out of my way, YOU FREAK!"

"I'm holding you at finger point," came the retort.

"I don't dig dudes who shoot blanks, you hear?"

"Oh, baby! You're a wild woman; I could get lost in your long blond hair."

"Watch me choke you with it," Barbarino said, as she tried to move past him to get to Cody.

But Cal was entranced, as I'd never seen him before. "Let me rustle up some grub for you, lassie. Roast beef with Yorkshire pudding? Red bliss rosemary roasted potatoes? Persian love cake? Pumpkin torte? Chocolate mousse?"

"I don't eat all of that fattening crap. That's why I'm a size four."

"Sexy slender baby of mine. May I then interest you in a crudité?" Cal said, gesturing toward the mound of raw vegetables with his right hand.

"I'll show you crude," she said, making an obscene gesture at him. "I'd like to take that green goddess dressing and slime your face with it, loser!"

"Oh, baby, let me dip my cucumber in it instead."

"LOSER FREAK!"

As Cal and Barbarino went at it, drawing an audience of their own, I noticed that Alan, Muriel, and Max had all gathered around me to make sure everything was okay. Muriel, assessing the situation with Cal and Barbarino, made a beeline for them as the sparring continued.

"Maybe you'd like to munch on my carrot," Cal offered.

"Who do I look like, you decrepit dickweed? A frickin' gay Bugs Bunny? Go chomp on your own carrot."

"Oh, baby!"

"Cal," Muriel said, interrupting them. "Speaking of carrots, maybe someday you'll buy this lovely lady a twenty-four-karat gold ring."

Barbarino looked at Cal, and then turned to Muriel. "Right, like this bird crap on my windshield could afford to do *that*!"

"Isn't she breathtaking?" Cal gushed.

"Don't be so hasty, honey," Muriel told her. "This is Cal Leighton, one of the heirs to Leighton Technologies. He's the vice president of Leighton Computer. Want to rethink the windshield thing?"

Barbarino stopped and looked Cal up and down.

"Hey, baby," Cal gushed, "want to turn my software into hardware?"

Before Barbarino could utter her next "LOSER FREAK," Cody, noticing her momentary distraction, made a decision on the spot. "Molly, you're right. Tonight's not gonna work. But I'm calling you tomorrow, baby, and we're gonna work this out, My world has stopped you-know-what-ing since we split. I miss you like nobody's business."

And with that, Cody raced out of the ballroom more quickly than he'd come dashing into it. Before Barbarino could go after him, he was gone. But Cal wasn't.

"You LOSER FREAK! Now he's gone. My man is gone!"

"But I'm here, snugalicious one."

"Why don't you go snuggle up with a trash compactor? Or better yet, date another freak like Molly Hacker!" Barbarino stomped over to me, with Cal trailing at her spiked heels. "FREAK, MEET FREAK!"

"We've met," Cal said. "But this perty lady is already married to that guy," Cal pointed to Max, and everyone in the near vicinity went silent again. But not for long.

"What the #@$*?" Tony said.

"Molly!" Claudia shouted. "You don't have a double life, girlfriend. You've got a triple one. I don't even *know* you."

"EVERYONE," Max said loudly. "Calm down. Molly and I are *not* married. We're friends."

"That's not what they told me," Cal said to Barbarino. "They said they were married … with kids."

"Oh, yeah? Tell me everything that man-stealing skank said."

As Barbarino stepped away to gossip about me with Cal, not a second went by before Randy and Kyle began to mix it up, though I must say, they kept their exchange on the down low.

"Perhaps you'd like to tell me why you didn't come clean with me last night," Randy said to Kyle. "Was I not worthy of a simple explanation as to why you saw fit to succumb to the manipulations of Ms. She-Devil? Or that she was even behind this mess? No, you merely offered your 'profound regret' and left me groping in the dark for explanations as I, with dread anticipation, prepared to cancel the many plans that had been weeks in the making."

"I was with the Benchleys until quite late," Kyle said, trying to keep his voice low. "I had no privacy whatsoever."

"I'm quite sure they didn't come home with you!" Randy countered. "Or did they?"

"It was *very* late when I got home," Kyle said.

"As if I got any sleep!"

"I'm so sorry," Kyle said. "I shouldn't have let any of this happen. It's all my fault."

"No, you should *not* have let any of this happen. Why didn't you just tell the she-devil that you were in a relationship?"

"Because … "

Randy jumped on Kyle's pause. "Say not another word. It's all too clear."

"No, Randy, it's *not* all clear. Not at all. I've got a lot to tell you, but this isn't the time or the place. Tomorrow. Tomorrow night we'll talk it all through."

"Tomorrow? The sun'll come out tomorrow, bet your bottom dollar. Wait, better *not* bet anything. The sun isn't coming out at all. The sun appears to be in the closet!"

Randy's last line had not been as quietly spoken as the rest of the conversation, and the overstimulated crowd, still anxious for entertainment, turned toward Randy and Kyle.

"Nothing to see here, folks," Kyle said loudly. "Just two gay men having a lovers' spat. Let's move it right along."

The she-devil was not too distraught to react. "Oh, my goodness!"

"What a waste of testosterone," Ginger snickered.

"I told you to butt out of his life," Art said to his wife.

"How dare YOU chastise *me* for anything!"

"You ruin people's lives for sport, Naomi. You've made mine a living hell. I wouldn't *have* another woman if you'd given me the least amount of happiness. Looks like the next matchmaking you'll be doing will be for yourself."

The crowd twittered as I turned my attention back to Randy.

Kyle's public declaration was definitely a plus, but not enough to subdue Randy's hurt and anger. "I am so out of here. Molly Rose, I could censure you for not telling me the truth, but I would have done exactly the same thing, not only to save your job but to save you from acting on foolish impulse. You truly are my best friend."

Randy kissed me on both cheeks and refusing to even look at Kyle, headed out through the madding crowd.

AND THAT SHOULD HAVE BEEN THAT ... BUT!

Don't you think enough happened to end this chapter already? The drama was ongoing, as there were still two people (Barbarino doesn't count) who were angry with me: Tony and Claudia. Tony, though crushed to find out I had been seeing someone, understood why I had not told him. Claudia? Not so much.

"Well, Molly, aren't you going to run after your *best* friend? The one who isn't surprised by a *thing* and the one you tell *everything* to as you leave me out in the cold."

"Claude, don't you think we've had enough reality TV here tonight? Can't you and I get together soon and talk?"

"Sorry, I'll be busy with my *real* friends," she said, motioning for Colin to refill her champagne glass. "Dina, Candy, and Ellie. Remember them?"

"Don't be ridiculous," I said. "Can we please get together soon and talk?"

"Not interested. I don't care if you lead more lives than Captain Jack has. Tell someone who cares."

I was crushed and devastated by Claudia's public condemnation. It didn't matter that she was filled with the other kind of bubbles—the not-so-flattering ones. I was a wreck. Muriel, friend to all, stepped forward to console me.

"My, you look weary, Molly."

"Yeah," I told her. "I'm spent."

"Do you have your car with you?"

"Yes," I said, as the band resumed playing and the various personal dramas played out beyond earshot and eyesight.

"Someone should walk Molly to her car," Muriel said, her voice slightly raised.

"I will," Kyle, Tony, Alan, and Max said in unison.

"Well, there you go," Claudia said. "A virtual cavalry."

265

"Molly is my date," Kyle piped up. "I'll walk her out. *If* she's ready to go."

"Oh, yes," I said. "Beyond ready. Thank you, Kyle."

Muriel gave me a big hug. "I hope to see you again, Molly. You're A-okay with me."

"I'd love that," I told her. I turned to Tony. "Please call me tomorrow. I'm so very sorry."

MALFEASANCE HAS ITS JUST DESSERTS AFTER ALL!

And just as I thought *nothing* else could happen, the evening's pièce de résistance came to be. Kyle and I were seconds away from leaving when he stopped cold. "Oh, Molly, I think we have another party crasher, and I think she's trouble."

I turned to see a sharply coiffed woman standing just a foot away from Ginger, who was busily comforting BFF Naomi. She looked familiar to me, but I couldn't place her.

"Who is she?" I asked Kyle.

"Her name is Ariel. Randy and I met her at a private party one night. She works for a plastic surgeon named Dr. Miller. She moved here from LA with him: he's her lover *and* her boss. We couldn't make sense of most of it. Seems she's working as the doctor's office manager and for some bizarre reason has marginally tolerated his engagement to a woman named Ginger. She was wasted the night we met her and spilled way more to us than she probably should have."

"Oh, my God, Kyle."

The woman, whom Kyle identified as Ariel, had indeed spilled more to Kyle and Randy than she had to me. She had been my "confidential informant" aka "the source," but I was not at liberty to share that with Kyle. When I had met her just days before, she was without makeup, without a name, dressed in jeans, a flannel shirt, baseball cap, and dark sunglasses. What she had told me was that, while practicing in LA, Dr. Miller had performed some illegal and unsafe procedures on several high-profile clients. With pressures mounting, he relocated from Los Angeles to Swansea in hopes of finding patients of privilege while simultaneously avoiding the glare of big-city lights. That was *all* she told me in two hours of conversation that did nothing but circle. She was angry with him, but she was clearly in love with him, too.

Exasperated by her failure to deliver as promised, I had gone to the library to try to find a record of his practice in Los Angeles, and to my chagrin, none had existed. I then got sidetracked by more important issues and put the project on hold.

"Molly Hackerrrr!" Ariel shouted over the crowd.

"She's drunk again," Kyle told me. "I'd recognize that slur anywhere."

As she called out my name, Naomi, Art, Ginger, Max, Alan, Muriel, Claudia, Cal, Barbarino, and others gathered around. Oh, and a suave-looking snake with a square face and mustache, who I presumed to be Dr. Miller, was panicked by her presence.

"Sorry, Molly," she said loudly. "I'm not your confiden-shal source anymore. I'm Swansea's new town crier."

"For God's sake, Bill," Ginger said angrily to her fiancé, "her place is at the office ... and with her mouth shut. Why is she even here? She's an administrative employee."

Ariel spun on her heels and faced Ginger. "I think your mouth is the only part of your face left that can still move. Why do you think Willem never takes you out for candlelit dinners? He's afraid you might melt. Oh, and then there's the part about him not giving a rat's ass about you."

I heard Barbarino burst out laughing, and Cal began laughing, too.

"Who the hell is Willem?" Ginger snapped.

"Your fake fian-sssssssaay" Ariel said gleefully.

"Stop, Ariel," the doctor yelled.

"This is enough!" Naomi screamed. "No more!"

"Oh, I'll bet it issssssss waaaaay enough! You're not having a good night, are ya, Naomi? Well, issss about to get worser!" She turned to Ginger. "Meet Willem Klaus Marswicki, aka Bill 'I'll-pick-a-common alias' Miller."

"No wonder I couldn't find a record of him," I said softly to myself.

The crowd began to buzz.

"Anyone for some low-grade silicone in her face? Here's the doc for the job. Got a pig nose? I mean a big nose? He'll replace it with a pig snout. Lips too thin? He'll blow 'em up for ya and then some. Ha! Oh, the good doc did some bad things to some famous ladies out in Los Angeleeeeeeeeeeees. Why else do you people think a famous LA doc would relocate to this burb? And why, um, why do you think he'd pay big bucks to someone to help him set up a practice, change his name, and find him a big-bucked babe with Play-Doh for a face to practice on? Think, peeeeee-pull!"

The buzzing crowd grew silent.

"Yep, folks, thissssssss con game is coming to an end." Ariel turned to the doctor. "You shouldn't have ssssssssset a wedding date with her. You weren't sssssupposed to go *that* far."

"She was relentless," he said, nodding at Ginger as he spoke to Ariel. "I would never have gone through with it. Ever."

"What?" Ginger shrieked.

"Ssssssaid he wouldn't have gone through with it, bitch," Ariel told her. "You deaf?"

Barbarino burst out laughing again.

Ariel continued her rant. "Naomi here is the one who set him up. Took a wad of cash and offered up her best friend."

Ginger turned in horror and looked at Naomi. "You knew Bill wasn't Bill? You sold me for a price? You helped a quack set up a practice in this town and hooked *me* up with him? You would have watched me marry him. Been my matron of honor?"

"Maid," Art interjected.

"Yesssssssssssss she did, and yessssss she would have!" Ariel said.

"And you love a man like this?" Ginger asked Ariel tearfully. "Knowing what you know?"

"He's not an easy man to get over," Ariel said. "You'll ssssee."

"My God, Naomi!" Art said. "Why would you get involved in something as heinous as this?"

"It's all *your* fault. I knew you couldn't be trusted. I was afraid we wouldn't last. And I refuse to give up the lifestyle that I've become accustomed to! I needed some insurance. And I was tired of Ginger complaining about not finding the right man. So I bought her one!"

Ginger screamed in horror. Barbarino, with a glowing Cal at her side, burst out laughing again, this time incurring Naomi's wrath. "Who the hell is that gangly blond bimbo?"

"I'm the REAL DEAL, FREAK! I'm pure woman. I got BITCH FIRE!"

Seething, Ginger stared down Naomi. "How dare you blame your vulgar behavior on me or on Art for that matter? You are despicable." She walked toward the dessert section of the table and grabbed the Persian love cake from its stand.

"I did it for all of us," Naomi blathered.

"Well, I'm going to do *this* for all of us!" And with that, Ginger slammed the cake into Naomi's face, twisting it clockwise with all her might. The white icing and little pink rose petals clung to Naomi's neck, her ears, and her devil-red dress.

"You take the cake, FREAK!" Barbarino yelled.

"Ahhhhhhhhhhhh," Naomi screamed as Barbarino grabbed the Pumpkin torte and handed it to Ginger, who smashed it with a vengeance on top of Naomi's head.

"Malfeasance shall have its just desserts," I said.

"What?" Kyle asked, stunned by what he was witnessing.

"Malfeasance shall have its just desserts," I repeated. "That's what Randy told me. He's so prophetic."

"I've got to get him back," Kyle said, as a Japanese beef and scallion roll barely missed his forehead en route to Naomi's face.

"Watch out!" I said, as a maple-barbecued chicken leg came whizzing by our airspace.

One would think, from everything I've written about the she-devil, that I would have wanted to stay and witness every glorious moment of her social demise. I'll admit, I didn't feel sorry for her, but neither Kyle nor I wanted to spend one more moment ducking gourmet food and watching the bedlam before our eyes. It almost made me prefer the façade of the feigned, the ersatz world of privilege, and the skilled dance of the disingenuous. Kyle grabbed my hand, and we ran for the coat checkroom in the lobby, passing security guards on their way in.

As Kyle ushered me through the crowd, I heard Barbarino yell, "GOOD RIDDANCE, FREAK!" as Cal quickly announced to the disapproving assemblage, "She's with me!"

From what I heard the next day, every piece of food left on the buffet table ended up in flight. Every man and woman in Swansea, especially those who had visited "the good doctor," were furious with Naomi for bringing him to town for her own profit while simultaneously putting them at peril.

The foundation party was one that will live in infamy forever. More secrets were exposed than I could ever tell here. Someone else will have to write that book. For me, it was the night they brought old Swansea down, the night Naomi stopped interfering in people's lives, and the night before I tried, once again, to mend my wholly unsettled life.

Chapter 32: THE AFTER-PARTY: MY LIFE RESUMES

I needed a break from everything. However, time, irreverent little fiend that it is, refused to stand still, marching on instead in measured increments and dragging my life with it. While some days it politely tiptoed and whispered (a gracious measure of goodwill on my behalf), it refused to make like a bear and hibernate. Still, I plodded on, and as did my nearest and dearest.

Tony, relieved to finally be in the know about Vicky's life, happily forgave me for canceling the date. Shortly after Christmas, we rescheduled and had a beautiful evening together at the Wellington Inn. There were moments during the fireside repast that I felt butterflies in my stomach (on steroids, none the less), but considering Tony's impending divorce and Noah's impending siblinghood, it didn't seem like the best time for Tony and me to upgrade from coach to first class. That didn't stop Tony from asking or me from considering what unknown joys might lie in wait, but waiting seemed wise. And you know me well enough by now to appreciate the market price of my wisdom, yes? Would you give me two bucks for it? Moving right along …

Cody and I traded apologies and agreed to see one another with limited "world rocking." I can't say Cody was keen on having learned that I was still out there looking, but it also freed up the part of him that wasn't quite as ready to settle down as he thought. Besides, his daughter needed a lot of attention, and he was eager to give it to her. Yes, I'm happy to report we salvaged our relationship like adults. And adults, especially consenting ones, do like to have fun. Despite an invitation to spend New Year's Eve with Tony, I accepted Cody's offer to hear his band at a club. Loud music is a great way to drown out feelings, doubts, and unnecessary musings. Okay, yes, if you must know, we rocked one another's world until early morning of the following year. Satisfied? I was.

Alan. Now there was a conundrum of a man for whom I had a growing soft spot. A couple days after the party, he called me. Mutually appreciative of the fact that Naomi would not be throwing diamond-studded wrenches into our respective lives, we bonded further. Alan, however, upon realizing just how many men I might be considering as lifelong partners, hid his insecurities about as well as the emperor had hidden his new clothing. Metaphorically naked, Alan confessed that he felt foolish upon learning that my joke over dinner, the one about making love to a long-haired rocker, was quite obviously the truth. A case of the guilts crept over my conscience. While it's no secret that I had several issues with Alan (some justified and some not), I never meant to be cruel. I only meant to give back what I thought I was getting. It all seems rather foolish in retrospect, but then again, what does a person have when she tosses her spark and feisty individualism down the drain? A dulled clone of her former self? A door prize better left at the door? A disappointing prize in a Cracker Jack box? A letter addressed to "occupant"? You choose. I was not about to lose myself. Therefore, I was content to be a flawed, sometimes-confused person who continued to navigate this phenomenon called life.

My friendship with Max continued to evolve. I could talk to him, not quite in the raunchy tell-all style that I enjoy with Randy, but in a heartfelt, cozy, knowing-you-won't-be-judged way that feels like a superplush chenille blanket on a blustery winter day. And though I couldn't identify it at the time, we had a life-changing bond that neither of us was quite ready to admit, yet recognized in one another before we recognized it in ourselves.

Before I move on, let me say a few words about Randy and Kyle. After the party, I expected Randy would have a tough week and then slowly soften toward Kyle. But Randy took Kyle's concealment of the truth, the whole truth, and nothing but the truth to be indicative of the adage, both real and colloquial, that if you find one cockroach, there are always many more. I didn't want to see the trust monster kill Randy and Kyle the same way it had Leo and me. I had no doubt they loved one another, and though I didn't know Kyle the way I know Randy, he was about as perfect for Randy as a man could be. It didn't matter to Randy that Kyle was "out and about"; it just mattered way too much that Kyle had made the dreaded mistake of withholding full disclosure from the get-go. Do any of us want to disclose *everything* from day one? I am certainly guilty of not doing so and of being angry when truths were concealed from me. To this day, despite all that has happened, it's still anyone's debate as to when doing so is a good idea and when it's not. It's a tricky timeline no matter who you are. I tried telling Randy that life had no definitive rule book, but he couldn't get over the feeling of being betrayed. He didn't even see Kyle for two weeks, and then it was awkward and clumsy, despite the overwhelming love they shared. Then they spent New Year's Eve apart. That broke my heart. And it only seemed to crumble from there.

One of the nice things to come out of the horrid event, however, was my blossoming friendship with Muriel. And for me, one of the saddest things was the seemingly irreparable damage done to my friendship with Claudia.

LADIES ROOM MATINEE

While I stand by my decision to withhold recitation of certain love interests from Claudia, that doesn't negate the fact that I was still sad at having hurt her. Two days after the party, I called her, but she would not respond. I waited. Then, before Christmas, I tried again, with the hope that we could get together and talk things over, but she still wouldn't take my calls at her office or return the ones I left on her cell.

I decided to give up for an indefinite period of time. I had asked myself what I might do if our situations were reversed. Answer to self: Hurt or not, I would have definitely listened to what she had to say. Yes, I *so* would have given her the courtesy of explaining her side of things to me. I may or may not have understood, but at the very least I'm as fair as the justice system, and her day in court would have been granted.

Toward the end of January, Muriel and I had picked a day to get together for some lunch and shopping. The stores in the Swansea Mall were having a major end-of-season sale. Not a great day to avoid crowds, but a great day to save money. Yeah, I know, that's some flawed logic right there. It's kind of ridiculous to spend a lot of money shopping so you can bask in the afterglow of how much you've "saved." I do realize that abstaining from the procurement of goods offers the primo savings of all, but I'm not always programmed to be at one with that tiny sliver of reality.

We had eaten at Micelli's, a popular Italian eatery in the mall, and were restoring our faces in the ladies' room mirror when in walked Claudia.

Muriel, divinely friendly soul that she is, remembered Claudia from the party and immediately turned to greet her.

"It's Claudia, right? I'm Muriel Hall. We met at the Christmas catastrophe."

Claudia's effusive countenance dissipated when she realized that I was standing three feet away at the nearest sink reapplying my lipstick.

"Oh, yes, of course. Hello, Muriel. You were with Alan, of course. One of the many men Molly was, or God only knows is, still dating."

"I don't think—"

"Molly is so secretive, you never know *who* she might be seeing! Let's just hope they're all single. In fact, I heard a rumor she'd been seeing Santa Claus until Mrs. Claus—"

"Oh, my God, Claude," I said, stepping away from the sink. "I can't believe you're being so rude and so cruel. Not to mention insanely ludicrous."

Claudia refused to look at me, ignoring the other shoppers in the room who were eyeing us all curiously. Addressing Muriel, she continued, "Someone in this room is thinking that she has a right to speak to me. Once, I thought I had a very best friend. But that friendship is gone." She walked toward each stall and with the palm of her hand pushed on every stall door. "Let's see, where's my friendship with Molly? Not in this toilet. Nope, not in this one."

Muriel looked at me as if to say, "I'm sorry," but she had nothing to be sorry about.

Claudia, now on a roll, pushed open a third stall. "Nope, not in here. What am I thinking? My friendship with Molly isn't *in* the toilet; she's already flushed it away!"

"Be reasonable," I pleaded.

"Reasonable? I thought I heard someone say 'reasonable.' I'll check one last toilet." Claudia took the palm of her hand and punched open the last door without paying any attention to what she was doing. It wasn't until she heard the loud scream that she realized the stall was occupied.

"YOU SPAZZOID FREAK!" screamed the blond queen from her throne as the door slammed shut. "HOW DARE YOU! You broke the lock, you VANDAL BITCH!"

For a moment, Claudia looked at me helplessly out of instinct, desperately wanting to join forces against the wrath of Barbarino. Realizing her momentary slip, she quickly turned away from me and faced Barbarino, who was now emerging from the stall and putting on quite a show for the other shoppers.

"I'm so sorry," Claudia said.

"You're pathetic. Poor you. Upset with freak Molly for not telling you she was #@$%ing *my* man!"

Claudia, once again, out of instinct, turned to me for backup, then turned away.

"Oh, why don't you two FREAK BFFs kiss and make up? Losers ought to stick with losers."

"Have you heard from Cal?" Muriel asked Barbarino. "He took quite a fancy to you."

Barbarino stopped in her tracks and stared at Muriel. I don't think I mentioned that Muriel had lost twelve pounds since the party, let her long, bunned hair down only to cut and highlight it, and was dressing with a casual flair to mix it up with the best of them.

"Don't tell me you're the same freak who was wearing that green velour dress with the party lace. My kid had a Mrs. Santa doll like that when she was five. Chic North Pole fashion, for sure. Chic Freak."

"Oh, I was a freak," Muriel said. "Still am and proud of it. How do you like my new hairstyle?"

"It beats that dinner roll you had sticking outta your head. Your hair was pulled back so tight your eyes were on the side of your head."

"Oh, honey, I have eyes in the back of my head."

"Yeah, well, so do I. And I see the FREAK they call 'Bubbling Brown Sugar' trying to make a run for it."

"Look, beeotch," Claudia snarled, "I can show you BOILING BROWN SUGAR, and trust me, sweetie, it's SCALDING HOT! Unless you want to scar your questionably pretty face, you'll accept my apology and get over it already."

"You don't scare me," Barbarino shouted.

"Why don't we all take a chill pill?" Muriel suggested.

"I am *so* out of here," Claudia said. "Nice to see you, Muriel. Enjoy your new BFF while you can."

Barbarino, who had been washing her hands, grabbed a towel and scrunched it into a smashed ball. "This is your head, Molly Freak Hacker!"

In seconds, both Claudia and Barbarino had left, and the rubbernecking shoppers hurried into the vacant stalls. I turned to look at Muriel. "That went well."

"Didn't it, though?" Muriel said. "Come on, Molly, I need your fashion acumen. My shrinking physique is having a trendy attack. Take mercy on me."

"Right behind you," I said, wishing that Claudia could be a part of it all.

SUNDAY RECONCILIATION

When Claudia called the next morning at 10:00 a.m. to ask me if she could come over, I didn't hesitate. I called Tony to ask him if we could turn our brunch date into an early dinner, and he was thrilled for me. He knew how much the demise of my friendship with Claudia had been eating away at me.

Claudia insisted on bringing sustenance, so I did little more than set the table, dress myself in a clean pair of jeans, and proudly sport the cozy but chic Big Apple sweatshirt that Randy had generously given me, among other things, on Christmas Day at my parents' home.

"Good morning," I said, opening the door as Jack nuzzled my leg. "I'm happy you came, Claude."

"Tea sandwiches, salad, and assorted berries," Claudia said, handing me a bag from Swansea's premier gourmet shop. "Oh, yes, and the best chai ever."

Captain Jack mewed loudly at her.

"Oh, mon petit orange," Claudia said, "you know I'd never forget you. There are gourmet goldfish for felines in the bag, I promise. I love my little Jackie. Now, remember Auntie Claude's name is spelled C-L-A-U-D-E, not C-L-A-W-E-D." Claudia looked at me. "You remember that too, Molly."

I laughed. "Take a seat. As you can see, I'm all set up and ready. Just let me know what you want to drink."

Claudia pulled a bottle of water from her bag and sat down. "I'm fine. I think. Sit down, Molly. Before I lose my courage. And I won't get any from drinking spring water, either."

"Do you want me to start?"

"No. I need to go first, or I might just 'bubble over.' Listen, I'm not going to pretend for even a millisecond that I'm not hurt by your secret life you've chosen not to share with me. I'm certainly ready to hear your explanation and accept your apology. But first, I owe you one. I acted like a fool. Yesterday, when I made that remark about you messin' around with Santa Claus and then began attacking stall doors … honestly, that was the precise moment that the enormity of my idiocy whacked me on the head. And perhaps being at the other end of that screaming blond banshee illuminated my insanity even more. And you know I can get emotional, but I've never busted in a bathroom stall before. I guess losing my best friend hasn't worn well on me. Nobody *gets* things like you do, Molly. I kind of thought we were a team. Honestly, it never bothered me that you and Randy were so close until I figured out that for some reason, you trust him more than you trust me." She looked at the bag of food on the table. "Oh, for goodness sake, let's open this and dig in already."

I reached in the bag and took out the various delicacies that Claudia had so kindly brought over. "These tea sandwiches look fabulous," I said.

"The one you're holding is a delectable combo of grilled portobello mushrooms and roasted red peppers with a spicy hummus spread. To die for. Where was I? Oh, yeah, at the part where I was wondering why you trust Randy more than me."

Finishing the tiny sandwich, I reached into the bag and pulled out the romaine and watercress salad, carefully taking the plastic lid off and laying my salad tongs on top.

"Jump in any old time, Molly. Today would be good. Now would be even better. But don't rush. You pick a time to answer that feels all warm and fuzzy to you. Don't mind me. Jack and I have plenty of catching up to do. In fact, lil' whiskers here can probably fill me in on pretty much everything."

"I'm sorry," I said. "I'm a little nervous. You did say you wanted to go first. And you did tell me to take the food out of the bag."

"I ought to have suggested you let the cat out of the bag, too. And not Jackie. The other cat. The keeper of secrets."

I bit my lip as I frantically tried to figure out exactly how to explain myself to Claudia.

"Speaking of cats, has one got your tongue?"

"Okay, okay," I said, steeling myself for action. "Claude, I know you have the biggest heart in the world. And since time immemorial, it seems like best friends, of the real and female kind, do want to help one another on the path to true love."

"Well, of course. That's the true definition of a friend. Anyone who veers from that course is a jealous beeotch. Please don't tell me that you ever doubted my motives because I'll be crushed beyond repair if you do."

"I never doubted your motives," I assured her. "And that is said with complete sincerity. You have always been an advocate for me to live my most awesome life."

"Whew! Well, glad to at least know that much. So where did I go wrong? What did I do that made you think you couldn't trust me?"

"Claude, I'm going to tell you. But before I begin, you have to understand that, first and foremost, I blame myself. Okay?"

"For what, Molly?"

"For losing Leo."

"Friggen' A! This is about *Leo*?"

"Claude, I know you remember those days when Leo was secretly visiting his ex-dying girlfriend, Luciana."

"Luciana Grace," Claude said. "I remember, you found the name 'Grace' on his cell phone and thought he might be having an affair."

"Right," I said uncomfortably. "And then there was that day Dina saw Leo on the street and *purposely overheard* him talking to her. Remember? She couldn't make sense of what she had heard, so she went directly to you. And you came straight to yours truly, pressing me for information. Reluctantly, I told you about the number I had found, and you urged me to give it to you. I shouldn't have. But I did. My God, I hate reliving this. You called the number. From a blocked phone using a British accent. Remember?"

"Of course, Molly. I remember."

"And then months went by, and Leo was still taking overnight trips. And then you, Dina, Candy, and Ellie all decided I had a cheater on my hands. And then—"

"I gave Dina the number, and she called. She asked for Leo and the woman said he was coming to see her that weekend. And that alone convinced me that we were right. And it convinced you."

"But—"

"No. Let me finish. Your besties helped you to lose the love of your life. Just say it."

"I can only blame myself. I should have trusted Leo. And he should have trusted me. I don't want to forget that part. But I wonder now: was he worried about *me* believing him or all five of us believing him? Maybe he figured his odds were better just keeping everything under the radar."

"I'm so sorry."

"I can't blame you for what was ultimately my decision."

"Does that mean you can never trust me again? Any of us? Are you afraid we'll destroy something you've got going on now?"

"Oh, Claude, I don't know. It's taken me so long to get this far. And I finally have some awesome men as prospects."

"Well, I know you've always adored Tony."

"Yes, and now he adores me, too. But we've been friends forever, and I want to be very sure before I commit to him. Cody is amazing, and I guess it's been easier for me to get sexually involved with him because I don't run the risk of losing a lifetime friendship."

"He looks like he's *way* hot in the sack. I couldn't notice that his hands are—"

"Awesome with a guitar … and a paintbrush."

"And Max and Alan?" Claudia asked, scoffing at my not-so-subtle admonishment.

"Two totally different men. Friends, but definitely with the potential to be more. I just don't know. I'm working on it. One thing I never want to do and that's to rush into anything or anyone just for the sake of having a permanent attachment. I'd rather be 'picky Molly Hacker' forever than go that route."

"So, you didn't tell me, or any of us, because you were afraid we'd mess with your life?"

"I needed to do this alone."

"With a little help from Randy."

"Okay, yeah, with a little help from Randy. Claude, I love you to pieces. It's not like I was planning to never confide in you again. I just needed space to make my own mistakes this time. It's just different with a male friend. You know that. Let's not forget you have a husband to confide in."

"You're right. I do. As for the rest, say no more. The memories are flooding back to me. I think we were all so caught up in what we *thought* we had found out that we did not handle it with care. If you hadn't confided in us, in *me*, you'd be married by now. Molly, I can't bear that I did this to you. What can I do to fix it? There must be something I can do."

"Leo is my past, Claude. And maybe one of these guys I'm seeing is my future. I don't know. What I do know is that if Leo and I had trusted one another, as we should have, this never would have happened. I can't blame my friends, but at the same time, I'm glad you understand why I've become a bit gun-shy about divulging every detail. And trust me, I do *not* tell Randy every detail either."

"I'm so sorry."

"It's okay. Just let it die. Let me move on. Let me sort out my feelings and when I find true love again, I promise I'll let you know."

"I'm glad to hear that. I just feel so bad."

"It's okay."

"But Leo was your soul mate. You were engaged. You guys were like sunrise and sunset. You completed one another."

"That was another lifetime," I said, tearing up. "I have to live in the present. And that's exactly what I'm doing."

"I guess you are, girlfriend. No one can accuse you of not living. I just feel so bad."

Chapter 33: THE DEATH OF 1,000 INFANTRYMEN (AND ME)

It was Friday, February 6, exactly one week and change before Valentine's Day and approximately two weeks since Claudia and I, through intelligent, amiable dialogue, had patched up our friendship. Additionally, Muriel and I continued to pick up speed in our newfound sisterhood, and nobody was more surprised than me to find a Hall I could call "friend."

Since the holiday party had forced my secrets out into the open, life became simpler in many ways. At the very least, my playing-the-field status helped me to keep unwanted commitment at bay.

Say what? Isn't her whole freakin' story about this chick who wants commitment? If you haven't figured it out yet, her story is that of an extraordinary woman who is seeking everlasting love with her soul mate and who will settle for no less: good looks, sexuality, social prominence, and other fine traits be damned. She wants to make very sure of what she's doing, as she has no intention of writing a sequel about her divorce and subsequent recovery. It should be added that she is intent on proving how virtuous patience can be (even with "world rocking") and at present is wondering how she meandered into the third person. She will now yank herself out and continue. But before she does, she wants you to know that perhaps she's acting strangely because this is the part where she writes about the worst day of her life. No joking: it was.

One look at Randy's face when I stepped off the elevator that morning told me that life, as I knew it had shattered into tiny pieces. Whatever he had to tell me was far worse than the latest manipulation of a controlling socialite, a lost job or the threat of one, or a crisis in the newsroom.

"Molly Rose."

"Something horrible has happened. Is it Kyle?"

Randy shook his head.

"My parents? Hannah? Claudia? Tony? Cody? Max?"

"Molly Rose, let's go into your office. And no, it's none of those people."

"Thank God," I said.

Randy took me lovingly by the arm. Small beads of sweat were forming on his forehead, and he was biting his lower lip. He was scaring me. As we passed through the newsroom, I saw Ana and Ray and a couple of others looking sorrowfully at me. Once in my office, Randy closed the

279

door and helped me off with my coat, then led me to my chair. Grabbing one of the visitor's chairs, he wheeled it around the desk so that he would be no more than inches from me.

I was standing in the middle of nowhere on a dark road. A truck with blinding headlights was coming straight toward me, and I could not get out of the way.

"I don't know how to tell you this," Randy said.

"Just tell me."

"I *don't* know how to 'just tell you.' It's too tragic."

"Tell me!" I screamed, as the truck was just seconds from hitting me.

"Oh, Molly Rose, I'm so sorry."

"Now, Randy!"

The truck was not going to stop.

"This came in late last night. Ana gave it to me earlier. Thank goodness she looked at it and didn't just leave it on your desk."

I saw that he had a printout in his hand. "Thank you for your kind preamble, but now would be the time to hand over whatever it is you're holding," I said tersely. Randy handed me the paper, and my right hand began shaking uncontrollably.

With no mercy, the truck rolled over me, and I lay flattened on the road, holding a piece of paper upon which were printed the most horrific grouping of words I had ever read in my life.

Leonardo Pierluigi Millefanti, 34, formerly of Swansea, born in Turin, Italy, died in a car accident on February 5. Millefanti, well-known political essayist and environmental pioneer, is survived by his parents, Emanuele and Giuseppina, and his sister, Isabella.

"NOOOOOOOOOOOOOOOOOOOOO!"

"Molly Rose, I am so sorry."

"No! No way! Leo is not dead! No way, Randy. No way! I'll never believe this."

The lone EMT tried to comfort me and lift me from the path of more danger. "I don't want to believe it, either. He was such a superior man."

"Don't talk about him in the past tense. This is just a stupid piece of paper. It means nothing."

"Oh, Molly Rose. It didn't just materialize out of the ether."

I burst into tears. "I don't believe it! I don't believe it for one minute. I want to call his parents. They have an estate in New York. It's in the Hudson Valley. It's, um … "

"I know exactly where it is," Randy said. "I contacted a former colleague who works at an area paper. He told me that the Millefantis, Leo's parents, sold that place and moved back to Italy nearly a year ago. He didn't know where they were now, only that they were from Turin, in the region of Piedmont."

"I know. It's in northern Italy. Leo was going to take me there on our honeymoon. We used to talk about living there someday. Maybe down the road, maybe a few months out of the year. We never got to figure it all out. There were so many things we were going to do, Randy. So many. We were so much in love. I ruined it all. If I had trusted him, he would have stayed in Swansea and be alive now. No, he *is* alive now. I don't even know where he was last living. Maybe he went back to Italy with them. I don't know. I should have trusted him. That's what I *do* know."

"Oh, Molly Rose. Don't even begin to think about blaming yourself."

"One thousand infantrymen have not died," I said through my tears.

"What are you talking about, Molly Rose?"

"Leo's last name. Millefanti. It means 'a thousand infantrymen' in Italian. Leo once told me that when he died, 999 infantrymen would die along with him. But they're all alive. I know it. The army lives on, Randy."

Randy put his arms around me, and I sobbed into his shoulder. He didn't even care that I was getting makeup on his clothing. He didn't notice that I was broken and bloodied after being run over by a truck. After a half hour of sobbing, I looked at him. "If his parents are living in Italy again, there would be a notice in the Italian papers, too. Right?"

"I have no idea, child, but I would certainly think so. Let's Google it."

I was too shaky to type, so Randy typed Leo's name into the search box. To my devastation, the following appeared at the top of a long list of hits:

Un nostro connazionale, originario della sicilia, Leonardo Pierluigi Millefanti é venuto tragicamente a mancare in un incidente d'auto il 5 Febbraio. Lo annunciano con grande dolore i genitori Emanuele e Giuseppina e la sorella Isabella.

"Oh, my," Randy said. "My Italian is remedial at best, but I can read *this*."

"NOOOOOOOOOOOOOOOOOOOOOO!" I wailed loudly, as I read the Italian announcement for myself. "My Italian isn't much better. It just says pretty much the same thing. It's just a lie in another language."

Randy began to frantically click on different links.

"What are you looking for?" I asked, as the tears fell.

"I'm trying to find some recent writings by Leonardo, but everything seems to be a couple of years old. I thought maybe he'd have some kind of blog or social networking page."

"Are you serious?" I asked. "No way! He stayed under the radar every opportunity he got. I mean, he *stays* under the radar every opportunity he *gets*. He might not even *be* writing now. He could be using a nom de plume. He does so many things, and none of them for personal glory. He's so brilliant ... and humble."

"Oh, Molly Rose."

"Don't tell me I have to accept this," I cried, reading Randy's face.

Randy bent his head down and looked at the floor. "I'm so sorry. Life can take some tragic turns."

"What do you know? You have a wonderful man who is very much alive and in love with you, and you're going to be stubborn until the end of time. You have a chance to make everything right, and you're just going to let a beautiful relationship die. How stupid is that?"

Randy looked at me, shaken by my words and my grief. I knew right then he would resolve his differences with Kyle. Leo's death made them seem so insignificant.

I was so lost. I wandered off into the forest. It was thick and dense, and night was falling. It was cold. Finding my way home seemed impossible. I wanted to gather the leaves and branches around me and make a nest. I would just curl up and die. That way, without a doubt, Leo and I would be together again.

"Molly Rose, let me take you home. Ray's got us both covered. I'll stay with you."

I heard some kind of creature rustling around in the leaves. I couldn't help but remember that day in the park when Leo hid under a mound of leaves for fifteen minutes, just waiting for me to arrive so he could scare the daylights out of me. Now, all daylight was gone, and I didn't know what kind of nocturnal creature lay in wait for me. I was petrified. Perhaps I'd better not stay after all.

"Please, Randy ... get me out of here."

"I'll get your coat, Molly Rose."

"Oh, Leo," I cried softly as darkness embraced me.

AND THE WORLD KEPT ON SPINNING

I held Captain Jack for a tearful ten minutes before the low warning growl came forth from his throat. As I've told you, Jack's tolerance for being held (when he is not the initiator) is about three minutes tops. For a cat to go seven minutes beyond his or her limit, well, that's an eternity in the feline world.

When I released Jack from my arms, he didn't go far, snuggling up against me on the couch. It was his way of protecting me from the world. Randy, who spent the entire day at my side, covered me with my grandmother's afghan, bought me homemade soup and bread from the local gourmet shop, and held my hand, literally and figuratively, until I insisted on releasing him from active duty. I knew that the news of Leo's death had changed his perspective about Kyle. I wanted him to go find his man and be happy.

There was a changing of the guard at 5:30 when my sister, Hannah, came over. She was the only person I had allowed Randy to call. The rest of the world would know soon enough. I wasn't ready for a deluge of sympathy, nor did I want to discuss Leo with the men in my life. And after my reconciliation with Claudia (and our conversation about her peripheral role in our breakup), I wasn't ready to even consider the possibility that she might blame herself. I was very content to remain alone in my misery and until I figured out how to transition back into my life.

If there was anything positive in Ray's coerced complicity with Naomi regarding the holiday party debacle, it was that he was now bending over backward to please me. Ray had no issue with allowing me to use an unused week of vacation from the previous year for grief leave. And grieve I did.

I WISH YOU KNEW HOW MUCH I LOVE YOU

In case you're wondering, yes, Cody, Tony, Max, and Alan all called me during my week in exile. As Tony was the only one of the four who had known Leo, I felt compelled to listen as he expressed his sorrow. I don't want to sound ungrateful; it was just painful to even talk about Leo being gone—to anyone. As for the others, to varying degrees, I stated my need to deal with my pain in a personal matter and asked for some time alone.

I mustered up the courage to call Claudia. Had she heard the news from anyone but me, she might have thought I was dismissing our friendship again. Having her back in my life meant everything, and I wasn't taking any chances. I was relieved that she didn't cast blame upon herself, but the tone in her voice said otherwise.

Thankfully, Valentine's Day fell on a Saturday. Had it and my scheduled return-to-work day been one and the same, I would not have held up. I was not so thankful, however, to whichever one of the men thought to send me another Porter Williams bouquet, this time, with a card that read: "I wish you knew how much I love you." The flowers were exquisite and made me feel comforted, but I didn't want to ruminate about who might love me, though I had my hunches. I just wanted to touch my pain with every part of my being. Only by embracing it did I have any chance whatsoever of even the tiniest diminishment.

Chapter 34: FAST FORWARD TO AUGUST

What happened to Molly between Valentine's Day and August? Is that the end of her story? Leo died and she was left to figure out what to do with her life and with whom to spend it? I just read this whole freakin' book, and this is the satisfaction I get?

Okay, one question at a time. Please.

A whole lot happened to me between February and August. I learned the most important lesson I shall ever know: the precise moment when you feel your life has ended may be the precise moment when your life begins anew. The key to my happiness was right under my reporter's nose. I just had to look for it. (To be explained.)

When I started writing this semi-lucid memoir, Chapter 1 began at Susan Decker's wedding and ended a year later, just as my beautiful younger sister was about to marry the love of her life. In case you're so inclined to flip back the pages to refresh your memory, I'll save you the trouble. Here's where I left off:

> *So here I sit today, August 27, just about a year after Susan's wedding, on a bright and beautiful summer day, glammed up in my dress, as I watch my younger sister, Hannah, get her hair pinned up with flowers for her big day. Hannah is bursting with joy. She's only twenty-six and is marrying her long-time guy, Matthew. Nobody ever told Hannah she was too picky.*

What I failed to mention in that first chapter was that Hannah was not the only one wearing a wedding dress. Yes, that's right. I was wearing one, too. The Hacker sisters were having a double wedding, right in our parents' backyard. (Kind of apropos, don't you think? That *is* where happiness lies.)

My parents' large, white, post-Victorian home was the most beautiful setting imaginable. The expansive backyard had a huge tent set up for the reception, and there was still enough room for the 300-plus guests in attendance to sit during the ceremony.

The lily-trimmed altar was exquisite. Hannah and I each had a matron of honor and five bridesmaids. Claudia, radiant in her pale pink gown, was my matron of honor, and Muriel, Ana, Dina, Ellie, and Candy served as my bridesmaids.

As the music began, Hannah began her walk down the aisle, beaming with joy, as she finally took her place next to Matthew, radiant in his tux. And now it was my turn. Here comes the bride ... again.

Happiness was oozing out of my pores. My endorphins were jitterbugging, my adrenaline was racing like an Olympic runner, and my hormones were on fire. The walk down the aisle, with over 600 eyes watching me (none of them belonging to Naomi), was the most amazing, spine-tingling thrill I had ever experienced.

As I approached the altar, I looked at Tony, so handsome in his finery, and thought about all of the years I had known him and all that he had meant to me. I was so lucky to have him in my life. I was so blessed to be marrying the man of my dreams—the man whom I had loved for so long. And there he was, standing next to Tony, love overflowing.

You know all the things they say at weddings, and as this was a double wedding, there was twice as much. Hannah and Matthew exchanged vows first. Then it was our turn.

"Leonardo Pierluigi Millefanti, do you take Molly Rose Hacker to be your lawfully wedded wife? To live together in marriage? Do you promise to love, honor, and keep her? For better or for worse, for richer or poorer, in sickness and in health? And forsaking all others, be faithful only to her as long as you both shall live?

"I do," Leo said, the sunlight dancing in his big brown eyes.

"Molly Rose, do you take Leonardo ... "

"She does, she does!" Randy whispered, as Leo's other groomsmen laughed.

I'd heard the words so many times in my dreams, in my head, and at other people's weddings, that in my excitement, they almost floated over me. And as we exchanged rings, I almost melted under the late August sun. But when the minister said, "I pronounce you husbands and wives," my heart swelled with happiness, and as Leo and I kissed, something came to my mind—something so integral to my life and to everything that had happened.

I'd spent years enduring all of the good intentions and certainly the evil ones, too. I'd heard everything that they said about me. Well, almost everything. But now it was my turn to have the last words, if even silently. As Leo and I, as man and wife, walked up the aisle, my eyes swept the crowd. Thank goodness Molly Hacker was so picky, I thought. Thank goodness.

Don't worry, I'm not going to let you close this book without knowing how it all came together. I've got the *most* amazing epilogue writer. I'm off for my honeymoon. Thanks for sticking with me; I

appreciate your ear, my friend. More than you will know.
And now, I am *so* outta here!

EPILOGUE: BY RANDY F. GOODRICH

Isn't she something, that Molly Rose Millefanti?

Okay, on the oh-so-obvious meter of life, I have a lot of loose ends to tie up for Molly Rose's readers. There is much to dish, but clearly, the first order of business is to explain what happened between Leo's "death" and subsequent marriage to Molly Rose.

Please, do have a modicum of patience with me. This isn't *my* memoir, so I have to absorb myself into every nook and cranny of Molly Rose's narrative in order to provide a fluid transition into my own charming and elegantly crafted prose.

As you are well aware, after her breakup with Leonardo, Molly Rose found it prudent to distance herself from the "helping hands" that inadvertently had once helped her slip the noose around her own neck. Not that Leonardo Pierluigi was without complicity in the unfortunate outcome, for it does indeed involve two for tangoing, but he had only his own flawed thinking to blame. Molly Rose had way too much help.

Allow moi to continue. At the end of January, when Claudia Porter-Bellman, aka "Bubbles" or "Bubbling Brown Sugar," missed BFF Molly Rose sufficiently to jump-start their rapprochement, the poor child was swathed in guilt upon realizing her share of culpability in the breakup. Believe Randy, the "Bubbles" sobriquet has not been unjustly earned. While keeping her true intention from Molly Rose, she was indeed going full bubble thinking of ways to reunite her best gal pal with the love of her life despite the fact that said very same thinking had caused so much trouble in the first place.

Leonardo, meantime, had been living in New York, seeing a woman insanely unsuitable for him in myriad ways I shall not delineate at this time or any other. What you should know is that he had been miserable with this wench, who, to put it most delicately, was a conniving beeotch desperate to hold on to the nothingness that bound her to Leonardo, well aware that her remaining seconds with the man were numbered.

Try this on for size: the lovely Ms. Bubbly, through her vast network, tracked down Leonardo's cell phone number. With nary a thought to any consequence except for the most pleasant one, she left an effusive voicemail urging him to reclaim his rightful position in Molly Rose's life before one of her many suitors stood in permanently.

288

I'm sure it will be no surprise when I reveal that the calculating, unworthy wench clutching desperately to Leonardo intercepted the message, listened carefully, then erased all trace of it. Bad Queen Wenchilass (BQW), I shall call her, wasted no time in employing her knight in shining searchliness, Sir Google, to track down Molly Rose (whose name was already known to her) on the Internet. Within seconds, she not only confirmed Molly Rose to be a features reporter at the *Swansea Herald*, but stumbled upon something that Leonardo himself did not know: Molly Rose is also an obituary writer. Do you see the evil plot forming?

BQW wrote Leonardo's obituary and emailed it to the *Herald*. Of course, being fully cognizant of Leonardo's deep ties to Italy, the significance of planting a fake obit in the Italian papers was not lost on BQW. And, yes, this twisted deception was executed just so that Molly Rose would take the Italian obit as confirmation that her beloved had indeed perished. Of course, the truth could not be squashed forever, but BQW figured that if indeed Molly Rose discovered Leonardo among the living a year or so down the line, she would have already married one of the "suitors" Claudia bubbled on about in her message, and BQW herself falsely envisioned that she would be married to Leonardo. Oh, don't you just wish, you brazen hussy of despicable character!

BQW had just one little pesky problem with the Italian obit: Leonardo's family and friends live in Turin (in the NORTH of Italy), and placement in a Turin paper would have would raised many an Italian eyebrow, to say the least, and her evil plot would have been Napoleon blown apart.

Here's where I have to take some responsibility and admit to my own failings (gasp!). As there was never any reason to question the greatly exaggerated reports of Leonardo's death, I failed, along with Molly Rose, to notice one little phrase in the obituary that waved a big red flag: originario della sicilia. After Molly Rose had cried her eyes out for two weeks, she was rereading the Italian obituary when it occurred to her (smacked her in the face!) that Leonardo was *not "originario della sicilia (originally from Sicily)"* and had no ties there (in the SOUTH of Italy) whatsoever.

BQW had simply added that little tidbit so that *La Gazzetta Siciliana* would publish it, thinking Leonardo to be a Sicilian native. So, once Molly Rose's reporter's nose sniffed out that discrepancy, it didn't take long for the truth to be uncovered and the lovers to be reunited. (And I hear it put Cody's "world rocking" to shame, though Molly Rose was quite ladylike in only hinting at, but barely revealing to me, the grand magnificence of their blissful reconnection.)

And here's what presses against my heart: Leonardo had been sending Molly Rose flowers since November. You may recall that Leonardo is a great lover of Halloween, and Molly Rose was always such a good sport about his antics. And so, on the first of every November, Leo dedicated that day to his beloved. When she received the first gift, a stunning arrangement sent from out of town, she assumed that it was "a plant from a plant" sent from Mr. Cressman, who was indeed out of town when it arrived.

Leonardo had just assumed, because of the date it had been sent, that Molly Rose would know it was he who had sent it. But alas, she did not. But Leonardo persevered and tried again. This time, his gift of the first Porter Williams (Chocolate Bliss!) bouquet arrived during the week that Molly Rose had requested solitude. She assumed it was one of her suitors. Do you remember what the card said: "I'll just say I love you and I miss you—with flowers. And I'll deny that I sent these until you say that you love me, too. I'll be waiting." Again, Molly Rose assumed it to be one of her suitors, and Leonardo assumed he was being ignored. Oh, Molly Rose! Oh, Leonardo! We all know what we are when we *ass*ume.

And lastly, on Valentine's Day, while Molly Rose was grieving and believing the worst, Leonardo's third attempt at winning her back went unnoticed. Yes, another Porter Williams (Yummy Man!) masterpiece with a simple note, "I wish you knew how much I love you."

All from Leonardo. And there you have it. Not only did two soul mates find their way back to one another, they did so with greater maturity, immense personal introspection, a true understanding of trust, and a whole lot of time to make up for. This is as good a place as any to state that, in my radically humble opinion, the most fabulous thing to happen in Molly Rose's quest for true happiness is that her "journey" (possibly the most trite and overused word in today's parlance) served as a catalyst in bringing so many others together.

You may now be wondering what happened to the other men in Molly Rose's life, so with my usual aplomb, it is to that purpose to which I segue.

In scrambling to familiarize myself with this memoir, I see that Molly Rose had hinted about having a bond with Max that each recognized in one another before they had done so in themselves. Ah, so true. They were each still deeply in love with their exes. When Max congratulated Molly on her good news, she suggested, with the delicate forcefulness of a sledge hammer, that it was half past the time that he needed to reunite with Phyllis, let go of his pride, and rid himself of eligible-bachelor status as soon as humanly possible. Molly Rose, knowing the signs of being in love with your ex, had recognized the same in Max from early on. But in order to confront him, she would have had to confront her own feelings. We know how icky and tricky that can be when one is not prepared to stand in the raw—emotionally speaking, of course. But all's well that ends well, as trite as that may sound. I'm happy to announce that Max and the lovely Phyllis remarried this past July.

I interrupt my scheduled narrative here to speak of the lovely Ms. Muriel Hall, a woman for whom I have developed a great affection. Since the ill-fated holiday party, Muriel, who endeared people to her the way her cousin Naomi repelled them, decided to give her life a makeover. The dear girl got herself a personal trainer slash nutritionist and shed an amazing sixty-eight pounds. As Molly Rose has already shared, Muriel learned that hair is to be cut and styled, not bunned à la spinster. The woman is a knockout. She is a sparkling spitfire with more appeal than her cousin Naomi ever had—and imagine this—people like her, too. I indeed mean no rude or lewd pun here, but the square-pegged Alan T. Cressman proved to be the perfect fit for Muriel's round hole. Did I say that? I hope it will not be edited out by some puritan who thinks I'm being naughty. Simply, it is the truth. They are planning a spring wedding, and Molly Rose will be the matron of honor. Oh, and that sixty-eight pounds that Muriel seems to have misplaced? I'm afraid that in her misery, Naomi has found them. Alas!

I return to the subject of Molly Rose's suitors. Cody Cervantes did not take the news of Molly Rose and Leonardo's reconciliation well. Aside from his genuine feelings of love and lust for Molly Rose, he had some other ideas. Big ideas. Our girl was being considered as the stepmother to his daughter, Donatella, and as I perceive it, a secret weapon for him in the seeking of custody.

As it turns out, and this should come as no surprise, Donatella will have a new stepparent after all in the form of a finger-gun-pointing scion known as Cal Leighton, Jr. Molly Rose, the unwitting catalyst for so many romantic hookups, was not spared invisibility in this great love affair. Let Randy explain.

You see, the FREAK-screaming banshee had convinced herself that Molly Rose was the only thing standing between her and everlasting love with Cody. So, when Molly Rose proclaimed her love for Leonardo and announced her wedding plans, Ms. "YOU FREAK!" had to recognize that the father of her child was not making a U-turn back home and that the former Miss Hacker was not the roadblock she had perceived her to be. In reassessing the not-unhandsome looks of Mr. Leighton, the vast fortune, the social status, and the hole left in Swansea society by soon-to-be-divorced Naomi Hall-Benchley, Ms. "YOU-FREAK!" saw the wisdom in accepting the huge piece of ice placed on her finger by the slobbering, smitten scion.

As for the minor child, I believe a joint custody arrangement will be pending. Good luck to all. And may Swansea society enjoy their new addition. The soon-to-be Mrs. Cal Leighton will surely be old money's worst nightmare.

Last but hardly least in Molly Rose's circle of admirers is Tony. As Molly Rose has revealed, he served as Leonardo's best man: a true show of happiness for his old friends. Despite his feelings for Molly Rose, one look at the enormity of her grief and the overwhelming elation in discovering that Leonardo's death had been a mere ruse was enough to quell his pursuit of happiness as it pertained to Molly Rose. Not to speculate, but I do believe Tony may have a new love interest. I saw him chatting up Isabella Millefanti, Leonardo's exquisite younger sister, at the wedding, so perhaps Molly Rose and Tony may end up in the same family some day after all. 'Twould be nice, methinks.

Oh, Randy, you're not going to end Molly Rose's book with nary a word about yourself, are you? Why, of course not.

As Molly Rose has revealed, the greatly exaggerated news of Leonardo's death changed my world in a heartbeat. The simple remembrance of a love divine and the harsh reality of how it can instantly be gone—forever—were more than enough to get me out of the kitchen and away from the huge pot of stubborn soup that I had been stirring.

This is not my memoir, so I shall be ever so brief. When I met Kyle, I was thrilled to find someone so right for me that in my appreciation for our many commonalities, I was, dare I say, a bit intolerant of our differences. I didn't stop to realize that the things that make people dissimilar from one another don't have to be negatives at all. In fact, they are the gifts that we give one another. If we were all the same, on the inside and outside, what would we have to teach one another? How would we grow? How would we evolve into greater beings? How would we ever learn the true meaning of "For better or for worse"?

Kyle and I had a different set of challenges. Although we arrived at the same destination, our routes were vastly different. As I see it now, had we traveled along the same road, it wouldn't be much fun to compare the scenery.

I learned so much from Molly Rose because she has always been passionate and unapologetic in her quest to "get it right." No matter how picky, quirky, or overwrought she finds herself, she wipes her tears with one hand and claws her way out of purgatory with the other. She inspires me, but if you tell her I said that, I shall vehemently deny it.

As Molly Rose and Leonardo enjoy the enchanting land of Turin on their honeymoon, I sit here with an orange furball shedding upon my lap. I do not mind. However, should you choose to tell Molly Rose I said *that*, it too will be denied. Just like Kyle and me, Captain Jack and I have our commonalities and differences. For example, we both have claws, though Jack doesn't use his as often as Randy does. Oh my, did I say that? Both are fiercely protective of Molly Rose. Captain Jack has nine lives, whereas I only have one. And I will live it to the fullest.

And now, please join me in raising our glasses to the newlyweds …

THE END

1

Made in the USA
Middletown, DE
08 July 2016